WHO PAYS THE FERRYMAN?

BY PAT MONTHEATH

A Quill Publishing Book

Published by Quill Publishing in 2003

ISBN 0-9545914-0-2

First published in 2003 in the United Kingdom by
Quill Publishing
The Haven Eskdaleside,
Grosmont,
Whitby, North Yorkshire YO22 5PS.

Printed and bound in Great Britain by HPE Print, Pickering, North Yorkshire YO18 7JB

To Crispin,

Read, enjoy but whatever you do — do not underestimate the enemy!

Pat Manteath

2003

Acknowledgements

This would not have been possible without the unwavering support of Anne and my family who have had to put up with my many late nights and lack of time spent with them whilst writing this book. Nor would it have been possible without the main characters that shall remain nameless to protect their anonymity, but they know who they are. I would also like to extend my thanks to Richard for his help in proof reading the finished item and also his constant badgering to get it published.

Introduction

To the right, rising out of the undergrowth, stood two giant concrete blocks, the remains of an Anti Aircraft Gun emplacement from the war. Directly ahead were nothing but bracken and trees stretching into the distance. To his left was a small clearing where the bracken and undergrowth lay completely flat. The sun splashed through the leaves overhead. The breeze caressed his face. Although it was only 08:00 hours it was already warm and had the makings of another hot day. Again, he scrutinised the sector, scanning carefully from right. To left. He paused as his gaze fell on the small clearing, then out of the corner of his eye something caught his attention, and he quickly turned to concentrate on the area in front. (Did something move?) Was it the light playing tricks? He screwed up his eyes against the light, concentrating his gaze even harder. There it was again. Taking no chances, he dropped into the prone position. Slowly, ever so slowly to avoid attention, he slithered deeper into the undergrowth, easing his Browning 9mm from its holster. He cautiously parted the bracken so he had an uninterrupted view of where he thought the movement had been. He lay concealed just watching a point directly ahead but nothing moved. All was quiet. Maybe he'd imagined it. His body slowly relaxed and again, he looked towards the clearing, watching, always watching for any sign of movement. In the peaceful surroundings first one rabbit cautiously hopped from the undergrowth into the clearing, paused its ears erect like radar scanners listening for the slightest noise. It sat poised ready to run back to its hiding place, its nose constantly twitching as it sniffed the air around it. Then a second rabbit hopped into the clearing momentarily poised with ears erect listening for any noise that would send alarm signals. They were oblivious of the man concealed nearby as they ate their fill of new succulent shoots. Again the man scanned the area. Suddenly his whole body tensed, his gaze attracted to a spot left of the old gun base. He watched intently concentrating hard. Was he seeing things? No, there it was again, this time he was certain. It was not the breeze, nor had he imagined it. He stared at the place about forty-five metres away. There again was an imperceptible movement of bracken. The rabbits sensed danger and bolted for cover. He slowly raised his weapon and took careful aim at the spot. With a gentle squeeze of the trigger the peace was shattered. A loud crack rang out, and suddenly everywhere was thrown into pandemonium. The whole woodland screamed out. Hundreds of unseen birds screeched their warning to each other... all around was panic... beating wings clattering together as birds took fright... everything was running just to get away...

"Quebec Romeo 1 from Control - Proceed with caution your back up on the way. Acknowledge. Over."
"Roger Control message timed at 08:15 hours. Out."
The car swung off the main road and proceeded along a narrow, bumpy track before halting at a closed gate. The passenger alighted from the vehicle and fastened back the gate allowing the car through. The driver gently edged the car along the track until they came to a clearing adjacent to a radio mast. There, he stopped and switched off the engine.

The radio, crackled into life, "Quebec Romeo 1, this is Red Leader ETA at Radio Station five minutes. Proceed as planned. Stake out and observe only. Repeat observation only. Acknowledge. Over"

"Red Leader from Quebec Romeo 1. Message received and understood. Message timed at 08:25 hours. Quebec Romeo 1 out."

As the noise in the clearing abated, the man with the Browning slowly edged his way through the undergrowth. He paused from time to time, listening, watching for any other movement. There was nothing, everywhere was still. Then he heard the short staccato message over his personal transceiver, "Alpha, Whisky, Bravo 1 down."

He quickly depressed his call button and replied, "Alpha." He lay still, taking a further recce of the area, then moved slowly forward. Inch by inch he skirted the clearing moving deeper into the woods. He continued moving through the undergrowth until confidant that he had sufficient distance between himself and the clearing. He was now directly opposite where he had started. From here he scanned the woods ahead and to the left of the clearing. Nothing. He could detect no further movement.

The man now lying prone in the undergrowth scanned the area ahead through his telescopic sights gradually swinging his high powered automatic rifle around in a smooth arc - still nothing. He was sure that was where the he had heard the shot. However, he could have been mistaken. Again, his weapon described a smooth arc through the air as he carefully looked through the sights. In the distance a radio crackled into life, but too far away to hear any message, then all was quiet save for the occasional beep, beep from his personal radio.

At 08:28 hours precisely a convoy of assorted vehicles turned off the main road and proceeded at speed along the bumpy narrow track. Passing through the now open gateway and on through the woodland until the radio mast came into view. At 0830 hours precisely, the lead vehicle (Red Leader) pulled in behind the car already parked and the other vehicles pulled up alongside, the truck bringing up the rear. Doors flew open and the noise of running feet filled the air. A senior officer issued clear concise orders to the various individuals. Two of the men were to conceal themselves at the entry to the lane from off the main road and act as observers, advising mobile control should any vehicles turn into the lane. The gate having been made fast. Four men concealed themselves among the trees to cover any approach from either side. Their orders were to apprehend and question anyone attempting to enter or leave the woods by this route. Within minutes, they cordoned off the whole area. Each man was now in position and acting under strict orders, no more than a pawn in this large-scale game of chess where the hunter was soon to become the hunted. The waiting game had begun!

There was something, the person, hidden by tall bracken, carefully surveyed the area near the old gun emplacement. There it was again, a fleeting movement through the trees, which, even to the trained eye was difficult to discern against the backdrop of foliage and undergrowth. He quickly brought the high powered rifle up to his shoulder, trained the telescopic sights on a point near where he thought he had seen the movement and slowly scanned the area for any further evidence. Yes, there it was again, a definite movement. He hurriedly adjusted the cross hairs of his telescopic sights bringing the outline of a man into stark focus. As he carefully studied the target ahead of him, he moved his line of potential fire from the body to the head, focusing his attention on point just above the ear of the target. One gentle squeeze of the trigger is all it would take, but his orders were to observe and report only. He felt for the send button on his personal radio and in a hushed voice called his control, confirmed his position and that he had visual contact with target. The net was closing.

At 08:40 a grey Ford car turned from the main road and onto the bumpy lane. The driver did not appear to be in any hurry as he drove at a leisurely pace passed the two carefully concealed observers and on towards the gate. The observers called their control to advise of the car's approach. The four armed men at the gate their readiness to intercept. The grey car came into view and slowly approached the closed gate. It stopped a couple of feet from the closed gate and the driver got out to open it. Having now fastened the gate open he turned to go back to his car only to find his way was blocked by two armed police men. They carefully levelled their high powered rifles directly at his chest. He stood motionless as he heard the footfalls of the others behind him. They roughly manhandled him towards his vehicle and forced him to lay face downwards spread-eagle on the ground in front of it. Whilst in this position, he was curtly asked if he was 'tooled up' and was quickly yet thoroughly frisked - these men were professionals and had carried out this operation many times before. Having been relieved of his Browning 9mm pistol, they roughly pulled his arms across his back and a pair of handcuffs deftly snapped about his wrists. Whilst still lain in the position he was told that he was under arrest, advised of his rights and was dutifully cautioned.
"Control from Delta Bravo, we have detained Target one. A White Caucasian awaiting further instructions? Over."
"Delta Bravo from Control - good work hold there and await car out."
"Roger Control."

Alpha now crawled forward more confidently. As he approached the point near the gun emplacement where he thought the hit was, he stopped and as a precaution brought his Browning 9mm up in front of him, parted the bracken carefully and viewed the scene. It was a positive. The target was down. At this point, he stood up. Replaced his pistol in its holster and called out to someone who was concealed, telling them that they could no longer take an active role in proceedings as they had been discovered and subsequently shot. He pulled out his transceiver.
"Whisky, Alpha, Bravo 1 down confirmed. Returning base." The acknowledgement came back.
"Whisky." With that, Alpha moved off into the woods.

The observer quickly put out a call to his control to advise them that Target two was now on the move through the woods, he gave them the necessary details and advised he was following at a distance. Later that morning two men were apprehended an operation that had used a number of armed police officers from the tactical operations unit; in addition to other officers, drew to a successful close.

"Well gentlemen it's your lucky night." The custody sergeant quipped sarcastically as he escorted two men in combat gear from the police cells at Canterbury. "Don't ask me why, but I've been told you're free to go."
"What about our stuff?" The shorter one of the two asked.
"I'll sort that out for you both in a minute," replied the police sergeant.
"What about our weapons?"
"I believe that's all in hand. Here sign here," the sergeant made a cross on the sheet where he wanted the men to sign. Both men scrawled their respective signatures on their respective sheets and returned them to the custody sergeant who returned one copy for their retention. "Now gentlemen is there anything further?"
"Yes one question are we on bail?"
"No, you are totally free. All charges have been dropped."
"Why?"
"Because I believe we have been directed to do so. The expression is 'not in the interest of the public.' Now if you'll excuse me gentleman, I'll arrange for someone to escort you from the premises."
"Our weapons?"
"The Armourer will sort those out for you."

"Mmm, that's nice", the shorter guy said as he took a deep breath. "Out of those stinking clammy cells and into the fresh air at last. Do you know we've been banged up in that place for over twelve hours." He took another deep breath. His friend didn't say a word.

It is always at this point that I waken still with the overall pictures of that day strongly held in my mind's eye. These pictures, which happened in 1985, have mercifully all but obliterated some of the worst flashbacks.

So why did the police arrest the two men? Why were they taken to Canterbury police station for questioning? What was the police operation all about? Who were the men dressed in combat gear? Why were the men later released with all charges dropped?

Chapter 1

A shaft of light penetrated the inky blackness as he gripped the pencil torch between his teeth. One last heave should do it. He grunted as he struggled to manoeuvre what appeared to be a dead weight into position.

"How you doing Pat?" A whisper with a sense of urgency filtered through the surrounding darkness from his small transceiver.

"Be done in a couple of minutes and you?" He called back in a low voice.

"Yeah I'm through." Then silence. There was a dull clang of metal on metal, a half-whispered oath then silence once more. A few seconds elapsed and the disembodied voice floated through the darkness once again.

"What's holding you up? Come on man let's go." There was silence. "Pat are you ok?"

"Yeah I'm ok." He muttered in the cold night air as his hands deftly twisted a pair of wires together in the small beam of light from his torch. "There that should do it." He said to himself, he then depressed the send button on his transceiver and in a hoarse whisper said; "Right I'm through. Come on we're out of here." He scrambled back up the bank to the wall and gave a low whistle, which was answered by another barely fifty yards away and a small circle of light momentarily flashed in his direction then it was gone. Within seconds his partner joined him.

"Ok Pat I've taken my trip wire across the road at a height of six inches and tied it off. I've concealed it as best I can under the soft earth. What do you reckon, will it work?"

"It should do, I see no reason why it shouldn't. Right lets get back to the van and wait." It took the pair of them five minutes to reach their British registered ex-royal mail van concealed down a farm track well away from the main road and prying eyes.

"How long before we detonate it?" Pat looked at his watch it was three o'clock.

"Well I reckon they should be able to see the flash about now." With that he pulled up the antenna of a small transmitter and pressed a tiny red button. The effect was instantaneous. There was an almighty roar as a wall of flame shot about twenty feet upwards and culminated in a loud explosion which ripped the sub-station apart. He calmly pushed the antenna back down and started the engine. "Well that should keep them busy for a few minutes looking for candles. I don't see them getting the power back on today." In the distance could be heard the plaintive wail of a two-tone horn as the patrol headed with speed to where the wall of flame had occurred. In a matter of minutes they would be dead or dying but they were not to know.

As the Land Rover rounded the bend the driver spotted what appeared to be a wire at about six inches above the ground stretching across the road in front of him. Too late he realised what it was. He slammed on his brakes locking all four wheels as he did so then everything went into slow motion. With all wheels locked up the vehicle slithered forward over the surface of the road. The driver saw the wire disappear from view. As the front wheels made contact and he sensed the wire go taught there was a blinding flash of light and an almighty BOOOM, then blackness. The force of the explosion picked up the Land Rover and tossed it in the air as if it were a toy. It landed a broken twisted wreck upside down some forty feet along the road. The blanket of silence that followed was almost deafening as the pitch black of the night closed in once again.

11

Fifty miles away to the south a small group of men worked in the glare of arc lights loading bulk bins of apples onto an articulated truck. The time was just before three in the morning. It was always the same routine; the truck would arrive in the early hours and be loaded in the dead of night. The driver could never understand the reasoning behind this, but the pay was good and he, like many people in this area, needed money so it didn't pay to ask too many questions. Word had it that the man in charge was exceedingly wealthy and was a very powerful man, with friends in high places. Rumour was that he was the hidden force behind certain union personalities and that he indirectly controlled their actions, but of course it was only rumoured. Still he was only a truck driver so far be it for him to question even the rumours. When he had first been told about the job he was somewhat sceptical and being a good Protestant he was even more dubious at the prospect of working for a Catholic family. Especially in the present unpredictable environment and in particular the geographical local he found himself in. I wonder why they want me here just for apples at this hour, the driver thought to himself.

"Right that's the last of them," someone shouted. There was a swish and rattling noise as the Tautliner curtain was pulled along its runners then a series of clumps as the clips were locked into place. Someone banged on his door.

"Ok mate all yours." Colm, that was the drivers name, wound down the cab window took the clipboard that was being proffered, signed the paperwork keeping his copies then passed it back. All this time the big man stood with his Irish Wolfhound by his side, watching just watching. Colm had been told he was the boss but he'd never spoken to him.

"Ok Colm see you in a couple of weeks." The man with the clipboard said. Already the arc lamps were being extinguished one by one. Colm hit the ignition and there was a deep muffled roar as the powerful engine kicked into life. In a matter of minutes he was pulling out of the leafy lane and turning right heading northwards. Colm whistled along with the radio as it played 'Danny Boy' quite happy at being on the move at last. But I wonder had he known the real reason behind those early morning pickups would he have been just as happy?

In 1972, not long after 'Bloody Sunday', my good friend Paul Jones and I started work on my fathers fruit farm in Kent. This was a far cry from the excitement I had yearned for when we had both joined the Parachute Regiment some years previously. During our stint in the Para's we had served our time for Queen and country to the best of our ability but I somehow still found something missing. In a way it was nothing like I had expected, don't misunderstand me I really enjoyed my time, but it was not as exciting or as glamorous as I had expected or had been portrayed. Maybe it was I. Perhaps I had read too many war books or possibly I was just plain naive. Anyway, upon our discharge Paul went back to Kent to start his life as a civilian once more, whereas I still thirsted for excitement. The thought of fruit farming held as much appeal to me as watching paint dry, so I set off in search of a more stimulating life elsewhere. I didn't have far to go. In fact Dorking was the place that beckoned to me. I had heard on the grapevine that a Major Paul Leonard was looking to recruit ex-military personnel with a view to building up a mercenary force to send out to Angola. This sounded like the life to me, a bit of action, good money, and foreign lands. Yes excitement, the very thing I craved for and the very thing I had expected to find in the Para's but didn't, so no sooner had I heard about it than I was there. Unfortunately I was not the only one to learn of Major Paul Leonard and his band of merry men. The British Government had also heard about his mercenary force and learned of his intentions to ship out to Angola with them. This, the Prime Minister felt, was not in the best interest of the country therefore some gentlemen paid our Major a visit one-day and that was that. Once again I, Richard James, found myself back in civilian life with any prospect of foreign countries, good money and excitement fast disappearing over the horizon. Left with no income, no excitement I had no alternative but, like Paul, to return to my native county of Kent and join him working for my father.

It was whilst working for my father we devised, or should I say stumbled on, a better and much quicker way of grafting fruit trees. Our method showed great promise and it wasn't long before our reputation started to spread throughout the local fruit growers and farmers. Very soon the trade magazines started to take more than just a passing interest in Richard James and James Fruit Farms. A number of articles started to appear in various trade magazines and journals tracking our progress and praising our new innovative approach to fruit growing and management but most of all they showed a particular interest in our method of tree grafting. Then, completely out of the blue and apparently in response to one such article, I received a telephone call from a man called Breandán O'Shea.
"Hello, would that be Mr James?" a man with an Irish accent enquired, "Mr Richard James of James Fruit Farms?"
"Yes, I'm Richard James. Who am I speaking to?" I asked.
"My name's Breandán O'Shea and I'm..."
"Sorry Mr O'Shea should I know you?" I asked cutting across his conversation.
"I wouldn't have thought so Mr James, but if you'll just allow me to finish I'll explain why I'm calling you this evening."
"Sorry Mr O'Shea. Please continue."
"Well it's like this now. I've just been reading this latest article about your grafting technique...." He then went on at great length about the different articles he had read about Paul and I. How he had followed our progress with interest and watched how we had become celebrities in our own field, so on and so forth. In fact I would say he was full of the Irish blarney, I was only half paying attention to what he was saying, trying to work out how to get rid of him without appearing rude, when he dropped the proverbial bombshell. "...So you see, if you were prepared to come over here, and of course you can guarantee your work, then I'm prepared to offer you two hundred punt plus all expenses paid. Oh and that would also include hotel accommodation. What do you think now?"
"Sorry Mr O'Shea I didn't quite catch all of that. Would you mind repeating the last bit?" I couldn't believe my ears.
"I'm sorry Mr James. What I said was, if I was to pay you two hundred punt would you be prepared to come over to my place and do some work for me?"
"How much?" I asked in amazement still not believing what I had heard.

"Two hundred punt, that is of course per week."

"You did say two hundred pounds?" I asked again incredulously.

"Yes, two hundred punt plus expenses and hotel accommodation." I still found what I was hearing incredible because what this man was offering was way above what we could earn here.

"I'm sorry Mr O'Shea, but you did say plus accommodation as well didn't you?"

"Yes that's right. Two hundred plus accommodation, that's hotel accommodation you realise, not some back street guesthouse you know. So what do you think?" I was so taken aback I didn't know what to say. "Hello, Mr James are you still there?" This was too good to be true.

"Yes Mr O'Shea, I'm still here. I'm sorry can you hang on a minute?" My hands were shaking with excitement as I covered the mouthpiece and whispered to Anne. "This blokes offered me two hundred pounds to do some work for him."

"What, two hundred!" She exclaimed. "But for how long?" She asked as common sense prevailed.

"I don't know." I replied.

"Well the money's good if it's only a week or two, but any longer than that then you could earn more here at home."

"No I couldn't. You must be joking. Where would I get two hundred a week?"

"What! A week did you say?" Anne like me just couldn't believe it. "Did I hear you right, two hundred a week?" She repeated the question.

"Yes that's what I said."

For a minute she stood there eyes wide and mouth open, then she shook her head in disbelief as she said, "Bah I don't believe you, you're having me on." I shook my head to let her know I wasn't and mouthed the amount again as I pointed at the telephone. She thought about it and laughed. "Richard James you are pulling my leg?" I shook my head.

"I'm not," I whispered "He's offered two hundred a week plus expenses and hotel accommodation." I looked at her for an answer.

She stopped laughing and realised I was serious. "Richard you are serious aren't you?" I nodded. "Two hundred a week plus expenses, well what are you waiting for, take it, take it." She said with a sense of urgency.

"Are you sure?" I asked, but she did not have time to reply as the softly spoken Irishman was now pushing me for an answer.

"Mr James, hello are you still there?"

"Sorry Mr O'Shea I'm still here."

"Well Mr James are you interested?"

"Well yes, the question is how long will you want us over there for, and I presume you mean for both of us to come?"

"Two of you?"

"Well yes of course. Is that a problem then?"

"Well hmm..."

"Well it takes two of us to do the work and I presumed you realised that." I caught sight of the look of disappointment in Anne's face as she sensed that things were starting to go slightly pear shape.

"Oh I'm sorry Mr James. No I hadn't realised that at all, but of course. If that's what it takes to do the job then that's a different matter. I thought you wanted to bring your wife or someone that's why I was a little hesitant." His voice held a note of relief in it. "Now can you come or not?"

"For two hundred..." I must have sounded slightly hesitant or something for he cut me short before I could say anything further.

"Three hundred and that's my top offer. Yes or No?" The man had just upped the price by a further hundred a week. What I wasn't sure of was this for two men or was this pay per man. So trying to keep my voice on an even note and business like, which I now found increasingly difficult, I asked him.

"The three hundred and all expenses, including the hotel, is of course per man isn't it?"

"Of course." The line went quiet for a second before he started to speak again, "So is it a deal then?"

"Yes. It's a deal."

"Good I'm relieved to hear it. Now Mr James what's your partner's name?"

"Mr Jones, Paul Jones." I added, "I look forward to receiving your confirmation in writing Mr O'Shea."

"Oh I'm sorry Mr James, let's just say my word is my bond. I will of course be sending you the ferry tickets nearer the time so that in itself will be some form of confirmation." He paused as if waiting for me to speak.

"Ok Mr O'Shea, you leave me with no option but to accept what you say at face value. So will you be contacting us again, with the necessary information as to where we will be staying?"

"Sorry Mr James, an oversight on my behalf. You'll both be staying at the Tara hotel. I'm sure you'll find it more than adequate and I will of course need to speak to you again before you come over, just to go over some of the finer details. In the meantime take it as read that you have a contract at three hundred punt a week for each of you plus hotel and expenses. Is that ok Mr James?"

"Yes certainly Mr O'Shea, three hundred a week per man and staying at the Tara Hotel." I repeated the salient points more for the benefit of Anne than anything else. "I can't think of anything I've missed Mr O'Shea." I paused as if I was thinking then added, "No that's fine, more than fine."

"Good, then I'll not take up anymore of your time, and thank you Mr James good bye."

"Thank you Mr O'Shea and I hope to speak to you again soon, good bye for now."

A big grin spread across my face. Anne couldn't believe her ears. She rushed over grinning like a Cheshire Cat and gave me a hug.

"Wow, three hundred pounds a week. Umm just think of it. Oh I love you I love you. Hey wait 'till you tell Paul and your dad. Brilliant, absolutely brilliant, three hundred a week! Can you imagine it? Three hundred pounds a week! Where does this wealthy man live Richard, I want to meet him?"

"Ireland."

"Ireland did you say?" Her voice suddenly changed. It was now tinged with fear, she knew about Ireland all right from my time in the 'Mob'. Although Paul and I had never done a stint over there many of our friends had and some had never returned it was this aspect that worried Anne. "Where, not Belfast is it?"

"No, it's south of the border near Dublin."

"But it's still Ireland." She said looking concerned.

"It's not the same Anne, it's the Republic and quite safe." She still looked worried so I tried to reassure her. "Anyway it's different when you're a civilian. We'll be all right don't worry." I gave her a reassuring cuddle, and went on to explain to her that the trouble was in Ulster and not in Eire. Once she had grasped the difference between Ulster and Eire she cheered up.

"So when will you go?"

"Oh not until next Spring."

"But that's months away, oh Richard I thought it would be sooner than that." She looked disappointed. Suddenly she grinned, "Still it gives me time to work out what we can spend all that money on!"

"Slow down girl, I haven't earned it yet."

"Don't worry I have every faith in my man." She gave me another hug and a kiss then disappeared into the kitchen humming.

We arrived at our destination much later than anticipated on that fateful Saturday in March 1973. It was our first visit to the Republic. The town we found ourselves in, was a small town north of Dublin located deep in the heart of the 'Valley of Kings'. It is here where the River Boyne gently meanders its way between luxurious grassy fields and thickly wooded banks. In the distance the rolling hills and mountains form a backdrop to this beautiful area. It is here that one finds the very heart of Eire, where history, legend and folklore come together and are so entwined it is difficult to discern the ending of one and the beginning of the next. The valley is rich in Irish history and is home to such places as that of the Hill of Slane where it is reputed St Patrick lit his fire, a beacon to Christianity, and the ancient Hill of Tara the seat and burial ground of the 'High Kings of Ireland'. However, for all its natural beauty I, unfortunately, remember it more for the sinister secrets it holds and the events that took place during my period there.

Having reached the town, all we needed now was to find the hotel that was booked for us. Hopefully we were not too late to meet with Mr O'Shea as arranged. It was not long before we turned off the main road into a tree flanked lane sign posted to the Tara hotel. We passed through a large gateway and into the hotel grounds. The drive swept round in an arc passing in front of a wide flight of stone steps leading up to a paved terrace area. The steps were flanked on either side by a solid looking stone wall behind which a steep grassy bank rose up to meet with a low wall that surrounded the paved terrace area. The entrance to this magnificent flight of stone stairs was guarded by two rampant lions each one holding an ornate outdoor lamp post between its paws. At the top, where the steps gave way to the terrace, there were two further lions lying facing down the steps. The sweeping drive finally opened up into a large rectangular car park. The whole area was encompassed within a high stone wall.

"Hey, would you take a look at that." I said as Paul pursed his lips and gave a low whistle in sheer disbelief at the size and grandeur of the building set before us. Even the main hotel door was imposing in itself, a huge solid oak door. "Isn't that something else. Look at that flight of steps, it's like, like... well I don't know what its like. It's brilliant just like..." I was lost for words but Paul came to the rescue.

"A Georgian manor house." He said in a matter of fact way.

"Yeah, that's right. You've got it, a Georgian manor house." I was like a wide-eyed kid in a candy store. I was amazed at the opulence the building portrayed; after all I had never been fortunate enough to stay in a place like this before. We parked the car and made our way up the stone steps, through the huge oak door and into reception where we checked in. I had never, in my wildest dreams, expected anything quite so big and grandiose as this.

Being dazzled by my surroundings and unaccustomed as I was to such luxury, I had completely forgotten about our host, that was until I started to unpack, then I remembered, we were supposed to meet Mr O'Shea for dinner. Rushing from the room I knocked on Paul's door.

"Paul" I called with a sense of urgency, but there was no reply. I waited, then knocked again. "Paul" even more urgently this time. I waited and waited but still no answer even though I could hear him moving about. "Paul" I shouted as I banged on the door in desperation.

"Yeah. Who's there?"

"It's me hurry up."

"Hang on, hang on. What's the problem, is there a fire or something?"

"Shit Paul come on hurry up."

"All right, all right I'm coming hold on. Anyway what's the big deal?"

"Nothing much only that I forgot to tell you that we're supposed to meet O'Shea for dinner."

"You what," he shouted back from the other side of the door. "Did you say we were to meet O'Shea?"

"Yeah. Sod it Paul come on leave what you're doing and let's get down there." There was a crash from inside the room.

"Shit!"

"What's up?" I called to him through the closed door.

"Nothing much it's only that my bloody case has slipped off the chair and tipped all my pissing clothes on the floor. Tell you what, why don't you go down to find him and I'll see you in the bar."

"Ok, but don't be too long then." I went back to my room grabbed my wallet and my keys then rushed off downstairs slamming my door behind me.

As I approached the desk, the receptionist, a pretty Irish girl with an oval face and beautiful long fair hair and the biggest brown eyes I had ever seen, looked up from what she was doing and smiled.

"Good evening sir, can I help you?" She asked. For a minute this beautiful girl transfixed me as she smiled and waited patiently.

"Sorry I was miles away, what did you say? Oh yes, I mean of course, I..." I stuttered and stammered like a schoolboy, "I just wondered if you could tell me where I can find

Mr O'Shea?"

"Would that be Breandán O'Shea you'd be after?"

"Yes." I answered still spellbound by this pretty cailin.

"In that case he's away to the Dining Room with some guests. Was he expecting you?" I snapped back to reality.

"Yes. Unfortunately we arrived later than anticipated."

"Just a minute sir I'll check if there's any message." With that the young lady disappeared into the office, to reappear a moment later with another pretty Irish girl.

"Good evening sir, my colleague told me Mr O'Shea was expecting you."

"Yes we were supposed to meet him for dinner but we arrived later than we had hoped. I gather he's already has gone into the Dining Room with some other friends."

"That's correct sir. Now tell me would you be one of the two Englishmen he was expecting?"

"Yes, I'm Mr James, Richard James. How did you know?"

"The accent, it's a dead give away. Now sir if you'll excuse me I'll let Mr O'Shea know of your arrival"

"Excuse me," I called after her, "Excuse me." She turned and smiled, "I'm sorry sir, did you want something else?"

"As Mr O'Shea's gone into dinner could I book a table for two?" She glanced at her watch and I did likewise. It was getting on for 9.30. She gave me an apologetic look, which summed it up. I was out of luck.

"I'm sorry Mr James, the restaurant takes last orders at 9.00 o'clock." My annoyance must have shown in my expression because she smiled and said, "I know it's not the same, but I could organise some sandwiches or maybe a salad or something. Or perhaps the night porter could recommend somewhere to you." I was hungry and that was all there was to it. To go somewhere else would mean more driving and I had done enough of that for the time being.

"No don't worry him, sandwiches will be fine. What can you offer?"

"Chicken, cold beef, prawn, ham or should I get the kitchen to prepare a small selection?"

"A selection please."

"Thank you Mr James I'll organise that now for you. Would you like them in the lounge, or maybe the bar?"

"The bar thank you, and could you make that two plates please."

"Certainly Mr James and I'll tell Mr O'Shea you're through in the bar then." She then rang the bell and the night porter appeared almost immediately.

"Ah Noel, would you show Mr James the way to the bar and arrange for a selection of sandwiches for two."

"Certainly. Now if you would be so kind as to follow me sir."

"Thank you."

"Is this your first visit to Ireland then or have you been before?" He asked as I followed him through the lounge to a comfortable looking bar.

Paul and I hadn't long finished our sandwiches when a smartly dressed well-built man approached our table.

"Hello, I'm Breandán. Breandán O'Shea." The stranger announced in a soft Irish accent. "I trust you had a good journey here and no problems. Let me get you a drink. Seamus," he called over to the barman, "Bring over an orange juice for me and whatever these two gentlemen are drinking."

"Yes Mr O'Shea."

He pulled out a stool and sat down at our table. "Now gentlemen, that's the priorities sorted out, so which one of you is Richard James?"

"Sorry Mr O'Shea." I extended my hand in greeting, "I'm Richard and this is my partner Paul Jones."

"Pleased to meet you Paul. Now lads this is the deal. You'll be here in the Tara Hotel as my guests whilst you're working on my farm. The pay, will be as agreed during our telephone conversation and is a contract price. If I am pleased with your work then there will be an additional bonus at the end."

"How much are we talking?"

"Let's just say you will not be disappointed."

"Yes, but what do you mean by we won't be disappointed. Exactly how much are you paying?" I asked.

"What exactly do we have to do to earn this bonus?" asked Paul.

"Just do a good job Mr Jones that's all."

This puzzled me. We had agreed a price for the contract, three hundred pounds a week, a figure that was seven times above the national average and put us in millionaire's row figuratively speaking. So why should this man now offer us a bonus on top? It didn't make sense.

"Why would you want to pay us a bonus Mr O'Shea, what's the catch?"

"There's no catch Richard. However to earn your bonus I expect loyalty and a fair days work." He paused, "Is that understood?" He looked first at me then at Paul. We both nodded our agreement, but deep down I felt for all his apparent honesty there was something he was not telling us.

"That's that sorted then. Now what do you know about the area around here?" He asked.

"Nothing much" I replied.

"Well we are situated in the area known as the 'Valley of Kings' and it is the 'Tara Kings' that this hotel is called after. Did you know that the Tara Kings burial grounds were discovered not a million miles from here?" he asked as he took a look at his watch. "Gee is that the time I'll have to go otherwise my guests will wonder what's happened to me. Sorry lads I'll have to tell you about the area some other time, oh and I'm sorry I couldn't meet up with you tonight but there'll be other times." He got up to go, then as if with second thoughts he sat back down. "By the way, if you're interested there's a dance on in the nightclub tonight."

"The nightclub?"

"Yes Richard, we've got a nightclub here as well. Of course it's a separate business to the hotel, also a separate entrance."

"Do hotel guests get in free?"

"No, they pay the same as the locals have to." He smiled and gave a wink. "That way we get two bites at the cherry. After all we have to earn a crust! But don't worry lads you go in free, as my guests I can arrange things, if you know what I mean." He gave another sly wink and continued, "After all it's no good being the boss if you can't have some perks is it?"

"Is this your hotel?" I asked.

"Technically no, but in practical terms yes. I hold the major interest and my wife is my sleeping partner, in more ways the one," he smiled at the pun, "So I suppose I do own it really, anyway enough of that. So what about this dance would you like to go or not?"

"Well what do you think?" I asked Paul.

"Sounds all right to me."

"Good, that's settled then, I'll arrange it with reception. Oh yes, I almost forgot." A slight edge crept into his voice as he continued, "There is one other thing you need to be aware of whilst working on my farm. You'll no doubt hear and see certain things, which have nothing to do with you. No matter what they are you will not say a word to a soul." He looked from one to the other of us. "Do I make myself clear? Not a word." His smiling Irish eyes had suddenly lost their charm and became cold and threatening. We both nodded showing we understood. "Because if you do repeat anything it could be very unhealthy for you and all concerned." He paused to emphasise what he had just said before speaking again. "Also whilst we are on the subject, there are certain pubs in the town that you should avoid, especially after the British Parachute Regiment murdered, yes and I mean murdered, many of our people." He paused staring into the distance as if he were somewhere else. His eyes cold and filled with hatred. I broke the spell.

"Mr O'Shea, I know what happened." I said in a quiet voice. He turned and looked straight at me. "I think you are referring to what the press called Bloody Sunday. Now I really don't want to get involved in a discussion about that, especially as it has nothing to do with us, or why we are here." An uneasy silence descended on the three of us sitting there. Breandán shook his head as if to clear it and blinked.

"All right then," he said, his voice taking on a lighter note. "I understand what you're saying but both of you must also understand how feelings are running high here in the south. Some people see it as the blatant murder of innocent people living in the north." He heaved a sigh. "Anyway as I was saying, there are some pubs in the town you must avoid, especially after last year. They are somewhat on the rough side and in view of what has happened I would strongly advise you to stay well away. They do not take kindly to outsiders, especially Englishmen," he paused and his eyes said it all. 'Yes Mr O'Shea.' I thought to myself, 'I certainly know all about Bloody Sunday.' The fact of the matter was that had we both stayed on in the army we would almost certainly have been in the thick of it. I could see O'Shea's words had well and truly struck a chord with Paul. Seeing that look in O'Shea's eyes I just could not help thinking back to the bonus he said we would get paid, it just went to confirm my uneasy feeling that he was hiding something from us. Then, just as if someone had thrown a switch O'Shea's mood changed.

"Come on lads, drink up. No harm meant it's just my Irish humour. Warped." He looked at both of us in turn, threw back his head and laughed aloud and his eyes danced with a look of friendly mischief about them. "Seamus," he called across to the barman, "fetch us some drinks, these lads are thirsty and we need to welcome them to our beautiful land. Oh and Seamus let's liven up the place it's like a morgue. Put on some good Irish music."

"Yes Mr O'Shea. Straight away."

"Now lads where were we, are yes I was telling you about the 'Valley of the Kings' and a little of our Irish heritage."

"What about your guests Mr O'Shea?"

"Oh they won't mind a little longer wait, they know me well enough. Anyway they're Irish and as long as I'm paying the bill it doesn't matter, they'll have a few Bushmill's whilst they patiently wait. That's one of the things we have a lot of here in the south, patience. Things always have a way of coming right in the end, so why worry."

The room was suddenly filled with the strains of a traditional Irish jig, and the atmosphere warmed, but no matter what happened from now on, deep down I knew that Breandán O'Shea meant what he had said and would be a force to contend with. My military training warned me that he was a very dangerous man and that we should always take care, treating him with the utmost of respect.

"I give you a toast," he raised his glass and looked first at Paul then at me and said. "May you both have a long and happy stay in the Republic and may we all do well."

"Cheers Mr O'Shea, I'm sorry we seemed to get off on the wrong foot, but here's to our future."

"Yes cheers Mr O'Shea," said Paul.

O'Shea drank his orange juice. "Well now, if you'll excuse me," he said as he stood up and shook our hands. "I must return to my guests in the Dining Room otherwise they will wonder what's happened to me even if I am paying the bill. I'll catch up with you both later."

Chapter 2

It must have been nearly half past eleven when the beautiful brown-eyed receptionist came over to our table.

"Hello Mr James I'm Fionnuala." I couldn't believe my luck.

"Fionnuala did you say?"

"Yes that's right. Well done. You got it right first time."

"That's a nice name, is it Irish?" I asked.

"Yes it means fair shoulder," she replied.

"Pretty appropriate I would say."

She laughed at this. Her eyes danced with laughter as she flirted with me. "Why do you say that?" she asked.

"Well your long fair hair and..." I was once more lost for words. Paul, who had been sat there, watching me make a fool of myself coughed, then cleared his throat. He could be so annoying at times like this. It wasn't often I got the girl when he was around because he seemed to have this knack of pulling birds. I'd start the ball rolling and he'd reap the rewards. I guess the fact that in a girl's eyes he was good looking. He was tall with dark curly hair; muscular body kept in trim by constant weight training. He had a Roman shaped nose and blue eyes, and an attitude. In fact some people would say he was good looking but knew it. A bit of a Greek god, but arrogant with it. That was Paul. An arrogant self centred bastard and good-looking to boot, but I love him. The only thing that I had advantage over him was that his hair was slightly receding so the chances are that given a few more years he will be going bald. Thank goodness for that. Perhaps then he wouldn't be so 'bloody' arrogant. He certainly could piss me right off with his attitude at times, especially around pretty women like now. The spell had been well and truly broken.

"Well aren't you going to introduce me?" he asked.

"Sorry mate, Fionnuala this is Mr..." but he cut me short.

"Paul. My name's Paul. Fionnuala is it, pleased to meet you can I get you a drink?" he asked.

"No thanks Paul. Mr O'Shea asked me to come and find you both and escort you through to the club."

Paul was beginning to monopolise the lady and this was annoying me so I cut in again, "Are you sure you wouldn't like a drink? It's no trouble honestly."

She looked at the small gold wristwatch then looked up and smiled. "Are you sure Mr James?"

"Please call me Richard, and yes of course I'm sure, so what may I get you?"

"As I'm finished now I'll have a Vodka and lime please. Thank you Richard." Once again she flashed that beautiful smile.

"Here Paul," I said giving him a five-pound note, "I'll have a whisky, a vodka and lime for Fionnuala and whatever you want." He gave me a filthy look but I ignored him.

"Here Fionnuala sit down," I said as I pulled another chair across from a nearby table. "Do you live locally?" I asked.

"No I live in Corke Abbey near Dublin."

"So do you commute every day?" She laughed.

"Of course not silly. I live in but go home on my rest days. It's too far to travel backwards and forwards." Just then we were interrupted by the return of Paul and our drinks.

"Vodka and lime for you Fionnuala, Bushmill whisky for you and a lager for me. So Fionnuala are you coming to the club with us?"

She smiled and said, "Afraid not I'm just the escort to show you the back way."

"Go on come in for a few minutes."

"Sorry guys, some other time maybe."

But I wasn't to be put off that easily. "Well just for one dance then, that won't hurt would it now?"

"No Richard thanks all the same."

"Why?" I asked.

"I've got to be up early as I'm early turn tomorrow and it's already getting on for ten to twelve." I shrugged my shoulders and looked mortally offended. She laughed and touched my hand; "There'll be other nights."

It was nearly midnight as Fionnuala showed us around the maze of corridors and down a flight of stairs to the back of the club. We could now hear the faint murmur of voices and the strains of the band as the sounds drifted through the door up ahead. Fionnuala opened the door for us and after the relative quiet of the bar upstairs the sound that now greeted us was deafening. Fionnuala shouted something to me but I didn't hear so she leaned forward her breasts pushed hard against me as she shouted in my ear.

"Well this is it. This is where I leave you." Her lips brushed my cheek. I leaned forward to speak to her; I could smell the delicate smell of her perfume.

"Do you ever come down here?" I shouted in her ear. She shrugged her shoulders.

"Sometimes why?" Once more I could feel the outline of her breast as she pushed against me to speak. Once more my feelings stirred deep down in the pit of my stomach then it all came to an abrupt halt as a young barman, who must have been about six foot tall, came over.

"Hi Fionnuala who've you got here then?"

"Oh this is Richard and Paul. Both are guests of Mr O'Shea and I've been told to bring them down to you. Mr O'Shea says they can come in this way as tonight should be a good show for them ok to leave them with you?"

"Ok Fionnuala see you." With that she smiled sweetly and waved as she disappeared back along the corridor.

"Right guys, do you want to go through." He held the bar flap up to allow us through to the dance floor. The club was heaving. Packed with locals leaving little or no space save adjacent to the bar.

"Paul," I shouted to make myself heard above the raucous strains of 'I Can't Get No Satisfaction', "See if you can spot O'Shea."

"What did you say?" he shouted back.

"Can you see O'Shea?" He shook his head pointing to his ear. It was obvious he still hadn't heard.

"Hang on until the group stops." He shouted back in my ear.

I waited until there was a slight decrease in the volume and tried again.

23

"I said, can you see O'Shea?" He screwed up his face and shrugged his shoulders. "In here, you must be joking?"

"Well have a look anyway." I shouted back to him.

"What?" he shouted back.

"I said, have a look..." Just then the band stopped.

"Why you shouting I'm not deaf," he said grinning at me. "Anyway you've got to be joking to find anyone in here is going to be like looking for a needle in a haystack."

"Well just have a look anyway."

"Ok I'll have a look over this way if you look over your side." We both set about searching for O'Shea. In a matter of minutes having drawn a blank Paul returned to the bar.

"Anything your way Richard?" I shook my head.

"No, I can't see him anywhere. Like you said it's like hunting for the proverbial in a haystack." I shouted to make myself heard above the noise.

"I told you it would be."

"So much for..." I started to say when the band cut me short as they went into their next number.

"What d'you say?" Paul shouted next to my ear.

"I was going to say so much for finding O'Shea."

"Oh right." He said then drank the last of his pint. I quickly downed what was left of my drink as Paul tried to attract the attention of the barman.

"Here, I'll get these mate." I said as the barman approached Paul.

"Yes Sir."

"Two pints of Smethwicks please." The number the band had been playing came to an abrupt halt and silence reigned.

"Phew that's better, now sir was that two pints of Smethwicks?"

"Yes and a packet of crisps please."

"One packet?"

"Paul do you want some crisps." I never did hear his answer because the band burst into their rendition of 'Twist and Shout' and people immediately started to flock back onto the dance floor once again. He put his thumb up so I assumed he meant yes.

"Make that two." I shouted to the barman and held up two fingers. As more and more people took to the floor we found the crowd at the bar started to thin out. I passed Paul his pint and took a mouthful of mine then motioned to him to move away from the bar so we could take a look around. Just then a young women with the shortest tightest pair of hot pants I'd ever seen caught my eye. I nudged Paul.

"Here Paul take a look at her." I indicated the girl wearing the hot pants, "What could you do with her?" I asked.

"Hmm, lovely legs." He said.

"Lovely arse," I said as she bent over to pull up one of her calf length leather boots. She straightened up and made her way towards the bar and where we were stood. She stood alongside us and waited patiently until the barman came to serve her.

"Yes love, what would you like?" he asked. As she leaned forward to order her drinks and her top fell open to reveal her natural beauty.

I nudged Paul and nodded in the general direction.

"Well mate, what do you think?"

"Got to be a thirty-eight and no bra. Lovely."

"Come on Paul it's not good for you. It'll only get you frustrated. Lets have a look around." He followed me reluctantly.

"I could happily spend an hour or two with her and keep her amused, couldn't you Richard. Now that's what I would call a decent bit of stuff!" We slowly managed to edge our way to the dance floor and found a table where we could sit and watch. The place was packed, but I suppose that would be true of anywhere on a Saturday night. We stayed at the table for a while watching the people on the dance floor.

"What do you reckon to the group?" Paul shouted to me.

"What d'you say?" I shouted back.

"The group, what d'you reckon?"

I shrugged my shoulders. "Not bad I suppose. I've heard a lot worse. What do you think?"

"I think they're good."

I just nodded and finished off my beer; "Do you want another beer?"

"Yeah please."

"Come on let's get back to the bar then." It was then I noticed the two guys. Both were wearing black berets and dressed in what looked like some sort of uniform. At first I thought they might have been from a local army base.

"Looks as if we've got a couple from the local mob in."

"Have we where?" Asked Paul. I pointed to the two blokes in berets. It was then that he noticed the others.

"Look there's some more over there."

"Must be a local barracks around here somewhere, anyway Paul never mind them, let's get the beer." With that we made our way back towards the bar, not giving our friends a second thought.

"Two pints of Smethwicks please." I shouted to the barman.

"Two pints was that sir?" I gave him the thumbs up sign.

"Paul," I shouted to my mate.

"What's up?"

"See any toilets?"

"No mate."

"Two pints of Smethwicks, anything else sir?"

"Yeah, can you tell me where the toilets are?"

"What was that sir?"

"Gents. Where are they?" I shouted to him again.

"Toilets. Over on the far side in the main lobby." he pointed across the dance floor towards the front entrance. "You'll see. Gents on the left Ladies on the right."

"Oh, is that where the main entrance is then?" He gave me a quizzical look.

"Yes sir. How did you get in then if not through the main entrance?" I smiled.

"Don't look so worried mate. Fionnuala..." ah Fionnuala I thought. "Yes Fionnuala the receptionist, she brought us through the back way."

"The back way?" he gave me another of his quizzical looks.

"Yeah. You know, through the bar. Mr O'Shea arranged it." Immediately I mentioned O'Shea's name the puzzled expression left his face.

"Oh right. Now I understand. Yes of course Fionnuala the receptionist. So you're friends of the boss. That explains it then."

"Explains what?"

"Why you didn't know where the entrance was. So you must be the Englishmen we've been expecting."

"If you say so." I said nonchalantly.

"Good. Are you enjoying it?"

"Yeah. It's ok." I replied. "Yeah it's good."

"Best around these parts, unless you go into Dublin. But Dublin's a bit of a drive from here, especially if you've had a few. Yes sir, it's a good crack in here most times. In fact Mr O'Shea hoped there would be a good crack especially tonight." He grinned, "Anyway as I said the toilets are over in the foyer across the other side. Take care now sir."

"Cheers mate." I picked up my beer and called Paul to take his.

"Well did you find out where they are?"

"Where what are?" I asked.

"The toilets."

"Yeah, they're over the other side where the main entrance is." I answered, then took a large swig of my beer.

We made slow progress as we pushed our way through the crowded room towards the entrance and the toilets. I had never seen such a heaving mass of humanity - I'd hate to think what would happen in a fire!

"Excuse me mate" I shouted to the big guy in front of me as I gently pushed my way through. He must have been at least six feet tall and was built like the proverbial.

"Who do you think you're shoving about then. Englishman?" He growled.

"Hey, come on! What's your problem? I'm only trying to get through." I continued to gently push by him.

"Not so fast Englishman." He snarled as he grabbed hold of my arm and yanked me back. I spun round to face him. Looking first at his face then at his hand grasping my arm. I snatched my arm free and transferred my stare back to his face.

"Look pal I don't know what your problem is, but..."

"Shut your face Englishman." He shoved his face closer to mine. He then started to prod me in the chest with his extended finger "You'd better be careful who you're pushing around or you could be in big trouble."

"Hang on mate. I did ask you to let me through but you chose to ignore me didn't you?"

"I'm not interested in what you have to say. Just watch it that's all. Now piss off." With that he turned away.

"Hey pal! Your threats don't worry me." Once again he turned and glared at me.

"Oh I see, cocky little bastard. So, are you looking for trouble, or is that you just enjoy hospital food?"

"Piss off." I shouted and started to push my way through the crowd, but too late.

People close by had heard the altercation and sensing a fight started to clear a space and formed a circle around us. I was now isolated. I didn't want a fight. Besides I sensed that I would get a severe kicking so I gave him a parting look and moved off in the direction of the toilets again, only to have my way barred for a second time by another big Irishman. He, like the first, glared at me.

"You best apologise to my mate, unless of course you would be wanting to enjoy that hospital food." What was it about me? Had I got 'Englishman looking for trouble' or something similar tattooed across my forehead. "Leave it out friend." I once more turned to walk away.

Again he confronted me. "I said apologise."

The band finished the number they were playing and suddenly everywhere was silent. More people, now hearing the rumpus, moved to where the small crowd had gathered, curious to find out what all the commotion was about. For a second time in a matter of minutes I was being forced down the road to a fight. I could feel the tension building. My heart was thumping. The inside of my mouth was dry. Somebody somewhere started to chant

"Fight, fight, fight."

Others joined in until everyone around was chanting. The chanting grew louder and faster until it reached a crescendo then it stopped just as suddenly as it had begun.

The Irishman came closer and seemed even more threatening as he looked at me then spat on the floor next to me. "Apologise to my mate or die you English Bastard!" He said. Each word was emphasised by a poke in my chest with that outstretched finger of his. "I said apologise."

I stood my ground. My tongue started to cling to the dryness in my mouth. I was coiled like a spring waiting for his next move. My sight was filled by this man's ugly visage. The stench of bad breath filled my nostrils. We stared at each other without flinching. Everyone around us was silent. It was as if time stood still, waiting with bated breath for something to happen. You could have cut the atmosphere with a knife. Then the spell was broken as someone shouted.

"Go on Damian, hit the bastard." The crowd once again was starting to chant.

"Fight, fight, fight, fight..." I was being forced along a path I did not wish to go. In my heart I knew I was beaten so I tried to extricate myself from a difficult situation before it got out of hand.

"Look, I don't want any trouble mate. All I'm trying to do is get over there." I indicated towards the entrance. The chanting stopped. I turned to walk away, but once more the Irishman blocked my path.

"I've just said, I don't want any trouble. Now if you don't mind." I pushed forward. He blocked my path again and somebody in the crowd shouted out.

"Oh, he doesn't want any trouble."

"Did you hear that lads." The big Irishman said with derision, "The Englishman doesn't want any trouble." He looked around at his audience and laughed as the crowd started chanting,

"English, English, English..."

He thrust his face even closer to mine and through his clenched teeth he muttered, "Englishman. If you don't want trouble, then, apologise."

I knew I was going to have to fight my way out of this, but where the hell was Paul? "Shit," I muttered under my breath, "Where the hell are you Paul." Again I tried to reason with him and I repeated what I had said before. "Look friend, I asked your mate quite politely to move before I started trying to get through. So what am I supposed to do?" I desperately looked about for my buddy, but he was nowhere to be seen. My mind began to race. "Look mate," I continued, "I'm here to enjoy myself like you and your mate, so let's not spoil it. Look, all I'm trying to do is get across to the bog to have a slash. All right?"

The crowd pushed forward hoping to escalate the situation.

"Get on with it." Someone shouted.

Then just when I thought my time was up Paul arrived. He quickly weighed up the situation. "Everything all right mate?" He stared long and hard at the two Irishmen, then glanced at me.

"Yeah, no problem."

"Hmm, are you sure? It looks far from ok to me!"

"Yeah fine! Just a slight misunderstanding wasn't it guys?"

The Irishman gave a sardonic smile. "Yes, that's right Englishman, just a misunderstanding."

The first of the two Irishmen then turned to look at Paul. "Yes, just a slight misunderstanding by your mate here, but I think he's got the message now. Don't you Damian?"

"Yeah, I'm sure he has." Damian then reached out and patted my cheek grinning. "Yeah he's got the message all right."

"What's your problem Pal?" Paul squared up to Damian.

"Leave it Paul."

"No, I don't like this blokes attitude," he called back to me over his shoulder, then continued talking to the Irishman. "Do you know Pal, you and your mate seem to think because you're big the whole world should jump when you're around, but I've got news for you, Pal. It's a real world outside and if you want to live in it you had best learn some manners first."

"Very good Englishman and are you going to be my teacher?" There was a slight tinge of sarcasm to the reply.

"Come on leave it Paul."

Paul started to draw back his arm. I quickly grabbed hold of it knowing this was not the time or the place. "I said, leave it Paul."

He lowered his arm and began to relax. "Ok, sorry Pal, we don't want any trouble". There was the trace of a smile on his lips, but his eyes never flinched once. I knew that smile. The Irishman stepped aside and let us pass, but as we made our way towards the toilets he called after us.

"That's right friend, I should leave it before you both get hurt. Oh, and don't forget arsehole, you're in my country now. In my town and among my people and what's more, you're English. So, if you want to carry on living be careful Pal."

Paul stopped and turned but before anything else happened I grabbed his arm and moved him away. "Come on Paul there's O'Shea over there."

He glared back at the Irishman and shouted. "It'll keep."

"Oh it'll keep all right, just keep looking over your shoulder pal that's all. Do you hear me? Just keep looking over your shoulder that's all."

"Yeah, yeah, yeah. It'll keep all right. Anytime you fancy your chances pal." Paul shouted as I dragged him away. "What a pillock." He muttered.

"Yeah he's a pillock, but leave it for now Paul. Let's go."

"Ok, ok I'm coming," he said sullenly as he followed me. Slowly the tension within me subsided but still I had an uneasy feeling about the night. Why? I just didn't know. Perhaps the recent confrontation had unsettled me. Who could say?

The excitement now over the crowd slowly started to disperse, and the band struck up with another of the Stone's numbers.

"Where's O'Shea then?" Paul asked.

"I dunno. I thought I saw him but I must have been mistaken." I lied glibly.

Paul gave me a knowing look. "Don't you mean it was only an excuse to get you away Paul?"

I grinned. "Something like that mate. You're not annoyed are you?"

"You bastard!" he said jokingly, "D'you know, if it hadn't of been for you saying that about O'Shea, I would have smacked that Irish pillock."

"I know you would. Then we would've had a problem wouldn't we?"

"How d'you mean? Problem my arse. What's wrong with you, getting soft in your old age?"

"No. Just sensible."

"Sensible. What a load of crap."

"It's not crap and you know it. There are too many unknowns here to start anything. Anyway we'd end up getting a good kicking and for what?"

"I suppose so, but I'd still have a go. Wouldn't you?" he winked and laughed out loud.

"Yep, nothing's changed." I started to laugh at the absurdity of it all as I pushed open the door labelled 'Gents'. The refreshing feel of cool air from an open window greeted us as we entered into the comparative calm of the toilets. As the door gently closed behind us the noise from the dance floor subsided to an imperceptible level. Out there was another world.

"Damian come here."

He roughly pushed two smaller guys aside as he made his way over to his friend. Both men talked in a conspiratorial way and every now and then Damian would look in the general direction of the Gents toilet and nod. Suddenly his mate laughed and slapped him on the shoulder. Then they both moved off through the crowd towards the entrance where they joined a small group of young men wearing the black berets. They then started talking to the group. After a few minutes of discussion, two of the young guys removed their berets placed them in their pockets and broke away from the main crowd. They casually made their way towards the door labelled 'Gents' where they stood outside chatting. A few moments later another two from the same group removed their berets and joined them. The four looked over to Damian and his mate and nodded. They then took a casual look about them. No one took any notice of the four young men entering the 'Gents'. Well why should they?

As I flushed the toilet the comparative calm was shattered by the strains of the 'Hippy Hippy Shake' as somebody else came in. I could just make out someone talking in a low conspiratorial tone. Then there was a different voice. No matter how hard I listened, neither of the voices was loud enough for me to make out what they were saying, but I had a distinct feeling that they were up to no good. Their quiet conversation continued for a short time then there was silence. I unlocked my cubicle door and walked over to wash my hands. A young man about twenty years old was stood in front of the mirror, combing his hair. As I washed my hands, I studied his reflection in the mirror as he carefully and purposefully pulled the comb slowly through his slicked back hair.

"Not a bad band," I commented as I rinsed my hands. He didn't reply, but just stood there combing his hair. "Do you come here each week?" I asked as I pulled out the plug in the basin. Once more I was greeted by a stony silence. Then, as I heard the click of the lock from Paul's cubicle, I saw the reflection of two other lads as they appeared as if from nowhere. As they moved rapidly towards me, I glimpsed the reflection of another person as he moved over to the door. I knew trouble with a capital T when I saw it. A chair, near to the door, was skilfully jammed under the door handle so effectively locking it. He then stood guard.

"Hey lads what's the game then?" They didn't say a word. "What's the problem?"I asked again as they started to close in on me. In the distance you could just hear a faint drone of voices. The band had stopped playing. The lad, who had been combing his hair, stopped. Still they didn't speak. He moved closer towards me. One of the others stood the other side of me. The third behind me. The forth in front of the entrance. Out of the corner of my eye I saw the door to Paul's cubicle move slowly open. I turned. I faced my assailants. "I asked what the problem was? Why the hassle?" My eyes darting back and forth from one lad's face to the next. I was watching for who was going to make the first move. Then, as if in answer to the silent question, the one on the right brought his hand quickly into view. I momentarily saw a flash of light as it was reflected back from a glass bottle. He brought his hand swiftly down against a corner of the wall. The bottle exploded. He jabbed his hand towards my face. That was Paul's cue. He threw back his cubicle door and shouted, "Come on you little bastard," and launched himself at the one with the bottle. The sheer impetus took the lad off his feet and knocked the bottle from his grasp. The bottle crashed to the floor and shards of glass flew in all directions. He dragged him to his feet; slammed him against the basin; twisted his arm up his back; forced his face hard up against the mirror. Any fight that was in him had now been knocked out of him completely. A kick from me brought the one that had been combing his hair crashing to the floor in agony. I jabbed my elbow back as hard as I could hopefully to make contact with the one behind. A sickly crunch and a yelp of pain from somewhere to my rear confirmed that I had found my mark. I spun round just in time to see blood spurt through the fingers of his hand that cupped his now broken nose. The guy by the door took flight. He kicked the chair away, but in his hurry to leave ran straight into someone coming in.

"What's your hurry pal?" The stranger then saw the carnage. He grabbed hold the escapee and slammed him against the wall. It was then that he saw the bloke on the floor being dragged to his feet by Paul. "Ciaran, what's going on?" The new arrival asked.

30

"Yes Ciaran, what is going on?" Asked Paul.

"Who the hell are you?"

"Never mind me, but more to the point, do you know this little shit?" He glared at the lad in his grasp.

"Yeah. That little shit as you put it, is my brother so I suggest you let him go before you get more trouble."

"Oh yeah? So who's the other little bastards with him?"

I checked to reassure myself that any fight in the other two had long since disappeared, then I chipped in. "Hang on Pal before you start shouting your mouth off. Your so called brother and his three pals here started all this by threatening me with a bottle."

Ciaran's brother looked at me then at Ciaran releasing his grip on the lad he had pinned against the wall as he did so. The lad immediately made a dive for the door but not quickly enough. Ciaran's brother slammed him against the wall, then threw him across the floor. "Now you little bastard get over there and stay over there." He then stood in front of the door and turned his attention to Paul. "You."

"Are you talking to me Paddy?"

"Yes I am. Let him go and we'll get to the bottom of this."

Paul quickly glanced in my direction. I slowly inclined my head in agreement with the stranger. "Ok Paul let him go."

"But he tried to bottle you Richard." Paul protested.

"Leave it Paul. I said let him go, it's not worth it."

"Ok, if you say so." Paul released his grip on Ciaran.

"I should fucking well think so." He sneered at Paul and started to walk towards the door.

"Oi where d' you think you're going? Come here." His brother shouted.

"Piss off, I'm going back to the dance."

"No you're not." His brother grabbed him and twisted his arm up his back.

"Get off. Let go. It's nothing to do with you."

"Oh isn't it. Well I've just made it my business and if you know what's best for you you'll tell me what's going on."

"Leave it Fergal." The lad with the broken nose spoke for the first time.

"Oh, who've we got here then? Don't I recognise you?" His brow furrowed as he struggled for the lad's name.

The lad with the broken nose looked at him and shook his head slowly. "Fergal, please stay out of it." He spoke almost in a whisper. Fergal was not in the mood to take any prisoners.

"Ah yes! Little Shane O'Rielly isn't? Right you two start talking and talk fast, what the bloody hell is happening?" He started to bend his brother's arm up his back until Ciaran was begging him to stop. He looked first at O'Rielly then his brother. "Well I'm waiting."

Ciaran yelped in pain. "Fergal stop you're hurting me."

"I'll stop when I get to the bottom of this, so come on Ciaran what's occurring?"

"Hang on Ciaran," Shane said forgetting all about his nose. "I'll go for Damian." He then made a dash for the door. Too late, Paul was there before him. Once again I grabbed hold of Shane and slammed him against the wall.

"Who's Damian?" I asked, but he didn't answer.

Fergal twisted his brother's arm further.

"Arrh...let go Fergal. Please let go you're hurting me." Fergal did not release his grip.

"If you want me to let go then tell me what this is all about." With that he gave Ciaran's arm another quick twist.

Ciaran's face was now distorted with pain. "Ok, ok I'll tell you."

"Shut up Ciaran, don't be stupid." Shane shouted to him.

"What do you know Shane?" I asked as I pushed harder across his windpipe with my arm.

"Nothing. I know nothing."

"I don't believe you." I pulled back my fist to hit him again.

"Ok, ok. Ciaran knows the details don't you Ciaran?" His voice low and muffled.

"Well Ciaran tell me then." His brother asked bending his arm up his back again.

"Ok let go. Let go and I'll tell you."

"Good. That's better Ciaran. Now you tell me little brother what is going on and then I'll let you go and everyone can go. That way no more will be said. Understood?"

"Ok. It's big Damian and his mate, they told me to get a couple of mates of mine and to come in here. He said there was two strangers in the toilets that were causing trouble and needed to be warned off. Given a bit of a working over so to speak. He told me nothing too obvious though."

"You what." Paul interjected, "I would say bottling someone was a bit obvious wouldn't you?"

Ciaran looked at Paul wide eyed with panic. "It wasn't like that."

"Oh and what was it like then?" Asked his brother.

"The bottle was only to scare them off," interjected Shane. "We were told that they weren't welcome here. That they would be trouble for our families and us so we should scare them..." Ciaran cut him short.

"Yeah, and there was forty punt in it for us."

"That's all and that's the truth." Shane said petulantly.

"I see, so Damian McGuinnes offered to pay you forty punt to scare these two guys. Why I wonder?" he relaxed his grip on his younger brother and turned his attention to us. "What's your version?"

"We are completely in the dark as to what is going on. We arrived here today and that's all there is to it."

"On holiday?"

"No we're here on business."

"What sort of business?"

"We've got some work to do for Breandán O'Shea. Do you know him?" I asked.

"Who doesn't." He replied, "he's the biggest landowner around here and the wealthiest to boot." He put his mouth close to his brother's ear. "Did you hear that little brother" he snarled, "they are friends of The Big Man."

"We didn't know. Honestly we didn't."

"You're lucky it's me then and not these two. I think you might apologise to them little brother don't you?"

"Piss off, I'm not apologising to anyone." Fergal gave the arm another quick twist.

"Owww let go. Let go."

32

"Well apologise then." He said twisting the arm further.

"Ok, ok. I'm sorry. I'm sorry." With that he released the lad's arm.

"Now you and Shane had best piss off back to the dance and take these other two unfortunates with you. What's more keep out of mischief."

"All right." Ciaran replied sullenly as he left us.

"I'm sorry for all this trouble my brother's caused you and I'm sure when Mr O'Shea hears about they'll be a few more who'll be sorry to. By the way those two guys, not the youngsters but Damian McGuinnes and his mate, are bad news really. It's best to stay on the right side of them."

"Who are they?" I enquired.

"Just a couple of local thugs. Wherever they go there's always trouble. They don't usually come here though. Now I wonder what's brought them here tonight there must be something going on."

"How do you mean?"

"Never you mind." He appeared deep in thought. "Hmm, I don't like it."

"Like what?" I asked, but he didn't reply straight away and when he did it was as if he was thinking aloud.

"Why would McGuinnes and his mate be here unless... Oh shit no. Quick you must get out of here, there's going to be trouble. Big trouble?"

"How do you mean? What do you mean by big trouble?"

He was already opening the door to leave. "Haven't time to explain. Must find Ciaran and get out of here. You must go also. Go now. Go." With that he was through the door and gone.

"What did you make of that?" I asked as Paul and I started to make our way back towards the bar.

"I dunno. It seems that our friend Damian and his mate are a couple of right arseholes if you ask me."

"Hmm I think you're right. Still let's forget about it and enjoy ourselves."

Soon the episode in the toilets had been forgotten about and we once again started to enjoy ourselves. We even managed a couple of dances, but our enjoyment was short lived.

Suddenly as if from nowhere half a dozen or more individuals wearing black ski masks and carrying Self Loading Rifles (SLR) appeared in the club. The main entrance was slammed shut and bolted.

"What the f..." I looked at Paul.

"Jesus it's a raid or something." He yelled at me.

Women in the lobby were screaming. One of the masked individuals threw open the door to the ladies toilet and brandishing a handgun signalled to any women to get out into the dance. One woman who was a little slow was thrown bodily into the lobby.

"You bastard," she screamed at the top of her voice then started to cry.

In the gents' toilet a similar scene was being re-enacted, but the blokes were being more vociferous, shouting abuse at the masked gunman.

Paul and I watched as people were herded into the main body of the club.

"Richard, for Christ's sake it's the IRA. Let's get out of here."

"I'm with you buddy. Go! Go! Go!" I shouted back to him at the top of my voice as I started to push my way forward.

"Which way mate?"

"Head for the bar." I called, "But keep close."

"Yeah, ok, just go Richard, go!" He shouted back to me as I shoved and manhandled people aside, but it was all to no avail. The masked individuals had very quickly and very efficiently taken full control of the club; there was no retreat. Our way was successfully blocked.

"Shit we're stuffed. What now Richard?"

My mind went into overdrive, but I didn't have any answers. Events quickly took over as everyone was herded onto the dance floor. Once again the band started to play but their heart was not in it.

"Haven't a clue but we are definitely stuffed, and I reckon this was what Fergal meant when he said McGuinnes was big trouble!"

"Maybe. Perhaps he knew something. So where are those two bastards?" In all the commotion I had forgotten all about our little tête-à-tête with the two Irishmen, a lot had happened since then, but come to think of it they were now conspicuous by their absence.

Suddenly a couple of yards away a girl screamed as two of the masked men grabbed a guy and started to drag him away. She screamed at the top of her voice, "Leave him, leave him alone!" She threw herself at one of the men. He tossed her aside, "You bastards leave him." Again she threw herself at the masked man. Punching and kicking him she launched into a tirade of abuse. He once more threw her aside. This time she fell to the floor sobbing, "You bastards, you rotten murdering bastards."

Another masked man roughly hauled her to her feet and bundled her ahead of him as he shoved and pushed his way through the crowd following in the footsteps of his two compatriots. Nobody moved, everyone just stood where they were rooted to the spot while the band played on. Suddenly the spell was broken by a loud crash followed by the sound of breaking glass. People push backwards. Women sobbing and screaming. The band finally gave up.

"What's going on Paul?"

"I don't know. I can't see from here. Watch my back while I try to find out."

"Yeah ok, I'm behind you." The whole place erupted. For a minute I lost sight of Paul. A number of people closed in around me. Suddenly I felt very vulnerable. Shit, where are you Paul. Again I felt we were in deep trouble. Something told me we were to become the focal point of whatever it was that was going on. "Paul, where've you got to?" I muttered under my breath. This was not good. "Paul." I called in the general direction I thought he was. "Are you over there?"

"Over here mate, where are you?"

I gave a sigh of relief. I could hear his voice, but could not see him for people milling around in blind panic.

"I can hear you mate, but can't see you as yet." He must have caught a glimpse of me through the crowds.

"I'm through here." The bodies between us muffled his voice. "Try to make your way over to your right."

I pushed first in one direction then in another. "I'm not getting anywhere, too many people." I called back.

"Well you stay there and I'll try to get through from here."

I waited for what seemed an eternity but still no Paul. "This is not working Paul." I was now beginning to feel just a little isolated.

"Hang on. God there's so many bodies."

"Paul...still can't see you," I shouted.

"Richard I'm over here."

I could still hear his voice over to my right but the crowd, if anything, was getting worse. I was gradually being forced further and further away from where I was sure he was. The panic going on around me was causing me a problem and I was having to keep my mind centred otherwise I could feel myself slipping down the slippery spiral into that maelstrom of panic. I still couldn't see my buddy. Shit Paul, you may have an attitude and you maybe a good looking bastard and get more than your fair share in women, but I'll forget all about that if only I could find... Suddenly the crowd seemed to thin a little and I felt someone grab me by the shoulder. "Who the f..." then to my relief I heard the dulcet tones of Paul.

"Christ mate, you're jumpy," he said.

"Shit Paul, for a minute there I thought you were that Irish bastard again." He laughed.

"It's no joke mate I could have seriously damaged your pretty face, then what would the women do then?"

He shrugged his shoulders. "Yeah, yeah, yeah. I should say so."

"What's going on Paul?" We started to push our way forward through the milling crowd. "What's happening? Can you see anything?" I asked sensing something was wrong.

"Nothing at the moment," he said. Then suddenly the crowd in front of him seemed to melt away. "My god!"

"What's up Paul."

"Quick, get back Richard. Get back. Get out of here. Get out."

"What's up?" was all I managed to say before Paul was unceremoniously bundling me away.

"You don't want to know, just move. We've got to get out of here" There was a sense of urgency in his voice. Without question I started to push and shove my way back. All thoughts of the incident in the toilet had been banished from my mind. When I turned to speak to Paul his ashen face shocked me. Whatever he had seen had certainly shaken him and this only served to spur me on.

"Come on you bastards let me through" I uttered through my gritted teeth, as I pushed and shoved. Suddenly the crowd surged and I found myself being carried with it. I looked for Paul but he wasn't there. Again the crowd surged. Again I was swept along. I tried to stop myself. "For god's sake." I tried to force my way back to where I thought Paul was and for a split second I caught a fleeting glimpse of him. Then suddenly there was a gap. I was through. The area ahead was clear. I was free to move unhindered. I moved forward then froze. For there, in front of me, lay the body of a man. I recognised him as the man who had been hauled from the crowd just a few moments ago. His girlfriend was covered in red spatters as she tried in vain to staunch the flow of blood as it pumped from a jagged wound in his chest and formed a red sticky pool about him.

"Someone please help me." She looked around at the crowd, her eyes wide with fear. "Can't you see he needs help." Her eyes said it all, but no one offered. "Please, someone, anyone please help." She implored. "Hold on my darling, You'll be all right." She cradled his head in her arms, but then with a gurgling gasp his life ebbed away.

Although I was an ex-military man and had witnessed death before somehow this was different. It was on a more personal level. The sight of this man and his girlfriend would remain a vivid picture for a long time. The pained expression on her face. The look of fear in her eyes. The way she beseeched strangers to help her. The way no one did all made up the horrific picture. My mouth became dry and I felt sick deep down in the pit of my stomach. Time stood still. Why had no one gone to his aid? The noise of the crowd seemed far away and everything felt like it was closing in. I had to do something. I knew it was hopeless nevertheless I forced leaden legs to move. Then, as if in slow motion, I moved forward to help this woman. In the depths of my mind I could hear someone calling.
"Richard, leave him. For Christ's sake come away. It's not our problem."
I felt someone pulling my arm and I turned as if in a daze. It was Paul.
"Leave him Richard. It's not for us. Come on quickly, come on. Richard," he shouted frantically. "I said leave it, now let's go, come on let's get out of here."
I blinked my eyes. "Shit Paul, what's going on?"
"I don't know, but let's go, let's go."
I shook my head to clear my mind, but too late. Before we could move two burly Irishmen in ski masks grabbed us.
"Stand still Englishman and keep quiet if you know what's good for you."
Although I couldn't see his face I was sure it was McGuinnes. I'd recognise his voice anywhere. Then it was confirmed when the other one addressed Paul.
"So Englishman, when you said it'll have to wait I don't suppose you thought it would come round quite so quickly did you?" With that he twisted Paul round to face the stage.
I tried to break free but I was held in a vice like grip. "Face the stage, and stand still." Suddenly I felt a sharp jab in my ribs. I looked down to the glint of steel and felt a second jab. In his hand McGuinnes grasped a very thin bladed knife. It was probably the very same one used on the man lain before me.

I looked across at Paul and down to my side. His gaze followed the direction of my eyes to the knife being held by McGuinnes. He just nodded and this served to confirm what I had thought. As we looked on, another of the masked brigade made his way to the stage. He summoned a member of the band and after a quick discussion the band started to play 'A Soldiers Boy'. The main doors were re-opened and two masked men escorted a stranger to the stage. This man commanded respect. He moved forward unhindered. He climbed up onto the stage and silently surveyed the scene. As the last note of 'A Soldiers Boy' died away he summoned those wearing the black berets to come forward. Suddenly I realised the significance of the black berets. It was the badge of an IRA soldier how stupid we had both been. It all now began to fit into place. The black berets, the murder and the armed persons wearing ski masks were all IRA.

"All of you selected men," the guy on the stage started to speak, "will upon command, form a line shoulder to shoulder in front of the scum on the floor. You will stand facing the main entrance with the corpse to the rear. Understood?"

"Yes sir," They replied in unison.

"Good." He paused, took a breath, then in a voice that a Drill Sergeant would have been proud of, barked out the command, "Men, men fall in."

The black berets quickly and silently did as they were ordered while the armed ski masked individuals watched on.

"Death to all Protestants for they are all murderers. Let this be a lesson to all of you present. This is how we deal with these murderers and their families. Let it be known that in the north our cousins are fighting day in and day out against these murdering bastards." Again he looked around. Nobody moved. The club was silent. Not a murmur to be heard. This man was a force to reckon with. He was not only controlling them and the band, but it seemed he controlled the very heart and lifeblood of this community.

"Are you thinking what I'm thinking Paul?" I asked in a low whisper.

"I hope not or we're dead." He whispered back.

"Shut your mouth you English bastard or it'll be the last thing you say." Once again I felt the sharp point of the knife jab me again in the ribs. The cold point of the steel blade against my flesh gave me a chilling reminder that he meant what he said. I would give anything right now to be at home having a quiet pint in my local, but that was a long way away. Our chance of survival depended on our staying undetected and the longer we stood here the more optimistic I grew. However my hopes were quickly dashed and my euphoria short lived.

This man was arrogant. He was smug and had a look of self-satisfaction as he surveyed the scene before him. He even allowed a fleeting smile to touch his lips before turning his attention to us. How foolish of me to allow myself to be lulled into a false sense of security, thinking that perhaps, that just maybe, this person did not realise we were here. I had broken the cardinal rule; that of underestimating the enemy. Yes he was thorough all right; he had not missed a trick.

"Look at the bastard Paul. He's really enjoying this isn't he?" I whispered.

"Shut your mouth Englishman." I felt another sharp pain in my side as the point of the knife was pressed home.

"Yeah you're right." Paul whispered back. "What a scheming, arrogant bastard."

There he stood silently staring first at Paul then at me.

"Release them." I felt McGuinnes relax his grip on me and withdraw the knife from my side. "Provided you both return to your rooms by the way you came and stay there, then no harm will come to you. However let this be a warning to you," He paused and looked around the room and addressed everyone, "In fact to all of you present let this be a warning. Do as you are told...otherwise..." He left the rest unsaid. "Escort them back to their rooms."

Once inside my room the full impact of what had happened hit me: the picture of the blood spurting incessantly from a gaping chest wound; the girl cradling her boyfriend in her arms as he died. It could quite easily have been me lying there and it was that more than anything that hit home. As a soldier, death I could handle, but this time it was different. All I wanted was to earn some money then go back home. I shouted at the wall. "I don't need this! I really don't need this!"

For the first time in my life I was scared, real scared. I thought about home and how safe it was there. Suddenly it seemed so far away as if in another world. That was it, the money was no longer so attractive. I opened the wardrobe and started to pack, I wasn't prepared to stay a moment longer. All I wanted to do was run. I was scared all right.

I was just putting the last few items into my case when there was a knock at my door.
"Who's there?"
"It's me."
"Paul! Is that you?"
"Yes you daft bugger, open the door. Come on quickly before our minders return."
I unlocked the door and opened it just wide enough to enable me to check that Paul was on his own. "Where've they gone?" I asked as Paul came into my room.
"I don't know, all I know is that they've gone. One thing for sure I'd feel a lot safer in a public place rather than stuck in my room, wouldn't you?"
"Yeah, I guess so."
Just then Paul noticed the case. "Haven't you unpacked yet?"
"How do you mean?"
"The case, it's still full of gear."
"Oh err, yes." I said lamely.
Paul gave me a quizzical look. "How come?"
"Silly of me. I was in such a rush to get down to find O'Shea earlier I hadn't even had chance to unpack. Then with everything else it had clean slipped my mind."
Paul looked at me, then back to the case. "Oh I see." He said unconvinced. "I suppose our little experience couldn't have affected your err, memory in any way?"
"No." I paused looking away from him. "Well maybe slightly. Oh shit Paul, what do you think? We come over here to earn some money and..." My voice tailed off.
"Yes, and what?"
I shuffled about uneasily suddenly feeling very foolish for my moment of weakness. There was an embarrassing silence.
"Come on Richard, I think we could both do with a drink."
"Yeah your right. Sod 'em all, that's what I say." Suddenly I felt a lot better.
"That's right don't let the bastards grind you down!"
With my heart pounding I slowly opened the door to check if our minders had returned, but I had no need to worry. They were long gone.

We had been in the bar for a good hour, when the local Gardai arrived in answer to a call about a disturbance in the club. Of course they were far too late, the body and all traces of blood had been removed whilst we were there. From what we could overhear they found everything, as it were, normal. The band playing, people up dancing and enjoying themselves just as if nothing untoward had happened. Obviously they questioned everyone even the people in the hotel bar, but they drew a blank. Being strangers and English they paid particular attention to us. They questioned us at length and like everyone else we denied everything, claiming we had been in the hotel all evening.

"So you say you had been in the hotel all evening sir?"

"Of course, we only arrived today. In fact I didn't even know there was a nightclub until you said. Is it here in the hotel then?" I innocently asked.

"No sir. It adjoins the hotel."

"Then how would we know anything?" I lied.

"Sir, I assume that as two young men here on holiday you would..."

"But who said we are on holiday?" Paul interjected.

"I'm sorry sir I assumed you were. Anyway, as I was saying about the nightclub..."

"If it's not in the hotel then how would we know about it?" I asked.

"It is well advertised in the hotel's brochures. Now can we press on?"

"I'm sorry, but because it's well advertised in brochures doesn't mean to say we have read them does it?" I said a little curtly.

"Are you telling me that you have not read them, or seen anything about the club?"

"That's right. We haven't, have we Paul?"

"Nope."

"That's a little strange don't you think sir?"

"Why?"

"Well sir, when you stay in a place on holiday, then I would have thought you would like to know what the place has to offer, wouldn't you sir?"

"Yes, but my mate has already told you we're not here on holiday."

"I'm sorry sir, but your friend did not state that. He asked the question..."

"Ok, but surely you would assume from his question that we are not on holiday?"

"It pays not to assume anything sir. So you are not here on holiday, then what are you here for?"

"We're here on business."

"I see sir. What business?"

"We're working for Mr O'Shea and we are here as his guests."

"He'll confirm this of course?"

"Yes, why don't you check with him?"

"Don't worry sir, we will."

"So have you done officer?"

"For now sir, but I may need to speak with you both again." He then turned his attention to the other guests in the bar.

"Do you think he swallowed it?"

"Dunno Paul. I hope so!" I just hoped that our excursion into the nightclub had gone unnoticed.

Sometime after the night's events I found out that the night porter had for some reason confirmed our story. I have no idea why he should do such a thing unless Breandán O'Shea had instructed him to keep a weather eye on us. Even to this day it still remains a mystery.

Chapter 3

I was awakened by the telephone ringing.

"Good morning Richard, it's eight o'clock." The soft Irish lilt of female's voice was music to my ears. Suddenly I was awake.

"Is that you Fionnuala?" I asked.

"To be sure it is," she gave a little giggle, "I did say I was on early or don't you remember." I remembered all right, how could I forget such a pretty girl.

"Of course I hadn't forgotten." I tried to sound convincing. She gave a little laugh.

"Bye Richard." I lay there savouring a picture of Fionnuala with her long fair hair tumbling about her shoulders and her dancing brown eyes. I swung my legs out of bed and made my way to the bathroom. As I ran the shower the events from last night came flooding back, what had I got myself into? As I took my shower once more my thoughts turned to Fionnuala. How could such a lovely girl as her be involved in something as bad last night? I wasn't convinced that she or, for that matter, anyone in the hotel was. Unless, of course I counted O'Shea, but that had to be ridiculous, or were it? It didn't matter how many times I turned it over in my mind I still could not come up with any real answers.

"Come on then, if you're going for breakfast." I checked to make sure I'd got my keys and joined Paul. "What do you reckon last night was all about?" he asked.

"I don't know and you?"

"I'm not sure what to make of it."

"Well I've turned it over and over in my mind and I'm still puzzled as to who's behind it. I know before you say anything, I'm certain it's IRA driven but I thought only things like that happened in Ulster. Anyway let's change the subject."

"It may not be IRA."

"How do you mean?"

"It could be the UDA."

"What d'you mean UDA? Absolute rubbish! That bloke had to be IRA."

"Why?"

"You heard him. It was a sectarian killing, he was on about Protestants wasn't he?"

"Yeah good point. So it must be IRA."

After a good breakfast we drove down to O'Shea's farm and took a look around the orchards.

"Looks as if we've got our work cut out here Richard."

"Yeah. So where shall we start?"

"I don't mind. Near the house?"

"Ok, near the house it is." Whilst Paul collected what we needed from the car I went to the house to let Breandán O'Shea know we were here, but got no reply.

It was late morning before O'Shea came to find us. "Morning Richard, morning Paul. Hotel all right? Did you sleep well?"

"Yeah, fine." I tried hard to sound nonchalant.

"Good, so they're looking after you then?"

The idle chitchat went on for a few minutes and I sensed he was leading up to something.

"How did it go in the club last night, did you enjoy the dance?"

"Yes, it was fine. We looked for you but couldn't see you anywhere."

"Was the band any good?" He asked changing the subject.

"Yeah they were all right weren't they Paul?" Paul just grunted and nodded his approval.

"Good. I'm pleased you enjoyed it." He paused, then it came. "Was there anything special that happened there last night?"

I looked up from what I was doing. What did he mean by that I wondered? Did he know about the stabbing? I searched his face for a clue. I looked at Paul and raised an eyebrow. I thought about it only for a second.

"As it happens there was."

"Oh, and what was that?" He waited patiently for an answer looking first at Paul and then at me. My gut feeling was that he already knew.

"We were witness to a stabbing." I looked straight at him, studying his face intently to see if there was the slightest hint that he already knew.

"What? A stabbing!" He exclaimed with mock concern.

"Yes, a stabbing." I repeated and I looked straight at him but he never flinched, he just looked me straight in the eyes.

"I suppose some of the local lads fell out over a girl or something, that's usually the most common reason for fights and the like. Still it couldn't have been that serious, otherwise I would've heard about it wouldn't I?"

I was convinced he knew something, but I couldn't prove a thing. "Actually, I don't think it was as simple as you like to make out. It was not just a fight over some girl. In fact I don't think it was even a fight among the local lads that got out of hand as you put it. I think what Paul and I actually witnessed was premeditated cold-blooded murder!" I glanced at Paul then back at O'Shea. "Yes Mr O'Shea that's it, cold-blooded murder! In fact I would go as far as to say I think that what we saw was the work of the IRA. An IRA killing." That must have hit home, but he never flinched. We stood there in silence. O'Shea's face impassive as always, not a flicker. Suddenly he bellowed with laughter, which caught me totally off my guard. I quickly recovered my composure and continued on the same tack as before reiterating what I had just said. "I'm serious Mr O'Shea. I think it was the work of the IRA." He laughed even more. I suddenly felt very foolish. Perhaps I had made some terrible mistake. Perhaps I was wrong about him.

Then he stopped laughing. His eyes became cold and calculating as he said. "We always put on a good show, especially for the English." A flicker of a smile, then it was gone. He turned on his heel and walked off towards his house.

"Phew, well what did you make of that Paul, was that for show or what?"

"Hmm, I'm not sure, but I don't like it whatever it is."

My mind was in turmoil. Was it just an act by O'Shea? Had we witnessed a sectarian killing, or had the whole thing been stage managed from beginning to end? I had no answers, just questions, questions and even more questions.

After the episode in the orchard neither of us felt like talking much so the evening meal was a relatively quiet affair. There was a certain air of despondency, a big black cloud of doom. I was still in two minds whether to call it a day or not and Paul was keeping his own counsel on things. Both of us had come here with high hopes and the promise of big money, but now, because of what had happened it all seemed irrelevant. I broke the silence and started to air my thoughts and my niggling concerns.

"I don't know Paul, maybe we ought to call it a day. I know the money's brilliant, but money's not everything is it?"

"Huh, you've soon changed your tune. It wasn't long ago you were the one who was saying we've got to take it because of the money so I agreed. Now we're here you want to toss it all away. Why?"

"Bloody hell Paul, I can't believe I'm hearing this. Some great Irish thug and his mate have threatened me..."

"Just a minute," Paul interjected angrily, "You've been threatened, oh dear. Well in case you've not noticed, you weren't the only one there."

"All right then we've both been threatened, if that makes you feel any better, by two Irish thugs as well as a gang of youngsters and then to top it all we're implicated in a murder."

"Leave it out Richard. Implicated in a murder my arse. We saw a stabbing. We've not been implicated in anything. What a loud of bullshit."

"Ok so we witness a stabbing. Stabbing or murder what's it matter, the guy's still dead."

"Yes, I hear what you're saying but we're not implicated." He said with exasperation.

"Aren't we. Was it my imagination or not about that copper giving us the third degree last night?"

"Now you're being stupid."

That did it. "Stupid am I? Piss off Paul. You know what I'm saying is right, we are implicated." My temper was getting the better of me.

"Woo, woo, woo. Calm down, Calm down." Paul looked at me and grinned. "It's me, Paul, remember. What's bugging you, come on tell me. What is it?" Paul waited for my reply, but instead I just sat there in stony silence. "Come on Richard, it's not worth falling out over, but I do think you're getting paranoid." He grinned and winked, "So we had a bit of a run in with some likely lads, that's all." I opened my mouth to speak. "I know, I'll say it before you do, we also witnessed a killing. Not an everyday occurrence I'll grant you, but unfortunately we were there. As for the copper, well what can I say?" he shrugged his shoulders, "after all he was only doing his job."

"I suppose you're right. Perhaps I am paranoid; I'm just a little tired. I didn't sleep too well last night, so maybe that's something to do with it."

"That's better mate. Anyway what's happened to your sense of adventure. After all you were the one, who joined up with the Angola brigade to see the world, take some risks and earn good money. So Ireland isn't Angola but at least the money's good and we are almost certain of staying alive."

I had to smile. "Yeah, I suppose you're right and of course there's always Fionnuala." God how I fancied that girl and if for no other reason than that I was prepared to stay. "Come on let's get to the bar I feel like a drink."

Chapter 4

"So how long are you here for?" enquired the barman.

"Any ideas Richard?"

"We don't really know, could be a matter of weeks, or even months. Depends on how much work Mr O'Shea gives us."

"You're working for Mr O'Shea then." He said, as he looked up from washing some dirty glasses. "Have you been to the Nightclub yet?" he asked as he dried his hands.

"Yeah, we were there last night, it was absolutely heaving."

"It always is," he stated in a matter of fact way as he examined the glass in his hand for traces of lipstick. "Mind you, they do get some good bands though." He picked up the last few glasses and walked down the bar to put them away.

"Where else is there to go?" I asked as he placed the glasses on their respective shelves.

"In this area?" He thought for a minute, "Depends on what you're looking for. There are pubs of course, but the real night life is in Dublin or the club here." He walked back to the glass washer and turned it off. "All right so there's the odd pub that puts on a duo or something, but nothing special."

"So it's Dublin or here."

"I guess that sums it up." He disappeared through the door at the back of the bar to reappear a few moments later with a small crate of tonic water, which he proceeded to stack on the shelf. "So you don't fancy going again tonight then?"

"I don't really think so do you Richard?" Paul gave me a wink.

"No. I think we'll give it a miss."

"That's a shame," he said as he busied himself slicing up some more fresh lemon. "It should be a good night tonight. Good band and it'll be less crowded. Saturday night's good but it's always packed out and for some reason the bands are never anything that special. That's one thing I would say about Sunday night most of the young crowd you know the sort, two pints of Guinness and big enough to take on the world, have already spent most of their money so it's less crowded and less trouble. Also more chance of, well you know, getting a bird less lads you see."

"Excuse me, could I have two whiskies please." Someone called from further up the bar.

"With you in a second sir. Sorry was it two Bushmill's you wanted before I disappear?"

"Yes please."

After a lengthy discussion and couple more drinks we decided to go to the club again

The barman had been right; the club was not as crowded and I thought it was much better. We both stood at the side of the dance floor, as blokes do, just looking. Eyeing up the local girls and generally weighing up our chances. I suppose we must have been in there about an hour, when Paul gave me a nudge.

"Look, over there Richard, what about those two?" he indicated two quite pretty girls sitting at a table not far away from where we were standing. They must have both been in their mid to late twenties. I think they knew what we were about and every now and then one of them would glance in our direction.

"I reckon we're in there with a chance. What d'you think?"

"Maybe." Paul said trying to appear laid back about it.

"Come on lets get over there and ask them for a dance." I suggested trying to coax Paul into doing something.

"I dunno mate. I'm not sure." He wasn't convinced.

Just then the group launched itself into a medley of the Beatles numbers. This was our chance. "Come on Paul, let's go." I said, once more trying to coerce him to make a move.

"Hang on. Let's wait for something a bit slower. Here give me your glass." He said changing the subject. "I'll get another pint in." Paul wasn't being coerced and headed off towards the bar. I kept on looking over to the girls, then they were on the move. The one closest picked a shoulder bag up and slung it casually over her shoulder. They both made their way towards the centre of the dance floor where there was another group of girls. I sensed we were about to miss our chance but I wasn't giving up that easily.

As Paul returned I pointed to where the girls had been sat.

"Let's take a casual walk over there mate." I suggested.

"Ok, then what?"

"Well..."

"Ok, well what?"

"Oh I don't know. See how things develop."

"Ok I'm up for it." He replied to my surprise and with that we casually strolled over towards the girl's table. We stood there watching the girls dancing, they were totally immersed in what they were doing and oblivious of us. They slowly moved from the main group. Dancing their way across the floor eventually ending up not far from where we had been standing earlier. There two or three others joined them. Closer and closer they got to the edge of the dance floor and the deserted tables. This was our chance. Putting down our drinks on a table nearby we moved in for the kill!

The girl with the shoulder bag paused in her dancing and took out a steel comb with a long pointed handle; the type sometimes used by ladies hair stylists. In one swift movement she swung her hand upwards and plunged the pointed shaft deep into the stomach of the other girl. For a minute I couldn't believe my eyes, then as the girl swayed I reacted. I ran towards her as she screamed in agony. With a look of disbelief she staggered drunkenly backwards into the tables. She tried to regain her balance, staggered again, then collapsed.

A crowd of girls that had quickly gathered around her became a wall of venomous jeering women as I tried to get through. One woman even managed to land a kick that brought me up short. Another grabbed a handful of my hair. This was quickly becoming a re-run of last night. Women were shouting and screaming. The place was in uproar.

"Fuck off and go back to where you come from." A woman shouted.

I continued to push my way through. Suddenly I was face to face with the girl who had done the deed. Funny, I thought, only a few minutes ago I fancied a dance with you. My thoughts were interrupted as she looked at me and calmly said. "Yes, you I mean. Piss off back to England and take your sidekick with you." I then realised it was her who had shouted earlier. I just stared wondering how she knew we were from England?

"Come on Richard let's get the hell out of here and quick, before it gets worse." Paul calling me brought me to my senses and both of us headed for the main entrance and the cool night air.

"Well mate," I said between gasps of breath, "Mine was all right, but I didn't reckon much to yours!"

Paul sucked in a deep breath and looked at me. "Bastard," was all he said and all I could do was laugh.

"You bastard," he repeated, "What's so funny?"

"Shit, I don't know. Nothing I guess." My breathing steadied. "Well what now Paul, any ideas?"

"Nope, have you?"

I was beyond caring. We stood looking back from where we had just made a rapid exit.

"I know one thing, we best get back in the hotel a bit swiftly like just in case. Then you can buy us both a drink."

"Oh yeah, and what are you going to do?" Paul asked.

"I'm going to reception to phone for an ambulance."

"Are you mad? That'll mean we'll get implicated"

"No I'm not mad, that girl needs an ambulance."

"Leave it Richard, it's nothing to do with us."

"Hey, don't worry. I'll handle it. We'll be ok." I hope I sounded convincing, but I wasn't at all sure how I was going to play it.

"Richard, one thing."

"What?"

"Before we go in there," Paul nodded towards the front door of the hotel, "I want to know how you intend to get help without us being involved."

"Easy" I said, my mind working overtime, "I'll use O'Shea as our lever."

"What?" Paul was taken aback, "O'Shea!"

"Yes O'Shea" I said thinking on my feet.

"How do you think that'll help?"

"Easy he's our protection." It wasn't much of a plan, but it might just work.

Paul looked at me in disbelief. "You must be mad. How do you work that out?"

"Don't you see it? It's easy because everyone around here knows O'Shea don't they?"

"Well yeah. So how's that help us?"

"Not only are we working for him, but he also owns the hotel and the club. We are here as his guests and I bet no one is going to cross him."

Paul thought about this. "What makes you so certain no-one will cross him?"

"Would you cross him?"

"No but..."

"There's no but to it. It's a cinch."

Paul was still not convinced. "I'm not so sure you're right." He was silent as he mulled it over in his mind.

"Come on Paul it'll work. Trust me!"

"It's not you. I trust you. I just don't trust him."

I knew he had a valid point and I couldn't really argue with him on that score so I did the next best thing, I agreed with him. "I'm not suggesting you trust him. I am suggesting you trust me. Like you I don't trust him either. But one thing I do know or should I say, suspect, is that he is very powerful in these parts. I don't know what he's up to but I do know we've had some very close encounters haven't we?"

"That's exactly my point," he said.

"Yes but each time we've come out of it unscathed. Now why do you think that is?" I didn't say anything further I left Paul to think about and it seemed to work.

"Hmm. I see what you're getting at. Mind you I hope you're right otherwise we could be in deep, deep shit."

I don't think he was totally convinced so I tried to reassure him. "Trust me, that's all I can say. Trust me."

"Ok. But Richard...."

"What?" I asked a little brusquely.

"Nothing." He turned towards the entrance as if to go in but I grabbed his arm and stopped him short.

"No come on. Out with it!"

"Be careful that's all. Be very careful." He quietly stated in a matter of fact sort of way. I released my grip on his arm and nodded.

"Of course I will." We stood for a moment longer.

He smiled and slapped me on the arm. "Yeah of course. I'm sorry. I'll get the drinks in." With that he walked off in the direction of the front door.

Having decided my plan of action I repeatedly banged on the bell until the receptionist appeared.

"I'm sorry sir is something wrong?" The receptionist asked totally unflustered by my constant ringing of the bell.

"Yes, we need an ambulance urgently."

"Oh I'm sorry sir. I didn't realise is someone ill?"

"Yes a girl has been injured in the club and they need an ambulance straight away."

"In the club you say?"

."Yes, come on hurry up now."

"Please calm down sir."

"I am calm but an ambulance is required urgently for this girl. She needs hospital attention I think she has been stabbed in the stomach."

"I'm sure your mistaken sir."

"No I'm not mistaken." I replied sharply getting annoyed with her and her patronising manner. "Don't you understand, this girl has been stabbed and needs urgent attention, now I demand you send for an ambulance straight away."

"But sir, if it is as you say then the club would already have sent for the ambulance. So you see your concern, although it is appreciated is, maybe a little misguided?"

You snotty cow I thought to myself. "Now look. I'm not in the habit of calling ambulances willy-nilly and in this instance I'm not convinced that anyone has sent for one. Now do I make myself clear or do I need to spell it out to you. Call an ambulance."

"I hear what you're saying sir but I am sure someone in the club would already have telephoned for an ambulance. "

"Good God, how many more times need I say it? Young lady how would I know if they've sent for an ambulance or not? Even if they have does it matter? All I know is that the poor girl needs urgent medical treatment. Anyway I'm sure the ambulance control centre will sort it out even if you phone and the club phones." I took a deep breath to calm down.

"I'm sorry sir be that as it may but I'm sure the club will handle it quite adequately. Now sir unless there's anything else?"

I slammed my fist down on the reception desk. "This has gone beyond a joke. Where's the manager?"

"The manager isn't available at the moment. I'm sorry sir."

"Why is it I get the distinct impression that you are going out of your way to be obstructive?"

"I'm not." She answered sourly.

"I think you are." I said raising my voice; "First of all you have refused to send for an ambulance when requested to do so, then when..."

"But I have tried to explain..."

I held up my hand and interjected. "As I was saying, then when I ask to see the manager he is not available. So how about telephoning across to Mr O'Shea?" I paused to take a breath; she didn't say a word just stood there glaring back at me. "Well come on then how about it, because I know he'll be there."

"What I was going to say sir if you had let me explain was that the general manager is not available, but Alison the duty manager is. So would you like me to get her for you?"

"Yes please then perhaps we can get somewhere." My exasperation must have registered because Alison appeared from the inner office before the so-called receptionist had moved.

"Good evening. Mr James isn't it?"

"Yes it is and perhaps I can get some sense out of you." I replied curtly.

"What seems to be the problem?" She calmly asked ignoring my curtness. I repeated to her what I had told the receptionist and once again requested for her to summon an ambulance.

"I'm sorry Mr James, but I'm sure Siobhan has already explained to you that should an ambulance be required by the club for some reason then a phone call would have already been made by them. I see no point in us making another call. After all it's nothing to do with us in here is it now?" She flashed a disarming smile, but I was not in the mood to be fobbed off that easily.

"Listen to me," I started to speak to her quite calmly. "As I explained to Siobhan, I think that's what you called her, I don't know whether or not anyone in the club has sent for an ambulance, but what I do know is one is required urgently for an injured girl. Now perhaps you'll call the emergency services."

"Now Mr James, if what you say is true, and I've no reason to disbelieve you, then why come all the way up here to make an emergency call? Why didn't you phone from the club? After all there's a public telephone down there, surely common-sense would have been to phone from there wouldn't it?"

I now had the distinct feeling that the prevarication was no more than a cover up. There was definitely a hidden agenda here. "Look does it matter whether I phone from here or down there? The girl needs attention. So will you please telephone for an ambulance."

At this point her disarming smile faltered and disappeared. "With all due respect sir, I don't see it being any of your business, and what's more I would suggest you leave it to those downstairs. Now if you don't mind I've got work to do." With that she turned on her heel and started to walk away.

I lost my temper completely and shouted after her. "Right, if that's how you wish to play it, then I'll telephone them myself." I slammed up the flap of the reception counter and reached over to unbolt the small door in order to let myself through.

"Just a minute if you don't mind." she rushed to bar my entry and slammed the flap back down and bolted it. "Mr James, you will remain that side of the desk please."

"In that case I suggest you telephone the ambulance and Gardai then I may consider it." People nearby heard our raised voices turned to see what the commotion was all about.

"Sir, will you please refrain from shouting." She said through her clenched teeth as she started to colour up with embarrassment.

"Certainly. Provided you telephone the emergency services. However, should you and your colleague continue to refuse then you will leave me with little or no alternative but to have to SHOUT. Do I make myself understood, or will it be necessary for me do the job myself?" I glared at her across the front desk.

Her reply was one of quiet determination, "Like I said sir, you are involving yourself in something that you know nothing about. So please mind your own business." Then in a softer almost apologetic tone, "Please sir leave it."

I was no longer in the mood to listen to neither excuses nor the whimpering of a receptionist. "Now you listen to me. I've been here less than forty-eight hours and so far my mate and I have been threatened twice in one night by local thugs. I've witnessed two people being stabbed, and now you are telling me it's nothing to do with me! What the hell is going on round here? Now phone for that ambulance do I make myself clear or not?"

"Yes sir, but you are out of your depth. Please sir, leave it." Her eyes implored me.

"I don't care about what you say. I say again. There is a young lady who has been stabbed and needs medical attention. If you are not able to send for help then find me someone who will."

"But sir...."

"You do realise that both Mr Jones and I are guests of Mr O'Shea. That is Breandán O'Shea your boss. After all he is the man who owns this hotel, so if you don't want me to tell him how his receptionist refused to get an ambulance when I asked her then, ring for one. "

She gave me a long hard look, then reached under the desktop for the telephone. "Yes. This is the Tara Hotel, Ambulance please."

"Hallelujah, at long last! Thank you." I held her eyes momentarily then marched off to the bar muttering to myself about 'stupid bitches' and how annoying some people could be. Perhaps if I hadn't been so hasty things may have been different.

Both of us sat there in silence, wrapped up in our own private thoughts. I was thinking back to what I had just been witness to and judging from what Paul said it wasn't far from his thoughts either.

"Richard."

"What?" I gave an involuntary jump.

"Where were you then?" Paul enquired.

"I was just thinking about that girl and that stupid receptionist."

"Funny, so was I."

"Yes, and what?"

"What you'd said last night."

"About what?"

"About packing up and going home. Were you serious?"

"I was last night." I paused and looked at him. "Why?"

He didn't answer. I knew there was something wrong as he just kept tapping the edge of the table with a beer mat. I waited for moment or two for an answer, before pursuing it.

"Well come on. What's niggling you?"

He stopped what he was doing and carefully put the beer mat down. "What would you say if I said I agree with you?"

"How d'you mean?"

"What I say, I agree with you."

I gave him a quizzical look. "About what?"

"About packing it in and going home of course."

"I don't believe I'm hearing this. Less than twenty-four hours ago, after we'd been threatened, you inferred I was soft in the head even to think about such a thing. Now here you are talking about packing it all in just because someone else has a problem! Bloody hell Paul I just don't get you!"

We both sat there in stony silence as the strains of some easy listening music floated to us over the hum of voices in the bar. I felt angry and let down by Paul and the recent turn of events. I then thought about the money.

"Shit Paul, do you realise you're talking about throwing away three hundred pounds a week that's serious money. Can you afford to give that sort of money up?" He just shrugged his shoulders. "Well can you?" I tried hard to cover up my disappointment. My problem now was how to persuade Paul to stay. "Look Paul, perhaps I was a little hasty earlier, but can you really afford to give up that sort of money. I mean three hundred a week, well it's a lot of money isn't it and if the truth be known I'm sure you could do with it as much as I could." I paused to see if that had any effect. "Look Paul I've got to be honest. I just can't afford to pass up this sort of money." Without him there was no question at all, the job was doomed, just as it would be for him without me. I thought about it for a moment or two more then decided to try another tack.

"Listen, I know last night I said I was prepared to forget the whole contract and I know you talked me out of it." Shit this sounds pathetic, come on Richard you've got to do better than this. I paused, thought a bit more about how to put it, then started again. "Look Paul, what I'm trying to say is maybe, just maybe I was a little hasty then and perhaps you're being a bit hasty now." Paul opened his mouth to say something but I blundered on. "As you said to me we're here to earn good money, and three hundred a week is pretty good. No, I would go further and say it was bloody good wouldn't you?"

"Yes but..." I cut him short.

"There's no 'buts' Paul. It's bloody good and you know it is." I felt that he was weakening so I pressed on with the advantage, "It's far more than we've ever earned before and probably far more than we'll ever earn in the future." I took a swig from my glass.

"I agree it's bloody good Richard, but is it good enough to get killed for?"

"Well if you put it like that..." I paused just long enough for Paul to read into that my uncertainty so he was sure that he already knew my answer.

"Then you've answered the question."

I shook my head. "Hang on you didn't let me finish what I was saying."

"All right, so what were you going to say?"

I had to think of something quickly that would not only sound plausible but would also present a reasonable argument. I thought for a second then I had it. "What I was going to say before you interrupted me was..." I paused.

"Was what Richard?" He enquired in a low but meaningful voice.

"Well what I was going to say was that when we were in the mob we got paid a hell of a lot less and were then expected to die for Queen and Country."

"Yeah, but it was different then wasn't it." The tone in his voice showed that his resolve was faltering.

"Of course it was different. We got paid a pittance by comparison." Once again I used the financial argument, because if there was one thing about Paul, it was he was no fool when it came to pound notes. He knew which side his bread was buttered, but he still wasn't giving in without a fight.

"You know what I mean Richard. We didn't have a choice. We had to do it because we were in the Army."

"But that's my point." I lowered my voice, as I wasn't sure who maybe listening, "That's exactly my point. We are trained military persons. Ex Para's, the elite. We've been trained to stay alive under adverse conditions. Now you can't call this adverse conditions can you? You know we've less chance of being hurt or killed now than ever we were in the mob. I reckon if we keep our heads down we'll be ok."

He sat there in silence, obviously thinking about what I had said. I watched his face.

"Yeah I suppose your right." He answered resignedly.

I had at last got him agreeing with me. "Plus of course we'll be earning three hundred a week." I looked straight at him. "You know it makes sense. Besides it makes life interesting and for three hundred a week I suppose we have to take some flak. So what about it?" I waited with bated breath, had I convinced him? My gut feel told me yes, but I wasn't sure.

He lit a cigarette and inhaled deeply, held on to the breath momentarily before allowing a stream of blue smoke it to escape through his pursed lips. "Right you've persuaded me, we stay."

Boy was I relieved. "You're sure?"

His face broke into a wide grin. "Of course I'm sure." He winked and took a long drag on his cigarette. "Come on drink up its my shout."

It was our third drink when suddenly Paul remembered about the girl in the dance. "You did say that Reception had sent for an ambulance didn't you?"

"Yes, why?"

"I just wondered because I hadn't heard any siren." He paused and lit another cigarette. "I'd have thought we would have heard it in here wouldn't you?"

"Yeah strange that. We're not that far from the main road are we?"

"I suppose it could have been and gone without us noticing." I wasn't convinced though and I don't think Paul was either. Conversation faltered and we sat there in silence. Paul finished his cigarette and the last of his beer then said, "I think I'll call it a night, what about you?"

"No, not just yet. I think I'll just stretch my legs and get some fresh air before turning in. I'll see you in the morning."

"Ok see you then." He left me to ponder on the night's events.

The incident about the ambulance had been bugging me. There was something not quite right, but what was it? Why hadn't we heard it arrive? Then it dawned on me. We hadn't heard anything because in reality no ambulance had been called. I had been duped. Oh yes, the receptionist had spoken on the 'phone all right, but she wasn't connected to anyone. Of course I could see it clearly now it was too late. When she picked up the 'phone it was out of sight under the top desk and all she had to do was with her other hand hold down the receiver rest while she spoke into the mouthpiece. Idiot! Why didn't I see it? Damn that receptionist! Because of my stupidity anything could have happened to the girl. One thing was certain, if last night's episode was anything to go by she was no longer in the nightclub.

I searched every inch of the car park. Every dark corner but I had drawn a blank. I was at a loss as to what else I could do. Then I overheard a chance comment made by a young couple talking to some friends. "Did you get caught up in that accident near the entrance?"

"No. What accident?"

"It was terrible, it looked as if someone had been run over."

"Was the ambulance there?"

"No."

"Did you stop?"

"No, there was already a small crowd. Anyway it was nothing to do with us."

That was enough for me and with their words still echoing through my brain I set off to find the accident!

From where I stood I could see a small crowd of people gathered on the opposite side of the road near to where a truck was parked. Obviously that was the place. I now needed to see the girl. The question was how? I decided to walk a short distance along the main road, cross over, and walk back towards a lane on the opposite side. I would then be able to see what had happened.

As I reached the small group of people I paused just long enough to take in the scene. A young woman in her twenties had been run over. I was certain it was the girl from the club and a quick look at her face confirmed it. From what I could see, she was beyond help now and it would only be a matter of time before the poor girl passed away. From what little I heard it seemed as if she had been dumped from a car in the path of the following truck. The truck driver didn't stand a chance and neither did she. I had seen all I wanted and started back to the hotel.

I must have been away longer than I had thought because, to my consternation, I found the front door of the hotel already locked.

"Shit!" I said out loud because I now had to ring the bell for the night porter. That was a nuisance but not the end of the world. My main concern was to avoid a lot of awkward questions from PC Plod should he come to the hotel. You can't imagine my relief when the door was opened by Noel, the friendly night porter from last night.

"You look terrible. What an earth happened to you sir? "

"It's a long story."

"I see sir. Can I get you anything?"

"Hmm. Any chance of a drink?"

"For you sir, of course there is. Come in, come in." I walked into the main reception area. "Just take a seat in the lounge sir and I'll be with you." I wondered through to the lounge and sat down. I could still picture that poor girl in my mind's eye. "Now sir, what can I be getting you?"

"A large Bushmill's please?"

"Certainly sir. Just give it a couple of minutes for the last of the non-residents to leave."

"Sure, no problem Noel."

"Thank you sir."

The last couple of non-residents left and Noel went over to the porter's lodge where he unlocked a cupboard. It was this cupboard that housed the night bar, not a vast stock, but a superb collection and a nice little earner for Noel. In fact he bought the stock out of his own money then resold it to us, the residents and at times some non-residents. It was, like many things around here, all very irregular and of course illegal.

"Now sir, a large Bushmill's coming up."

"I'm surprised you get away with your drinks cupboard Noel."

"Why sir?"

"Well in England you wouldn't be allowed to sell drinks without a license."

"Well the hotel's licensed sir." He answered seriously.

"Yes but..." I was about to embark on telling him what I meant when he couldn't contain himself any longer.

He exploded with laughter. "Well sir, It's just the same over here. I'll tell you what, no one's complained so far!"

"How do you get away with it?" I asked.

"I suppose the meal and the beer I give the local Gardai at two in the morning may have something to do with it!" He grinned from ear to ear.

"Yeah I suppose it could." I answered thoughtfully.

After a couple more large Bushmill whiskies, Noel came and joined me. I was now beginning to feel the effects of the whisky and I slowly began to relax.

"If I may say so sir, you're now looking a lot better than when you first came in."

"Well thank you Noel. Did I look that bad?"

"Well let's say I've seen people look better."

"Very diplomatic of you."

Noel laughed. "We try not to offend sir. By the way I told the Gardai that you and your friend had been in the bar all evening last night, I assume you had told them likewise."

"How do you mean Noel?" I was at a bit of a loss as to what he was driving at.

"You know sir, when there was that, err, slight problem in the club. I'm sure sir wouldn't know anything about that though, especially as he was in the hotel bar all evening, now would you sir?" He just gave a knowing smile.

"You're right Noel, I don't know anything about that." With that I downed my whisky in one. Perhaps I was wrong but I didn't trust him.

"How much do I owe you Noel?"

"That's all right sir, have that on me."

"Are you sure?"

"Yes that's fine."

"Oh well cheers Noel, I'll see you tomorrow."

Chapter 5

"Morning Richard. Christ you look rough. A good night was it?"

"In your dreams."

"Well if it's not beer, why the hangover?"

"It's not a hangover. I just didn't sleep too well. In fact I nearly came and knocked you up."

"Why?"

"I'll tell you later, too many people listening in here."

Paul looked puzzled. "Has something else happened?"

"No not really. Wait till we get out of here and I'll tell you then." We continued our breakfast in silence.

The morning was dry and it looked as if the sun would break through as we made our way up the lane towards the farm.

"So, what happened after I went to bed?"

"Well, you know I said I was going out to get some fresh air?"

"Yes."

"That was only half the truth."

"I guessed as much, but carry on."

"After the cover up on Saturday and the incident at reception I was certain they would try and get away with it again, so I decided I would look for the girl."

"What? You must be mad. Why get involved?"

"If only it were as simple as that."

"Like I said why get involved?"

I ignored his last comment. "Anyway I hunted everywhere. Anywhere that I felt they could hide a body until later. I had just about given up when I overheard a young couple's conversation about some accident down on the Dublin road."

"So what did you do?"

"Well I took a look of course."

"Did you find anything?"

"Yeah, I found something all right. A truck parked and a small crowd gathered on the opposite side."

"Didn't you have a nose then?"

"Yeah, I walked up the road and crossed over just passed where the truck was parked."

"Why didn't you just cross over by the lane?"

I held the gate to the orchard open for Paul to walk through. "Think about it Paul. I didn't want to be conspicuous did I? By walking up the road and crossing over I could then walk along the other side passed where the crowd was without standing out as being plain bloody nosy. That way I could also get a good look at the victim."

"Never thought of that. So did you see who it was?"

"Yes. It was the girl from the club all right."

"How was she?"

"I would say she was way beyond medical help."

"So what had happened?" By now we had reached where we were working.

"From what I heard the truck driver say, it seems she was dumped out of a car right in his path. Poor lass never stood a chance."

"The bastards!"

"You're right."

"So, dead people tell no tales."

"That about sums it up. Then just to make matters worse I got back to the hotel only to find the door locked."

"Oh shit. So you had to ring the bell."

"My sentiments exactly, but I was in luck. It was Noel, the same night porter as Saturday night, and to cut a long story short, I had a drink and he started talking to me about Saturday."

"Oh yeah, and what was he saying?"

"It wasn't so much what he said, it was more what he didn't say that concerned me. He was very keen to find out what we knew or what we had seen." We made our way over to the row of trees we were working on.

"What did you tell him?"

"Nothing at all." I then told Paul about my conversation I had with Noel. Paul listened in silence until I had finished.

"Do you reckon he's on the level Richard?"

"I'm not sure whether to trust him or not."

"Hmm," Paul thought for a moment or two before answering. "I think we'll play it by ear for the time being. Perhaps he means well. Who knows he maybe genuine, but I think we tread carefully for now. Remember the old adage, don't underestimate the enemy, otherwise we could be in deep shit."

"Ok, so perhaps this evening we see what we can find out from him, what do you think?"

"Seems logical to me."

"Top o' the morning to you Richard, top o' the morning." I looked up from what I was doing to see O'Shea heading my way.

"Good morning Mr O'Shea." He seems full of the joys of spring I thought to myself as he strode across the orchard towards me.

"Now Richard how's it going?"

"Ok. No major problems." Well not with what we're doing anyway I thought to myself, which was more than I could say for last night.

"Did you have a nice evening last night?"

"It was ok." I was fairly non-committal about my answer, wondering how much he knew about last night?

"Did you go to Dublin then?" As we had never mentioned Dublin it seemed a strange question to ask.

"No. Why do you ask?" He ignored my question completely.

"Oh so did you had a quiet night in then?" Why the interrogation, what was he after? I decided to play along with him.

"No we went to the club again." I watched his face for some reaction. Some indication; but nothing.

"Was it a good night then?"

"Yes not bad, they had a group on."

"Any good?"

"They were ok."

"I expect there was less people in there than Saturday. A bit more room to breathe no doubt."

"There was certainly less people, but it was just as exciting, wasn't it Paul?"

"Definitely." Paul had picked up on cue.

"How do you mean exciting?" He asked raising one eyebrow. Huh, I thought to myself, as if you don't already know Mr O'Shea, but I'll play your little game!

"Oh, haven't you heard?" I asked a little sarcastically.

"Heard what?" He seemed genuinely surprised, but I wasn't so sure.

"I'm sorry Mr O'Shea I assumed you knew."

"Assumed I knew what?"

"Assumed you knew about the girl who got stabbed!"

"What?"

"I said there was another stabbing, two girls had a go this time and one of them ended up being stabbed. Don't tell me you didn't know Mr O'Shea."

"Of course I didn't know." He answered angrily.

"Oh I am sorry Mr O'Shea, I didn't realise." I feigned surprise at his not knowing.

"I can assure you I had no knowledge of this."

"Well what can I say? I just thought you might have arranged yet another good show, especially for us English, as you put it." I answered with more than just a hint of sarcasm in my voice.

He exploded with rage. "We had no problems until you arrived. There again, maybe it's you two causing it. What do you say to that?"

"What did you say?" I asked in disbelief.

"That perhaps it's you two causing the problems!"

"Are you suggesting that we are the instigators, because if you are then you can poke your contract right up your arse."

"No I'm not saying that at all, I'm..."

I cut him off mid-sentence not giving him chance to finish I stormed on. "We came over here to do a job, and all we've had since we arrived is trouble from you lot. What is it with you?"

"Ok, ok you've made your point. Perhaps I am being a little unreasonable."

"Unreasonable; I should say so. If ever there was an understatement you've just made it." My point had not gone unnoticed.

"I'm sorry for my outburst just now." He quickly regained his composure, but being a man who was used to being obeyed, even though he had apologised, there was still little give in his attitude. "Mind I'll tell you now, stay out of trouble, and from now on confine yourself to the hotel bar."

His attitude incensed me and I quickly made it known. "I'm sorry but isn't it up to you what we do in our free time."

There was no mistaking my annoyance at his dictatorial attitude and he tried hard to make light of it.

"I'm sorry, I didn't mean it quite like that." He looked down at the ground and shuffled his feet uncomfortably.

"Well what do you mean?" I asked.

He looked back up and said in a quiet voice. "What I mean is, that I need my friends alive. I need to look after my investment. I've a small fortune invested in you two." He then continued almost pleading with us, "So please, stay alive until you've finished." He gave a strange little half laugh.

"We don't have a problem with that do we?" I said looking over to my mate.

"No. I don't have a problem with it."

"There Mr O'Shea we both agree. We have no intentions of becoming dead meat. Now are you suggesting that we are only safe if we stay in the hotel every night, because if that's the case then we need additional compensation."

"Of course you do." He said almost enthusiastically and pulled out a thick wad and started to peel off hundred punt notes. "Shall we say four hundred punt each as a fair figure?"

I winked at Paul. "No Mr O'Shea."

He looked up in amazement. "No. Surely that's enough?"

I shook my head. He studied my face for a moment or two. "Let's say six hundred each Mr O'Shea just for the trouble!" He stared at me in disbelief, but like him, my expression had hardened and I was equally determined as he was. "Six hundred Mr O'Shea, that's the deal, no more, no less. Take it or leave it."

He was not convinced that I meant what I said so started by calling my bluff. "What if I say that's outrageous and four hundred is my maximum."

"That's up to you Mr O'Shea, but if that's your final offer then tell me."

"Ok that's my final offer."

With that I picked up my gear and Paul did likewise. "Thank you Mr O'Shea, but no." He had called my bluff and it was now my turn to call his and I could be just as determined.

"What are you doing Mr James?"

"I thought it was obvious, packing up. We're going."

He watched us as we set off in the direction of the hotel.

My bluff paid off because we hadn't gone far before he called after us. "Ok, six hundred punt."

I paused and slowly turned to face him. I looked straight into his eyes and said, "That's six hundred each Mr O'Shea."

"Of course. Six hundred each." He walked over to where we stood and started to peel off twelve crisp one hundred punt notes and pushed them into my outstretched hand. "There...twelve hundred punt. Jesus Richard you're a hard businessman that's for sure. I won't ask you if that's enough or you may ask for another couple of hundred or so." This was definitely the way to do business I thought as I put my gear back down on the ground. I looked at the crisp notes in my hand then back at O'Shea. "You're sure this is legal tender?" I enquired. He just laughed.

"Of course it is. It's more legal here than Stirling." Suddenly he was a different man. The coolness that had been there was gone and I felt the barriers between us melt away.

Chapter 6

The bar had been closed for over half an hour and the last of the non-residents departed. Noel, the night porter, was pottering about behind the scenes as Paul and I finished our drinks. Earlier we had agreed that this was start of a new era and our motto from now on was do not underestimate your enemy. At the time we did not realise how much we would need to rely on this motto in the future.

Our first objective was to assess where Noel was in the grand scheme of things, but how we could achieve this I wasn't sure. As it turned out Noel inadvertently solved the problem and played right into our hands.

"Good evening gentlemen. Can I get you anything?"

"Yes can we order some drinks?"

"Of course you may sir. Just give me a minute and I'll be with you." He then disappeared into the Dining Room only to reappear a few minutes later. "Sorry about that gentlemen, just getting my dinner organised. Now what may I get you?"

"A large Bushmills for me. What about you Paul?"

"I'll have a pint of lager."

"Certainly sir. So that's a pint of lager and a double Bushmill. Thank you." A few minutes later he reappeared with our drinks on a tray. "Shall I charge them to your rooms?"

"Can you put them on a tab please and I'll straighten up with you later."

"Of course sir." With that he produced a little black book from his pocket. "Anything else gentleman?" He asked pencil poised.

"Would you like a drink with us Noel?" I asked.

He made a point of looking around as if making sure there was no one else about and nothing left to do before answering. "Well to be sure that's very kind of you both. May I have a little one with you?"

"Of course Noel, have what you want. In fact why don't you bring the bottle of Bushmill's and join us," I suggested hoping he would take up the offer.

"Well I must admit that sounds very civilised and I'd be surely tempted but I've still some things to do yet. Thank you all the same sir."

"No problem Noel. See how things go, perhaps later then?"

"Maybe. Now I'll just away and get your drinks, so if you'll excuse me."

"For a minute there Richard I thought we had a bite. "

"I think he was tempted. Never mind there'll be other times."

At just after midnight Noel surprised us by suddenly appearing with three glasses and a bottle of Bushmill's.

"What have you got there Noel?" I asked, trying to conceal a smile.

"Well I've finished all my jobs. Had my dinner, or should I say breakfast, so I thought I'd take you up on your offer if it still stands?"

Bingo, I smiled to myself. "Of course it does Noel. Pull up a chair." I looked over to Paul and winked, he smiled and gave a knowing nod, so we had game on.

Noel placed the bottle and three glasses on the table between us and sat down. I poured out three drinks, making sure Noel got an over generous measure.

"Really sir, you have short changed both yours and your friends."

"Not really Noel, after all you've got some catching up to do."

"Well I suppose if you put it like that it's all right then, but I still think you're short changing yourselves."

"Stop moaning Noel and drink up." I raised my glass. "To you Noel cheers."

"Yes cheers Noel." Paul raised his glass. "Here's to a long and happy friendship."

"Gentleman, here's to you both. May you both have a long and happy stay in Ireland" He took a large sip from his glass and placed it back on the table.

"The other night Noel, you were saying something about the club, can you remind me what it was?" I asked him as I topped up his glass.

He leaned back in his armchair and relaxed as he took another large sip of his Bushmill's. "Was I sir?" He frowned.

"Yes don't you remember?"

He took a minute or two to think before answering. "No. It's no good. For the life of me I can't remember what it was now." He fell silent as if he was deep in thought about what it may have been. He then took another mouthful of his drink. Again I filled up his glass. "No. Sorry sir it's gone completely. You'll have to remind me."

I took a sip from my glass and stared at the floor as if I was pondering about what it was he had said. After a few moments I looked up as if I had just remembered. "Ah, that was it. It was something about Saturday night and what you told the Gardai."

"Yes it's coming back to me now sir. I told the Gardai that you had both been in the bar all evening. There had been some trouble or something in the club hadn't there?"

"I don't know Noel, had there been?" I asked with an air of innocence.

"Of course there was, but you knew that didn't you sir?" He said giving me a strange look.

"How would I know about that?" I asked, still keeping up the air of pretence.

"Oh come now sir, of course you know after all you were both there weren't you?"

"Of course we weren't." Paul said almost convincing me. "I think you must be mistaken Noel. We weren't in the club were we Richard?" He kept a dead pan face as he blatantly lied.

"Paul's right; Noel you're mistaken." I said as I leaned forward to refill his glass. "So what happened at the club that we are supposed to know all about?"

"Well from what I heard, and of course I don't know for sure, but what I heard was that there was a fight and someone got stabbed."

"Well?" I asked.

He looked at me quizzically. "Well what?"

"Well what else?"

"Come on sir, you were both there I know you were. You know you were so let's stop beating about the bush." He paused and took another drink from his glass. I once again filled it. "You both know what really happened don't you?"

I looked at Paul and he gave a slight nod. "Supposing, and I'm not for a minute saying we were, but just supposing you're right. Then tell me Noel, why tell the police or Gardai or whatever they're called that we were here in the hotel bar all evening. What's your angle?" This was the crunch question.

Noel's eyes flicked from me to Paul and back again before he answered. "That's exactly the point I'm making," he said his speech slightly slurred, "Surely if I'm prepared to lie for you when all the time I know you're in the club then that in itself should say something about me."

"In what way?" I asked.

"No I don't see where you're coming from Noel." Paul stated then winked at me. "Do you Richard?"

Noel tried to focus first on Paul then on me. I again topped up his glass. He immediately took a mouthful. "You don't see what I'm getting at?" He slurred. "I would have thought it obvious. I did it because I trusted you, surely you must know to trust me?"

"Slow down; not so fast. All you did was to tell the police that as far as you were aware we had spent the evening in the hotel bar. You didn't lie for us."

"It's Gardai sir, not police; and I did lie." He said petulantly.

"How do you make out you lied for us?" I asked.

"Because the Gardai checked with reception as to who was staying here and the whereabouts of each of the guests. She told them that you had gone to the club, I told them she must have been mistaken as you were both here all evening. Fortunately I happen to know John the local sergeant very well indeed and he took my word as being correct. So now d) you believe me?" He asked angrily and slumped back in the chair.

"If that's the case Noel, then why?" I wondered if there was some sort of hidden agenda here.

"Because I like both of you as people and whatever happened in the club I did not agree with you being implicated; it's as simple as that and that's the truth."

Was he telling me the truth? I looked across at Paul. He shrugged his shoulders. I thought about what Noel had said but I wasn't totally convinced so I tried another angle. "So what if we were there Noel, what is it to you?"

"All I would say is be very careful. Watch your backs, because you don't know who's who around here."

Once again I topped up our glasses. Playing with the drink in front of me I thought long and hard about what he said. I turned the glass first one way then the next, not sure which way to jump. I took a long drink from the glass. In the end I decided. He had to be telling the truth because what had he got to gain from lying to us. For some reason, best known to himself, he was trying to help us in whichever way he could. With this in mind I decided to tell him what had happened on both nights.

"So there you have it Noel, both Paul and I are convinced that the..."

Noel interrupted me and said in a low conspiratorial tone, "The IRA."

"Yeah. The IRA."

Noel leaned forward in his chair and put his finger to his lips.

"Shh! Keep your voice down. You never know who maybe listening around here." He continued talking in a hushed tone, "I'll tell you gentlemen, they are an evil force to contend with. Their strength is fear. The problem is nobody knows who is a member and who's not. You really would be surprised at how powerful they are. It's what I've always imagined the Mafia to be like in Brooklyn or Chicago, so as I said you can't be too careful."

"I see, so what about Sunday night? Would you say that was IRA?"

"I don't know for sure, but it has all the trade marks of it?"

"Do you think you would be able to find out more?"

"Oh I don't know about that sir. It's too dangerous. Hush." He got up and walked over towards a window that overlooked the car park. "Just as I thought and dead on time. I'll have to go now. It's John the local sergeant's come for his break. A word of warning, don't ever say much in front of him."

"Why shouldn't he be told?" I asked.

"Because he is great friends with your Mr O'Shea who is a very powerful man in these parts. Yes a very powerful man indeed. Now I really must go."

"All right Noel. Oh how much do I owe you?"

"Don't worry about it now sir, you can straighten up with me later."

"You sure?"

"Yes no problem." He picked up the remains of the Bushmill's and the three dirty glasses and walked towards the Dining Room door.

"Noel." I called after him.

He paused and turned. "Yes sir?"

"Thank you. From now on I'm Richard and this is Paul." Paul nodded in acknowledgement.

"Pleased to make both your acquaintances I'm sure." He gave a little dip of his head and continued into Dining Room.

"Paul I think we've found an ally don't you?"

"I think you could be right."

Chapter 7

Tuesday proved to be a somewhat uneventful day, with no sign of our Mr O'Shea. We managed to work through to late evening and by the time we'd showered and eaten it were quite late. So in line with our agreement with O'Shea, we retired to the hotel bar to have a couple of drinks before going to bed. Well that was the plan anyway. By eleven thirty the bar was clear of everyone except for us.

"I'm going to call it a night."

"Yeah, me too Richard."

"Oh hell, I forgot."

"What?"

"I still owe Noel for the drinks from the other night. I'd best try and find him otherwise he may get the wrong idea." I looked everywhere for him and was about to give up when he appeared. "Ah Noel there you are, I've been looking all over for you."

"Sorry about that sir, err, I mean Richard. Is it some drinks you're after?"

"No, not really, unless you want another Paul?"

"I don't mind, it's up to you."

"Well maybe just the one then, but that wasn't the reason that I wanted to see you, it was to..."

Noel cut me off in mid sentence. "A large Bushmill's was it?"

"Yes please, but Noel I need to..."

He ignored me and again cut me off in mid-sentence. "What about you Paul, a pint?"

"Yes please Noel."

"Noel I need to..." but he was gone before I could finish, leaving me standing there with my money still intact.

"I shouldn't worry about it Richard 'cause he's obviously not."

"Yeah I know, but I wanted to sort it out and get a reasonably early night."

"Well, just have this one, sort your tab out, then go to bed."

"Ok."

"Here we are then, a large Bushmill's for you Richard and a pint of lager for Paul, and a Bushmills for myself." He placed the tray on the small table and sat down in the chair opposite to me. He raised his glass. "Good health to both you now, cheers."

"Cheers Noel." We both raised our glasses and took a drink.

"Now Noel, how much do I owe you from the other night?"

With a flourish he pulled out his little black book and proceeded to add it up. "Sixteen punt and thirty pence please." I offered him a hundred punt notes and his eyes nearly popped from their sockets. Even his voice went up an octave when he spoke.

"I see..." He gave a little cough and cleared his throat. "I see Mr O'Shea has paid you then!" He then proceeded to hunt through his pockets for change. "I don't suppose you have anything smaller?"

"No I'm sorry that's all I've got."

At which he took the hundred-punt note and quickly stuffed it into his pocket "I'll just pop to the office and see what I've got in change. I won't be a second." Before I could protest he was gone. A few minutes later he reappeared looking very apologetic, "I'm sorry Richard I haven't enough change. Could you settle up tomorrow or will it be ok to give you your change in the morning when the office is open?"

Perhaps I was stupid, but I gave him the benefit of the doubt.

"Oh, by the way I've a few friends dropping in later for a bit of a get together. Nothing special just a few drinks perhaps you'll both join us?"

"What d'you think Paul?"

"It's up to you mate."

"Ok, thank you Noel."

"Good that's settled then. I'll give you a call about two o'clock, It won't be before two because of John."

"John; who's John?" I asked.

"You know, John the local sergeant."

"Ah of course, the local Police Sergeant."

"Gardai, if you don't mind"

"All right Noel so it's the Gardai. Anyway I thought you said they didn't mind?"

He smiled. "I know I said the Gardai turns a blind eye to my little perks, but I don't want to be rubbing their nose in it do I now?"

"In that case we'd best finish our drinks and get off then." I picked up the remaining Bushmill's and tossed it down my throat.

"There's no rush. You can stay up drinking all night you're a resident. I just thought you may like to disappear before he gets here in case he starts quizzing you about...you know...." His voice tailed off leaving a question mark hanging.

"About what?" asked Paul.

"Well, about the club and all that. Especially as I told him you were here all night."

"Why should he want to quiz us again, is there a problem then?"

"Yes why would he do that Noel?" I asked.

"No reason." Noel looked a little concerned and seemed agitated about something.

"Noel, are you sure you're being totally truthful about things. I have a strong feeling that there's something you're not telling us. Now come on out with it."

"No honestly Mr James, sorry I mean Richard. There's nothing more than I told you."

"Hmm." I studied his face for a while longer. I wasn't sure. "What d'you think Paul?"

"Are you sure you've told us everything Noel, 'cause if I find out you've been telling us porkies, or you're trying to set us up, then we'll just have to let it slip out to Mr O'Shea about the rumours you've been spreading about him and the IRA." Paul gave him a knowing wink.

"What rumours?" Noel was indignant, "I've never said anything about him and the IRA. You're making it up."

"That's not the way we see it, is it Richard?"

"No it's not."

"Honestly Mr Jones, I, I mean Paul." He stammered, "There's nothing else to tell. I've told you everything, well nearly everything..." his voice trailed off. We stood there in silence for a few minutes. Noel looked away from Paul's piercing stare.

"Well Noel, you best be telling us what else was said, hadn't you."

Noel darted a look in Paul's direction then back to me.

"When I was asked about the other night, it seems as if someone had already spoken with John. Someone in high authority around here."

"You mean his boss?" I interjected.

"No. I mean someone more important than that. You just don't get it do you? The IRA is all powerful and you can't be too careful nowadays because you never know who's who around here."

"So do you mean O'Shea, is he involved?"

"Maybe, sorry I mean no, well I don't think so." Then in little more than a whisper he said, "All I know is that your name was linked with the nightclub. Someone, somewhere is asking a lot of questions about you."

"So are you suggesting that we pack up and leave?"

"No, not at all. I'm just saying John was asking a lot of awkward questions as if he knew more than he was saying. In fact I know he knows more than he's letting on about, because he suggested that I may find myself in a spot of bother if I didn't co-operate with him."

"What exactly did he mean Noel?"

"I guess he wanted to find out a lot more about you. Your background and so on."

"So how's it been left?" asked Paul.

"I told him that there was nothing I could tell him except that you were over here working for Mr O'Shea, and that you had been in the hotel bar all evening. That's all I swear."

"What sort of bother do you think he means then?"

"I'm not sure, unless he means with Mr O'Shea."

I wasn't convinced, but it could be possible that was what was meant, especially as Noel worked for O'Shea and this John was a so-called great friend of the man. Anyway it really wasn't worth pursuing, so I let it go at that. "Ok Noel, you're right. I think it best if we make our selves scarce and wait for your call. So two o'clock then." I turned towards Paul, "Come on mate drink your beer."

Ten minutes later we were in my room well away from any eavesdroppers. "Well Paul, what do you make of that?"

"I think we have unwittingly dropped right in the brown smelly stuff, don't you?"

"Yep, I think you're right, so what do we do about it?"

"Nothing we can do apart from don't under..."

"I know, don't underestimate the enemy and I'm not, but do we stay or do we quit?"

"Don't know what to say. Let's look at what we've got. We witnessed two murders, so the Gardai would regard us as material witnesses. Then again which side of the fence is this John character? The geezer in the dance, you know the bloke shouting his mouth off, is obviously some high up in the IRA, or we assume so. He knows we are here. Having said all that, if they wanted us dead I think we would have been six feet under by now, don't you?"

"Yes I agree, so why aren't we?"

"It only leaves our man, O'Shea. Now let's assume he is what Noel intimated at, in which case the bloke in the dance is small fry by comparison. It doesn't make sense." An uneasy silence followed.

Suddenly it occurred to me. "Got it. O'Shea is our protection."

"How?"

"Don't you see Paul? If he is the main one, then he's pulling the strings and if that's the case, he knows exactly what's going on around here."

"But why is he protecting us?"

"It's obvious. John, or whatever his name is, is straight and he knows we are working for O'Shea, so if we suddenly disappear then O'Shea would become prime suspect."

"But Noel reckons this John is a great friend of O'Shea's. I think out of them all, the only one who seems more or less trustworthy is our friendly night porter."

"Hmm maybe. Just as long as we keep our wits about us then we'll see what the next few days bring. Anyway I wonder what this so-called party is all in aid of? It could prove quite interesting"

"Yeah. I think you're right. It could prove to be very interesting for all concerned!"

Dead on the dot of two, the harsh jangle of my telephone roused me from a light sleep. I swung my legs over the side of the bed and made my way across the room to where I had placed the phone earlier that night. "Hello, yes, yes. All right Noel, I'll tell Paul. Yes of course on my way now. Bye." I hung up the phone and made my way to the bathroom to wash away the last vestige of any drowsiness. I picked up my keys on my way out and carefully pulled my door closed behind me. Gently I tapped on Paul's door and quietly called to him so as not to disturb other residents.

"Yes, who's there?" Paul's voice sounded drowsily through the door.

"Are you ready it's two o'clock?"

"Two o'clock. Won't be a minute." Came the muffled reply from Paul. In no time at all he was up and we were on our way back downstairs.

We were the first ones there but seeing we were already on the premises that was not surprising. Within ten minutes of our getting downstairs others started arriving, and within half an hour all those invited had turned up. In all nine people, including us, gathered in that lounge at two o'clock in the morning. It seemed a strange affair, here we were, sort of thrown together with all these Irishmen, none of whom we knew, in the early hours having a drinks party. I can honestly say that out of all of them there, there was only one who really stuck in my mind, another Noel. I think the only reason I remembered him was because of his name. He was mid-forties with a really craggy face. It had that 'lived in look' about it with that unhealthy ruddy complexion you see in people who are heavy drinkers. Not one of them had much to say about their self, but everyone wanted to know plenty about us!

"So you say your working for Mr O'Shea then. What would you be doing for him then?" One of them asked.

"We're grafting fruit trees."

"Surely, there's men here in the twenty-six counties that could be doing that work?"

"Well not really..."

"And why not may I ask?"

"Well, we've developed a special method..."

"What method?" Someone else interjected.

"It's a new method that..."

"Surely grafting is grafting?" A younger man asked.

"Not quite as simple as that."

"Well tell me then, because I do grafting."

"Are you sure you are over here grafting, or is there some other reason?" With this last question, a hush descended on the room. I looked at my inquisitor and could feel all eyes were turned on me. "Well, is there?" The soft voice spoke again.

"How do you mean?" I enquired.

"Just what I say. Are you sure you're only over here grafting?" I started to feel a little warm. It must have been the drink. "Of course we are." I paused, "I'm not so sure I like your tone. Do you Paul?"

With that Paul tried to reduce the tension. "Oh I don't think he means it like you're taking it Richard. Look mate," Paul turned to speak to the one who had raised the issue, "We're not taking work away from the locals if that's what is worrying you." The questioner looked from me to Paul then back to me again.

"No my friend." It was Noel, the one with the craggy face who spoke, "What he is meaning is; this is a little difficult. Hmm, let me see, have you..." Suddenly someone else cut him short.

"Are either of you in the military, because a lot of people are saying you are?"

"No neither of us are in the military." Paul answered before I could say anything.

"Well, have either of you been in the military then?" Now that was the sixty-four thousand-dollar-question and caught us both totally unaware. I looked at Paul then looked around our audience. "Well, what do you say then?"

"I'd say," I was grabbing at straws now. "You're all great people and I like it over here. Now do we look like military types?"

Saved by the bell, Noel the night porter came in with some food. "Now, now gentlemen. This is not the Spanish Inquisition or is it? Leave the poor men alone, they've already answered your questions so let it drop. Come on; food up."

"But Noel, my friend, it's important to know what's going on around here, and more important to know who is on whose side. Wouldn't you agree?" the soft voice asked. There was a ripple of approval from around the room.

"I agree with Noel." Noel with the craggy face put his two-penny worth in, "So let it drop."

"No I disagree, we've a right to know?" Soft voice again. Noel looked at both of us and gave a shrug of his shoulders.

I could feel beads of sweat beginning to form. What was I to say? What should we do? I took my time. Once again I looked around the room. Once again all conversation ceased and all eyes were on me. Suddenly I knew what to say. "You asked a straight forward question, and you deserve a straight answer, even though I don't know where all this is leading, so before I give my answer I ask all of you two questions. Why do you want to know if we've been in the military, that's my first question and my second is what if we had been in the military?"

"Well if you lived here you would know the answers to both those questions."

"No, come on friend. Tell me what is so important about our background and us. Then I'll answer your question. After all we've nothing to hide." I only hope that we were right in assuming O'Shea was our protection.

"You say you are working for Mr O'Shea. Now Mr O'Shea is a highly thought of man in this community and some strange things have been happening recently. Especially since you two arrived here. Does that answer your question?"

"Not really, but I take your point. We are strangers to you all and from what little we've seen you have a very tight knit community here." I was waffling convinced there was some ulterior motive to all this. "However I will answer your question, which I believe was, had either of us been in the military." I paused, took a deep breath and looked straight in the eyes of the main questioner. "No." The warmth in that room suddenly felt overbearing and out of habit I undid my shirtsleeves and started to roll them up when Paul caught my eye. Just in time to stop my revealing two tattoos that I had. One was the Parachute Regimental badge, the other which depicted the word paratrooper. Suddenly all the tension evaporated and everyone was trying to speak at once. The atmosphere was convivial and friendly towards us with everyone wanting to introduce himself and shake our hands as if we were long lost friends. The drinks seemed never ending and the food Noel had put on would have been enough for a banquet.

In the distance I could hear a knocking sound, this was closely followed by a strange noise. It was a scraping noise, like something brushing against something metallic. Suddenly the sun was shining and there was rabbits playing in a field, ah so that was the noise, someone loading a twelve bore. The person's face was blurred, but whoever it was they were calling me.
"Richard, Richard." They kept calling my name it echoed. Who was it?
"Richard, it's 7.30." Why, what there it is again, no it's a different noise now. Suddenly everywhere is bright and I'm awake.
"Good morning Richard, it's 7.30 and I brought you up some breakfast." So that was it. I had been dreaming. It must have been Noel knocking at the door before letting himself in. "I thought you might appreciate this after last night and you don't have to rush down to breakfast. This way you can just take your time and blend into the morning. I'll just put the tray over here and I'll see you later."
With that I struggled to open my eyes properly. "Thanks Noel, you're a pal."
"No problem. I trust you slept well?"
"Yeah, too well if you ask me." Then I remembered I hadn't had my change. "By the way Noel, what about my change?"
"I've left it on your tray."
"Do me a favour Noel, pass me the tray." He placed the tray on the bedside table.
"Some more of my friends are coming over tonight if you're interested."
"Maybe, we'll see how it goes." I picked up my cup of tea just as Noel made his way to the door. "Noel, what's this?"
"What Richard?" He looked at the three ten punt notes in my hand. "Where's the rest of it?"
"That's all there is Richard."
"Come on Noel, you told me my tab was around sixteen punt, so where's the rest?"
"Well that was before last night. We all had quite a bit to drink and plenty of food."
"Hold on Noel. There is no way food and drink, even with what I had owed you, came to seventy punts. So where's the rest?" Suddenly my head cleared.
"Well as I said, we all had to pay towards the drink and food. I couldn't afford to lay that on out of my own pocket now could I?"
"No but I didn't expect to pay for everyone else's!"
"That's not fair Richard. You only paid for Paul and your share."

"Well if that's the case I'm not sure I can afford to come again tonight. Your hospitality is out of my price bracket Noel."

"Honestly Richard I only took what you and Paul spent." I remembered how he had lied for us earlier so I suppose I was being a little harsh on him but that should not be an excuse to rip me off.

"You enjoyed it last night didn't you?"

"I'm not so sure about that, what with twenty questions and what it cost, I don't know. I'll have to think about it." I started to drink my tea. Just for that Noel, I think I'll make you sweat a bit. Noel hovered by the door waiting for my answer. I took my time drinking my tea. All this time Noel tried to persuade me to go to this, his second party. In the end, having finished my tea and eaten my toast I agreed.

"Great, same time as last night then. Same arrangement."

"On one condition Noel."

"What's that?"

"I'm not paying for everybody else and we all settle up at the time."

"All right then it's a deal." On that note he left. I couldn't believe that I had just agreed to another late night party.

Chapter 8

Slowly the persistent ringing penetrated my brain. I wish someone would pick that damn phone up. Suddenly I was awake. Realising it was my phone I grab my watch and look at the time. It's eleven thirty. "Ok, ok I'm coming," I shout at the phone as I stumble out of bed. My head is throbbing. My mouth feels like the bottom of a parrot's cage. I'm suffering from a king-size hangover and the incessant ringing of the phone doesn't help. I grab the phone to my ear. "Hello. Who...?" I answer it brusquely.

"Hello, Richard it's Breandán O'Shea here."

Oh shit! I think to myself. "Hello Breandán what..."

"I was just wondering if there's any danger of either of you putting in an appearance today?"

You sarcastic bastard I thought to myself. "Yes of course..."

"Well just as long as I know. Is it likely to be before teatime do you think?"

"Of course."

"What happened to this morning then?"

"This morning?" My brain still wasn't functioning at full speed.

"Yes, this morning, or hadn't you noticed that its eleven thirty?"

That's it, there you go again Breandán, sarcasm is the lowest form of wit. "I know it's eleven thirty, but something urgent came up at the last minute."

"Oh, I see! Unexpected was it?" He said mockingly, "It wouldn't be that you slept in or something would it now?"

"No it wouldn't, and yes it was unexpected. I was awake at seven thirty this morning and we would have been there as usual if this hadn't have come up." Of course I wasn't lying when I told him I was awake at seven thirty, I just left out the fact I went back to sleep.

"So when can I expect you?"

"Straight after lunch. Sorry I didn't let you know," I added with a hint of sarcasm.

"I'll see you then." With that he put the phone down.

I was annoyed at going back to sleep and getting caught out and I certainly wasn't happy with the pounding in my head. "Shit, shit, shit." In fact I was just down right annoyed about everything. Perhaps something to eat would help. I lifted the cover from off the tray, took a look at the cold egg and bacon with all its trimmings and decided against it. Nice thought Noel, but it seemed as if lunch was now the favourite.

As the afternoon wore on the pounding in my head subsided to the merest ache. With my sleeves rolled up and totally immersed in my work I was oblivious of O'Shea's approach. How long he had been stood there I hadn't a clue.

"So you made it at last!" I looked up with a start.

"Jesus! Mr O'Shea, how long have you been there?" I suddenly remembered my sleeves and hurriedly started to roll them back down. Too late, he had already seen my tattoos. I expected him to make some sort of comment, but he didn't.

"Did you both enjoy yourselves last night then?" Instead he was more interested in Noel's impromptu get together.

"How do you mean Breandán?" I was sure he must say something about the tattoos, but his face remained impassive as he continued talking in the same vein.

"At Noel's little get together."

"I don't know what you're talking about." I tried bluffing my way out, but Breandán was having none of it.

"Come on now. I know you were there. Why man you've only got to look at you, something urgent cropped up indeed! Huh, what do you take me for?"

I thought I'd better quit whilst I was ahead. "Well, it was unexpected," I said lamely.

"So what time did you finish this little soiree of Noel's?"

"Late."

"Was there many there?"

"About seven besides us. Why?" He ignored my question completely.

"Can you remember any of their names?"

"Why the third degree? Look, he's having another tonight and it'll probably be the same crew. Why don't you come and find out for yourself if you're that interested?"

"Maybe. Now can you remember any names?"

"There was one bloke I remember, a bloke called Noel."

"Tell me about him, what did he look like?"

"Look what's this all about?"

"Never mind what it's about, just tell me about this Noel. What did he look like?" His voice seemed to have a slight edge to it.

"He was tallish with a rugged well worn face. You know sort of lived in look. Ruddy complexion as if he had high blood pressure. A heavy drinker's look."

"What was his line?"

"Line?"

"Yes, his job?"

"I don't think he said. Well if he did I don't remember."

"Interesting. Yes very interesting, I might just come along tonight."

"Do you know this Noel then?"

He chose to ignore my question. "Those tattoos," he pointed at my arm and I'd thought I'd got away with it. "Were you a military man then?"

Damn it I thought. I don't want to admit to being in the Para's. I took my time and thought carefully about my reply. "Yes, some time ago."

"Oh, what were you in?" He asked with an unhealthy interest.

"I was in the army."

"Interesting." He frowned and looked at me through half closed eyes. "Very interesting indeed." He added nodding his head. I suddenly felt nervous of this man and certainly very exposed. I hurriedly tried to extricate myself and take the heat off.

"But I didn't like it much," I lied.

"How long were you in?"

"Oh...only a short time."

His eyes narrowed again. "I see...so when you say a short time do you mean you bought yourself out then?"

"No, no. I served a couple of years." I hurriedly tried to qualify my answer. "You know the minimum. As little as possible." It wasn't an outright lie; I just bent the truth a little.

"Oh I see. Well if you disliked it so much, why did you get the tattoos done?"

Oh dear, I thought to myself, what now. I said the first thing that came into my head.

"Went out with the lads. Got pissed and ended up with tattoos." It sounded a bit lame but that was the best I could come up with on the spur of the moment.

O'Shea nodded. "Yes. I suppose we all do stupid things from time to time don't we?"

"Especially when you're young and I've regretted it ever since."

"Young!" He exclaimed. "Huh, I still do silly things. Now what times this party?"

At last he seemed to accept my story and I felt the tension gradually subside. "Party, what party? More like a piss up if you ask me."

"Well what time?"

"If last night's anything to go by I would say about two thirty."

"I'll be there." He looked at us both, shook his head and grinned. "You know, I'm not sure which one looks the worst, you both look pretty awful. You had best call over to the house for a couple of shots of 'Irish Dew' that'll cure your hangover and set you up for tonight. See you now."

We had caught up on the backlog and feeling more than just a little weary, we called it a day. We trudged slowly across the orchard in the direction of the farmhouse to sample Breandán's wonder cure - 'Irish Dew'.

A ferocious snarling and barking greeted my knock on the door. Eventually this was replaced by a lot of sniffing and snuffling at the bottom of the door. This lasted but a short time and a further cacophony of barking ensued. I could just hear someone shout sternly "Quiet! Enough!"

As the door opened the largest Wolfhound imaginable confronted us. Held fast by a choke chain grasped in Breandán's right hand, the dog again started barking. "I said quiet! Enough!" Breandán pulled on the dog's chain. "Sit." The dog immediately sat and quietened. "Come in, come in. Don't mind the dog, he's had his fill of Englishmen this week!" We were ushered into the large kitchen "Here take a seat." He indicated to a couple of sturdy looking pine chairs at the table Three whisky tumblers and a colourless liquid were placed on the table in front of us. The dog now started nuzzling my hand wanting me to make a fuss of it.

"Now that *is* unusual, he's never done that before. You're honoured he's usually very anti-social. A one man dog so to speak."

"Here boy." Paul patted his thigh but the dog didn't move, so he tried again.

"Here boy, come on boy." The dog's heckles rose. Baring his teeth he started to growl. Slowly, ever so slowly he crept towards Paul. With each step his growl grew in intensity.

"Bed! Go and lie down!" Breandán commanded the dog in a stern voice. The dog went to his bed and lay there resting his head on the side of the bed, but his eyes constantly watching Paul. "Now that's his usual stance." Breandán said as he poured out some of the colourless liquid into two of the tumblers. "Help yourself lads."

"Aren't you having one?" I asked.

He shook his head and pointed to a small stickpin in his lapel. "I've signed the pledge."

"I see. Well cheers." I took a large mouthful of the liquid.

"Yes cheers Breandán," said Paul doing likewise. We both started coughing and spluttering together. I nearly choked as it burnt its way down my gullet. I even had tears rolling down my cheeks. It fairly took your breath away. Breandán was helpless with laughter.

"Shit Breandán. What the hell is this stuff? Paint stripper?"

Breandán guffawed again and again until he had tears in his eyes. "That my friend, is what we call 'Irish Dew'. It's Poteen."

"Poteen. What the hell's Poteen?" I asked.

"Poteen is a liquor distilled all over Ireland. True Poteen is illegal and is the strongest drink you can get anywhere."

"What's it made from?"

"Ah, that's a secret."

"Isn't it potatoes?" asked Paul.

That started Breandán laughing again. "Potatoes. I like it, Potatoes indeed. No Paul not at all, that's a total misconception. What do you think to it Richard?" He asked with a twinkle in his eye.

"My honest opinion?"

"Yes."

"Bloody awful. If this is the main drink in Ireland I'm not surprised you're on the wagon."

Breandán once more started to laugh, again the tears rolled down his cheeks.

"I'm sorry Richard," he said as he wiped the tears away, "But I did say it would clear your hangover, I didn't say it was tasty." Once more he erupted into more laughter. "Ah dear, I've not laughed as much as that for a long time, the look on your face. I wish I'd a camera. Anyway a jokes a joke, now would you like a Bushmill's to take away the taste?"

"Best not, especially if tonight turns out like last night. Thanks anyway." I glanced at my watch time was getting on. "We'll get off if you don't mind Breandán."

"Ok Richard. Probably see you both later."

"Yeah sure. Are you fit Paul?"

"Yes mate. I'm sorry Breandán but I don't reckon much on your 'Irish Dew' so if you don't mind I'll leave you with this."

"I can't imagine why you'd want to do that Paul, can you Richard?"

"Do you fancy a beer?" Paul asked as we came out of the dining room.

I looked at my watch and it was getting on for ten. "Just the one maybe. Hang on a minute there's Noel and I ought to let him know that O'Shea's coming over tonight."

"Ok, I'll get the drinks in whilst you see to that. What do you want, a pint or a whisky?"

"A pint please." I walked off towards the porter's lodge to catch up with Noel, but he wasn't there. My next stop was reception. "Excuse me love." The receptionist looked up, "Good evening sir. Mr James isn't it?"

"Yes that's right. You've got a good memory."

"It pays to have sometimes. Now what can I do for you?"

"I was looking for Noel the night porter. I thought I saw him come this way."

"Is he not in his lodge?"

"No."

"Oh dear, I don't know then. It's really my night off and I just popped in to see someone, but if you hold on a minute I'll ask my colleague if she knows where he is." She disappeared into the inner office to re-appear a few seconds later. "Evidently he has just popped up to one of the rooms on the first floor with some drinks, he shouldn't be too long if you care to wait, or maybe you'd prefer to sit in the bar. We'll send him over to you when he returns."

"No, that's all right I'll hang on here for a few minutes."

"If you like, he shouldn't be very long. Ah, talk of the devil, here he comes now. Noel, Mr James would like a word with you."

"Hi Noel, I thought I'd let you know Breandán is coming over tonight."

"Breandán O'Shea?"

I didn't know whether I imagined it or not, but for a minute he appeared quite shaken by my news. "Hey Noel, are you all right?"

"What? Oh, yes I'm fine." He quickly gathered his composure and smiled, "Now what did you say?"

"Breandán O'Shea said he would join us tonight. That's all right isn't it? If not I could always ring him and..."

"No, no that'll be fine."

"Are you sure you're all right?"

"Yes, yes I'm fine really I am. Now if you'll excuse me I must get on I've a lot to do."

"Sure, no problem, I'll see you later." He rushed off towards the kitchen as if he had a train to catch. Strange I thought, Noel never rushes anywhere.

"So why did you think it strange, perhaps he had a lot of work to do."

"No Paul, you didn't see the look when I told him O'Shea was planning on coming. Honestly Paul, I'm not exaggerating, he was visibly shaken."

"He was scared?"

"Well if not scared then he's certainly hiding something."

"Well, well, well. Look who's just come in to help tidy up."

I turned in my seat to see Noel helping the barman putting up the grills. This was probably a good chance for me to find out a little more.

"How about another drink before the bar closes?"

"Ok if you're having one?" I picked up our glasses and went over to the bar.

"Your just in time sir, what will it be?"

"Pint of Smethwicks and a lager please."

"Thank you sir, anything else?"

"No thanks would you put it on my room please."

"Certainly, what is your room number?" I gave him my room number and turned to speak to Noel. "Hello again Noel that was unlike you earlier."

"How do you mean sir?"

"Well rushing off like that."

"Oh err...yes, I'm sorry about that. It's just that I'd suddenly remembered something that I had to do urgently." He then spoke in a low whisper, "Look I can't talk now, but when everyone's gone I'll explain everything..."

I cut him short as the barman approached. "Would it be possible to have some cheese and biscuits?"

"Certainly sir. If you would take a seat in the lounge I'll bring it through to you."

"Thank you Noel." I gave him a wink.

Gradually the other residents drifted away to their respective rooms and we had the lounge to ourselves. It wasn't long before Noel appeared with a tray of freshly made coffee. He looked about him nervously and sat down. "I'm sorry Richard that I couldn't talk to you earlier, but..." He once more looked around the room making sure we were the only ones present.

"What's wrong Noel?"

"Nothing." He licked his lips nervously. He seemed very agitated about something.

"You're joking aren't you?"

"There's nothing wrong I tell you." He licked his lips and again he looked around the room.

"You're very nervous for a person who says there is nothing wrong."

"No I'm fine. Just fine."

"Come on Noel cut the crap. You're absolutely shit scared. What's going on?"

"The two killings you saw..." He faltered

"Yeah, what about them?"

He leaned forward in his chair, his voice little more than a whisper, "Well like I was saying, the two murders you saw were, as you suspected, IRA killings."

"Well what's that got to do with tonight?"

Noel took a deep breath. He looked ashen, his face glistened in the light and beads of sweat started to form on his brow. Again he licked his lips and once more in little more than a whisper he spoke. "Whatever I tell you tonight, you must promise. No swear on your life that it is not repeated to anyone else, otherwise I'm a dead man and so are you. Do you understand?"

"Get on with it Noel. Tell us what you're on about." Paul answered brusquely.

"Not until you both promise not to breathe a word of this to a soul. I'm risking my life telling you anything!" His eyes pleaded with us as he wiped his hand across his sweating brow. We realised then he was deadly serious about something, something that worried him immensely.

"Ok you have my word Noel."

"Paul, what about you?"

Paul nodded.

"No Paul swear to me you won't breathe a word."

"I nodded didn't I?"

"That's not good enough, I need your word." He started to get up from the chair.

"Hang on Noel. Come on sit down again."

"But you don't understand. It's my life at risk and...well you'd be the same."

"Yes I do understand." I answered softly to reassure him. "Now come on Noel sit down and tell us what it us that's worrying you so much."

"Only if Paul gives his word as well."

"Sure he will, won't you Paul?"

"Of course I will Noel. I won't breathe a word to anyone. On my mother's life I promise."

Noel pulled a handkerchief from his pocket and wiped his face and eyes, then sat back in the chair and gathered his composure.

"Well Noel we're waiting." I said as gently as I could.

He shuffled in his seat, took a deep breath and with hands shaking he started to talk in a whisper.

"Sorry Noel we can't hear you. What did you say?"

"I said, please don't tell anyone will you."

"Noel, listen to me. We have both given our word. You need to trust us on this one."

He was petrified. It was obviously something very grave indeed. He took a deep breath. "Well, it's Mr O'Shea. You know your farmer friend. Breandán O'Shea. The man you're working for. He is IRA. He is one of the top officials. The main man. There are others but he has the final word. My friends be very, very careful. Careful of what you do and what you say in front of him. Please be on your guard at all times. Don't trust him."

I couldn't believe what I had just heard. "Are you telling us that we are working with, or for a... a terrorist. Is that what you're saying Noel?"

"I've told you. Please be very careful."

"No, no, no. I don't, I won't believe it!" Oh shit, I thought, what have I got us into. We sat there in silence mulling over what we had just been told. I remembered O'Shea seeing my tattoos and that could be a problem!

Paul pursed his lips and gave a low whistle. "Richard, we're right in the shit."

"That's not necessarily true."

"How d'you mean Noel?" Paul asked.

"Surely to be forewarned is to forearmed. Just carry on as normal then you'll be all right. You're only in the shit if you suddenly change."

"I don't follow you."

"I do. What Noel is saying is if we didn't know then we would happily carry on working. Yeah?"

"Yes so?"

"We do exactly that. We carry on working, because, if we just pack up and run then O'Shea will know we know something."

"I see, and if he suspects that we know who he is then...well dead men tell no lies."

"Exactly."

Paul was silent A look of consternation on his face as he thought about the implication of what Noel had said. He looked at me with a rebellious look in his eyes and said, "Bollocks! There's only one option then; we stay."

"Are you happy with that Paul?"

"I'm certainly not ecstatic. If you ask me we're right in it up to our eyes with little chance of extricating ourselves. Shit, I need a drink to get used to the idea. How about you Richard?"

"Yes I'll have a large..."

"Bushmill's, and lager for you Paul?"

"Get them out of this." Paul handed Noel a five punt note but he refused to accept it.

"No you won't I'll get these." Then, before Paul could say anything he was gone.

"What do you honestly reckon Richard?"

"If what he says is true, then we could have a problem tonight."

"Why tonight?"

"Because Breandán saw my tattoos today. Do you reckon last night's lot were IRA then?"

"I don't know why?"

"Well they were very interested in whether or not we had a military background?"

"Good point. We'll just have to be very careful tonight especially if it's the same crowd."

Just after two in the morning a small group of men gathered in the lounge of the Tara hotel. Breandán O'Shea was conspicuous by his absence. Apart from two, who looked very young, most of the group was in their late thirties to forties.

"Do you recognise anyone Paul?" I asked as we walked into the lounge.

"No, do you?"

"I'm not sure, but I think those four were here last night." I indicated the four men deep in conversation. Paul looked across at them.

"Maybe, but I'm not too sure. What about those four over there on the settee?"

"The two young blokes and their mates?"

"Yes."

"Definitely not. You'd think those young blokes would be out with a couple of girls wouldn't you and not stuck here with this lot?" It was getting on for 2:15 and as yet our arrival had gone unnoticed.

"No sign of O'Shea yet Richard."

"Perhaps he's decided not to come."

"You hope!"

"Well stranger things have happened. Where's Noel?"

"There he is just coming from the bar."

Noel saw us and came over. "What would you like to drink?"

"I'll have a Smethwicks. What do you want Paul?"

"Lager please."

"Ok, I'll bring them over in a minute.

"Noel, who are they?" Paul indicated the four blokes on the sofa; "They weren't here last night were they?"

"No, I know them vaguely. I think they're friends of Noel."

"Who's Noel?" Paul asked.

"You know Paul. The bloke with the red craggy face."

"Yes, I remember. So they're his friends."

"Hasn't Breandán O'Shea's arrived?" I asked.

"Not yet, but there's time."

"Has he called you Noel?"

"No, not a word but that doesn't mean a thing."

"Still I suppose no news is good news."

"Hmm. Look, why don't I introduce you to those four blokes and have a chat with them whilst I get your drinks?"

"Ok." We followed Noel over to the four guys on the settee; he was about to introduce us when the front door bell rang. My heart missed a beat, because deep down I knew it had to be O'Shea.

As Breandán O'Shea entered the general hubbub ceased. You could hear a pin drop. I took a deep breath. This could be one hell of an evening. Breandán smiled benignly. Shaking hands. Greeting everyone except for the two youngsters. For them a curt nod of acknowledgement. They only spoke to him in response to a question. On the odd occasion he did speak to them they jumped to their feet and addressed him as 'Sir'. After the niceties were over Breandán summoned the night porter. Placing his arm around Noel's shoulder he guided him from the main body of the lounge and spoke to him. A few minutes later Noel reappeared with a tray of drinks for everyone except the two youngsters. We were still the centre of attention with someone always wanting to know something either about us or about our work, but as the night wore on gradually a subtle change took place.

We found ourselves being subjected to a course of indoctrination. The main thrust was a two-hour lecture on Irish political history competently delivered by the two youngest members. They gave a well-rehearsed and polished performance. They started with the atrocities perpetrated by Oliver Cromwell, when he all but committed genocide against the people of Drogheda. They then continued up to the present situation that existed within Eire and Ulster. Every now and then they would stop and look to us for our approval on certain aspects. Of course when asked for our views it paid us to agree with what they said rather than say what we really thought!

"Well gentleman, I think it's been very interesting for all concerned, especially our English friends, wouldn't you agree?" There was a murmur of approval from the small group, and then Breandán turned to me. "What about you Richard, what did you think?" He looked at me through half closed eyes.

"Hmm, interesting, but I think it's way passed my bedtime."

"I see, and what about you Paul, what do you think?"

"Like Richard, I'm tired and yes it was hmm, interesting."

"I'm glad you both appreciated it." Once more there was that benign smile that we had seen earlier. "Good God, look at the time! Come on you lot time to go."

"Noel, how much do I owe you for Paul and my drinks?"

"Don't worry about it I'll settle up with Noel tomorrow." Breandán said as he walked with the others towards the front door. "By the way, are you working on Saturday afternoon?"

"No why?"

"Well in that case we're going for a little trip."

"Who?"

"You and I."

"But..." I was more than just a little concerned after what we had learnt earlier.

His eyes narrowed. "There's no buts about it. We're taking a little ride on Saturday, and remember..."

"Remember what?" I answered a little nervously.

"Stay in the hotel otherwise you'll be in more trouble. I'll let you know at what time on Saturday. Goodnight."

Chapter 9

Saturday morning and still no word from O'Shea. I felt as if a great weight had been lifted from my shoulders and for the first time since Wednesday I was relaxed. I felt on top of the world as I descended the stairs. I called at reception to pick up my morning paper en route to breakfast. Little did I know that my mood was to be short lived?

"Good morning Mr James."

"Good morning." I answered as I picked up the 'Daily Mail' newspaper. "Has Mr Jones come down yet?"

"Not as far as I know." I gave the receptionist my keys at the same time she handed me a small envelope. My heart missed a beat. I knew straight away who it was from. With shaking hands I withdrew a piece of paper. I read the single line. 'Pick you up at reception one o'clock.' I stared at that sheet of paper.

"Is everything all right Mr James?"

I heard her voice as if in a distance, but didn't register at first. My thoughts centred on that piece of paper. What was I going to do?

"Mr James, excuse me." The voice sounded like an echo in the distance. "Excuse me, Mr James."

I looked up. "Sorry, I was miles away."

"I just wondered if everything was all right?"

I gave her a weak smile. "Yes just fine why?"

"I'm sorry, it's just that I couldn't help noticing...

"I'm fine honestly."

"It was just that you seemed quite shocked. Not bad news I hope?"

"No it's something I've been expecting." I said rather lamely. I stood there for a little while vaguely conscious of her soft Irish voice prattling on but I was more concerned about the cryptic note I held in my hand. I looked at it for the last time then screwed it up in controlled anger and shoved it with the envelop into my pocket, gave the receptionist a fleeting smile and thanked her before making my way to the dining room for my breakfast.

"Good morning Richard."

"Huh." I grunted and fell into a sullen silence.

"What's up with you, a bit touchy this morning aren't you?" I didn't reply but carried on reading my paper. A few minutes of a moody silence ensued then Paul tried again.

"Richard."

"What?" I replied crabbily.

"What's bugging you? Come on tell me, you're like a bear with a sore head?"

He was right, I was like a bear with a sore head, and it was unfair to take it out on him. If the truth were known I was scared. I didn't know what O'Shea was after and I was beside myself with worry.

"Have you heard from O'Shea?" Paul asked.

I didn't answer him but passed him the screwed up piece of paper.

"So this is why." Paul said. I nodded. Paul straightened out the paper and read the cryptic message. "Why are you so worried?"

"Come on Paul, knowing what we know, then wouldn't you be?" I snapped at him.

"Well, put like that I suppose..."

"There's no suppose about it. I know you, and you would react exactly the same way. So don't try telling me otherwise."

Paul shrugged his shoulders and looked at the note again. We sat in silence immersed in our own thoughts.

"Richard listen to me." I looked up from my paper. "We've been over this time and time again and we agreed that if the IRA wanted us dead then they would have killed us by now. The first night we were here they could have done it. In fact anytime they could have. Anyway, why would they kill us, after all we're not a threat to them are we?" I thought about what Paul said and had to admit that it made sense. Paul continued to press home his point. "Listen if we were some powerful individual, something to do with the military, a spy for Special Branch or something like that then I would be the first to panic. But we're not so loosen up Richard. Relax, nothing's going to happen to us. After all it was you that convinced me there was minimal danger to us, so what's happened to change your mind?"

"Breandán O'Shea."

"How d'you mean Breandán O'Shea, what's different?"

"Well up until now we didn't know where he fitted in."

"Crap. You said yourself that you thought he was behind all this, and Noel certainly intimated that he was involved. So we as good as knew."

"That's rubbish Paul I never said..."

"Maybe not in so many words, but when I said I had a sneaking suspicion that there was an element of truth in what Noel was intimating, you agreed. Also we've discussed the possibility of him being IRA many times and you always said that because we were of no threat to him, or his organisation, then there was little or no threat to us. Right or wrong?"

I was left with no option but to agree.

"Yeah, you're right."

"Well, nothing's changed has it?"

"Yes it has."

"Bollocks, what's changed?"

"Our suspicions have been confirmed." I added somewhat lamely.

"So what." He retorted angrily. "Richard, The bottom line is that we are no threat to him or the organisation, surely you of all people see that?" He didn't wait for my reply but continued with his line of argument, "We are still earning a lucrative income from this contract, and we are still..."

"Paul" I cut him short. "I can't argue with anything you say, but it still doesn't make me feel any the less nervous about this journey."

"Ok, but you said earlier, should they, or O'Shea, want either of us taken out they would have done so by now. Look at what happened in the club in front of all those witnesses. Doesn't that prove that they have no scruples? If they want someone out of the way, then they'll just do it, they won't give a toss."

"I agree but..."

He cut my protestation off in mid sentence. "There you are then, you agree. It's a trip, so what? A business trip to discuss possible additional work."

I tried to interrupt "But..."

Paul was having none of it. "Now listen to me it's a business trip. For Christ sake Richard, get real. He's hardly likely to knock you off even if he wants to. After all everyone will know that you went off with him so he's not going to be that stupid is he?"

I thought about what he said. "Your right. I guess I am being a little paranoid about things."

"That's an understatement if ever there was one."

"Ok, it's just that after what Noel told... "

"Let's forget about it all right?"

Back in my room, my military intuition took over and any doubts I may have had about this trip had disappeared. I threw off my working clothes and got out my suit and a clean shirt and tie. I had just finished tying my tie when the phone rang. I glanced at my watch; it was 12:58. "Hello." It was reception advising me that Breandán O'Shea had arrived.

At 13:00 precisely I walked to the reception desk and handed in my keys.

"Ah there you are Richard."

I swung round to face O'Shea. "Afternoon Breandán."

His eyes twinkled and I sensed he was having a bit of a laugh at my expense, as he looked me up and down. "To be sure you're looking very smart indeed, but a little over dressed for what I've got in mind for you."

"What have you in mind for me?" I asked a little worried.

"You'll find out soon enough." He looked me up and down again and started to laugh. "You sure look real smart Richard, I'll give you that. Still not to worry it's too late to change now. You'll have to come as you are."

As we left the hotel foyer there was a large gleaming Mercedes parked nearby. Thinking it was his I started to walk over to it.

"Where you off to?" Called out O'Shea.

I turned to see he was walking up the car park towards a beaten up old car parked at the far end. "I thought this was..."

He cut me off short. "You forget that I'm a poor farmer. I can't afford that sort of luxury for a farm car now can I?" He winked and gave me a big grin. As we got into his beaten up old Fiat I smiled to myself. I could picture the pair of us, me in my best bib and tucker and him in his ragged old clothes, climbing into some old heap of a car surrounded by rubbish. It may well have appeared like a heap of scrap metal, but as soon as it started I realised that it was far from it. We pulled out of the lane onto the open road there was no mistaking the fact that this was no ordinary car, but a highly tuned piece of engineering. He gently pressed down on the accelerator and the gentle purr became a deep-throated roar as we accelerated to over 80 mph in a matter of seconds.

We hadn't gone far before heavy traffic forced us to slow to a snail's pace. It was patently obvious that something major had happened.

"Do you think it's an accident?" I asked.

At first Breandán did not reply. Then as we coasted to a standstill he said in a matter of fact way, "No there's no accident."

"If it's not an accident, then what is it?" I enquired.

"It's the Gardai," was all he would say.

"How do you mean it's the Gardai?"

"What I say, it's the Gardai. The Police."

"Why do you say the Police are causing this?"

"It's a roadblock that's all."

"How do you know it's a roadblock?" I asked.

"Because they do it the same time, the same place every day of the year."

"Why? What are they looking for?"

"Terrorists."

I was surprised by this disclosure and couldn't help repeating it, more as an exclamation than anything else. "Terrorists!" How do you mean terrorists?"

"Like I said, terrorists. Surely you've heard of the IRA haven't you?" He asked with a tinge of sarcasm.

"Of course, but I didn't think the Republic were involved in such activities." I replied equally as sarcastically.

"You've changed your mind then."

"How do you mean?"

"Well it was only the other day that you told me that you had witnessed two IRA killings in my club. Or perhaps I mis-heard."

"Now hang on a minute you're taking things out of context."

"Well, didn't you say you had witnessed two IRA killings?"

"Yes I did say that the other day but..."

"Well there you go then."

"Yes but what I said then and what I just said a minute ago are two different things."

"I'm intrigued, please explain."

"Well, I didn't think the Police in the Republic actively looked for IRA suspects. Well, not as a matter of course." I shot him a sideways glance.

"Well, they do and they don't." He said in a fairly non-committal sort of way.

"How do you mean?" I asked.

"Well Dublin's only paying lip service to London."

"In what way?" I asked, but before I could get my answer we entered the roadblock. As we stopped Breandán wound down his window.

"Good afternoon sir. Ah Mr O'Shea and how are you?"

"I'm fine." The young man on duty gave a cursory look into the back of the car then glanced in my direction. "Would this gentleman be a friend of yours Mr O'Shea?"

"Yes, this is Richard. Do you want to check the boot?"

"As it's you sir that won't be necessary. Have a good trip." With that he waved us on.

"I see what they mean by lip service. If that's how they check for terrorists than that's a farce." I said sarcastically.

"Of course that's not their normal routine. It's just that the local Gardai all know me from the hotel."

I bet they do.

"So do they search other cars?" I asked.

"Some of them. Some they just look through the windows and check the occupants. It helps them keep tabs on undesireables."

I smiled. "You mean like Englishmen?" I tried to sound as if I was joking but I really meant it. He didn't bite.

"No. I mean undesirables."

"But according to you, you never get stopped and searched. So am I right in saying that provided you are extremely wealthy, own the local hotel and a landowner to boot, then you are above suspicion. A regular pillar of society so to speak. Bah, that's ridiculous." I could see by the look that on his face he didn't like what I had said.

"Why do you say that?" he asked.

"Well some of the top spies portrayed exactly that, until they were caught that was, but had it not been assumed that they were so squeaky clean then I would suggest that they may well have been caught a lot sooner. Wouldn't you?" I thought I had made my point, so left it at that.

"Hmm, an interesting philosophy," was all he said. We continued in silence.

We were just passing through the last town before the border when I broke the silence.
"Where are we heading for?"

"My other farm."

I heaved an inward sigh of relief. At last I felt a little more relaxed about things. I didn't know exactly what his plans were, but it seemed that he wasn't planning on knocking me off not just yet anyway. "I didn't know you had two farms. Where's your other one then?" Suddenly this journey had taken on a whole new perspective and I was very curious as to where we were heading.

"Where's my other farm, now that's a good question." He smiled at some secret joke that only he was aware of.

"Yes, where is your other farm?" I repeated the question.

"I'm not so sure you'll really want to know." He answered softly as if talking to himself. There was that fleeting smile again.

"Well?"

"Over the border, in bandit country." He looked across at me; "Does that worry you?"
I shrugged my shoulders. "Well does it worry you?"

"I suppose not. I can run bloody fast if it comes to it!" I said quite flippantly. He nodded his head and chuckled.

"You English, you're all too busy living in the fast lane so haven't a clue what life's really all about, but when we get there I'll show you." He started to laugh out loud.

"Yes my friend. Too busy and far too stressed out. Look at you for instance, you're up tight about something. Come on Richard relax enjoy the drive, tomorrow's another day." He was right I suppose I was up tight then I thought I had good reason to be.

Once through the town and heading for the border we started to slow. Breandán pointed out a single-track road up ahead.

I looked slightly puzzled. "Is this to your farm then?"

"No, not yet. I want to show you something." He said fervently.

He swung the car into the single track and slowed to a walking pace. We had not proceeded along it very far when an old boy waved us to stop. Breandán wound down his window as the elderly guy approached his side of the car. Meanwhile another shabbily dressed individual emerged from the shadows and casually sauntered up to my side of the car and signalled me to wind down my window. I never gave it a thought and did as I was requested. Suddenly I felt the cold steel rim of a gun barrel jammed against my temple. I froze. I heard the old man say something in what seemed to be a foreign language, probably Gaelic. Breandán replied. There was a small exchange of words then the older man addressed his mate and the gun barrel was withdrawn. All this time I had sat with my eyes straight-ahead, not daring to move.

"Sorry about that, but you can't be too careful, can you now." The voice was that of a young person. I turned in my seat to be confronted by a youth that could not have been much more than eighteen years old a mere youngster. His face broke into a broad grin as he said, "Sorry if I frightened you Sir, but needs must."

"Oh, that's ok. I understand." I said as I looked straight into the youth's eyes, but it wasn't ok and I didn't understand. The little bastard had scared the shit out of me. I really thought it was the end of the road.

"All right Paddy, we won't be staying long. Is Ryan here?" Breandán asked.

"To be sure he is. He's round with the others. He did say he was expecting you sir." The older guy stepped back as we moved off along the single-track road. We eventually came to a halt not far from a small Chapel of Rest situated in the middle of a large cemetery. Breandán switched off the engine.

"Now what?" I inquired.

"Just wait and see. I want you to see something."

So we sat there in silence for two maybe three or more minutes waiting for what, I wasn't sure.

Breandán wound down his window. "Listen can you hear it?"

I strained my ears listening. "Hear what?" I asked.

"Wind down your window and listen." I did as I was asked and listened. "Well can you?" he asked in an excited voice.

"I can hear the crows, if that's what you mean?"

He didn't reply straight away, but sat there in silence for a moment or two, as if treating my reply with contempt. There was something out there that he desperately wanted me to hear. Something that he found exceedingly exciting.

"There listen. Now, surely you can hear them?" He was so excited he was almost shouting at me. I listened and then I heard it.

"Left, left, left right left." It was very faint at first. Barely audible above the noise of the crows, but it quickly increased in volume, as round the corner of the chapel a column of about twenty men dressed in British Army uniform appeared. At the side of the column, complete with Pace Stick, was a guy wearing a red beret.

"Left, left, left right left. Left, left, left right left." There was no mistaking that accent; I could recognise a London accent anywhere.

"Squaaad, squad halt!"

The column came to halt in perfect time about twenty feet from where we were parked. I could now distinctly see that it was not any old red beret, but it was a genuine Para's beret.

"Squaaad. Squad right turn." The men turned to face the ex Para.

You despicable bastard I thought to myself. How can you train these people who ultimately will end up fighting and killing your fellow countryman? I was seething.

"What's he doing here?" I asked Breandán barely able to cover my anger. Breandán turned to face me and there was a strange fire in his eyes.

"I would have thought it obvious. He's training young men. Our young men." His voice was full of pride as if this was some marvellous spectacle to be held and revered the world over. I felt I would explode if I didn't say something. With Paul's words and our motto in mind I carefully chose my words and hoped my anger was not too obvious.

"I can see what he's doing, but he's a Para." I managed to keep my voice fairly steady so I don't think my anger showed.

"No, he was a Para just as you were. He's now a mercenary and earns good money by teaching others discipline and how to be good soldiers."

"Squaaad stand at ease." The ex-Para barked out the order and the men smartly brought their weapons down to their side into the 'At Ease' position. "Right men, in a minute I'll dismiss you for a ten minute break, let's try and get it right this time shall we!"

"Where are these lot from?" I asked managing to keep my voice steady.

"Oh we recruit from the local farms and villages around different areas. Now watch this Richard, this guy's done wonders for these young men. Just watch." I could see the fervour in Breandán's eyes and sense his restrained excitement at what he was watching.

"Squaaad, squad 'Shun." The squad snapped to attention.

"Very professional don't you think Richard?" Breandán's voice was full of emotion but I didn't answer.

"Squaaad, squad dismiss." The command from the ex-Para was barked out in a voice that any regular DI would have been proud of but the squad that was a different matter. Some of the men turned to their right others to their left all in all a total shambles. In that split second all my pent-up anger dissolved as these so called professionals made a complete idiot out of their so-called DI, it was hilarious to watch.

"What were you saying about them being professional," I managed to splutter out between bouts of laughter.

"It's because of the man's accent." Breandán replied angrily.

"How d'you mean his accent? Bullshit! They're incompetent and you know it."

"Bollocks! It's the man's accent I tell you. Anyway they haven't been training long with an Englishman and sometimes it causes a problem." After this petulant remark he got out of the car, angrily slammed the door and walked over to where the Drill Instructor stood.

"Good afternoon."

The Para turned around to see who was addressing him, came smartly to attention and gave a slight inclination of the head. "Good afternoon to you sir." Breandán looked around those lounging about on the grass.

"Ryan O'Malley, is he here?"

The Instructor gave a cursory look about the men, before answering.

"Yes sir. Do you wish to speak to him?" Breandán nodded, turned on his heel and walked back to the car.

"O'Malley," the dulcet tones of the acting Drill Instructor rang out.

"Yes sir?" A young man with premature grey hair shouted and jumped to his feet. "Return your weapon to the armoury. Collect your stuff and report back here. On the double man, come on move." O'Malley picked up his weapon, which I recognised straightaway as the SLR 7.62 mm as issued to the British Army, and ran off into the cemetery. Not only was an Englishman training them but also their weapons were British Army issued. The plot thickened.

O'Malley took from the canvas bag a screwdriver and what looked to be a pair of numberplates and proceeded to remove the Dublin registration plates from the car. In a matter of minutes the beaten-up old Fiat had become a British registered vehicle and now sported a Belfast registration. Sticking a British road tax disc, issued in Belfast onto the nearside of the windscreen, completed the illusion. We now had a brand new identity.

"Well what did you think of the training?" Breandán asked as we continued our journey northwards. I smiled at the question, surely he couldn't be serious, but he was.
"In all honesty Breandán if that's the best you can offer then I don't think the British Army has anything to fear from such a motley bunch. Anyway, why the false plates?"
He didn't answer the question. I pointed at the small disc of paper on the windscreen in front of me, "So I assume that's a forgery?"
"Maybe."
"Why, what's the point of it?
"It avoids awkward questions."
"Come on don't give me that! What d'you take me for?"
"It's true."
"I don't believe a word of it, there has to be another reason. You know I sometimes think, that you think, I'm stupid." He chose to ignore what I had just said and we drove on in silence, but I wasn't prepared to let him get away with it. "So are you telling me that you're going to attract more attention than anybody else with Republican plates? Rubbish! You see cars on both sides of the border with plates from Belfast and Dublin so what's the difference?" My argument was sound and he couldn't ignore my questioning any longer and he knew it.
"Well let's say if you are travelling from Dublin to Belfast with Republican plates, you will attract far more attention than if you have Belfast plates. Don't forget it's not the border crossing that's the problem, it's being in the six counties that's the problem."
"How do you mean?"
"In the six counties, it's highly probable we'll get stopped by either the UDR or RUC. With Belfast plates we avoid a lot of unnecessary hassle." I still wasn't totally convinced but I had to accept it especially when, a few minutes later, we crossed the border unchallenged. As Breandán gently accelerated along the Newry road I wondered where we were heading.
"Are we going to Newry?"
"No, we'll pass through it then out towards Armagh we've still some way to go yet." He was still playing it close to the chest.
I was lost in a world of my own when suddenly Breandán shattered the silence.

"Shit!"

"What's up?"

"There's a roadblock ahead."

"Is that all, I thought something was wrong the way you were shouting."

"Ah well that's life, fortunately there's not much traffic so hopefully it won't slow us down much." Breandán gave a resigned sigh. Three Land Rovers were used. The first was on our side parked across the carriageway. The second was across the opposite carriageway a little further on and the third was positioned on our side. The whole produced the effect of a chicane forcing vehicles to slow to a snail's pace in order to manoeuvre around the obstructions safely.

"Richard, have you got your driving license with you?" Breandán asked.

"Yes why?"

"Well give it to me quickly."

"But why?" I asked again.

"Don't ask questions just do it and I'll tell you why in a minute." His tone of voice held a sense of urgency. I pulled my wallet from my pocket and took out my license. Breandán glanced quickly in my direction then looked back to the road ahead.

"Because it's the UDR and they're nosy sods. They want to know the 'ins' and 'outs' of everything. They're bastards." I was confused.

"So how does it help having my license?"

"If I pass them both licenses together they will see you're English and they won't keep us there for long."

We didn't have to wait long before we passed the two soldiers armed with automatic weapons and into the roadblock proper. Breandán wound down his window as the UDR Sergeant approached.

"Good afternoon. Switch off your engine please. Pass me your driving license sir." He studied both, then addressed me. "I see from this you're from Kent sir."

I looked across the car to the face framed by the driver's window. "That's right." I said.

"I know it well. I've spent many happy days over there. Are you here on business or holiday."

"He's visiting my family, comes over from time to time don't you Richard?"

"Yes, every now and then I pop over."

"Open the boot please."

Breandán leaned down to pull the boot catch but as he did so I heard the click of the gun safety coming off.

"Don't move. Sit back in your seat and place both your hands on the steering wheel." Breandán slowly sat back in his seat placing both hands in full view. "Now both of you out of the car. MOVE. Keep your hands raised above your heads." We both got out slowly and raised are hands as directed. The Corporal covered me with his weapon and signalled me to move over to the parked Land Rover where I was placed in the capable hands of another soldier whilst he rejoined the Sergeant.

"Now sir," the Sergeant addressed Breandán, "I will ask you once and once only, do you understand?" Breandán nodded.

"Have you any firearms in your vehicle."

"No of course there are no firearms do you think I'm stupid or something?"

"In that case why did you reach down to the floor instead of taking your keys and opening the boot as we asked. What is it that you're concealing on the floor of your vehicle?"

I couldn't believe what was happening, I just had to say something.

"Look mate," I said to the soldier guarding me, "It's a bloody Fiat. What's up with your Sergeant. Doesn't he know that Fiats have the boot release on the floor between the driver's seat and the door?"

"Sergeant." The soldier called across from where he was holding me.

"What is it Jameson?"

"This bloke is telling me that the boot release is on the floor."

"Is that correct?" His question was directed toward Breandán.

"Yes. All Fiats have their boot release there."

"Check it out Corporal."

"Serge." The Corporal immediately opened the driver's door and with the thoroughness of an expert checked the interior of the car. It was clean.

"Well corporal?"

"Clean Serge."

"What about the boot release?"

"It's like they said, it's here." With that he pulled the release lever and the boot opened.

"Check the boot Corporal."

"Serge." Once again the Corporal gave the boot a quick but thorough check and found nothing. "Ok Serge, it's clean."

"Right. Corporal search this man."

The Corporal quickly and thoroughly frisked Breandán O'Shea for any hidden weapons and on completion nodded to the Sergeant.

"He's clean, what about his mate Sergeant?"

"Do him also."

"Jameson."

"Corp."

"Bring him over here."

"Yes Corporal." I was ushered over to where the Corporal now stood.

"Raise your arms." The Corporal commanded and as I did so he very quickly ran his hands along the underside of my raised arms and down my trunk. His hands moved swiftly yet firmly down my legs and up the insides of my legs.

"Clean." Only now did the Sergeant relax by lowering his weapon and pushing the safety catch home as he did so the other's followed suit.

"Your driving licenses sir you're free to go. Next time say what you're about to do. That way we can all save a lot of time and trouble."

As we pulled out of the roadblock Breandán passed me what he thought was my driving license. I was about to put it back in my wallet when I noticed it was in his name and issued in Belfast. Now why would a Dublin man have a driving license issued in Ulster? Ten minutes down the road we encountered a second roadblock.

"They're keen today Breandán, two roadblocks in the space of about ten miles."

"Hmm yes!" He said and gave a slight chuckle. Then in a quiet voice as if speaking a thought out loud, "I'd say they're very keen!"

From a distance it looked as if there was only a single control vehicle and no evidence of anyone being present. It seemed very strange. Breandán slowed as we approached the vehicle parked across our carriageway and still there was no one to be seen. We were about twenty five to thirty yards from it when two men wearing army style camouflage gear, black ski masks and black berets suddenly appeared in front of us. Both men were armed with modern SLR 7.62mm weapons. One of them signalled us to stop whilst the other aimed his weapon directly in line with Breandán's head. We coasted to a halt. "You keep you mouth shut and let me do the talking. These are friends of mine. Ok?" I nodded. Glancing over my shoulder I caught a glimpse of two more as they positioned themselves to the rear of the car. I managed a quick look in the nearside mirror and noted both had their weapons pointed directly at us. My mind was in turmoil. I was scared yet Breandán said they were his friends. It didn't make sense. If they were his friends why was one of them pointing his weapon straight at Breandán's head ready to blow his brains out? Some friend! There was no escape. Had Breandán set this up knowing of my connection with the Para's? Was this some form of retribution? All these and a hundred and one other questions flooded through my mind. Slowly Breandán wound down his window and the man who had stopped us shouted something that I didn't quite catch. Breandán replied, speaking rapidly in that strange language he had used previously. After a brief exchange, the two men lowered their weapons, stepped aside and waved us on. As we slowly manoeuvred around the vehicle parked across the road I turned and looked out the back. Nothing. The two men, who only moments ago had had their guns pointing at our backs, had completely disappeared. Once more they had melted into their surroundings.

"Are you all right then?" Breandán glanced across at me and winked.

"I'm fine. Tell me was that another little show for my benefit just like the rest?"

He thought that was hilarious and started to laugh uncontrollably. "You really thought that was staged for your benefit?"

"Well was it?" I asked.

Again he roared with laughter. "Not at all. That my friend proves a point."

"What point?"

"That for every roadblock manned by the UDR the IRA and its friends will match. For every patrol that they put out on any one-day, the IRA does the same. They may not be able to match them man for man but they will do their best."

Finally we reached our destination and stopped in a cloud of dust outside a large white farmhouse. Even before Breandán had chance to turn off the engine his door was wrenched open by a young man who was the mirror image of him.

"Well you old bugger how you doing?" Then he saw me. Who's he?"

"Richard, meet my younger brother Gerry. Gerry this is Richard" Gerry lifted his hand in acknowledgement.

"Pleased to meet you Gerry."

"Likewise Richard. Well come on Breandán move yourself Jenny's got tea on the go." We both got out of the car and followed Gerry towards the house. "Mum and Dad will be really pleased you got here at last. Come on Breandán, hurry up!" He gently chivvied his brother along. "I'm ready for something to eat how about you Richard?"

"I could do with a cup of tea thanks."

"So, what have you been up to big brother? What's new down in your neck of the woods?" I followed the two O'Shea brothers into a big flagstone-floored farmhouse kitchen. Opposite the entrance an open peat fire greeted visitors and in the centre of the room was a large pine kitchen table at which sat three men and a grey haired lady and a young fair-haired woman of about twenty-five. As we entered the young woman saw Breandán and pushing back her chair she shrieked with delight as she threw her arms about his neck and hugged him.

"How's things with my favourite man?"

"Couldn't be better and how's things with you Jenny?" Breandán said as he returned her hug.

"Don't mind them Richard, they'll get over it in a minute. Here Jenny put my brother down and say hello to our guest."

"Oh I'm sorry." She looked slightly embarrassed, smiled and said "It's just that we don't often see Breandán, well not often enough should I say."

"Oh that's ok. Don't worry on my account."

She looked up and smiled.

"By the way I'm Jenny, Breandán's sister-in-law, just in case you hadn't realised." She said as she offered me her hand.

"Pleased to meet you Jenny." I shook her hand gently.

"I presume you're Richard."

"Yes." It was my turn to be embarrassed. "Yes of course, how silly of me. I'm Richard."

"In that case, pleased to meet you Richard. Come on, come and sit down." She smiled at my embarrassment and pulled out a chair at the table. "Would you like a cup of tea?"

"Yes please I'd love a cup of tea."

"Well aren't you going to introduce us son." The lady with the grey hair addressed Breandán.

"Yes of course, I'm sorry mum. Richard this is my mother." I pushed my chair back and stood up proffering her my hand. "Mum, this is Richard."

"Pleased to meet you Mrs O'Shea." I said as she took my outstretched hand.

"Likewise Richard and please excuse Breandán's ignorance in not introducing us earlier."

"All right mum I'm sorry. Richard this is my father Dónall O'Shea." He indicated the man opposite where I had sat. "Dad meet Richard." We both shook hands across the table.

"Pleased to meet you Richard."

"Same with me Mr O'Shea."

"Just call me Dónall that's the same as Donald in England."

"Are you sure?"

"Yes of course, we don't stand on ceremony here. Anyway let me introduce two of our neighbours, this is Mike McCluskey."

"Pleased to meet you Mike."

"Mike's a close neighbour of ours," At this point Dónall leaned across towards me and in a conspiratorial tone said, "Mike's a Protestant, but don't ever let it be said that Catholics and Protestants don't get on, because we do." Mike smiled at Dónall's comment about his religious standing in the local community.

"Pleased to make your acquaintance Richard. Yes my farm backs on to Breandán's farm, Ross O'Toole, my friend here, is another close neighbour and also a Protestant to boot." He looked toward Dónall and grinned. "Isn't that right Dónall?"

"Of course Mike." He said and laughed at their private little joke.

"Pleased to meet you Ross." I raised my hand in acknowledgement to Ross who smiled and returned the gesture.

"Well that's got the formalities out of the way, now where's that tea Jenny?"

"Just coming dad, just coming." Jenny said as she poured out two more cups of tea for Breandán and I. "Did you have many hold ups on the way Breandán?"

"No, it wasn't too bad a journey, was it Richard?"

"No I suppose not."

"I hope Breandán's looking after you well Richard?"

"Yes he certainly is Mrs O'Shea, he certainly is." Little did she know, or maybe that was it, she did know!

"Still you'll be well looked after in the Hotel no doubt."

"Yes it's a very nice hotel Mrs O'Shea."

"Dad, Richard's the man I spoke to you about do you remember?"

"Of course I do, he's going to show us one or two things about grafting fruit trees isn't he?"

"Ok dad, you've made your point."

"Good, because I, for one, am looking forward to that and I hope you enjoy your stay with us Richard." What does he mean by staying and grafting fruit trees I wondered? It was all news to me. Nothing seemed to be making sense anymore. Here I was, an ex-Para sitting down drinking tea with a top IRA man, on a farm in Ulster. What was going on? Everyone was talking about this and that when there was a knock at the door.

"I'll get it," but before Gerry had even got up the door opened and in walked three big Irishmen all were over sixteen stone and even the smallest was at least six-feet tall.

"Hello everyone, we're not too late are we?" The smallest one said.

"No, Richard hasn't started yet."

"Richard hasn't started what Breandán?" I asked in surprise.

"Your demonstration of what you are doing on my farm in the south." He rapidly changed the subject. "Anyway let me introduce you, Richard these are my three cousins. This is Jim Devlin the eldest one"

"Pleased to meet you Jim." He must have been well over six feet tall.

"Hello Richard, these two are my younger brothers, this is Barry."

"Please to meet you Barry." Barry tall and broad like the other two nodded.

"This is Danny boy, the baby of the family."

"How d'you mean baby of the family."

"Well all right Danny, the youngest then, is that better?" Danny grinned.

"Danny, pleased to meet you."

"Likewise Richard."

What's this all about Breandán? What demonstration?"

It was Jim who answered my question. "Well Breandán told us you were coming up this weekend to demonstrate your grafting technique to us and a number of other farmers from around here that's all."

"Hang on. Have I got this right? Breandán, you've brought me all this way to give a demo?"

"Yes why?"

"Oh no. Not likely." I was angry that he had arranged this without asking me first.

"Give me one good reason why you can't." Breandán was equally as cross by my attitude, especially as he was paying me very good money to work over here, but that still didn't alter the situation as far as I was concerned.

"Oh I'll give you one all right. In fact I'll give you three. First of all I'm not suitably dressed. Secondly, I'm not equipped. In other words I've no tools with me and finally the light is failing fast. There are possibly others but I can't think of them right now. You see it's impossible, a complete waste of time." I was incensed and they knew it, but after a few seconds I had calmed down a little. "Look how about if I come back again to do whatever is necessary at a later date?"

"Sorry Richard this has all been arranged before hand, that is not an option." Breandán was determined to have his way.

"Then why didn't you tell me?"

"Because I wasn't sure that you would relish a trip north of the border."

I thought about it for a moment and recognised the predicament Breandán found himself in. "Ok I see your problem, but I still can't deliver what you want me to deliver."

"So you say, and you've given your reasons, but I fail to see that any of your reasons are insurmountable."

"But..."

He held up his hands. "No buts, let's just examine the reasons one by one. First of all the failing light - no problem we stay the night. You're not dressed for it." At this point he started to smile and I have to admit I could see the funny side to it. "Your dress sense is I would say a little eccentric to say the least, but we still stay. We still do the demo."

"Oh come on Breandán, this is stupid. All right I stay. I accept the point about dress and the light, but what about tools. Also I forgot to add, I need someone who is skilled in this technique to help. So as I said I can't do it."

"Hmm. Tools. Well what do you require we must have something here you can use?"

I shook my head. "That's no good. If I'm to do the job properly I need my own tools."

"All right Richard, I'll send for your tools, we'll sort out some other clothes. The light is failing so we stay. Problem solved."

Then I remembered the arrangement with Paul should I fail to return. I desperately needed to get a message to him before he contacted the Gardai. "Not quite."

"Now what?"

"I usually use Paul as my help when we are grafting and that way we take it in turns to do the preparation."

"Train someone here, give them a crash course. Do it. Problem solved." It seemed whatever argument I put up Breandán had an answer.

"All right, I give in, but I need to let Paul know what's happening."

"I'll contact the hotel and let Paul know what's going on and I'll arrange for anything you need to be here for the morning so just relax and have something to eat."

"Ok."

"Good that's sorted then." He then turned his attention to the two neighbours. "Would you both stop and have some dinner with us?"

"No thanks Breandán I must get back. I've a lot to get on with if you don't mind."

"Are you sure Ross, you know you're more than welcome?"

"No thanks, but I'd still like to come over in the morning if that's all right with you?"

"Of course it is. What about you Mike, are you stopping?"

"No thanks all the same Breandán, but like Ross I've got a lot to get on with at home, so if you'll excuse me I'll get off now and see you in the morning."

"All right see you both in the morning."

"Don't get up we'll see ourselves out. Goodbye all"

"Goodbye" everyone said in unison.

Chapter 10

"Has everyone had enough to eat?" Jenny looked around the table, "Speak now or forever hold your peace." There was a general mutter of approval from everyone. "What about you Breandán, have you had enough?"

"Yes thanks Jenny, I couldn't eat another thing."

"How about you Richard?"

"Yes thank you." Jenny started to clear away.

"Jenny. Dad and I will give you a hand here," Breandán's mother looked pointedly at her husband.

"Are you sure mum?"

"Of course dear."

"In that case Breandán why don't you and your cousins take Richard out for the evening?"

Breandán shook his head, "I'd love to Jenny, but the truth is I've got some business to attend to but I'm sure Jim wouldn't mind would you Jim?"

"Of course not. You know us Breandán any excuse eh lads!" Barry and Danny both grinned with approval.

"In that case the three of you must take him for a real mans night out," Breandán gave a slight smile and a knowing wink.

"By that d'you mean singing, music, plenty of beer and no women Breandán?" Breandán nodded. "In that case we know just the place."

"I thought you might."

"How about it Richard?"

I looked around the O'Shea household, "Well, if you're sure Jim. What about you Breandán, are you sure you can't come?"

"Unfortunately I've got too much to do but these three will show you a night to remember."

Jim slammed his foot down on the accelerator and the powerful Mercedes leapt forward spitting gravel as the rear wheels fought to get a grip. Once out on the open road the five-litre engine smoothly powered the car and its occupants off into the night.

Within minutes of our departure Breandán looked at his watch got up from where he was sitting and went through to the kitchen. "Well folks, I'm sorry to break up the party but time's getting on and I'd best make a move." He reached out and pulled Jenny towards him and gave her a hug, "As usual a lovely meal from the best sister-in-law in the world, thanks Jenny. As for you," he turned to his brother and hugged him, "look after her won't you."

Gerry smiled. "Of course I will. Look after yourself and BE CAREFUL whatever you do. I'll tell Mum and Dad that you've gone?"

Breandán paused as he went through the back door, turned and smiled to both of them before disappearing out into the night. A few seconds later they heard a quick blast of a car's horn as Breandán accelerated away from the farmhouse and out onto the open highway.

Jim Devlin looked at me through his rear view mirror. "Have you been in these parts before?"

"Around here do you mean? No never."

He studied my face in his mirror. "Not specifically here. I meant have you ever been to the six counties before say Belfast, Newry or even Armagh?"

Alarm bells rang, why should he specifically ask about the main areas in Ulster, was he fishing or did he know something? I wasn't sure. "No. Can't say that I have. Why do you ask?"

He didn't reply.

"So how long have you known Breandán?" asked the youngest brother.

"Are you Barry?" It was my turn to be evasive.

"No, I'm Barry," the brother sitting in the front passenger seat answered, "He's Danny."

"So, how long?"

"I'm sorry Danny, how long what?"

"Have you known Breandán?"

"Oh only a short while. So why did you ask if I'd been up here Jim?"

Jim looked at me in the mirror again. "No reason, just thought you may have been that's all."

I wasn't sure about him. In fact I wasn't too sure about any of them. "Where are we heading for?"

"Not far. It's a pub we use quite a lot. It's a good crack. Got good beer. Good music, singing and no women. You'll see soon enough it's a good night out." I wasn't going to get anymore than that out any of them.

We eventually slowed and turned off the main road down a quiet country lane, with hedgerows on either side. Finally the hedgerows became trees and we entered a heavily wooded area. The lane we had been following had now diminished to a narrow dirt track between the trees. Suddenly we appeared in a clearing and there in front of us hidden among the trees in the middle of nowhere was a small pub.

"Well here we are then, everyone out."

Danny was first out and made his way towards the darkened building. I began to feel a little nervous.

"This place looks closed, why are we here?" I asked suspicious of their motives.

"Looks can be deceiving."

"But it's in darkness." I replied even more worried. Then as if to allay my fears the faint strains of an Irish jig drifted to my ears from the darkened building ahead of us.

"You'd be surprised how wrong you are my friend!" an Irish voice came from somewhere off to my right as the whole region was bathed in light. Gradually my eyes grew accustomed to the brightly-lit area and I could clearly see Danny as he knocked on the pub's solid looking door. The response was immediate as a small wooden hatch was opened in reply and the sound of voices and the Irish jig could be heard quite distinctly. From where I stood I could see that Danny was talking to someone through the open hatch but because of all the other sounds it was difficult to make out what was said. After a short discussion Danny turned in our direction and beckoned us to join him at the door.

"Three of you, you said. I can see four." A voice said through the opening.

"Sorry we have a guest with us tonight, I forgot."

"Too bad Danny. You know the rules." With that the hatch slammed shut.

"Shit Danny why didn't you tell him about Richard?"

"Come on Barry I forgot. I'm so used to it being just us three..."

"Come out the way the pair of you and let me sort it out." Jim pushed through to the front and hammered on the door. Again the hatch rattled open and a pair of eyes peered at him.

"Yes. Oh it's you Jim Devlin. Now listen I've just told that young brother of yours..."

"Yes so I heard, but it's me you're dealing with and there are four of us. Ok?"

"Well I'm not sure..."

"Come on Pat stop messing with me and open the bloody door."

"Only if I can see each of you one at a time in front of the grill here."

"Fuck me Patrick what's the matter with you?"

"Sorry Jim but you know the rules as well as I do. After all how do I know that this guest hasn't got a gun in your ribs or something? He could be UDR for all I know. So line up in a queue and come to the hatch one at a time."

"Ok." Jim said begrudgingly, "I'll go first." With that we all lined up in a queue.

"Right, name?"

"Jim Devlin."

"Right-o Jim go to the back of the line. Next."

"Danny Devlin."

"Ok Danny. Back of the queue. Next."

"Barry Devlin."

"Thanks Barry. Next."

"Before that let me just tell you that Richard is a guest of our Breandán O'Shea and he has asked us to look after him for the night."

"Breandán's guest you say?"

"To be sure he is. I just thought I'd let you know Pat. That's all."

"Well thank you for that Barry. Next." Barry moved to the back and left me in front of the hatch. All I could see through the little trap door was the same pair of eyes that had stared out at Jim.

"Name?"

"Richard James."

"A friend of the man himself then?"

"I'm working for him and..."

He cut me short. "Thank you friend, back of the line."

As soon as I had moved the trap door was slammed shut and the area was plunged into darkness. A few minutes later the solid oak door was pushed open and the smell of beer and tobacco invaded my nostrils as we entered a packed bar.

"What was that all about at the door Barry?" I asked.

"Oh it's for security. Did you notice that the door opened outwards?"

"Yes."

"Well that's so no-one can easily force their way passed the doorman."

In that room was a mixture of men from all walks of life, there were wealthy landowners and lawyers rubbing shoulders with navvies and farm workers. Office clerks and doctors alongside teachers and factory workers, it was truly a place where there was no class distinction. As the evening progressed the drinks flowed more freely and the songs became increasingly more rebellious. These people were brought together by a common theme; they were all involved as either a so-called soldier in the IRA or belonged to the political arm, the Sien Fien. I found myself in the middle of a terrorist meeting place. An IRA stronghold. Suddenly I felt very isolated and vulnerable.

It was late when Danny Devlin made a drunken lurch at me, grabbing hold of my arm, he tried to pull my shirt sleeve up to display my Parachute Regimental Badge tattoo to those around us. "Here. Look here I'll show you all something..." he stumbled against someone and turned to apologise to them, "Sorry mate, here do you want to see something?" He turned his attention on me again. "Richard, come on give us your arm...Oops," he stumbled against them again. "Sorry," he gave them a crooked smile. Fortunately they didn't want to know this drunk and pushed him away. He grabbed at my arm again, "Here everyone have a look at..."
I wrenched my arm free and hit him as hard as I could in the middle of his chest.
"Now fuck off Danny. You're pissed."
He staggered backwards bumping into some other men, quickly recovered and started to square up to me. His eyes narrowed, but fortunately Jim grabbed hold of him.
"Come on Danny boy, I think it's time we went."
Because he was so drunk and his speech was slurred nobody had taken any notice, but I was now sure of one thing, the brothers knew about my past and that worried me.

Jim swung the Mercedes out onto the deserted highway and within a short space of time we were cruising at a high speed along the open road. The road started to twist and turn forcing a reduction in our speed and as we came out of the final bend we saw the blue flashing beacons of a roadblock in the distance. As we approached the roadblock someone was swinging a red light to get us to stop.
"Shit!" Jim spat the word out and once more we started to slow down. You could feel the atmosphere in the Mercedes as Jim braked and we slowed to a crawl. It was the RUC and as we approached the roadblock so slowly I was certain Jim was going to stop. Suddenly Barry shouted.
"Go, go, go."
Jim shouted as he floored the accelerator.
"Heads down and hold on to your balls, we're going through."
The engine roared. The car leapt forward. The wheels screeched as they fought to get a grip. Then like a Bat out of Hell, one powerful white Mercedes headed straight at the policeman. I was convinced we would hit him but somehow he managed to scramble out of our way. I instinctively ducked holding my breath and waited for the predictable hail of bullets and I was not disappointed. Jim killed the lights but a dull thud somewhere to our rear indicated that at least one bullet had found its mark. With no lights and the engine screaming we hurtled on into the night so putting as much distance as possible between ourselves and the RUC.

We seemed to travel at a breakneck speed without lights for an eternity before Jim gave a nervous laugh and switched them back on.

"Well, I guess that put the shits up them." Barry said.

"Never mind them it sure as hell scared me." I said still crouched low in my seat.

Jim just chuckled. "Is everyone all right?" he asked.

I gingerly raised my head and looked over his shoulder at the speed. "Phew Jim, what speed were you doing?"

He glanced up at the mirror. "I haven't a clue. What I do know is that it was a good job they were there and not further back."

"Why?" I asked.

"Well I know that the road here is dead straight for at least five miles or even more. Jesus that made me sweat a bit. I must be getting too old for this lark." He wiped the back of his hand across his forehead. "What did you reckon that thud was Barry?"

"Don't know but it sounded like a bullet found its mark."

"I think you're probably right. Richard, have a look out the back and make sure we're not being followed."

I turned around in my seat to look out of the rear window. "No sign of any lights."

"They still may have got our number Jim and called for back-up."

"Hmm, I suppose so Barry, I think I'll play it safe just in case."

Halfway up the hill Jim slowed right down to turn up a narrow dirt track that was hidden among the trees. We slowly edged our way bumping and bouncing along a bridle path deep inside the woods. For a second time since leaving the pub Jim switched off the headlights only this time we stopped and he switched off the engine. Winding down his window he stuck his head out.

"What have you stopped for?" I asked.

"Shh! Listen."

"For what?" I asked.

"Anything. Noise of an engine, Helicopter anything like that." We all sat quietly listening but all we could hear was the gentle breeze rustling the leaves.

Gradually the trees and undergrowth around us started to thin and the bumpy narrow track suddenly burst out into a large meadow. Jim turned the car along the hedge that now formed the perimeter of the field and picked up a well-worn farm track and at last we were able to make a reasonable speed. We passed through the final gateway and crossed a concrete farmyard. Then at speed we entered into a huge barn. Braking violently and with screeching tyres and the smell of burning rubber we halted. The engine was turned off and Jim leapt from the car and ran towards the entrance.

"Barry give us a hand to close the doors. Danny, once the doors are closed switch on the lights. Richard, get out of the car. Come on everyone move" There was a sense of urgency in Jim's tone that galvanised us into action. As the two barn doors closed with a metallic clang we were plunged in total darkness. Off to my left I could hear footsteps then a shuffling noise. Suddenly everywhere was bathed in a brilliant light as Danny threw the main light switch. Jim walked across to a large switch panel mounted on the back wall above the workbench and pulled down one of the many switches.

"Danny, move the car back into position. Richard, stand over there with Barry." The

Mercedes engine burst into life and slowly Danny reversed back.

"Whoa Danny. That'll do you." Once the car was in position Jim pulled down a lever protruding from the switch panel and somewhere deep below us a faint whirring noise could be heard. Slowly, ever so slowly, it appeared as if the Mercedes and a complete section of the floor started to sink and it wasn't long before the car, along with Danny, had disappeared altogether and all that was left was a large opening. Jim switched off the main lights in the barn and an eerie glow emanated from the aperture in front of us.

"Right, let's have a look at the damage then."

"It's ok Jim, don't bother coming down." The disembodied voice of Danny floated up from the hole in front of me.

"Are you sure it's ok Danny?"

"It's fine Jim, nothing major leastwise nothing that the man can't fix."

"So what's the damage?"

"Two hits, but three holes."

"In that case we'll get the floor in place. Come on then Danny get your arse out of there." Jim lifted the end of a steel 'T' section up. "Here Richard grab this while I switch the main lights on again." As the main lights came on I wondered what this long piece of steel was for, but didn't have to wait long to find out.

"Right Richard." He said as he picked up the other end of the 'T' section. "If you look at the edge of the pit you should see a slot just wide enough to drop your end into so the stem of the T points up." I looked around, but couldn't see what he was getting at.

"Have you found it?"

"No can't say that I have."

"Barry, show Richard where it fits."

Barry came over and took the end of the T piece that I was holding and slotted it in. He then picked up another 'T' piece with his elder brother and slotted that in place.

"Look I'll do these with Jim, if you could grab those sleepers with Danny." Once all the 'T' sections were in place then the sleepers dropped in neatly. The whole gave the effect of floorboards and by parking a tractor and a truck on them the illusion was completed. No one would ever dream of a car being concealed below the floor.

The face, panic stricken was framed in the window. The engine note now changed from a scream to a thunderous roar. It was deafening the most horrendous noise that I have ever heard in recent times. Suddenly I was awake and it was eight thirty in the morning. The noise was still with me as the threads of my nightmare receded into oblivion. Where was I? Gradually my head cleared and my mind began to focus as I remembered the Devlin brothers. The IRA pub. The roadblock. It all came flooding back. What the hell was that noise? I looked out of the bedroom window and saw, not one but two, Wessex helicopters hovering just above the ground and less than one hundred yards away. As I watched a number of armed security forces disgorged from the two helicopters and proceeded to set up a checkpoint adjacent to the dirt track leading here to the farm. I thought that this was because Jim Devlin had jumped the roadblock last night, perhaps they had been alerted by the RUC and they were hoping to catch the perpetrators.

I thought back to last night and the conversation in the Devlin's home after we had locked up the barn...

"So why did you jump the roadblock?" I asked.

Jim looked at me and just laughed. "Don't worry Richard it's a little sport here, everyone does it. It's a way of life."

Hmm a pretty deadly way of life I thought to myself! "Sure Jim. Now tell me the real reason." He ignored what I said and concentrated on driving the mini loaned to him by the man repairing his Mercedes.

"Is it that you don't want to tell me?" I asked.

"It's not a case of that. It's just that I don't see the point because you won't believe me anyway."

"Try me."

"Ok, a few months ago I got stopped in a roadblock. The normal routine. License and some form of I D - no problems. They then did a vehicle check convinced that it was a hot vehicle. An IRA vehicle, but it was clean. Still not satisfied they then searched the vehicle and found two kids transceivers belonging to my kids. The smart arse copper refused to believe me. He insisted I was IRA so arrested me."

"Why would they arrest you?"

"Search me?"

"That's stupid, there must be some reason."

"Search me. Perhaps someone had it in for me. Anyway I was hauled off to Belfast and held on suspicion of being a terrorist."

"What about your family, didn't they let them know where you were?"

"Huh, you must be joking," He said scathingly, "Do you know my wife was almost beside herself with worry. Everyone was kept in the dark for over two weeks about my arrest. They were determined to get me to admit that I was IRA and subjected me to all sorts of torture."

"What sort of torture?" Amazed to think that we would stoop to that.

" Different sorts of things. Not thumb screws or anything as crude as that. It was much more subtle, more of verbal and mental abuse than anything else."

"Why would they do that?"

"Because they were holding me on trumped up charges."

"So what did they hope to achieve?"

"I presume that they assumed if they pressurised me enough then I would admit to anything. Do you know, they even wanted me to give them details of IRA operations, but of course I couldn't."

"So why do you think they acted like that?"

"All I can assume is that someone somewhere had it in for me. Do you know up until then I had always been totally law-abiding, but after that I vowed I would never ever help the RUC again, and as for roadblocks, I am paranoid about them."

"When did your family find out?"

"Eventually the local RUC admitted to my wife that I had been arrested and was being held in Belfast."

I was amazed. I could not believe such things happened. "So what happened then?"

"They couldn't prove anything so they had to let me go."

No wonder he reacted the way he did. It had certainly made me think. I now wondered if the guys outside were looking for us. Had they been tipped off about Breandán? A knock at my bedroom door brought me back to the present. "Yeah."

"Hi Richard, Jenny has made some breakfast for you when you're ready."

"Thanks Gerry, I'll be right down."

I couldn't help feeling that there may have been an element of truth in what Jim had said, but after last night I could never be sure.

Chapter 11

"Morning Gerry, morning Jenny. I was just watching them setting up the roadblocks. Is that a frequent thing out here?"

"No, I can't say it is. There's obviously some reason for it though, unless of course the British Army are coming here to see your demonstration as well!" but for all Gerry's smile he looked apprehensive.

"Where's Breandán?" I asked.

"Breandán?" Jenny looked at Gerry and raised her eyebrows. "I'm not sure, I thought I heard him about earlier. Do you know Gerry?"

"Breandán?" he echoed her question.

"Yes love, Breandán," she gave him a sweet smile.

"Of course; yes Breandán. Sorry Richard I was miles away. Yes well umm, unfortunately Breandán was called away on business earlier." He made a show of looking at his watch, "Goodness, is that the time. In that case he should have been back by now."

"Perhaps he got held up somewhere, what do you think?" I asked.

"Could have, but I doubt it." Once again he looked at his watch with slight apprehension. "Hmm I wonder where he's got to?"

"Don't worry love," Jenny said, "I expect he'll be back any time now."

With Breandán missing I really didn't know what was expected of me, nor did I know what the arrangements were.

It was now late morning and still no sign of Breandán, and I was getting a little concerned about what was going on.

"Do you know anything about the demonstration?" I asked Gerry.

"Not really, but last I heard Breandán had everything in hand."

That's a fat lot of good I thought. "So, Breandán's got it all in hand has he, shame he didn't let me in on the secret then."

"Are you telling me you don't know anything about it either Richard?"

"Yep. That's right you've got it in one." I answered a little sarcastically.

"So there's nothing you can do until he returns."

"Correct."

"Well what should we do about all the people who have turned up."

"I give in Gerry. How do you mean, what shall WE do about all the people who've turned up? Don't you mean what should you do about all the people who've turned up? Don't count me in on this farce, it's nothing to do with me." I was getting just a little impatient with my situation. I started to drum on the table impatiently.

"Gerry, this is becoming somewhat embarrassing, are you sure Breandán has got things organised?" I asked more than just a little annoyed.

"Definitely, don't worry Richard I'm sure he'll be here." Gerry looked at his watch again. "This is unlike him to be so late. Jenny have a look up the lane and see if he's in sight will you?" Jenny went out of the kitchen door to reappear a moment later.

"Sorry love, still no sign of him. Oh I do hope he's all right. What do you think could have happened?"

Gerry shrugged his shoulders. "I don't know. This is totally out of character for him."
I was beginning to wonder if the man had shanghaied me, but why would he want to do that I asked myself. We all sat there in silence whilst even more people arrived.

I stared at yesterday's paper as Gerry drummed his fingers on the table.
"Gerry don't keep drumming on the table it's getting on my nerves" Jenny said testily.
"Sorry, it's just that..."
"Just that what?" she asked him.
"It's just that, there's nothing we can do until Breandán gets here is there?"
"Well, you could make yourself useful and put the kettle on. Would you like a cup of tea Richard?" She asked.
I looked up from the paper. "Yes please."
Just then the door opened and who should appear but the missing Breandán. "Why are you all sat in here with all those people outside and Richard why haven't you started the demonstration? Why is it that if I want anything done I have to be the one to make sure that it's done? What's wrong with everyone? I expressly said that we would stay the night and make a start in the morning and what do I find, loads of people outside waiting to see this wonderful grafting technique and you're all sat in here. What's wrong with you all?" he stormed.
"One problem," I spoke in a quiet voice, "I cannot start any demonstration without tools, and I have not got any tools. After all you promised that you would get them here for this morning, so where are they?" Breandán looked at me somewhat surprised.
"Haven't they arrived?" I shook my head.
"Nope, not one. So what do you suggest Mr O'Shea? Over to you."
He now looked somewhat sheepish. "Sorry I was sure they would be here." He thought about it for a moment, "Hmm what do you need?" he asked. I went over the list of tools for a second time. "Damn," was all he said, "Oh well let's have a hunt around up here and see what can be found."

Despite the various setbacks and not having Paul with me I had to admit that the demonstration had still gone exceedingly well and by the end I had managed to generate a lot of interest from all those present. So much so that it looked extremely positive for follow-on contracts. I felt really pleased with the outcome and it must have shown in my eyes.
"So you feel it was worth it then?"
"Of course Breandán and thank you for setting it up."
"I was only too pleased to be of service, after all there maybe something you can do for me at some stage, so don't forget you owe me!" I wondered what the payoff would be?

We had enjoyed another well-prepared evening meal and it was just after nine o'clock as Breandán pushed his chair back from the table. "Well Jenny, Gerry that was a lovely meal and I'm sure Richard has enjoyed your hospitality, but I'm afraid we'll have to make a move."
"What so soon Breandán, can't you stay for just a little longer?" Jenny asked.
"Afraid not Jenny. Are you ready Richard?"

"Sure I am, after all I've nothing else to take." I turned my attention to Jenny and Gerry, "Thank you both very much for everything and who knows I maybe back," I smiled at Jenny and shook Gerry by the hand.

"Come on let's go." Breandán gave his sister-in-law a hug, "Bye Jenny, say cheers to mum and dad for me. See you Gerry. Oh and sorry about this morning I got held up."

"That's ok all's well that ends well, bye now. Bye Richard."

You can imagine my surprise when instead of the old Fiat there was a reasonably new blue Volvo parked in its place. "Where's the Fiat?" I asked.

"Oh, I thought I would have a change," he replied quite nonchalantly. It seemed a little strange, but being the wealthy individual he was I didn't give it a second thought. At the main road Breandán turned to the left instead of right towards Newry. "You're looking a little bewildered, why?" he asked.

"I am. I thought Newry was off to the right?"

"It is, but you see I'm not going to Newry," was all he said.

"I thought we were going back south?"

"So we are." he said, "But there's more than one way home, so I thought I would take you on a different route, also this way is quicker than the way we came."

The winding road seemed familiar to me but it was not until we started to descend the steep hill did I realise it was the same route the Devlin brothers had taken last night from the IRA pub in the middle of the woods. We passed by the narrow lane that had eventually led us to their farm when we were on the run from the roadblock. At the bottom of the hill, we came out onto the straight flat section where we had jumped the roadblock, but tonight the road was clear, no roadblock or for that matter no traffic. We travelled on through the series of bends and then we were into uncharted territory. The car purred quietly just eating up the miles.

What with the heat in the car, the hypnotic drone of the engine and the soft music being played on the radio I could feel my eyelids grow heavy gradually I drifted off into semi-consciousness, hearing sounds as if they are far away.

"We are about to enter what we call the butter run." Breandán's voice sounded woolly and far off. Suddenly I realised he was speaking to me and I forced my heavy eyelids to open.

"Sorry, what was that?" I asked, "I was miles away."

"I said that we are about to enter what we call the butter run. "

"What's the butter run?" I asked as I tried to keep my eyes open and concentrate my mind.

"It's an old smuggling route over the border along which they brought butter and many other things that could well attract the unwanted attention of government officialdom. As the security forces hardly ever patrol here it serves as a quick and easy route by which to cross in either direction with minimal risk."

I couldn't believe what he was saying. "Let me get this right. You are saying that this route is rarely patrolled by security forces?"

"That's right."

"Well that means that anyone can come and go as they please!"

103

"Yeah, spot on."

"I don't believe I'm hearing this!"

"Well whether you believe it or not it is a fact."

"Well I'm absolutely amazed. In that case, all the checkpoints are useless."

"You're right."

"Here we are." he indicated a left turn down a narrow country lane, "The start of the 'butter run' and as I said no patrols."

The lane was flanked on either side by stone walls that over the years had fallen into disrepair. The walls gradually gave way to woodland on either side the whole being criss-crossed by hundreds of cart and bridle tracks. I could now understand what a mammoth task it would be to secure the border with all these different routes throughout the woods. Nonetheless I still felt that the security forces could do a lot more than they were, after all if this area is so well known by the locals then the RUC and the UDR must know it equally as well.

It was not long before we had crossed over that imaginary line between the province and Eire. It was just as Breandán had said it would be. No police. No patrols. No UDR. No check points. In fact it was deserted. Without warning Breandán turned sharply to the left down one of the minor roads.

"Where are we going now?" I asked.

"Ah, wouldn't you like to know?" he then smiled. "All will be revealed."

A few moments later we turned into the car park of a public house called 'The Border Inn', which was partially obscured by trees, and it was here we stopped.

"Why have we stopped?" He turned off the ignition and the lights.

"I won't be long. It's just that I've a little business to attend to in the pub." With that he was gone.

I sat there fiddling with buttons and switches, as you do, and casually switched on the courtesy light. Imagine my surprise, when a label I had noticed stuck to the steering column, revealed the true identity of the owner of this car as being one Dr James O'Shea with an address in Belfast. Who was Dr James O'Shea and why was Breandán using this man's car? Surely the doctor would need it for himself, unless he had alternative transport. My curiosity aroused, I started to rummage through the glove compartment and found that the good doctor was another brother. So why was Breandán being secretive about his brothers, unless it was to protect them from prying eyes?

I sat there staring at the name, Dr James O'Shea, and wondered how this information could be put to good use. There must be some reason why Breandán was being economical with the truth. Another thing niggling me was why was he driving this car? Why should he be taking it over the border to Dublin? It really didn't stack up, unless of course the car was hot property. Yes, perhaps that was it. The good Dr O'Shea had been fingered, I wonder? Hmm, maybe just maybe this information could be put to good use. A germ of an idea started to formulate in my mind, an idea that may just redress a little of the balance in my favour, it may even give me a bit of a hold over my host. I rehearsed my words over and over again honing and polishing my plan.

Ten minutes later Breandán had returned. "Right here we go, the last leg of the journey." The engine of the Volvo leapt into life and we pulled out of the car park to continue on to Dublin.

"Did you get your business sorted out?" I casually asked.

"Oh yes, no problem. Sorry if I was a little longer than I thought, but sometimes things get a little complicated in this life." Yes I thought, they sure do.

"Breandán?"

"Umm." He answered.

"Why you driving this instead of the Fiat, is there something wrong with it?" I asked casually.

"No not really, it's just that a friend of mine asked me to pick this up for him, why?"

"Oh no reason, apart from it looks remarkably like a car I know."

"Oh really! I would be surprised if it's the one you're thinking of."

"Oh but I'm sure it is." I watched his face carefully. "A friend of yours you say?"

"Yes, but I doubt if you know him."

"Oh but Breandán I do." He roared with laughter, because he knew that I could not possibly know his brother in Belfast, especially as he had not, nor had the rest of the family, ever mentioned him.

"Why do you laugh Breandán?" I asked. "You see this car is owned by one Dr James O'Shea, who lives in Belfast and..." He cut me off in mid-sentence.

"What did you say?"

Yes, just as I thought. Got you Breandán. Got you on the run at last.

"I said, this car belongs to Dr James O'Shea from Belfast. Then before I was rudely interrupted, I was going to say that the Dr James O'Shea I know is the brother of one Breandán O'Shea, hotelier and wealthy landowner who resides in the Republic of Ireland. James O'Shea has another brother, one Gerry O'Shea. Gerry O'Shea looks after a farm in Ulster, which is also owned by one Breandán O'Shea. In fact Breandán he is your brother." Breandán was very quiet. I could not resist forcing my point home in a very clear and concise way

"Yes, it belongs to Dr O'Shea in Belfast, your brother I believe!" That got a result. He savagely braked, the tyres screamed in protest as we slithered to halt. His face was a picture. His mouth worked but no sound came from it. The engine stalled and I nearly went through the windscreen. There was an acrid smell of burning rubber.

"Like I said," I turned the screw again, "I know your friend."

He had now recovered some of his composure.

"How the hell would you know him, especially as you have always maintained that you have never been to the north before. Is that it are you working for the British Government. Well are you?" He bellowed more with panic than any other reason.

It was now very important that I kept my cool and picked my words carefully before I answered. Not only did I need to convince him that I knew his brother. I also needed him to think that I had some power, just enough to make him unsure of exactly who I was and where I stood in this scenario.

"As I said, I know your brother in Belfast." I paused just long enough for effect, "So just be warned that I, like you, have very powerful friends. However, they are not necessarily in the British Government. So, should anything accidentally happen to me then I suspect some very senior, and powerful people in high places both here and elsewhere would have a lot of explaining to do. Especially your people, so be warned!" Just to add weight and under score what I had said I repeated it again, "I know your brother." I went on even more convincingly, "Now ask yourself a question how would I know him? Am I with the British Government, or could it be that I am with the Republican Government, the RUC, the UDR or perhaps a sleeping cell over in England. I ask you, can you be sure who I work for?" with that I shut up and held my breath.

"If what you say is true then what's your game?" He blustered. "What are you up to eh?"

"No game Breandán. I am deadly serious, regard it as a warning and let's leave it at that." I waited for that to sink in. then I continued talking in a meaningful way, "All I want to do is to get on with the job I came over here to do. The one that you are paying me for, so can we now stop playing this dangerous and political game and let me get on with my job without any further interruptions?" I had played my last card in a very dangerous game of brinkmanship using fear as the key. I only hope that I had won this battle. We sat there quietly for a minute or two longer. Breandán, with his eyes narrowed, looked at me as if trying to see into the very depths of my soul. Then with a shrug of his broad shoulders he turned to face the front and started up the engine and we set off again.

It was in the early hours of Monday morning when we stopped outside the main entrance to the hotel and as I opened my door to get out, he caught hold of my arm in a vice like grip. I turned and looked down at his large hand then slowly raised my gaze to stare unblinking straight into his eyes.

"I'm sorry." He mumbled as he quickly loosened his grip on my arm. He then looked away and said, "Richard, whatever you do please do not talk to anyone about the last twenty-four hours, I didn't mean anything by it, only business ok."

I looked at him for a moment and thought I saw a glimmer of a pleading look that in a flash was gone. From that moment, I knew I had his respect. My earlier bluff had been a pure gamble but had paid off.

"Ok Breandán." I paused for a moment then spoke softly, "Ok not a word I promise." With my promise he visibly relaxed.

"Thank you Richard. Sleep easy and goodnight my friend."

Chapter 12

Whilst I had been away Paul had managed to find himself a girlfriend called Sinead, a local girl by all accounts. I gathered that there had been some slight excitement involving a local farmer who had had one of his outbuildings blown up and had also been shot at. Someone must have pointed the finger at Paul, because the Gardai showed an unhealthy interest in his activities over the weekend but it obviously came to nothing. I had my own feelings about whom that may have been and Damian McGuinnes was not far from my thoughts. The last couple of days were pretty uneventful on the whole and we had worked damn hard to break the back of the contract, so this afternoon Paul had gone off to meet up with his new found love, and I was invited back for some tea at Breandán's.

The weather had been fine all day but by late afternoon, it was becoming dull and overcast with the distinct promise of rain. By evening fine drizzle came in from the west and the day had now degenerated and by the look of the sky there was worse to come.
"Is that the time?" I said glancing at my watch. "I had better make a move before Paul gets back to the hotel."
Breandán looked out at the weather. "What a miserable evening, you'll get soaked let me run you back to the hotel."
"No don't worry. I'll enjoy the walk. Besides I could do with some fresh air."
"Are you sure?"
"Yes honestly."
"Hang on a minute." Breandán disappeared through to his kitchen to reappear a few minutes later clutching a bottle of Bushmill's. "Here, take this back to your room with you."
"Cheers Breandán. Are you sure?"
"Of course I'm sure. Go on take it, there's plenty more where that came from."
I picked up the unopened bottle and stared at the label. "Well what can I say."
"Nothing. Now are you sure you wouldn't like me to drop you back?"
"No honestly. I'll enjoy the walk," and with that I set off. As I reached the gate I lifted the bottle aloft and shouted, "Cheers Breandán, I'm going to enjoy this. Bye now." In spite of the drizzle, it was nice to get out in the fresh air again and I enjoyed the gentle stroll back to the hotel. It gave me time and space to reflect on everything that had happened since our arrival.

Just after eight I went downstairs to the bar, Paul was already there deep in conversation with Noel, the union official. As I approached Noel turned.
"Hello there Richard." Noel slurred.
"Hello Noel, have you been here long?" I asked.
He staggered slightly and gave me a drunken smile. "Just a little while," he slurred, "Just long enough to have a few drinky-poos!" He then started to laugh. "Richard," he placed his free arm around my shoulder and started to whisper in my ear, "Richard, I want to give you this for safe keeping." With that he placed his glass down on the table and as he gently swayed backwards and forwards he pulled an envelope from his

pocket and thrust it into my hand. "Now, promise me you won't give it to anyone else." He gripped my shoulders and smiled that crooked smile again. "So you promise?"

I smiled back at him. "Ok, I promise Noel." He took a deep breath then let go of me.

"Good, then put it in your pocket." He watched me place the envelope in my inside pocket.

"There you are Noel, satisfied. It'll be quite safe there." I said patting my pocket.

"That's good then. Now it's time for a drink." With that he thrust his hand deep into his pocket and pulled out a number of notes along with some loose change that clattered to the floor rolling everywhere. He stood there just watching the coins as they rolled across the floor in all directions.

"Come on Noel, why don't you sit down Paul and I will get your money for you."

"Oh bugger it, just leave it there, I'll pick it up. Here get yourself a drink, one for Paul and I'll have a large hmm, a large Brandy." With that he sat down heavily in the chair. He looked at me again and said, "You understand, it's for you and only for you. Whatever else you do you must keep it safe."

I looked at him and asked. "What safe?"

He fell silent and tried to focus his eyes. He waved his finger in my general direction. "The envelop of course. The one I've given you." He then started to go through his pockets muttering, "You must keep it very safe. Very safe."

I watched him searching his pockets. "What are you looking for?" I asked.

"The envelope.

"Noel." I tried to get his attention. "Noel."

He looked up. "Yes Richard, what?"

"You gave me the envelope," I showed him it to reassure him.

"Ahh, I thought I had. Anyway put away again. You must keep it very safe, no one else to have it, no one else to know." He was now rambling on more to himself than anyone else. He stopped momentarily to take a drink from his glass, then started again, "Safe. Must keep it. No one to know." he paused again to take another drink from his glass. "Keep it safe and don't you be breathing a word of this to anyone. Do you understand now, not a word to anyone." He carried on about keeping it safe, it obviously concerned him so much that it had to be something very important and that intrigued me. I wanted to know what the great secret was. I took the envelope from my pocket to examine it more closely, but there was nothing to indicate what the great secret was, there wasn't any writing on it at all but my curiosity was aroused.

"What is in the envelope that is so important to you Noel?"

"Never you mind," he slurred, "just put it in a safe place. I know you can be trusted, remember not a word. Shh! Shh don't say a word to anyone. Now put it away" He pushed my hand holding the envelope towards my pocket as if trying to get me to put it away. He started to get quite agitated so I, once again, put the envelope out of sight in my inside pocket. "Remember, shh, shh not a word. It's our secret. So now my Englishmen, my friends, where's that drink? Paul get the drinks in."

The buzz of conversation around us suddenly faltered as into the room walked a monk escorted by two very attractive women. One was very petite and in a nurses uniform the other was dressed in a red suit. At first I thought that the monk and the nurse were dressed up to go to a fancy dress party, but how wrong can you be.

"Ah, there you are!" exclaimed the lady in red. Noel struggled to his feet looked towards where the voice came from and gently swayed with a crooked, drunken grin on his face.

"Hello dear." He slurred as he tried to focus his eyes on his wife as she purposely walked towards him. The whole room became hushed as all eyes turned in our direction. She marched up to Noel.

"How dare you 'dear' me. How dare you stand there with that stupid drunken grin on your face."

"But darling..." She slapped his face with such a force he staggered backwards and slumped back in the chair. She continued to give vent to her anger by shouting at him in Gaelic. Apart from her no one else in the room spoke. Then suddenly Noel gathered all his concentration and rose to his feet and started a torrent of Gaelic abuse at her which then culminated in him pulling back his fist to strike her, but just at the crucial moment the monk grabbed his arm. In no time at all he was being frog marched away towards the front door.

Noel's wife immediately turned her attention on us and proceeded to give vent to her feelings by hurling abuse in Gaelic at me, then at Paul.

"Please, please calm down. Calm down and tell us what this is all about." She carried on oblivious of what I had just said.

"Please, listen to me." I implored, "It's no good shouting at me in Gaelic as I haven't a clue..."

"What did you say?" She asked in English.

"I said, I do not understand what you are saying. I am English and I don't understand Gaelic."

"Oh, how terrible. I'm so sorry, you see, you see," but she suddenly burst into tears.

"Come on, what's the matter?" I asked gently.

"Yes there's no need for this," added Paul, "Tell us what's wrong and maybe we could help." Slowly her sobbing started to subside. "Can I get you a drink of something?" asked Paul.

"No thank you."

"Are you sure?"

"No honestly I'm fine thank you all the same." With the excitement over people soon forgot about us and got back to their various conversations and a sort of normality returned.

"How about a coffee or something?" I asked.

"Well thank you perhaps a coffee." She said having gained a little of her composure. I caught the attention of Noel the night porter.

"Yes Richard, what can I do for you?"

"Would you kindly arrange for some coffee please, and Noel could you find us somewhere a little less conspicuous?"

"I'll see what I can do." In a matter of minutes he was back, "Gentlemen and Ma'am, if you'd care to follow me I've found a table that I think will suit."

"Thank you Noel."

"This is so embarrassing," she said in her soft Irish accent. "You see I did not realise you were English. I was so mad at Noel I just let fly and assumed you were some of his so-called friends from Dublin. In my anger, oh dear how stupid, I heard you speaking but I was so annoyed it didn't register that it was English you were speaking. I bet you think me stupid. How embarrassing."

"I'm sorry about Noel being drunk but we've only just arrived and he was already in that state when we got here wasn't he Paul?"

"Yes he was."

"Oh dear, will you ever forgive me for my stupidity. You see Noel is alcoholic and when I saw him in that state I assumed that you were the ones who had been plying him with drink. I didn't even consider the fact that you weren't from around here. I just assumed..."

"No harm done." She drank the rest of her coffee and got up to go. "Must you go already?" I asked. She looked deep into my eyes with those grey green eyes of hers. I felt quite uneasy. I cleared my throat and she looked away.

"Will you ever forgive me for my outburst?"

"Of course, it's forgotten already. Now are you sure you won't stay for a little longer?"

"No thank you I must go. Thank you both for being so understanding." She turned to go then suddenly remembering, "I almost forgot to ask you."

"Ask us what?"

"Did Noel give you anything?"

"No. Should he have done?"

"Well it's just that sometimes when he's like this he does silly things and gives things away. If you know what I mean." She smiled innocently.

I was on my guard immediately, what did she know and what was she hinting at. Was it the envelope that he had given me? "What sort of things do you mean?" I asked equally as innocently.

"Oh money. He had a sealed envelope containing some money. You see when he's like this he never remembers who he's given things to."

"No, he didn't give me anything at all. Incidentally who was the monk?"

"Oh he was from the clinic."

"The clinic?"

"Yes the clinic. Oh didn't I tell you. I haven't seen Noel for some weeks now as he has been away in the country up near Belfast at a drying out clinic. It's a private clinic run by a monastic order. A very good friend of his, Mr O'Shea, he's quite well known about these parts, arranged for his stay." Interesting I thought, I wonder if that's where the brother Dr James O'Shea comes in?

"Tell me if you thought he was in the clinic, what made you come here?"

"Oh when I telephoned the clinic to see how he was progressing I was told he had disappeared. I was frantic with worry; they were doing all they could to locate him but had not managed to trace where he had gone. Anyway as I knew this was one of the places he gets to from time to time I telephoned here and spoke to Noel."

I raised a questioning eyebrow. "Noel" I said, "Your husband?" She laughed.

"No silly, Noel the night porter, the one who brought the coffee."

"Oh I see. Well I don't see really. Why Noel?" I asked.

"Well Noel knows my husband, he also knows about his problem. I told him that the clinic was trying to trace his whereabouts and I just asked him to watch out for him and let me know if he saw him."

"So did you expect him to come here?"

"Yes."

"Why?" I was curious as to what made her think he would come here, did she know something.

"I just did." She said lamely.

"And?" I asked.

"And what?" she asked.

"Well when did you find out?"

"You're very interested in all of this, why?" she asked.

"Well when I get accused by a beautiful lady of being party to something I know nothing about it just gives me a chance to get to know her better, that's all." She smiled and looked at me with those lovely eyes of hers, but I was not to be put off.

"So, when did you say you found out that he was missing?" She smiled again.

"I didn't say."

"Touché. Still if you don't want to tell me that's up to you." I said nonchalantly.

"No I don't mind telling you. I was told by the clinic last night. Then Noel telephoned me about ten minutes before I met you. Why do you ask?"

"Just curious. So you don't live far away." This was more a statement than a question.

"No not far." She looked at her watch, "Gosh is that the time, look thanks for the coffee and being so understanding but really I must go otherwise I'll be late." There was a quick flash of a smile as she turned to hurry towards the front door. "Bye Richard, and once again thanks for everything." She called back over her shoulder.

Now she had gone I withdrew the envelope from my pocket. I knew deep down from what she had said that she knew about the existence of this envelope. What did it contain and why was it so important to both Noel and his wife? I decided the only thing to do was to open it so I knew exactly what it was that I was keeping safe. Inside I found a small booklet consisting of four pages. Each page depicted what seemed to be a religious theme. On the first page a title 'The Seven Wonders Of Fore' which did not convey anything to me. After reading it through a number of times I noticed that in each case the description of the so-called wondrous seven items that were listed contained a mixture of letters and numbers plus an asterisk pencilled against it. It didn't take me long to come the conclusion that what I was looking at were different grid references on a map and the descriptions helped describe the specific areas. The real question was what was their significance and why had Noel given them to me? What with my trip and now this what did it all mean? The more I tried to make sense of it the less sensible it seemed. In the end I gave up and pushed the envelope back in my pocket.

As I went to draw my curtains I noticed in the distance a number of very bright lights which emanated from the direction of Breandán's farm. I was intrigued. I checked the time it was nearly two in the morning. This made me even more curious. I had not noticed these lights shining through the trees before, so what were they. I opened my window and listened intently. All that I could hear was the hoot of an owl and the call of a fox. I paused there for a moment or two longer then my curiosity got the better of me. I just knew I had to find out what it was. So with my thick jacket on to keep me warm in the chill night air. I quietly locked my door and stealthily made my way down the back service stairs to the kitchen. Every now and then, I would stop to listen carefully for anyone coming. I furtively looked through the door into the kitchen to ascertain that Noel was safely out of the way before I entered. I darted quickly through the kitchen and out through the staff entrance. Once outside, I deftly moved through the shadows towards the corner of the building. I once again carefully checked that no one was about before running across a narrow strip of exposed land to the trees. It was a cloudy night, so once in the woods there was little or no light to see by. My progress was slow as I forced my way through the brambles. Life would have been so much easier had there been a moon.

I must have been about halfway towards my target when I stumbled and tripped over a very primitive alarm system. Within seconds, a huge black shape materialised to my right. I thought this is it. My instinct was to run but before I could untangle myself from the trip wires and make off, the large black shape was upon me. I stifled an involuntary shout as my breath was knocked out of me. For a minute I thought the game was up. Then I realised that it was Breandán's Irish Wolfhound.

"Shh, there's a good boy, hush it's only me." It gave a low growl.

"Shh, good boy." It muttered a little longer, then recognition dawned and it gave a slight yelp of joy and proceeded to lick and slobber all over me.

"Come on boy," I whispered, "Up, let me get up." Eventually I managed to push the big friendly lump off and struggled to my feet. Then I froze. Someone gave a low whistle off to my right. I could hear dry twigs snap close by as someone walked towards me.

"Bloody dog, come here." It was Breandán's voice. "Here boy, where the hell are you. Come on boy." He whistled again.

"The bloody dog has tripped the alarm," someone shouted.

"Well switch it off." Breandán called back. "Come on boy, come on." The Wolfhound ran towards his master's shout and the footsteps receded. Now's my chance I thought. I followed the dog as it crashed through the undergrowth. The noise of its progress drowning out any noise I made. As I neared the edge of the copse I dropped to the prone position and slithered forward bit by bit. Then I froze. There, only a matter of feet away, stood Breandán with the dog now, I really appreciated the thick undergrowth and the lack of moon as I held my breath. It seemed an eternity before I heard Breandán call his dog to heal as he moved away. I waited a few more minutes listening for the slightest noise, but nothing. I cautiously raised my head to look. The coast was clear. I double-checked to make certain that there was no one else about and again moved stealthily forward in the direction of the lights.

The lights that I had seen from my room were in fact large arc lights, which illuminated everything around me making it easier to see. It also meant that I could be seen easier. I had to be very careful. Stealth was the name of the game. As I watched an articulated truck from Armagh was being loaded with bulk bins of apples from the cold store. I was even more curious now. Why would anyone want to load apples at the dead of night? Then my curiosity was rewarded as one of the men removed a side from one of the crates. Before any further loading took place they stacked into this a number of smaller boxes which took two men to lift between them. Having put several of these smaller boxes into the crate, a false bottom covering them was installed and a side was nailed on. Once this operation had been completed, the forklift truck driver brought a quantity of smaller crates of apples from the cold store, which they quickly transferred the contents of into the larger one with the false floor. This operation was repeated several times and they then distributed these 'special' bulk bins throughout the load. Eventually the operation was completed and the arc lights switched off. The truck driver started to crank over the powerful engine and it fired into life then with headlights blazing and a low rumble, the powerful rig moved off. I lay there quite still and watched as the men in their cars followed the truck into what was left of the night.

Chapter 13

I was just thinking to myself, I hadn't seen or spoken to Breandán for a while when he appeared as if from nowhere. He stood there in silence, sort of hovering as if he had something on his mind but wasn't sure how to broach the subject. A couple of times he looked as if he was going to say something then Paul came over so he changed his mind. In the end he smiled. "How's it going? Is everything ok?"

"Yeah it's fine, why?"

"Oh no reason, just making sure that everything's going ok and there's no problems, that's all."

"Yeah fine, couldn't be better."

"Ok, I'll let you get on then."

"Ok." What was all that about I wondered? Breandán started to walk away but, as soon as he saw Paul move off down the row, he came back and hovered again.

"Look Breandán I can't help feeling that something's bothering you. Is there something you want to see me about?"

"As it happens there is, but it's a little sensitive and I would rather Paul did not know." I checked to see where Paul was and decided he was well out of earshot.

"Ok Breandán, what's bothering you?"

He glanced briefly in Paul's direction before speaking.

"I thought you may like to know there's going to be a meeting at the Tara tomorrow which involves some very senior members of the Government."

I looked at him somewhat bewildered. "Well thanks for telling me, but I fail to see what it's got to do with me. Why should I be interested?"

"Well aren't you?" he asked, "After all it could do you some good if you were there couldn't it?"

"How?"

"Well to start with the Minister for Agriculture will be there and that means a number of very influential landowners and farmers will also be present. You never know, you could get some substantial contracts from them."

"Sure I could, and pigs may fly. Anyway how do you propose that I get these contracts because before anything else I would have to be at the meeting and that is the first stumbling block."

"It isn't a problem."

"Oh yes, and how do you propose I get into the meeting?"

"Just walk in?"

"Oh sure just like that." I replied rather scathingly. "So I just walk up to the guys on the door and say, Oh hello, I'm Richard James, and they of course would reply. Are you, well in that case you'd best come in." I said in a mocking tone of voice. "If you think that then you're not as clever as I thought you were Breandán."

"You may mock, but if you had let me explain before you started taking the piss you would have found out. Now if you had an official invite you have no problem."

"And where or from whom am I going to get this invite?"

"Don't worry, I can arrange it if you are interested." I looked at him incredulously,

"Breandán, are you telling me you can arrange an official invite?" I asked.

"Ah, changed your tune now haven't you?"

"Well can you?" I was suddenly very interested.

"It's no problem when you have friends in high places. Especially when it's your hotel and you're the organiser."

"Are you telling me you know the Minister for Agriculture? Huh, I don't believe you. Next you'll be telling me you know the Prime Minister!"

"I do." He replied in a matter of fact way.

"You're joking, aren't you?"

"No I'm not joking," he said seriously, "I know the Taoiseach." He looked straight at me and asked, "Well, think it over, do you want to go or not?"

I didn't need to think it over.

"Of course I do," I said enthusiastically. "If you're sure you can arrange it then I'll come."

"Oh I can arrange it all right. In fact I had already assumed you would be coming and made the necessary arrangements. There's only one minor problem."

"What's that?"

"I can't invite you to the official lunch, but everything else after that is taken care of, is that ok?"

I nodded enthusiastically. "Great, so what happens now?" I asked.

"Leave it all to me and Richard, this is just between you and myself all right?" I nodded. "Well that's settled then. Now changing the subject, on Sunday we're all off to Dublin to see the match. We'll have a meal and a few drinks. It's a good day out, do you fancy coming along?"

"I'd love to Breandán, but you know, next time maybe. I really need to get on with some letter writing." This was my excuse because here was my golden opportunity to have a good nose around the farm whilst they were away.

"You're sure now, 'tis a good day out? Everyone from around here goes so it'll be terrible quiet for you now."

"That's all right thanks all the same." I just could not pass up such a chance, football or no football. This was too good an opportunity to miss.

"You'll be missing a good day out with my family and friends. 'Tis an annual event. Everyone has a meal and a good drink, you know the crack, a laugh and a joke?"

"Honestly Breandán I've got too much to do. Thanks for the thought though."

We finished early for the weekend and I was so tired when I got in that I decided to crash out on my bed. It was whilst I was getting out my clean clothes, after my sleep, I realised that something in my room was different. I couldn't put my finger on it straight away, but something was not quite right. I looked carefully around trying to work out what it was. Then I noticed the wardrobe door was slightly open. I always locked the door out of habit because our wardrobe door at home would not stay closed unless it was locked. Now I knew I was not mistaken. Someone, apart from the chambermaid, must have been in the room. I carefully looked around, what else had been tampered with? I opened different drawers. Everything seemed all right, but I still had this feeling I had missed something. There was something not quite right. But what was it? I stood there wondering, could I be imagining it? I was puzzled. I was certain that the wardrobe door was locked when I left this morning. Then something prompted me to look in my bedside cabinet drawer. My photograph of Anne and her latest letter had gone. I was puzzled as I searched the drawer. A thorough search of my room did not uncover it. Now why would anyone want those? I turned out all my drawers wondering if I had made a mistake and put them somewhere else. Having checked everywhere and still nothing, I had to admit that it looked as if someone had taken them, but why.

"Hello Richard." I was so preoccupied I hadn't noticed Noel.
"Sorry Noel, I didn't see you there."
"By the looks of it something or someone's upset you, what an earth's wrong?"
"Hmm, you're right. Some bastard's taken some stuff from my room. "
"What stuff?"
"Never you mind Noel," I growled. "I'm going to see the receptionist. I'll get to the bottom of this."
"Richard, Richard. Wait. Listen to me."
I was in no mood for listening to Noel. "Noel leave it, ok!"
"But Richard hang on. Hang on will you."
I stopped and glowered at Noel.
"Right, now tell me what's happened."
"What good will that do Noel?" I snapped angrily.
"Maybe, just maybe I could find out what's going on, after all people talk to me, you know that. Besides the staff see things." He paused before going on, "Has it occurred to you that it maybe a certain person behind this." I had to admit the thought had crossed my mind but I had discounted it just as quickly. "Well what about it Richard?" I thought about his suggestion of seeing what he could find out and I suppose it made sense, but I was still fuming. I then made up my mind.
"Ok, mind you if you draw a blank..."
Noel interrupted me. "If I don't find anything out this evening, then by all means take it up with reception. Ok?"
I agreed. "So how long do you reckon you'll need?"
"An hour at the most should do it."
I had calmed down a little and started to think straight. "I'll come and find you in about an hour unless I hear from you before." I didn't hold out much hope of Noel finding anything out.

Forty minutes later as I was entering the Dining Room when I bumped into Noel on his way out." Richard I was just on my way back to the lodge to phone your room."
"Why?"
"I think I may have found out something." He took my arm and gently steered me away from the Dining Room and over to a quiet corner in the lounge. "It's as I thought, it's none of the staff."
"I see." I paused, "What are you suggesting then?"
"I'm not suggesting anything. All I'm saying is that I'm certain it isn't anybody here."
"What makes you so sure? Someone could be lying, couldn't they?"
"No. Nobody is lying."

"How do you know, and how can you be so sure?" I asked.

"Just something that was said that's all."

"Which was?" "I can't tell you. I need to speak to someone first. It's just something I overheard."

"Noel what did you overhear? I insist you tell me."

He considered what I had just said, then shrugged his shoulders. "I guess it doesn't matter, but I can't confirm it that's all."

"That's ok, just tell me what you overheard."

"Well there is a rumour that tomorrow some Government Ministers are coming here for a meeting and that we had some strange blokes here checking things out or something."

"Special Branch?"

"Dunno maybe. I'm not really sure." He thought about it for a moment, "I think there were some from Special Branch, but there was also others who came afterwards. They wanted a list of all guests staying here and keys to the bedrooms."

"What then?"

"From what I've heard they then checked out different rooms, perhaps they went in yours?"

"Are you suggesting that these Special Branch people took my things?"

"No I'm not, I'm suggesting that it is possible that the others did. The ones who checked the bedrooms."

"I thought they were Special Branch?"

"No, these were men from the Government."

"Weren't they escorted?"

"From what I've heard when the manager saw their Government ID cards he said he would accompany them, but they insisted that he went about his business and left them to get on with theirs."

"I see, and who told you all this?"

"I overheard someone talking, so it's only a rumour."

"Well who did you hear?"

"Well if you must know I was in the office when the manager was telling the duty receptionist what had gone on. He was fuming at this government bloke's attitude." From my knowledge of how things operate when places are being checked out for high-powered meetings Noel was not far off the truth. The only thing that concerned me was why would they take a photograph of my wife and her letter. I didn't like it, unless they weren't who they purported to be.

By the time I had finished my evening meal it was getting on for ten and the bar was busy with locals. I had managed to find a quiet table, in the corner of the lounge, where I sat with my drink thinking about what Noel had told me. It was then that I caught sight of two of the men I had seen the other night. They made a beeline towards me. Oh my God, I thought, I don't really need this. Then none other than Breandán O'Shea joined them. All three were now making a beeline straight towards me. "Bugger, that's all I want," I said quietly to myself, "Some self righteous jumped up Irishman lecturing me again on Irish history. Bollocks!"

"Hello Richard, thought we might find you here. Do you mind if we join you?" Before

I could answer him, Breandán had sat down and signalled the other two do likewise. "Richard you remember Eddie O'Rielly and James Paisley from the other night, don't you?" Each man gave a salutary dip of his head in acknowledgement. "Where's Paul, out with his new love?"

"Yes, I don't expect to see much of him over the weekend. Anyway what are you doing here?" I asked.

"Oh nothing special, just thought I'd meet up with my three friends that's all."

"Three friends?" I asked a little puzzled.

"Yes, you, Edie and James. Excuse me. Noel, I say Noel." He called to the night porter as he went by.

Noel half turned. "Just a moment sir and I'll be right with you." Then he realised it was O'Shea and hurried over to our table. "Sorry Mr O'Shea, I didn't realise it was you. Now what could I get you?"

"A round of drinks for a start. No bugger it. Bring me a bottle of Bushmill's and three whisky tumblers, plus a jug of orange juice, Not squash mind, but juice and a large glass. Tell the barman to book it down to me and I'll sign for it. Thank you Noel."

It was a couple of hours later and well after the bar had closed that James Paisley leaned over to Breandán and spoke in a low confidential way to him. I wondered what that was all about. I didn't have long to wait to find out. He looked straight at me, his eyes firmly fixed on mine.

"Richard I have something to ask of you. A big favour."

"Go ahead. Ask away it doesn't hurt to ask but whether I can help or not is another matter."

He gave a little nervous cough. "Well it's like this. Eddie and I came here with one purpose tonight and that was to see you. We have talked it over at great length with Mr O'Shea and he has agreed to this approach. So all three of us wish to put a proposition to you." He paused and took another sip of his whisky. "We are involved in a very special organisation which could make use of certain of your talents, and we wondered if... How should I say," he paused looking for the right words.

Eddie took over. "Well what James is trying to say is, we wondered if you would consider joining us in our struggle. The rewards, the financial rewards that is, would be very good indeed. In fact probably far greater than you could ever imagine." I went to say something but he hurried on. "There's no need to rush with your answer," He looked at his friends for confirmation. "No, there's no rush Richard so take your time and think about it." I looked at O'Shea and he nodded in agreement.

I could not believe my ears. "Am I right in what I just heard," I asked, "You're asking me, or should I say actively recruiting me an Englishman, to join your organisation?" I was completely thrown off balance by this and hadn't a clue how to answer. Once again I looked across at O'Shea. "Shit Breandán, I can't believe this."

"Just think it over that's all we are asking. Don't worry."

I took a deep breath. "I'm sorry I need to pay a visit." With that I got up and made my way to the toilet. I could feel three pairs of eyes watching me as I walked away from the table.

I paused by the wash hand basin with water dripping from my hands wondering how I was going to get out of this. Deep down I suppose I was proud to think that they trusted me enough to ask the question, after all I was an Englishman. I placed my hands under the hot air dryer still worried. Richard, you're going to have to come up with something. They're expecting an answer. Then it hit me, of course, the conversation I had used as a bluff against Breandán on our way back. That's it, you've got it my son. Use that and play for time. I dried my hands off and returned to my table.

"Well gentlemen, I would like to ask some questions."

"Of course, what would you like to know?"

"First of all I will be finished over here soon so I'll be returning to my home surely that would affect my, shall we say position, wouldn't it?"

"Not really, after all you will be returning back here, wouldn't he Mr O'Shea?" Breandán slowly inclined his head in a nod.

"What happens if I decline your offer, where do we go from here?"

"Nowhere." James Paisley answered. "That's right isn't it Breandán?" Breandán again gave a slight nod of his head, "However, should you decline our offer then it would mean we would have to re-think our plans, so please think about your answer very carefully before making a decision. Take as long as you want." Once again Breandán gave an almost imperceptible nod of the head.

"Hmm, I see. Well gentlemen I've got a very good idea as to what your organisation stands for and what it does so I will certainly need a considerable amount of time before I make a decision." Breandán stared at me and I stared back, "By the way Breandán you have not forgotten about our conversation already have you?" I paused, "You know, the one when I told you about my situation." A puzzled look crossed his face. "Don't tell me I need to remind you already, let me see, we were travelling..." He shook his head and frowned. "No there's no need to discuss it again. Of course I remember what you said. Eddie, James I think Richard deserves some space so let's leave him to think about things, after all it's a big decision we are asking him to make and I don't see any point in rushing him into anything." With that he got to his feet, "Well Richard, I feel you should take as much time as you want. The offer is there."

"Yes take your time Richard," said James, "I agree with Mr O'Shea don't you Eddie?" Eddie nodded his head, "Of course we do understand so take whatever time you need." I smiled politely. Inside my heart was pounding. Phew, what a relief I thought to myself. "Well gentlemen if you don't mind I've had a long week and I'm very tired. So would you please excuse me I bid you all a good night."

"Certainly," O'Shea replied and all three rose to their feet, "Goodnight Richard."

"Goodnight Breandán." I nodded to the other two and made my way to the stairs.

Chapter 14

Breandán had been right, everywhere was deserted. Everyone had gone to Dublin for the match of the year and all I had for company was the noise of the rooks as they roosted in the trees around me. It was Sunday morning, the sun was shining and it was a glorious March day. Just right for my unscheduled visit to the farm. Ever since I had seen them loading that articulated lorry in the early hours of Tuesday morning I had been looking for a chance to have a really good nose around and this was it.

As I made my way along the lane towards the farm my thoughts went back to yesterday's meeting at the hotel. Breandán had kept his promise to me and had indeed arranged for my own official invite and although, from my point of view, it had been a useful exercise, it raised more questions than answers. I still couldn't believe that the Taoiseach, the Minister for Agriculture and many leading Government officials were gathered together in the same room with the top IRA officials such as Breandán, Eddie O'Rielly and James Paisley. What was the connection, it just didn't stack up? I also kept thinking about Anne's photograph and letter, now why would the Republican Government want those? It was yet another question that I was unable to answer. I have to admit it; I just don't like loose ends. No matter how hard I try I can't come up with any satisfactory answers. Ah well think of something else Richard. I tried humming a tune to myself, but that didn't work, so I tried to think out what I would do when I got to the farm. Hmm, that's a point, I wonder if Breandán has gone to football or not? Was it just a ruse to see what I would do? I didn't think so. Careful Richard you can't be certain. True, I thought, on the other hand why would Breandán go to such lengths? Good question, I thought, he wouldn't unless he suspected that I had seen something. That's a point, I wonder if he suspects it was me that set off the alarm the other night and not the dog? Hmm, I wonder, will the farm be deserted or not? Come on Richard think positive, think of something else. How about what a beautiful day it is. No, ok, well hum a tune or something. Anything, just do anything, but get off these negative thoughts because they are not helping one little bit. I started to sing.
 "Come on come on, come on come on, come on come on come on. Do you wanna be in my gang my gang my gang? Do you wanna be in my gang? Oh yeah..." Very soon I had forgotten all about yesterday and all other thoughts as I started to get into the swing of Gary Glitter's song and there was now a definite spring about my step as I walked along the lane.

As I rounded the bend in the lane I was now totally immersed in my singing, all other thoughts were gone. I was on my Beetle's medley as I passed the low privet hedge that encompassed the small cottage. I had just got to the first line of the chorus "I wanna hold your hand..." when a girl's voice joined in.
 "I wanna hold your hand...." I stopped singing and looked over the hedge to see who my singing partner was.
 "Hello there, it's a grand day for a walk isn't it?"
 "Yes, it's beautiful." her pretty face seemed familiar but I just couldn't place it.
 "So you're a Beetles fan then." It was more of a statement rather than a question.

"I suppose so. Yes I am, are you?"

"I like most of their stuff, in fact I've a lot of their records," then suddenly she said, "Don't I know you?"

"I don't know, do you?"

"Yes of course, the other night remember?"

"Yes of course," I lied.

"No you don't do you?"

"How do you know I don't?" I asked.

"You've only got to look at the puzzled look on your face for that answer. Let me give you a clue," her blue eyes twinkled mischievously, "We met not far from here. Now does that help?"

"At the hotel?"

"Well done. So do you know who I am now?"

I thought about all the girls that I had seen in the hotel including Fionnuala and the other receptionists and of course that wasn't many. I even racked my brain about the girls I had seen in the club.

"Well do you remember?"

"I'm sorry, I know your face but I can't think how."

"Oh dear, now I'm hurt. Obviously I didn't create much of an impression," she feigned disappointment. I came to the hotel the other night with another lady to collect your friend."

"Ahh, now I've got it! You came to get Noel."

"That's right I am the nurse."

"Of course, I'm so sorry but..."

She cut me short, "It's no good apologising now, the damage is done. I'm mortally hurt that you didn't recognise me." She lowered her head in mock hurt.

"I should have known," I replied, "but you look so different out of uniform." She looked up and for a moment her blue eyes met mine, then she laughed. "Do you live here?" I asked then as an after thought, "Or are you staying with friends?"

"Oh no it's my place, or should I say I share it with a friend of mine. We live here on and off."

"What does your friend do? Does he work locally?"

"Firstly my friend is also a nurse and works with me. Secondly he is not a he but is a she and her name is Marion. We don't actually own it but rent it from Mr O'Shea and come here when we are off duty." She looked around the garden and sighed, "Ahh it's beautiful here you can see why people love this area can't you?" I nodded. "Did you know it's called the Valley of the Kings? Of course you do. I'm sorry, how rude of me, would you like a coffee?"

"No I've got to get on, thanks all the same."

"Are you sure, it won't take a minute."

I was surely tempted. I thought about my planned visit to the farm and looked back at the nurse. "Well maybe just a quick one then."

"Really so you like a quick one?" She said mischievously, "I personally like to savour it!"

"You do?" I said.

"Yes, I do" she said.

"Ok, I'll hold you to that."

She gave another of her smiles. "Right come on then." She grabbed my hand and pulled me towards the gate, "Coffee is served." I let myself be guided through the gate and taken by the hand up her garden path and into the front room of the cottage. "There you sit down and I'll put the coffee on." With that she disappeared into the kitchen, "Have a look and see if there's any music there you fancy." She called back through the open door. The room was comfortably furnished with a small cottage suite. On the walls there were some watercolour paintings of different landscapes. Over by the window was a record unit housing the stereo player, television and numerous LP records and singles I started to look through her record collection when she came over to where I was. She leaned over and looked over my shoulder her hair gently caressed my cheek as she did so. I picked out the 'Gentle on my Mind' album and turned to speak when once again her eyes met mine. I looked deep into her soft blue eyes and slowly ever so slowly stood up. Our lips met in a frenzied and torrid embrace. She slowly sunk to the floor pulling me down gently to lay with her. My resolve had gone and in one easy movement we were as one in unison with the strains of Dean Martin as the album 'Gentle on my Mind' played softly.

It was over an hour later when I eventually left the pretty nurse's house. I had never intended to stop even for coffee and I was now way behind in my plans.

"Bye Richard, I hope you enjoyed the coffee."

"Lovely" I said. She smiled as I closed the gate behind me. "Bye," I called back over my shoulder as I set off up the lane towards the farm in pursuit of my original aim. I could quite fancy her I thought to myself, and then a more sinister thought entered my head. Why was a nurse from an Ulster clinic renting a place right here and from Breandán O'Shea? What was the connection between him and the clinic in the north? Why was she here today of all days, was she a plant to keep me under surveillance?

It's now been over an hour and a half since I left the hotel. So allowing for my delay at the cottage then it should not be long before I'll be able to see the farm. From now on I'll have to be extra careful. Damn my stupidity for staying at the cottage I should have resisted, still the damage is done now. With these thoughts uppermost in my mind I veered off the lane into the woods and doubled back on my tracks towards the cottage just to satisfy myself that I was not being followed. I continued through the woods for a couple of hundred yards then carefully worked my way back to the lane, I paused and looked both up the lane towards the farm and down the lane towards the cottage. Nothing. Thank goodness for that. So perhaps she is genuine and not here to spy on me, but I still wasn't sure. Having made sure that the lane was clear in both directions I retraced my footsteps back towards the farm.

Ten minutes later I could see the dry stone wall that enclosed the first of the orchards, I now had to get my bearings as to where I was in relationship with the Cold Store and the house. Now the tricky bit, I ducked down and kept a low profile all the way to the wall. I gingerly raised my head until I could get an uninterrupted view. Damn, I'm too far up. I needed to be much closer to the lane than I was so that I could have a clear view of the house. Once again I ducked down and in a doubled-up position. Keeping the wall on my left I followed its line until I could just about make out the lane from where I was. Once more I cautiously raised my head above the wall. Great, I could now see the house as well as a number of outbuildings that I had never seen before. "Oh shit." I muttered under my breath, because there in front of the house was the red Mercedes and the blue Volvo. I thought you were going to this bloody football match. Hmm now what? I ducked back down behind the wall and looked about for somewhere to hide up whilst I gathered my thoughts. "Bollocks Breandán, so you were giving me a load of old crap the other day hoping to catch me out. Well it didn't work." I looked at my watch it was only just ten. When he had said they were going off for the day I had presumed they would have left by now. Perhaps kick-off is later over here or maybe the ground's closer to here than I had thought. If it is a ten-thirty then perhaps they'll be leaving soon. I soon found myself a good place to hole up for awhile where I had a good view of the lane but would be hidden from prying eyes. I decided to give it half an hour and if they hadn't left by then I would have a re-think.

I looked at my watch for the umpteenth time, it was ten twenty-five and still there was no sign of them leaving. "Damn you Breandán, if you're going go." I muttered to myself and settled back down for a further wait. I hadn't been waiting long before I heard the sound of an approaching car I checked my watch, it was just before ten-thirty. Easing myself up for a better view I was just in time to see the powerful red Mercedes roar passed and sweep off down the lane. At long last I thought to myself, and heaved a mental sigh of relief. A few minutes later I once again cautiously raised my head above the wall to check for any possible complications but all seemed quiet. Satisfied I stood up when suddenly the savage barking and snarling of Breandán's dog shattered the peace. I saw the huge Irish Wolfhound, with great leaps and bounds, heading in my direction. "Shit!" I hurled myself to the ground, holding my breath and praying it wouldn't find me. Gradually the noise abated. God, where in hells name were you? I hadn't spotted the dog, but he'd obviously seen me. I left it for a few moments before venturing to raise my head again. I peered over the wall, now I could see why he hadn't found me. He was securely chained up to the outside wall of the house. If nothing else it confirmed that there was no one at home. That was a plus. After a quick assessment of the situation I was left in no doubt at all that his chain was long enough to reach any of the outbuildings, and that put a different complexion on things. There was only one thing for it and that was to walk straight up the drive to the dog so he would recognise me otherwise he may just think I was a burglar and go for me. All I hoped was that he would remember me.

As I approached the house from along the lane the dog, once again, started to bark. "Come on boy," I called to him encouraging him to me, "Come on then, come and see me." I walked closer then waited for him to get my scent. I then held out a small piece of chocolate that I had found in my pocket. "Here boy, come and see what Richard's got for you. Come on, good boy. Who's a good boy then." Over he came, he wasn't too sure at first but gradually his barking diminished until it had stopped completely. He started to wag his tail and I moved further forward.

"Here boy, come on look what I've got." I held out my hand again, he sniffed at the chocolate, then gave it a lick. At first he wasn't too sure.

"Go on boy take it then. It's for you." At this point he gently took the chocolate and ate it in one gulp.

"There, did you like that?" I started to make a fuss of him.

"What's a matter then?" I said as I got out another small piece of chocolate. I made my way towards the outbuildings with the dog trotting happily alongside of me.

"Here you are boy," I gave him the small piece of chocolate.

"That's it boy all gone. No more now, it's all gone. Good boy, there's a good boy." I made another big fuss of him.

"Go on now go and lie down there's a good lad," and with that he trotted back to lie down close to the house. That's a relief I thought.

There were quite a few outbuildings, which I had never seen before because I had no reason to be down here and even on the odd occasion I had been to the house I was always on the other side. I had a good nose around them all. Some were quite dilapidated but regardless all had three things in common. All the windows were bricked up; each building had a large bell fixed to its apex inferring that they were alarmed and lastly they all were fitted with brand new solid looking doors. Intriguing I thought, now what did these buildings house that would warrant no windows, an alarm system and solid doors?

I spent time checking each building in turn to see if there was any way that I could get a clue as to what was going on. I was about to give up and concentrate my time on the cold store when I kicked something that had a metallic ring to it. Now what was that? I bent down and carefully moved the longish grass aside with my bare hands. "Ahh there you are," I said to myself as I reached down and picked up a black metallic rectangular object. It was a Browning 9.00mm magazine clip with a number of live rounds still in place. What a find, my heart was pounding as I got down on my hands and knees and started to diligently search the area inch by inch for further items of interest. My enthusiasm had now fully returned and it wasn't long before other finds came to light in the shape of a number of spent 9.00mm brass cases, very interesting I thought and put them along with the magazine into my jacket pocket for later. I checked my watch, come on Richard you'd best get a move on, time you were not here. I had been here for a little over two hours and there was no point in outstaying my welcome. I dusted myself off and started back towards the gate when suddenly the dog started a further bout of incessant barking. I ran towards the dog calling.

"Come on boy, there's a good boy," but all to no avail. Suddenly a Gardai patrol car appeared through the gate.

"Bastard. Shit Richard this could be very awkward for you. Here you are complete with live ammo in a clip trespassing on O'Shea's farm and the fuzz turns up," I muttered to myself.

The car stopped in a cloud of dust and one of its occupants addressed me. "Good afternoon to you sir, and now what would you be doing up here on Mr O'Shea's farm?"

"Well I was in the hotel grounds a while ago when I heard the dog making a commotion so I wondered if something was wrong."

"But with all due respect sir why would you be thinking something maybe wrong?"

"Sorry, how do you mean?" I asked.

"Like I said sir, why would you think something was wrong? Now please answer the question."

"Oh wrong," I gave a slight laugh, "I see what you mean," I said stalling trying to think quickly for something to say that sounded convincing. "Well I work for Breandán and I knew they were all going off to the match in Dublin, in fact they asked me to go, but I had some letters to write. Anyway as I said, I knew they were all out so when I heard the dog barking like he was I thought maybe there was an intruder or something so I came up here to investigate."

"Didn't I boy," I said patting the dog.

"Hmm, I see. So you say you were in the hotel grounds and heard him creating?"

"Yes that's right. In fact you could ask the lady at the cottage down the lane she must have heard him as well."

"Ok we'll take your word for it but we'll just check around and make sure everything's all right seeing we're here."

"Oh I've already done that and everything's fine. I checked all the buildings they're all secure. Besides they are alarmed aren't they and I would have heard the bells wouldn't I?"

The guy talking to me shrugged his shoulders and turned to his mate. "What do you think?"

"It seems ok, but you'd best still check it out Joe, just to be on the safe side." With that he opened his door to get out and that was an invitation for the dog to do his job. His heckles went up and he bared his teeth, rushed towards the car snarling, Joe or whatever his name was didn't need any further encouragement, he just swung his legs back in and slammed the door. The dog stopped short of the door and started ferociously barking.

"Well perhaps on second thoughts I think I'll leave it," he said to his partner. He then shouted to me. "So you're sure everything's all right then Sir?"

I looked at him and smiled pointing towards the dog. "What do you think?" I asked.

"Yes I take your point. So we'll bid you good day Sir and thank you for your help." I took that as my cue to leave.

Having walked a reasonable distance down the lane I glanced back over my shoulder to see what they were up to but their car was hidden from view. I pulled the ammunition clip from my pocket and thought about my next move. Scrambling up the bank from the lane I disappeared into the woods. There, away from prying eyes, I scooped out a shallow hollow in the soft earth. I took one last look at my trophies then lay them to rest. It suddenly registered with me how shiny the cases still were. That could only mean one thing and that was that they had not been there very long. Now come to think of it the grass where I had found them was still down flat where someone had been lying. Hmm, I wonder what they were up to? Other thoughts started flooding into my head. Who was it who had been lain there and on whose side was they? Had someone been shot is that how the spent cases got there and had they been discovered? Perhaps some sort of struggle had taken place and the ammunition clip had been dropped it. Once again too many questions with too few answers. Deep in thought I slowly covered them over with the earth placing old leaves and a stone on top to mark the spot.

Chapter 15

We are now enjoying something of an Indian summer here in Kent and the picking season is well under way. My memories and experiences of Ireland have already started to fade; even my trip to Ulster and the visit to the IRA pub now seem a lifetime away. I suppose I was a little disappointed when the work came to an end and I have to admit that I miss the excitement of Ireland. What with all the encounters and half-truths, by comparison, life back here is very mundane. However I was somewhat surprised that nothing further came out of our visit, still that's life isn't it?

I hadn't been in more than about ten minutes when the telephone rang. "Hello."
"Is that Richard?"
"Speaking. Who's that?"
"Hello Richard it's Breandán, Breandán O'Shea here. How are you keeping?"
"Hello Breandán it's a long time since I heard from you. I'm fine. How are you keeping?"
"I'm well."
"Funnily enough I was just saying to Paul the other day that I hadn't heard anymore from you. So to what do I owe the pleasure?"
"Well, it's like this. The grafting you did for me turned out better than I'd have ever thought possible and based on those results alone I need you to come back over with a view to discussing more work."
"But I'm right up to my eyes in it over here so is it really necessary for me to come over to Ireland just to discuss what you want me to do? After all you already know my terms." I was somewhat reluctant to go over there just to sort out some more work with Breandán O'Shea.
"Well I think it would be in your interest Richard."
"I hear what you're saying Breandán, but it's a helluva long way to come just to talk to you about your orchard, surely that can be sorted out over the telephone," he went quiet. "Well couldn't it?" I asked.
"That's the point Richard, it's not just my farm we're discussing, that's only the beginning. Since your visit everyone has been talking about the 'Englishmen' and asking when were you coming back. So you see it's not as simple as just sorting out something over the 'phone. The potential over here is huge, so when can you come?"
"Hmm, it's difficult at the moment I'll have to think..."
He cut me short. "No time for you to think Richard I need you over here now. You'll only need to be here for a couple of days to sort out the contracts."
"Yes but I'm extremely busy here and..."
"Richard this is big, very big. Now I can organise everything. Set up the meetings with people and arrange your accommodation. In fact do whatever you want, but I need you here and the sooner the better. So what do you say?"
"But can't you see Breandán I can't drop everything just like that, after all I already have commitments over here. As you know we're right in the middle of picking and it's one of our busiest times so I'm sorry but it's impossible..."
"How about if I pay your fare and all other expenses, book you into the hotel and so on."

"Breandán, the cost is not the problem, it's the time."

"Hmm," the line went quiet for a minute, "Is there no way you could get over just for say forty eight hours. Surely you could manage that."

"I'll speak to my father and see what he says, but I'm not promising anything."

"Ok, so when will you let me know?"

"Tomorrow night about this time if that's all right?"

"That'll be fine so I'll speak to you then."

"Good and Breandán!"

"Yes?"

"If my father agrees and I do come over it had better be as good as you're saying."

"Look Richard, if it isn't as good as I'm saying not only will I pay all your expenses but I'll also give you an extra three hundred punt for your trouble, that's how confident I am."

It seemed too good a deal to pass up, but what was the catch? "Hmm all right I'll phone you tomorrow," and with that I hung up.

I spoke to my father about the telephone call and he felt that it sounded like a good opportunity.

"What about here, are you going to be all right?"

"Of course we will. Anyway it's only two days and besides if we are going to get this contracting side really off the ground this could be the break we've been waiting for. No I think you ought to go."

"Well if you're sure you can manage without me?"

"We managed before when you were in the Army, so no doubt we'll manage this time. Besides Paul is here and we've got plenty of pickers in so I don't see a problem."

"All right I'll give him a call and tell him I'll be going over in the next couple of days."

"Hmm, on second thoughts it might be better to leave it until the weekend and we'll have got the bulk of the fruit away to the market before you go. What do you think?"

"That's a point. Yeah good idea, so I'll tell him I'll go at the weekend, if you're sure that's all right."

"Of course I am."

"Right I'll catch up with you later then."

"Oh Richard," he called after me as I climbed onto the tractor, "You had best tell Paul that you're off then he knows to cover for you here."

"All right." I shouted above the noise of the engine as it kicked into life.

It was six o'clock on the dot when I dialled Breandán's number. "Hello, Breandán it's Richard."

"So what's the news?"

"I'll come."

"Great, when?"

"At the weekend."

"Oh," his disappointment was obvious.

"What's wrong?" I asked.

"Oh nothing, it's just that I was banking on you getting here before then that's all."

"Well I'm sorry Breandán but you're lucky to get me at all. I had to really work on my dad to get him to agree to my coming over in the first place," I lied, laying it on with a trowel.

"Well if that's the best you can do then the weekend it is."

"I don't expect the ferry times have altered much but I'll check them out. I'll phone you again tomorrow and let you know approximately at what time I should arrive."

"The ferry did you say?"

"Yes. Is that a problem?"

"Well yes, it'll take you hours.

"Well unless you want to pay my air fare and hire car when I arrive then the ferry it will have to be."

"Like I said it will take hours, so catch the plane. I'll meet you at Dublin so there's no need to hire a car and as for the fare, well, it's peanuts."

"It certainly costs more than the ferry that's for sure."

"Yes but when you add on the petrol plus the fare there's not a lot in it. So come over by plane all right?"

"It's all right by me. I'll phone you tomorrow then with the details and I'll see you at the weekend."

"Ok Richard, speak to you tomorrow...cheers."

Having eventually got my flight booked I was just about to phone Breandán with the details when the telephone rang.

"Hello, is it true?" an agitated Irish voice shouted down the 'phone.

"Who is it, who are you?" I asked, but he ignored my question.

"Richard just tell me. Is it true?"

"First of all is what true and secondly who are you?"

"Is it true that you're coming over here again? I had heard that you were coming over to see Breandán, so is it true?"

"Slow down, first of all tell me who am I talking to?"

" It's Noel. When you do come don't forget the envelope will you?"

"Is that Noel from the Tara?" I asked. "What envelope are you talking about?"

"The envelope Richard, please tell me you haven't lost it?"

"What envelope?" I asked again.

"The envelope, the brown one I gave you at the hotel." He fell silent waiting for my reply.

"I'm sorry Noel, I don't know what you're talking about..."

He interrupted me. "You must remember, the brown one that I gave you on the night they came and took me away." He sounded desperate. "Don't you remember," he started to grab at straws, "It was when my wife came with a monk and the nurse and they..."

I interrupted him." That night! Yes of course I remember it's all coming back to me now. So where did I put it..."

"You haven't lost it?" he asked with a sense of urgency.

"Calm down Noel, of course I haven't lost it. It's in my jacket pocket where I put it."

"Thank goodness." You could almost feel him relax. "Will you bring it with you when you come?"

"Yes I'll bring it with me when I come."

"You haven't shown it to anyone have you?" Once again he was unable to disguise his agitation.

"Of course I haven't shown anyone why, did you think I would?"

"No of course I didn't" he sounded relieved. "Oh by the way, when are you coming?"

"Saturday."

"Saturday did you say?"

"Yes Saturday."

"Great," he almost sounded elated; "I'll see you then. Richard I'm sorry for doubting you."

"That's all right forget it."

"No I mean it, I'm sorry. I didn't mean to doubt you but if had I lost that envelope my life would not be worth living. I'll explain everything when I see you and perhaps then you'll understand. Cheers Richard."

"Cheers Noel." I replaced the handset and pondered about the conversation I had just had. The envelope seemed to be a major issue and when Noel had thought I'd lost it he was worried sick. Obviously this puts a different complexion on things. I think when I pick up my plane tickets in the morning I will get the contents photocopied, just as an insurance policy of course.

The telephone rang several times before Breandán answered.

"Hello Breandán. I'm booked on the Aer Lingus flight leaving Heathrow at 10:55 arriving in Dublin at 12:10 Saturday lunch time."

"Is that the best you can do Richard?"

"Afraid so. Everything was booked solid."

"Well that'll have to do then. I'll meet you at the airport. It was 12:10 wasn't it?"

"Yeah that's right."

"I'll see you when you arrive then. Bye for now."

"Cheers Breandán see you Saturday."

We hesitated momentarily at the start of the runway and what had been a fairly shrill whistling note from the engines perceptibly changed to that of a thunderous roar, the overhead air stopped flowing as the aircraft leapt forward and started to accelerate down the runway. The noise from the jet engines hit a crescendo then suddenly we were off the ground and climbing rapidly up through the clouds into a wide expanse of blue azure, leaving Heathrow looking like a small model airport in the distance. The plane banked sharply to the right then levelled off, the cool air once again played on my face. The engine note now changed to an imperceptible whisper as we moved almost silently along our flightpath.

"Good morning" the public address system clicked into life, "This is your Captain speaking and on behalf of the crew and Aer Lingus I would like to welcome you aboard Aer Lingus flight..."

"Hello, my name's Andrew are you going to Dublin?"

"Sorry, what was that? I was miles away."

"I said my name's Andrew, are you going to Dublin. No I know you're going to Dublin but what I meant to say was are you staying in Dublin?"

"Oh no."

"Family over there?"

"No."

"Going on holiday are you?" Nosy sod I thought.

"No. Why do you ask are you then?"

"No I live there." At this point I opened the 'In Flight' magazine and got absorbed in reading the articles in there.

It seemed no time at all before the tannoy once again came to life.

"This is Captain Hobbs once again. If you care to look out of your window you will see that we are just about to cross over the coast of Ireland and in a few minutes we will be arriving at Dublin International Airport. The weather is fine and the temperature is sixteen degrees. I would ask you all to return to your seats and place them in the upright position, fasten your seat belt and extinguish all cigarettes. Thank you." On came the 'Fasten seatbelts and the No smoking' sign.

It was after six thirty when I eventually got down into the bar. We had arrived at the hotel a couple of hours previously but Breandán had declined my offer to come in, saying he had some final arrangements to make before this evening, but he would see me later. I had checked in and then taken a leisurely stroll for an hour or so before returning to unpack. Nothing had changed; it seemed just as if I had never been away, still the same old faces working here. I was even back in my old room, which looked out towards the farm. As I entered the bar, I noticed a solitary person sitting drinking orange juice; it was Noel the union man. At first I did not recognise him as he looked quite a bit thinner than when I last saw him, plus I certainly was not used to seeing him drink orange juice. As I walked over to the bar, he stood up, made his way over to me.

"Hello there my friend I've been expecting you, can I get you to drink?"

"Thank you Noel I'll have an orange juice."

"Two orange juices please."

"Will that be all sir."

"Yes thank you." Noel passed me an orange juice and we made our way over to where he had been sat.

"Did you have a good flight?"

"Not bad thanks. You're looking well Noel, lost a bit of weight since I last saw you."

"You're right, I've lost over two stone since I gave up drinking. Anyway how are you keeping?"

"Oh I'm fine. By the way how did you know I was coming by plane and when I would arrive?"

He chose to ignore my question and immediately lowered his voice as he asked, "Well did you bring it? Have you got it with you?"

"What are you talking about Noel?" I looked bewildered.

"You know," he leaned towards me and in a whisper said, "The envelope."

Realisation dawned. "Oh yes of course." I felt inside my pocket and pulled out the manila envelope, "Is this what you mean?"

His face lit up as a big grin spread across it. "Thank goodness for that, thank you very much, you will never know how much this means to me." The tone of his voice said it all, but as he reached out to take it from me I pulled it away.

"Hang on Noel, not so quick. Now what's so important about this?" I tapped the envelope on my knee.

"Richard," he suddenly looked worried again, You haven't opened it have you?" I sat there in silence. "Richard please tell me you haven't opened it." From his tone it was obvious that my silence caused him acute problems.

"Yes, I have opened it." I eventually replied. "Why is it so important?"

He slumped back into his chair with the look of a defeat written all over his face. His eyes were the eyes of a frightened man.

I looked at him and said, "Listen Noel, the deal was you were to tell me what this was all about, so either tell me and get the envelope back or don't and well you know the rest." He sat there in silence. "Well Noel what's it to be?" I watched him intently for any signs, but he just sat there staring at the floor in silence. Then, just as I was to give up, he stood up and picked up his drink and without saying a word beckoned me to follow him. I followed him in silence over to a table in the far corner of the lounge, as far away from everyone as possible, he sat down and still without speaking motioned me to do likewise.

It was then he spoke. "Ok Richard. I feel I can trust you so you win." He still seemed a little unsure and once again wanted reassurance from me, "Richard you must promise never ever repeat what I am going to tell you to anyone." He paused and looked at me for some kind of undertaking.

I studied his face; it was the face of a frightened man that stared back at me. "Yeah, all right Noel, I promise. So what's all this about?"

He looked at me, his eyes pleading. "I hope you mean it Richard because I am putting my life in your hands, so please promise me on your child's life that you will not say a word."

"Noel I've promised, now do you trust me or not?" I asked. At that he looked me straight in the eyes. "If I had felt that I could not have trusted you I would never have given you the envelope, so please, I beg you don't let me down now."

"Ok Noel you've made your point. So I promise on my kid's life."

"Thank you Richard." Then in all but a whisper he started to talk. His voice was so soft I had to lean right forward in my chair to hear him. "Each one of the seven wonders, as you already know, is a description based on religion or folklore, for example it maybe describing a place of worship or a land mark. Then against each description there is a series of numbers, these are grid references and combined with the description they pin-point the seven different locations within the Republic that are ordinance dumps for the organisation and our lads." He took a drink from his glass then continued, "I was wrong to give it to you because as liaison officer I am responsible for it and should always keep it with me or in a safe place. The reason I gave it to you was that I knew deep down I could trust you. Even through my drunken haze that night, I still felt you were the person to trust. Even so, I should really have given it to Breandán O'Shea him being the main man and all, but with them arriving to take me away as they did there was no time and I was worried, especially as the clinic was north of the border. I didn't want it to fall into the wrong hands now did I?" He took another mouthful of his drink. "You could just imagine what a disaster it would have been for the organisation if the British Security Forces had got hold of it." He paused and looked up at me.

"So what makes you think that I'm any different. More to the point how do you know that I wouldn't pass on the information to Special Branch?"

"Because you worked for Breandán O'Shea and that makes all the difference. It means I can trust you." He now seemed oblivious of me he just repeated over and over again, to himself, what he had just said to me. To him I was part of the organisation.

"Noel," I interrupted his ramblings, "Noel listen to me."

He looked back at me. "Yes," he said in a flat monotone voice.

"Now listen to me. The fact that I worked for Breandán is just that, I worked for him. Get it, I worked for him, not for you or anyone else." Slowly as realisation struck home as to what he had done he grabbed my arm in a vice like grip and for a second time the look of fear returned to his eyes as he repeated the request.

"Please, please don't tell anyone what I have told you." I was now looking at a broken man. He started to talk again as tears welled up in his eyes, "Do you know Richard, my wife left me a while back." He pulled the back of his hand across his eyes to wipe away the tears, "All I've now got in the whole wide world is my few friends and the organisation. At least there, I could hold my head high that was until they found out about my alcoholism and some of them started muttering about me being a security risk. So you see if you say anything, then I am finished, not just finished but killed, shot dead." He then fell silent. In light of what he told me I thought long and hard about what I was about to do, I know what people would say, but I also know that this man was not the real enemy it was what he belonged to that was the enemy. Anyway I had already kept a copy for an insurance policy so I felt that I was not betraying anyone. I pushed the manila envelope into Noel's shaking hand; he just sat there and stared in disbelief at what I was doing. Then with hands shaking he tore open the brown envelope to reveal the original piece of paper entitled 'The Seven Wonders Of Fore'. He just could not believe it. He looked up at my face and the sheer relief was too much for him. He couldn't contain himself anymore as tears of gratitude rolled down his cheeks. "Thank you my friend." He unashamedly sobbed, "My dear, dear friend. Thank you very, very, much. I cannot begin to thank you enough for what you have just done. You have just saved my life. Thank you for understanding."

I stood up and gave him a friendly pat to his shoulder. "No problem Noel, just remember that you owe me one."

He just nodded and took out his handkerchief to wipe his eyes. "Thank you my friend, if ever you want anything just let me know."

"I will don't worry. Now don't you think you had best get out of here before anyone sees you."

"Oh, that's all right I'm at the meeting that Breandán has fixed up for later. It's the same one that you're going to. That's how I knew the time you were arriving."

So that was how he knew. Then I remembered something else that had been bothering me since my last trip and that was about the clinic. "Noel there is one thing more?"

"Yes, what's that Richard?"

"The clinic, you said it was north of the border, whereabouts exactly?"

"Just outside Belfast, why?"

"Does it have a doctor?"

"Well of course why do you ask?" He was beginning to look puzzled.

"What's the name of the good doctor, it wouldn't be a Dr James O'Shea would it?"

"Well of course it would he is after all Breandán's brother, but of course you would probably know that wouldn't you?"

"I thought it was. Does Breandán own the clinic then or is it his brothers?"

"I'm not completely sure, but I think Breandán is the sole owner, but maybe his brother has a stake in it. Anyway why the twenty questions?"

"No reason it's just something that I wanted to clear up in my own mind. Breandán had said about James and the clinic," I lied to my back teeth, "and I thought he had said it was owned by James, that's all."

"I could be wrong, perhaps it is, but it was Breandán who got me in there and the organisation funded my stay so I automatically assumed it was his clinic. What's this all about Richard?"

"Thanks Noel you've been very helpful."

"Why all the questions?"

"It was just that whilst I was here last time I met up with the nurse who came for you, she lives down here in a rented cottage and it just seemed strange her living here and yet working in the north. That was all. Now if you'll excuse me I best go back to my room I've got a few things I need to do."

"Ok Richard and thanks again."

Hmm I thought, so Mr O'Shea or his brother owns the clinic near Belfast. That would explain the blue Volvo and why Noel went to that clinic. It seems as if the good doctor may well have other links with the IRA as well as his brother. I wouldn't mind betting that he and his clinic have been used on more than one occasion to patch up the IRA Soldiers and that way they are not checked through the local hospitals.

I checked my watch for the umpteenth time and at last it was seven o'clock. At any time now Breandán and the others, whoever they maybe, should start arriving. I switched off the television, picked up my room key, and after a quick look around to make sure I'd got everything, I pulled the door closed behind me. I hadn't been in the bar long when Breandán arrived accompanied by the Minister for Agriculture and two other people whose faces I recognised from my last visit.

"Breandán," I called over to him raising my hand as I did so. He raised his hand in acknowledgement and guided the other three over in my direction.

"Evening Richard, let me introduce you. Minister, this is Richard James you possibly remember him." The Minister for Agriculture looked slightly puzzled; "He was over here earlier in the year when we had the luncheon here at the Tara. I introduced you then, do you remember?"

"Ah yes, yes of course. You were here with your partner I believe, something to do with this new technique of grafting you've developed wasn't it?"

"Yes, that's right."

"You see Breandán," he turned his attention to Breandán O'Shea, "My memory isn't as bad as you try to make out!" With that he laughed, "Plenty of life left in the old dog yet, eh Richard? Anyway pleased to make your acquaintance again." He said as he shook my hand.

"Pleased to meet you Minister."

"Richard, I'm not sure whether or not you've met Tom and Bill before, but anyway this is Tom O'Dowd, Tom this is Richard James from Kent in England."

"Pleased to meet you Richard."

"Likewise Tom."

"And this Richard, is Bill O'Grady."

"Pleased to meet you Bill." Bill nodded his head in acknowledgement. "Can I get you all a drink?" I enquired.

"No you don't Richard. You're here as our guest tonight so I'll get the drinks if you don't mind." I didn't object. "So what will it be gentlemen?"

As we stood there talking I noticed the bar started to fill up and I suppose after about half an hour there must have been a good fifty or so people.

"Are all these people guests of yours Breandán?" I asked.

He casually looked around the bar. "Well, not all but I would say a good two thirds of them. There's supposed to be slightly over forty tonight. I told you it would be worth it didn't I?"

"Yes. I must hand it to you Breandán you've done us proud."

Some of the faces certainly seemed familiar from my last trip, but there was still several others I did not recognise. Out of all those present there was one person that struck me as being out of place and that was a monk. I just had to satisfy my curiosity. "Breandán, What's a monk doing here?"

"Wouldn't you like to know? Well he's not here to give you absolution that's for sure is he Minister?"

"No he's definitely not here for that Breandán!" He replied.

"So who is he?" I asked again. "I'm interested because the last time I saw a monk here, he had come to talk to Noel, that's all."

"Be rest assured Richard that's not the case tonight."

"Actually Richard he is here at my request," said the Minister for Agriculture, "He is here to represent one of our leading Colleges of Agriculture believe it or believe it not."

"You do surprise me Minister."

"Do you remember on your last visit I asked if you would be interested in giving the odd lecture and running some short courses at an Agricultural College. Well the college I had in mind was the one run by a small monastic order and the monk is here as their representative. Does that clarify it a little?"

"Thank you Minister, very much so." I, once again, looked around the bar and tried to gauge how many were in the party. If it was true what Breandán had said then there was no way I could cater for all of these people. This concerned me.

"Breandán." I beckoned to him to follow me and moved a discrete distance away from the Minister and the other two.

"What's wrong?" He asked.

"These people."

"Yes, what about them?"

"Well are you telling me the truth when you say a good two thirds of them are probably your guests?"

"Yes why?"

"Well, I don't know how to put this, but we have a major problem because even if I could put three or more teams over here there is no way I can handle all these contracts this coming season. No way."

"So what's the problem, do what you can and the others will have to wait."

"But who decides which ones to do first?"

"Easy. Apart from the college, which you must do, we hold a draw. Richard, don't worry leave it to me ok?"

"All right, but I just hope you're right."

"Of course I am. Now let me get you another drink and then we'll go into the Dining Room."

"Gentlemen, if I may have your attention." Breandán waited a few minutes, but still people continued talking. To get everyone's attention he picked up a heavy glass ashtray and used it as his gavel giving a number of sharp raps on the table. "Gentlemen, your attention please." Gradually the talking subsided. He waited until everyone was listening then he introduced me. "Gentlemen, some of you already know my friend Richard, but to those who do not, this is Richard James, a very trustworthy friend from England. The fact that he comes from England should not deter you; he is a man of his word who knows our ways. I can vouch for him as a person to be trusted, a person who knows a lot about life, a person who has seen many things and will no doubt see many more things. He knows that not only do I have the deepest respect for him, but as a person, I also like him. I would also like to think that, one-day; he will count me as one of his loyal friends and remember me for that. Gentleman whilst he is in our midst I offer him my hospitality and yours, he is here to do a job of work from which we will all benefit in the end, so look after him well. Gentlemen, I give you Richard." Breandán motioned me to stand up, I had not been expecting this at all and felt a little foolish to say the least as I stood there. Were they expecting me to make a speech? All eyes were on me "Well I don't know what to say, except that I haven't prepared a speech or anything. I would however like to thank Breandán for inviting me over and of course all of you for coming." My embarrassment overcome I continued, "It's wonderful to see so many of you here and I assume that most, if not all, are looking to place work with James Fruit Farms contracts department which offers a complete management package, from replanting through to grafting. On the grafting side, as you are probably aware, we have developed a technique that has shown a marked improvement over what was known as the traditional method of grafting, but I'm sure you already know this from Breandán." I looked around the room and took a drink from my glass. "Unfortunately James Fruit Farms is only a small family business with limited resources so I will not have sufficient manpower to fulfil everyone's requirement next season." I took another drink as a low murmur ensued. "Now I know some of you will be disappointed but all I can say is we'll do our best. Gentlemen thank you for your time." Phew, I was glad to get that over with and sat down.

"Gentlemen." Breandán used a spoon as a gavel to get everyone's attention,

"Gentlemen please." He waited until everywhere was quiet before continuing; "Now in order for Richard to be totally fair to everyone here I suggest that we have a draw. How many contracts could you take Richard?"

"Well if I bring two teams over, Paul could run one and I'll head up the other, then perhaps six or seven depending on the size of contract and where it is. The problem is I've also got commitments back home."

"How about if we said, including the College, a total of four definite and I take a list of names and telephone numbers then if you have chance you take on more. If not then you can make arrangements for the following season."

"Sounds good to me."

"Right that's settled then." Once again Breandán used the ashtray as a gavel. "Well gentlemen this is the deal. Richard can undertake, including the College, a total of four main contracts." Immediately a barrage of questions started to fly.

"Gentlemen, gentlemen please." Once again the ashtray was used, "Thank you. Like I was saying, Richard will undertake a definite four contracts for next season and as he progresses he maybe able to take more on. However he has agreed to come back the following season if anyone wishes him to do so. Are there any questions?" Breandán looked around. "No, well that's settled then. Noel," he beckoned the union man over.

"Yes Breandán?"

"Go to reception and ask them if they could let you have some paper and pens. Also would you get the barman to bring us an empty ice bucket as our raffle box, thanks."

With all the pieces of paper filled in and duly placed within the ice bucket I was asked to make the draw.

"The first name from the draw is, Danny Murphy near Duleek County Meath." A great cheer went up as I passed the slip of paper to Breandán.

"The second name is," I fished around in the ice bucket and pulled out another slip. "Is Seamus O'Doherty from Trim." There were more cheers as I passed the second piece over to Breandán for his safekeeping. Once again I fished about in the ice bucket.

"This is for the last contract, all right Richard?"

"Ok everyone. Here we are." I pulled the last slip from the ice bucket, "It is Patrick and Kelly O'Connor 'The Holiday Camp' near Louth." A great roar of laughter went up. I leaned over to Breandán and asked him quietly. "What's this Breandán, 'The Holiday Camp' near Louth?"

"Oh that's all right, I put that in on behalf of my cousins as they were not able to get here tonight. It's called The Holiday Camp because no one seems to do any work there." Once more he banged the ashtray on the table. "Gentlemen please. Now if those who's names have been drawn out would like to come and see me then I can write down their telephone numbers and brief details of what work they are looking to be undertaken. Richard," he turned to me. "If you would like to get the details about the College I'll get the other information together for you then you can let the people know when you are coming over. I do know that the ones drawn out not only want grafting done but also additional work such as pruning and replanting. Anyway I'll give you the details and leave the rest to you."

"That's fine Breandán and thank you."

"Gentlemen, now if the rest of you would like to adjourn to the bar Richard and I will join you in a few minutes. Thank you."

People started to make there way towards the bar as Breandán turned to me.

"My cousin's place. Because of where it is I'll have to make special arrangements for you, so if you could let me know when you intend going there I'll put that in hand."

"What sort of special arrangement?" I asked.

"Oh nothing too drastic. It's just that the area where they are is a little sensitive so I need to advise the 'local co-ordinator.' It's no big deal. Once he knows you're working up there on my instructions then you'll have no problems."

It was well after two o'clock in the morning when the last of the group departed. "I've just thought, Richard, tomorrow, or should I say today I've got a problem. I can't take you back to the airport. Not to worry, I'm sure you wouldn't mind driving yourself. So if you pop up to the farm, you know like you did the Sunday we went off to the match, then you'll find the Mercedes in the yard!"

My mind raced as I wondered how long he'd known about my little excursion? I tried not to show my surprise as I asked. "What about the keys?"

"I'll leave the keys in the ignition for you."

"What shall I do about your car once I get there?"

"Just lock it up in the car park and stick the keys in a sealed envelope with my name on and leave it at the information desk in the terminal. I'll arrange to collect it later."

"Are you sure?"

"No problem."

"Well thanks."

"Goodnight then Richard and a safe journey. I'll telephone you in the next couple of weeks."

"Goodnight Breandán and I'll look forward to hearing from you." As I made my way back to my room my thoughts returned to his comment about my visit to the farm whilst he was in Dublin. I wonder who had told him? Was it the Gardai or was it the nurse? It had certainly brought home the point that I was going to have to be even more careful in the future.

Chapter 16

"Have a good weekend Richard and I'll see you on Monday."

"Yeah see you Monday." Paul got into his car as I walked over towards the farm office. "Richard," Paul shouted through the car's open window, but I didn't hear him. So he gave a quick blast on the horn, thinking that it was just to let me know he was off, I turned to wave to him. "Richard," he called again and gave another blast to attract my attention.

"What's up?" I shouted back to him.

"Have you heard anything yet from O'Shea?"

"Don't talk to me about O'Shea."

"Why?"

"I'm not that impressed."

"Why?"

"What, after him making out everything was so urgent and all."

"Do I take that as you haven't heard anything then?"

"You've got it in one."

"Why don't you give him a call?"

"Why should I chase him? He was the one who said it was so desperate and all his cronies wanted us over there wasn't he?"

"Yes I know but that was over a month ago."

"I'm well aware of that Paul." I said somewhat testily.

"I thought you said that he was going to be in touch in the near future?"

"That's what he said. Also two of the contracts included planting out as well as winter pruning"

"The pruning is no major problem, but if they want us to replant then we ought to be over there pretty soon. Certainly in the next month or two otherwise we'll be up against the early frost and that's the last thing we want."

"I know that and he knows that."

"In that case perhaps you ought to phone him just to find out what's going, what do you think?"

"Yeah all right then." I said somewhat resignedly.

"Unless you've got any better ideas?"

"Not really, it's just that it annoys me to think I rushed around to accommodate him and he hasn't even the decency to keep his end of the bargain." We both fell silent.

"Tell you what Richard, leave it for a couple of days then phone him." I thought about Paul's suggestion for a minute.

"How about if I leave it until this time next week and if I've not heard by then I'll give him a ring?"

"Yeah that sounds fair enough to me."

"Ok, that's what I'll do then."

"How do you fancy a pint later?"

"Why not, I might just take you up on that."

It was Friday night and by tradition the lads all met up at the local for a pint and just for a change I thought I would join them. I had just had a bath and put on my clean clothes when just by chance I glanced out of the lounge window. A car that I didn't recognise and carrying four people, pulled up in front of the house.

"Anne, are you expecting anyone?"

"No love why?" She called to me from the kitchen.

"It's just that there's some people just pulled up in a car."

"Where?" she asked as she came out of the kitchen.

"Outside the house."

"Show me." I pointed towards the car and its occupants. Anne looked and shrugged her shoulders. "I don't know who it is. I've never seen that car before, have you?" She asked.

"Nope! So you don't know them at all."

"No." With that she went back to the kitchen to her baking. I tried to get a better view of the occupants and it was then that I noticed the registration. I froze. The car had a Belfast number plate and four occupants, was it coincidental I asked myself, or was I just over-reacting. After my experiences in the Republic who could blame me for over-reacting if that's what I was doing. I felt more than just a little uneasy. I stepped back from the window. I could now view them discretely; safe in the knowledge they couldn't see me. Although I felt apprehensive I was curious about the strangers and could not resist watching their every move. All four just sat there talking but every now and then they would all look towards the house. It was obvious from their actions that our house or we was the object of their discussion. I wanted to know what they wanted? I had to admit this was real scary. Then the talking stopped. All four got out of the car and led by a big-built determined looking guy headed up the path to the door. The inevitable knock followed. I managed to manoeuvre myself into a position where I could get an uninterrupted view of our uninvited guests. Unfortunately it was of little use because the two tallest of the quartet stood with their back to me and as such obscured the faces of the other two. I once again slowly backed away from where I had been stood flattening myself against the wall and ever so slowly made my way towards the kitchen. A second knock came. Shit, I thought, for Christ sake stay in the kitchen Anne. I stretched out my hand seeking the door handle. My fingers groped around to eventually close about the handle. Gingerly I opened the kitchen door. The palms of my hands were clammy. I darted through pulling it closed behind me.

"For goodness sake what's the matter?"

"That car outside. They've come here."

"Well open the door then."

"You don't understand." The words tumbled out; "It's a Belfast car."

"So what. I don't understand what you're driving at."

"After what happened when I was at O'Shea's and what I saw whilst over there..." I left the rest unsaid as I had heard a noise of footsteps approaching the back door. "Shh! Hush love." I listened intently. "I thought I heard footsteps. Did you?" I whispered. Anne shook her head.

"No. I mean I don't think so," she whispered back. We stood there in silence. Just then there was another knock at the front door. We both jumped. "Richard, you're going to have to do something." Anne said her voice sounding strained with fear.

140

"What do you suggest?" I said between clenched teeth.

"Well I don't know, haven't you any ideas?" She asked.

"No sorry I'm fresh out of them." We held our breath and waited. All went quiet. I let out my breath between pursed lips. "Phew that was close." But I had spoken too soon. Suddenly there was a knock at the back door. "Shh, don't say a word," I mouthed to my wife and placed my finger over my lips.

"Hello anyone there," a voice with a strong Belfast accent called out.

"Richard, what are we to do?" Anne whispered in a strained voice.

"Nothing," I said. "Stay quiet and keep calm that's all we can do."

"Suppose they break in?" She said her eyes wide with fear. She had a point and I couldn't give her any answer, nor could I reassure her, but my gut feel was that they wouldn't.

"Shh, keep quiet Anne. They're talking out there. Keep down I'm going to see if I can hear what they're saying." With that I crouched below the window line and I stealthily crept close to the door. I turned and signalled to Anne to crouch down low and creep over to me. I could just make out what they were saying.

"I'm sure this is the address O'Shea." Someone told us in a broad Belfast accent.

"What's his name Richard Jones?" A second person asked.

"Not Jones, James. Richard James," the first voice replied. "Not to worry we'll have to leave it for now. I did say we should have phoned before we came over."

"I know we should but we didn't."

"It's a pity. It would have been nice to have got something sorted out on the grafting front whilst we were here wouldn't it?"

"To be sure it would, still we'll just have to leave a note for him."

"Good idea Ross, have you any paper?"

"No but Sean has got a notebook with this address in. Come on then it's no good hanging around he could be anywhere." Their voices and footsteps gradually receded.

"Phew, it's all right Anne. No need to worry. They're after me doing some work. I'll go around to the front door and see if I can catch them." Anne started to cry with relief.

"Oh Richard. Oh my God Richard. Don't do that to me."

"Come here," I said gently as I took her in my arms, "It's ok, hush, it's over everything's ok my love." But she just could not stop the tears of relief came flooding out. "Hush my darling, shh it's all right, it's all right." I held her tight.

"Go on, I'll be ok. You get the door," she sniffed. "Go on now otherwise you'll miss them."

One of the four was just about to push a note through the letterbox as I opened the door.

"B'Jesus! Yer made me jump. Are you Richard James?"

"Sorry about that. Yes I'm Richard I couldn't answer the door earlier because I was in the bath and Anne, my wife, must have been down the back somewhere. What can I do for you?"

"We wanted to talk to you about some contracts." The other three joined him.

"I believe you offer a contracting service?" the one whose voice I had heard around the back spoke.

"We certainly do, would you like to come in?"

"We would love to, how are you keeping Richard."

"I'm fine and how are you? I'm sorry but do I know you?" I asked.

"Yes, don't you remember? I was at Gerry O'Shea's" His face was familiar but I was terrible at names.

"Come on come in. Anne put the kettle on please" I called through to the kitchen. "Please, take a seat." Just then Anne came through. "This is Anne my wife, I'm sorry you'll have to remind me of your name..."

"Sorry, I'm Mike McCluskey pleased to meet you Anne. We met Richard at Gerry O'Shea's place."

"Pleased to meet you Mike."

"Of course sorry Mike now I remember."

"I'm Ross O'Toole, pleased to meet you Anne."

"Pleased to meet you."

"Richard, let me introduce another farmer friend, this is Jack Callaghan. Jack this is Richard." I shook the hand proffered in friendship.

"Pleased to meet you Jack, and this is Anne my wife."

"Pleased to meet you Jack."

"I'm Sean O'Donald." The big built Irishman introduced himself, "Pleased to meet you both."

"Yes Sean's a very good friend of ours but sadly not a farmer, but we don't hold that against him, do we lads?"

"Pleased to meet you Sean."

"Tea for everyone?"

"Yes please Anne." They all replied in unison.

"Now what can I do for you all?" I asked.

"Well," it was Ross O'Toole who raised the subject, "When you were up at Gerry O'Shea's farm you did a demonstration of grafting. We have now seen the results plus, from what I've heard, you also did a lot of work for his brother, which I'm led to believe, was tremendously successful. We would now like to discuss the possibility of you taking on some work for all of us."

"Hmm, that could be a problem."

"Why?"

"Well, it's just that we've got so much work on next season I don't think we could handle any more." Pat turned to his two farming friends and shrugged his shoulders.

"So what do you think? Next season?" Mike spoke.

"Are you sure you couldn't consider us we would pay you well?"

"How many trees are you looking at?" I asked.

"Between us I would say about thirty acres. What would you say Jack?"

"I would have thought it more than that."

"Well say forty acres then."

"That's out of the question then. We just haven't the manpower."

"What about if we had some done this season and the balance done next season. Would that help?"

I thought about it for a little while. "I'll tell you what, I'll speak to Paul my partner and come back to you on it." Then I had an idea. "Perhaps we could meet you tonight and

I'll introduce you to Paul." This suggestion was met by an embarrassed silence. Sean looked around the other three before speaking.

"Well to tell you the truth Richard, we haven't anywhere to stay around here and wondered if you could suggest somewhere?"

"Now that maybe a problem but I'll make a couple of telephone calls if you like and see what I can turn up."

"That'll be great if you don't mind?"

"No problem."

Twenty minutes later and after a number of telephone calls I had eventually got something in the nearby town.

"Well the only one I've managed to find with four single rooms with en suite facilities is The White Horse and Griffin Hotel. It's nothing very grand but it's comfortable and the food's good."

"How far is it?"

"Not far. I guess about three miles. Ten minutes at the most."

"That's fine then. How do we get there?"

"Give me a couple of seconds and I'll draw you a map." I proceeded to sketch them a quick map on a piece of paper that I passed to Sean as the driver. "Thanks," he looked at the map. " Right lads let's go."

"Ok," Ross looked at his watch; "I presume you told them we would want a meal didn't you?"

"No, would you like me to phone them back?"

"If you wouldn't mind. How about you, Anne and Paul joining us for a meal?"

"What about it love?"

"If you don't mind I've got some things to get on with here." Anne smiled at the other men, " Besides you don't want me there while you're discussing business. Thank you all the same."

"Are you sure Mrs James?"

"Honestly."

"Well if you're sure you won't join us?"

"It's fine. Richard and Paul will go I'm sure."

"Then six it is. Ok Richard; if you wouldn't mind phoning them again say about an hour. Is that all right with everyone else?" They all nodded their agreement. It only took a couple of minutes and it was arranged.

The meal at the White Horse and Griffin was up to its usual high standards and everyone seemed to have enjoyed.

"Well lads has everyone had enough?" Pat looked around enquiringly, "If so we'll away to the bar then."

As we made our way to the bar I said to Ross, "I had a quick word with Paul after you left."

"And?"

"Well..."

Mike McCluskey cut me short.

"Yes Paul, what do you think?"

"I've got to admit that my feelings are that we have already more than enough work on at the moment. We've contracts here and a load of work in the Republic, what with that and the trouble you've got in Ulster then I personally don't want to know." An uneasy silence fell on proceedings.

"What Paul means is that we have a lot of work on and it's going to be a little difficult fitting it in, isn't it Paul?" I gave him a stony look then smiled at the Irishmen present.

"But that wasn't what he said was it Paul? So what did you mean?" Asked Mike.

"What I said was..."

I cut him short. "A matter of speech. What he meant was it was really my choice in the end and as such he didn't really want to know right now on what I'd decided." I smiled once again at the party hoping they had accepted my explanation. I hurriedly continued before anyone could say anything. "As Paul and I haven't really had chance to discuss the overall planning he is not aware of the full facts involved. It might be pertinent at this juncture if we could be excused for a few minutes to discuss this. Paul, perhaps I ought to go over the schedule to date as I'm sure there has been something you missed."

"I'm sure I haven't it's just that I..."

"Paul, please. We need to discuss some additional facts that I think have been overlooked." The tone of my voice said enough for him to follow me out to the reception area. I did not give him chance to say anything before I verbally stuck into him. "What the fuck are you playing at, are you mad or something?"

"What do you mean?"

"Well fancy coming out with 'the troubles you've got in Ulster' and 'I personally don't want to know' and all that old shit. What's a matter with you, you daft bastard, are you really serious, 'cause if you are then I think we might as well call it a day now." I was fuming and Paul knew it. "To tell them we have already commitments here and added to the ones in the Republic means we are going to be stretched is one thing, but to blame the troubles in Ulster on us turning down their contracts is tantamount to suggesting we are in sympathy with the IRA."

"Bollocks Richard! How can you say that?"

"Well tell me Paul, you're so fucking wonderful then how would you view it?" I asked sarcastically. He didn't reply. "Come on Paul, you're one of them and you are bluntly told by an Englishman that because of problems in Ulster that the Englishman would rather work for a known IRA overlord than a fellow Britain. What would you think."

"If you put it like that I suppose your right."

"Fuck me, is there any other way to put it?" He was quiet. I just glared at him. He thought about what he had said and in the end he had to agree with me.

"So what now?"

"I'll tell you what now. We go back in there. We agree to undertake their work and by whatever means available, we try to regain their respect. Understood?"

"But however you look at it we have not got the manpower."

"Ok, I accept that. But with careful planning we can undertake part of their work in the coming season. What we can't get finished we complete the following Spring."

"So how do you plan to do this?"

"Right, now you're thinking sensibly. Let's think how we can do this."

"Hmm, what about if you take some of their forty acres Richard and any work that O'Shea has in Ulster?"

"Mmm that's fine, but what about the three others plus the college? I've still got to do the college"

"Ok. So if I take the two contracts in County Meath?"

"Which two?"

"The guy called Murphy and the other one at Trim?"

"O'Doherty do you mean?"

"I think that was the name you said."

"Fine in theory Paul, but we still haven't heard from O'Shea yet."

"Let's assume that those two plus the Holiday Camp, or whatever its name is, comes up and the College, then are you going to be able to handle all of that?"

"What about if I take the 'Holiday Camp', the College and we agree to fitting some of their grafting in somewhere. If I get stuck then you will have to take on some of the college work. How does that sound?"

"Sounds all right. So shall we go with that then?"

"Yes. Let's get back in there before they send out a search party."

All eyes turned towards us as we came back to the table. "Well gentleman?" Ross looked at us expectantly, "Have you sorted anything out?"

Paul answered. "Sorry about that gentlemen, my fault entirely, I got hold of the wrong end of the stick completely."

"Yes it was a misunderstanding, I think we can sort something out for you." I looked around at the party and smiled.

"Good, I'm so glad to hear it Richard, I was beginning to think that maybe you were IRA sympathisers or something!"

I laughed. "No not at all Ross, as I said it was just a misunderstanding wasn't it Paul?"

"Yes, sorry about that. It's just that I didn't realise that Richard had taken on some additional labour at the farm which will release some of his more experienced staff over to our contracts side."

"So you'll be able to take the work on then?"

"Well, it's not quite cut and dried yet is it Richard. Perhaps you would explain."

"All right. As we had not planned for your work I can't promise we'll be able to get the full forty acres done this coming season, but I will guarantee we will get a fair chunk of it done. Is that fair enough?"

"We understand and we appreciate the problems we have caused by leaving it so late, don't we lads?" Jack looked to the other two farmers for their approval. Both Ross and Mike nodded their heads. "Of course we're grateful for whatever you can do."

"We will of course review things as we go along and you never know, if the weather is kind to us we may even get the whole lot done, but no promises."

"Well thanks to both of you. Now what can I get you to drink?"

"So how did you meet up with the farmers Sean?" I asked.

"Well it was really Ross I knew."

Ross then took up the story. "I don't know whether you've already been told by the O'Shea family but I used to be in the B Specials before they were disbanded and so did Mike here. Then when they were disbanded we both joined the TA and that's really how the UDR came into being."

"What through the B Specials?" I asked.

"Well sort of," interjected Mike, "The vast majority of the B Specials joined the TA so the Ulster Defence Regiment was formed."

"So where do you fit into all of this Jack?"

"Oh my past is pretty uninteresting really. I've always been in farming and my family has owned the same farm for a hundred years or more. I'm the neighbouring farm to both Pat and Mike."

"I see and you Sean?"

"That's easy I'm in the UDR and knew Ross when he was in it, in fact it was he who invited me to their lodge and that was how I met Mike. Have you ever been in the forces Richard?" His question caught me on the hop.

"Why do you ask?"

"Just wondered that's all. "

"Yes both Paul and I were in the Para's together. What made you think we were ex-forces?"

"The short haircut, usually a dead give-away!" He smiled. I took a look at my watch.

"Is that the time? Sorry gentleman we need to make a move. Now don't forget we'll do the best we can during the season and get the balance in the following season."

"All right Richard. Thanks to both of you and nice meeting you Paul." Sean stood up and said to his fellow countrymen, " Will you excuse me if I take a walk outside for a minute I could do with some fresh air."

"No that's fine Sean, you go ahead."

"In that case Richard I'll walk to the car with you." He nodded to the others, "I won't be long, it's just that it's a bit warm in here."

"Of course Sean we'll see you in a minute. Goodnight Richard."

The night was cool and dry as we made our way to the car.

"Well Sean, it's been nice meeting you and good luck in the UDR. Remember us to Belfast when you're next there."

"Sure I'll drink a toast to you and absent friends when I'm next in the mess. By the way I'll be coming back again in a few weeks. UDR annual camp and all that."

"Where are you going?" I asked.

"Wales this time so I'll try to get the weekend off and pop down to see you, that is if you don't mind me stopping over for the weekend?"

"No not at all. Best just give me a call before hand in case something has cropped up."

"Of course I would, I wouldn't just descend on you. Anyway speak to you soon," he said as he shook my hand then turned and walked back to the hotel entrance. Just before he reached it he turned and called back to me, "By the way I didn't think you would mind after all you could very soon be one of us." I went to call after him, but too late he had already gone inside, so I stood there for a moment or two wondering what he had meant by this last comment.

Chapter 17

The trees stood gaunt and bare without their foliage and with the grey and heavy skies of winter fast approaching everywhere looked so tired and drab. It was only a matter of weeks since the Irish fraternity had visited, but even so, those warm balmy summer evenings now seemed a lifetime away and the nights were fast drawing in. Strange, the way Sean had been speaking about his annual camp I would have expected to hear something from him by now. Ah well, there's maybe a good reason why I had heard nothing. My mind drifted back to earlier days when I had been in 'The Mob' and the various camps I had attended and the different manoeuvres I had been on. There was one time in particular when Paul and I went to Germany and on a weekend pass we decided to visit Munich. What a weekend that was. Those German girls were great fun, hmm! I let the trace of a smile sneak across my face at the memory of the time spent with Anna and Heidi; yes those were the days. Suddenly I was brought back to the present by the ringing of the telephone. I looked at my watch it was eleven thirty, now who the hell would be phoning this time of night?

"Hello..."

The voice at the other end cut me short.

"Sean here."

"Well I be..."

"Richard how you doing?"

"Fine, how are you? Funny I was just thinking to myself that I hadn't heard from you and was wondering what had happened."

"Oh it's a long story I'll tell you about it when I see you."

"So where are you?"

"I'm in Herefordshire at the moment but we move out early next week on manoeuvres, up into the Brecon Beacons you know. Anyway I'm phoning because I've got a weekend pass so I wondered what you were doing this weekend?"

"Nothing really planned as far as I know, why do you want to come down?"

"Well I was hoping, but if it's inconvenient..." He left the sentence unfinished.

"I'm sure there'll be no problem. Hang on I'd best just make sure to be on the safe side. Anne," I called upstairs and waited. No reply so I called again. "Annie, Sean's on the phone."

"Sorry what did you say?"

"I said Sean's on the phone and wanted to know if it was all right for him to come for a couple of days."

"I should think so. When?"

"At the weekend."

"Not tonight then."

"You must be joking. He's up in Herefordshire."

"I was going to say. Tell him that'll be fine. Oh try and find out a rough idea of time."

"Ok. Did you hear any of that Sean?"

"Not really."

"Shouldn't be any problems. Oh Anne wondered when to expect you?"

"I don't know exactly..." the pips cut across the last part. "Sorry Sean didn't catch that."

"I've run out of change, see you tomorrow..." the phone went dead.

"What did he say Richard?"

"He's coming tomorrow sometime, but he ran out of money so I don't know what time."

"Oh well not to worry."

We were just about to sit down to breakfast when there was a rat-tat-tat at the front door.

"Now who the hell could that be at this time in the morning?" I looked at Anne as I got up from the table to answer the door. She shrugged her shoulders.

"I haven't a clue," She called after me, "Unless it's Sean."

"What already? You must be..." I opened the door, "Sean what are you doing here?"

"You said it was all right."

"I know but I wasn't expecting you at this time. What did you do drive through the night?"

"Who is it Richard?"

"You had better set another place, it's Sean. Come in."

Anne came through from the kitchen. "Hello Sean, you're earlier than either of us expected."

"Is it inconvenient?"

"No not at all, come in. Here put your bag down and give me your coat." Sean passed his coat to Anne. "Would you like some breakfast?"

"A cup of tea and a slice of toast will be fine thanks."

"Are you sure? It's no trouble to put some more bacon and eggs on?"

"Well if you don't mind, that would be great."

"So what have you been up to?" I asked.

"Oh not a lot really. Say how you both keeping?"

"Oh we've been busy with the farm. Sorting out a programme for the contracting, so on and so forth, nothing too exciting. Mind you just because it's autumn doesn't mean we can stop. There are still busy times ahead. This contracting business has really taken off and it won't be long before I'll be looking at organising my work schedules over in Ireland."

" When will that be?" He enquired with interest.

"When I say soon I don't mean we actually start over in Ireland next week or anything like that."

"Oh I see. I thought you meant you were going to be going over there in the next few weeks!"

"No, nothing quite as soon as that! I've still got things to do here. What I mean is that I've got to organise my work schedules, arrange cover here, get the teams together and so on."

"Quite an operation then. Nearly as bad as a war game eh!"

"Well not quite as complex as that type of exercise." I grinned at him, "But it still takes some organising though." Sean smiled back at me.

"So when do you expect to come over then?"

"A good question!" I thought about it for a few minutes before answering. "Hmm let me see. We've got to replant two orchards up near Louth, and they're big orchards, or so I've been told. We've a load of grafting to do. Another couple of orchards to replant south of Dublin, as well as some maintenance and winter pruning. That's just for starters."

"Quite a bit then?"

"Oh and that's without the stuff I've promised to do for the college, so there's more than enough."

"Are you doing anything more for O'Shea?"

"Not this trip, well that is not directly. Why do you ask?"

"No reason. Just wondered that's all."

"We're not working for him, but we are doing some major work for his cousins."

"Oh?" Sean raised his eyebrow and suddenly became very interested at the mention of O'Shea's relatives. "Who are they?"

"Just a couple of youngsters."

"I see." He looked deep in thought.

"Why? Do you think you may know them?" I enquired in all innocence.

"Not sure, where did you say they lived?"

"I didn't." I now began to wonder why the sudden interest. "What's your big interest Sean?"

"None really, just curious that's all." He fell silent for a couple of minutes then as if to change the subject. "Say how about all of us going out for a meal tonight?"

"Sounds good to me." I called through to the kitchen. "What do you think Anne?"

"Think about what?"

"Sean's asked if we would like to go out for a meal tonight. You've nothing planned have you?"

"Nope. Well nothing in particular."

"That's settled then. So where can you recommend around here?"

"How about the White Lion?" I called through to Anne.

"Yes if we can get in. I should give Tony a ring now otherwise it will be fully booked, if it's not already."

"Ok love." I got up to get the address book. "Trouble is the White Lion is one of the most popular eating places around here, so people book up well in advance. Still Tony and Sue are good friends so we maybe lucky. Oh, by the way, they're at Louth!"

"Who's at Louth?" He asked as a puzzled frown creased his brow.

"Why the cousins of course." I replied as I reached for the phone.

"Whose cousins?" He asked.

"Hey what are you like, O'Shea's of course." I watched his face as recognition dawned.

"Gee sorry Richard. Put it down to being weary. Ok I'm with you now. So he has relatives in Louth?"

"Yeah, they have an old farm up that way called The Holiday Camp. Mind you, it's pretty run-down from what I gather." I held my hand up as a voice at the other end of the phone answered. "Hi Tony?"

"Richard you old bugger. How you doing?"

"Tony you are such a smooth talking..."

149

"It's Richard love. How d'you mean Richard who? Richard James of course, how many people called Richard do you know? Sorry about that Richard it's Sue being nosy. How's Anne?"

"She's fine. How are you both keeping?"

"Oh we're both well. Listen mate when are you coming over to see us then?"

"Well that's what I'm phoning about. We wondered if there was any chance of a table tonight?"

"Hmm, that could pose a problem but hang on a second." The line went dead. "Yes, like I was saying, " I continued my conversation with Sean, "I gather from O'Shea that these two lads need the orchards really sorting out. As I said they live up in the Louth area..." Suddenly I was cut short as Tony came back on the line. "Richard it doesn't look too promising..."

"Oh..."

"Hang on..." I could hear his muffled voice talking to Sue... "No it's all right we'll squeeze you in. Is it for you and Anne?"

"Plus another, three altogether. Will that cause a problem?"

"I wouldn't have thought so." He paused, "No that'll be fine, after all if we can get two in we can get three in, especially when it's you. So what time can we expect you?"

"Eight, eight thirty, would that be all right?"

"That'll be fine. See you later."

"See you later Tony, Bye." I called through to Anne; "I told Tony eight o'clock, so if we leave here about seven we'll get a couple of drinks before we eat. "

"Fine by me. Is that all right with Sean?"

"To be sure it's all right," he called back to Anne. "Tell me more about your last trip to Eire."

"Where was I? Ah yes, as I was saying. Breandán O'Shea had kept his word, he had more people than enough interested in our capabilities but unfortunately he had left it so long before contacting me that we had already made other commitments over here. In fact if you remember that was the main stumbling block the last time you were here. Anyway to be fair to everyone O'Shea entered the names of those who wanted to place contracts with us into a draw, his cousins included. So that's how we ended up taking on their work, they were one of the lucky ones drawn out." I looked at my watch, it was now well after ten. "Shit! Look at the time, I'll have to go otherwise I'll not be finished this side of midnight let alone in time to go out. Anne?"

"Are you still there? Have you seen the time?"

"Yeah I know, I'm just going, so I'll see you later."

"Ok see you later. Do you want anything from town?"

"Not that I can think of, bye."

"Bye love."

"If there's anything you want Sean help yourself won't you. Oh, and if you want anything from the shops, newspaper or anything then tell Anne because it's her day for shopping. Must go dad will wonder where I've got to." I grabbed my wax jacket and went out through the front door. "Thanks Richard see you later."

Anne shook her head as she entered the room, "I don't know his dad will wonder where he's got to, still never mind. Now Sean is there anything I can get you from the shops?"

"Would you get me the Express please?"

"Sure. Anything else whilst I'm out?"

"No thanks Anne."

"Ok. Well make yourself at home. I should be back in about a couple of hours. If you want any tea or coffee just help yourself. You'll find the biscuits in a tin in the cupboard and the milk's in the fridge. I can't think of anything else. Oh if the phone rings, there's an Ansaphone so don't worry about it and I'll see you when I get back. Bye."

"Bye Anne. Oh there is just one thing..."

"What's that?" She asked popping her head back round the door.

"Would it be all right if I made a couple of phone calls?"

"Is that it? Of course you can," she said as she went out the door. "See you later." She called to him as she closed the front door behind her.

The room was quite a hive of activity. There was the constant murmur of voices and the light click of computer keys as the operators were constantly updating their information. At the far end of the room sat a number of printers constantly spewing out information of some form or another. A young Army Clerk removed the printouts and placed them into different coloured folders, which were then placed into various trays to be distributed throughout the system at some point in time. Some of the printouts were stamped URGENT and FOR IMMEDIATE ACTION, these were invariably passed through the system via different operators to their overlords for their action. Everywhere there was a constant low hum of whispered voices as people passed messages to and fro, from one section to the next. The whole area was one large room sub-divided into smaller units by hessian covered screens, each of these smaller units would have a sector number allocated to it. This was part of the eyes and ears of Military Intelligence.

A Colonel approached one of the many sectors and entered between the screens.

"Morning Frank, any news?"

"Morning Sir, no everything seems quiet. Mind we could do with some extra input south of the border."

"Yes, couldn't we just. What's in from Ulster?"

"Only routine. Oh one thing sir."

"What's that?"

"We've had contact from one of our cells over here on exercise. It seems as if there is some possible interest in a target south of the border."

"Is the target known?"

"Just getting it checked out will let you know as soon as I have the info."

"All right Frank as soon as possible then. Get some urgency on this one." The Colonel turned to leave when Frank stopped him in his tracks, "Excuse me Sir, there's something coming through now." Both men peered at the VDU as what appeared to be a string of mixed numbers and letters showed up on the screen in front of them. Frank quickly input a password and a menu appeared. He selected the encryption option and input a further password. Suddenly the screen went blank to be refilled by a written message.

'CONTACT WITH TARGET MADE. TARGET PLANS TRIP IN NEXT MONTH OR TWO WILL KEEP INFORMED. PLEASE ADVISE FURTHER. ANTICIPATE OPERATION IN LOUTH AREA.' Message timed 11:23.

"What do you make of that Frank?"

"Don't really know sir. All I know is our overview in the south is very sketchy indeed and we desperately need someone in there."

"I agree, but the problem now becomes how do we get close enough to O'Shea to be of use. The ideal would be to turn someone already working with him, one of his top men, but there's little or no chance of that so we have to use whatever means we have at our disposal."

"Well what about the target in this message?"

"Hmm, can't say for definite, but he is a possible. Mind you, we're still in the very early stages of this covert operation and anything could happen."

"Oh sure it could, but isn't he worth considering. Couldn't we do some exploratory digging, even if it was not a full p-vet at this stage?"

The Colonel stared at Frank for a minute. "You know Frank, you might just have something there." He looked back at the message on the screen and drummed his fingers on the desk. "Hmm." He suddenly stopped drumming on the desk, looked around at the faces that were staring at him, then back to Frank. "Ok, go for stage one and let me know. Get a message to Sector tell them to cultivate and observe. Check out any military background. This is to be a covert operation so close surveillance for next twenty-four hours, then withdraw. I want all information as it comes in. Oh and Frank, stage one only."

"Yes Sir."

The time was now eleven forty-five and Sean woke with a start from his deep sleep. It took him a minute or two to gather his senses wondering what the noise was, then he realised it was the phone. Without thinking he picked up the receiver, "Hello, who? No I'm sorry there's no-one here by that name." He put the phone down slipped on his coat and let himself out of the front door.

A car with a Belfast registration slowed down and stopped opposite the telephone box situated on the hill outside the old telephone exchange. A tall well-built man in army uniform got out and carefully locked the door. He checked both up and down the street before crossing the road to the public call box. Picking up the receiver he then dialled a number, waited a few minutes before speaking into the mouthpiece. He nodded his head on a number of occasions as if agreeing with someone without saying anything further. His parting words were "I understand mother and I will be in touch. Yes of course, I'd expect to be back home tomorrow sometime. Yes I'll let you know the time later. Ok, bye mother." Once more he checked both up and down the road crossed over, unlocked his car and turned it around and headed back the way he had come.

Chapter 18

"So Richard which way do I go?" Sean asked as he unlocked the doors.

"Turn left and at the main road turn right, down the hill then left."

"Left then right, down the hill then left?"

"Correct. We can take my car if you like Sean."

"We've already been over that one, just give me the directions ok. Are you all right in the back Anne?"

"I'm fine thanks Sean."

"You in Richard?" Sean asked as the engine came to life.

"Yeah, you can go now." I closed my passenger door and settled back in the seat as the car moved smoothly forward.

"Bugger." Sean swore and hit the brakes.

"What's up?" I asked.

"Sorry I've left my wallet in my overnight bag." I reached down to look for the door handle but Sean had all ready opened his door.

"I'm there Richard just pass me the front door key and I'll shoot in and get it." I passed him the key and settled back into the seat to wait for him. I could just make out the outline of his body as he disappeared through the front door.

"Richard you should have gone back with him."

"Why?"

"Well he may not be able to find the light switches."

"Rubbish. He'll be all right," and as if on cue we saw the light go on in the hall, then in the sitting room.

Sean quickly pulled a small pencil torch from his pocket and moved rapidly up the stairs to the master bedroom. He edged the door open gently making a mental note on its position before hand. In the light of the torch he could make out the outline of the telephone next to the bed. He picked up the receiver and dialled a number. He let it ring four times then replaced the receiver. He shone the torch onto the second hand of his watch mentally ticking off the seconds as he did. The phone rang. He grabbed the receiver.

"Hello, is that City Cleaners?"

"Yes, can I help sir?"

"Could I speak to Collections as I want to arrange for some express dry cleaning to be done."

"Anything in particular?"

"It's just that I'm here for a short stay and my mother would like a couple of things taken care of."

"That's fine sir. How soon do you want the cleaning done, we do offer an express service if you are in a hurry."

"Can you be sure to get them done in two hours at the most?"

"No problem sir. I'll arrange it now. Will you be there?"

"No I have to go out in the next ten minutes, but perhaps you can make the necessary arrangements just in case?"

"Fine sir, leave it to me." The phone clicked and he replaced the handset. Carefully he pulled the door to where he judged it to have been prior to his entering the bedroom and started back down the stairs.

Outside the night air was crisp as he made his way back to the car.
"Sorry about that. I thought I had left it in my overnight bag but I've hunted through all my things and can't find it anywhere, so it must be out here. Excuse me Richard." Sean leaned across and opened the glove compartment and after a couple of minutes of scrabbling around in the compartment he withdrew his hand triumphantly waving the wallet. "Well I'll be damned, it was here all the time, sorry about that folks. I must have left it there this morning after I paid the toll at the Dartford Tunnel. I really must get out of doing that otherwise one day I'll lose it for good. Anyway all's well that ends well so lets go. You did say left out onto the main road didn't you Richard?"
"Yes then at the 'T' junction turn right and go down the hill."

As Sean drove off in the direction of the hill a white van from 'The City Cleaners' reversed into the farm entrance. Two men dressed in dark clothing emerged carrying two cases. They walked to the front door. One of them tapped on the door. They waited there was no reply. Whilst they waited a blue Volvo stopped across the entrance whilst the driver studied his map. His passenger got out and made his way towards the farmhouse whistling 'Three Blind Mice' as he did so.
"You from City Cleaners?" He asked curtly.
"Yeah, where you from?"
"Oh my mother sent us to check that everything was ok." He answered, this time there was a definite trace of an Irish accent present.
"It's fine so you can leave us to it."
The stranger turned back towards the Volvo and started to whistle 'Three Blind Mice'. The door on the Volvo shut with a dull thud and the car moved off slowly towards the 'T' junction, but stopped once again a discrete distance from the farm entrance. The passenger once more got out and as if he had all the time in the world sauntered up to the 'T' junction where he withdrew into the shadows. There he stayed watching, just watching.

The car park of The White Lion was already quite full as Sean swung his car into an empty space.
"Well not bad it's only just after seven thirty, gives us time for a couple of drinks before we eat."
"Seems a popular place."
"Yeah, like I said earlier it's well known for its cuisine and people travel from quite a distance, don't they Anne?"
"Yes, but it's not only that. It's a typical 'olde worlde' country pub and people come here because they like the atmosphere."
Once inside Sean could see what we had meant by atmosphere. The whole ambience of this sixteenth century coaching inn was enhanced by the low oak beamed ceiling and the scent of burning apple wood from the large log fire roaring away in the Inglenook fireplace at the end of the bar. Just then Tony caught sight of us.

"Well hello my friend. Good to see you Richard." He leaned forward ignoring me as he took Anne's hand in his and pulled her forward to give her a light kiss on her cheek. "Hmm, you're looking well my darling. Look who's here Sue." Sue stuck her head round from the other bar.

"Hello strangers and how are you two?"

"We're fine," I called back, "How's life treating you?"

"Hang on a minute Richard and I'll come through."

"Anne, what can I get you to drink?"

"A white wine please Tony."

Just then the bar door opened and Sue appeared.

"Hello Richard," she kissed me lightly on the cheek. "Anne, lovely to see you." She gave Anne a kiss on the cheek. "It's been a while since we've seen you two, what have you both been up to?"

"Oh the usual things, nothing much."

"Now I know that's not true Richard."

"How do you mean not true?" I feigned a mock hurt.

"Of course it's not. I saw your parents in town the other week and your dad told me you've been over to Ireland. He was saying that it looks as if the contracting side is going to be quite big with you. Am I right?"

"Well, it's looking promising let's say that. By the way let me introduce a friend of ours from Ireland. This is Sean, Sean O'Donald."

Sue turned towards Sean and held out her hand. "Hello Sean, so you're from over the water then?"

"Yes."

"The Republic?"

"No Ulster. Why, do you know Eire?"

"Not particularly. Here let me take your coat."

"Thanks." Sean slipped off his coat to reveal his UDR uniform.

"Ooh," she said looking him up and down, "So you're in the army, I like men in uniforms!" She said rather mischievously. "Which division, or regiment or whatever they call it, are you in?"

"I'm in the UDR. The Ulster Defence Regiment."

"Is that what you were in Richard?" She looked at me and smiled. "No, of course not silly me, it was the Parachute Regiment wasn't it?" I nodded and grinned at her.

Things were progressing just fine until who should walk in but Chris O'Flynn a little worse for wear. He pushed his way through to the bar, barging his way passed Sean.

"Hello Tony I'd be having a pint of Guinness please." He pulled out a handful of coins and dropped them on the bar.

"Thank you Chris anything else?"

"No." He replied in a surly voice. He picked up his pint staggered slightly and knocked into Sean spilling some of his drink.

"Clumsy bastard, can't a man have a drink in peace without the army being everywhere..." then through his stupor light of recognition dawned. This was no local army lad, but a mountain of a man wearing a UDR uniform. He was the enemy. That was it Chris turned on Sean and let forth a tirade of abuse.

"You fucking UDR pig, piss off back to Belfast and the six counties. You're shit; you've betrayed your brothers. You're filth and..." His tirade was stopped in full flow as Sean turned on him and in a raised voice said something in what must have been Gaelic. People turned around to see what the commotion was. Sean then lowered his voice and spoke very quietly to Chris.

"Are you tired of living my friend, because you could be signing your 'teastas bais' if you're not careful and that of your family, so piss off before I embarrass my friends and really lose my temper. Understand?"

With that last remark Chris glared at Sean and with pint clutched in his hand he pushed his way away from the bar to a table as far away from us as possible. The excitement over, conversation in the bar returned to normal.

"Sorry about that Sean. You must think we are terrible. He's harmless enough normally."

"Who is he?" Sean asked Tony. "Oh that's Chris O'Flynn. He's one of the two local Irishmen who live in the village."

"Do you know him then?" Sean asked me.

"Yeah, everyone knows O'Flynn. Like Tony says, he's no real problem, well not normally." I cast a glance in O'Flynn's general direction "What did you say to him?" I asked.

"Oh just this and that." Sean was very non-committal.

"Well whatever it was you said Sean it seemed to have a devastating affect, didn't it Susan."

"I should say so Anne." Susan looked over towards Chris O'Flynn then back to Sean. "So what did you say Sean?"

"Oh I just pointed out he ought to be a little more careful otherwise he could be signing his death certificate and that of his family. That's all."

"Is that what 'teastas bais' means?" I asked.

"Yes Gaelic for death certificate."

"Who would like another drink?" I enquired changing the subject.

"I'll get these," Tony said, "So come on drink up. Anne what'll it be?"

It didn't take long before the front door clicked open and the two dark suited men from the 'City Cleaners' and carrying briefcases slipped quietly inside closing the front door behind them. One of the men made his way upstairs whilst the other carried his case into the front room and flicked on a pencil beam torch. He carefully and discretely shone it around the room making a careful mental note where everything was. Moving over to the telephone he placed his case on the floor where he opened it to reveal a comprehensive tool-kit. He took out a small screwdriver and gripping the torch in his teeth he deftly unscrewed the four screws holding the outer cover on. He proceeded to remove the cover from the telephone to reveal the bell, wiring and the associated circuit board. From his case he took out a small box containing a number of small rectangular blocks from which he selected one. Next he cut some short lengths of wire, stripped the ends and with a small wire-wrap tool he connected the rectangular block. He then proceeded to remove a number of the telephone's circuit connections from the connector block and reconnected these into the opposite side of the small rectangular block in his hand. The small flying leads he had previously connected to the block he now inserted into the telephone's circuit connector block. At the same time as the man downstairs completed his task his colleague upstairs did likewise. A last check to confirm all was connected and he replaced the cover and secured it. The whole operation had taken less than five minutes and was completed in total silence. The man from upstairs returned to the sitting room and now was the first time anyone spoke.

"Ok all finished upstairs."

"Right you cover in here, I'll check out the car and set that up."

"How we doing for time?" The first guy checked his watch.

"I would say no more than sixty at the most. Will that be long enough?"

"Plenty. Anyway it would have to do whatever."

"Ok." With that the first guy moved off in the direction of the kitchen.

"Lamp-lighter come in, over." The radio in the blue Volvo crackled into life.

"Hi Lamp-lighter go ahead."

"White Caucasian male heading towards target over."

"Roger. How far away over?"

"Hundred or more."

"Roger." The driver swept the area in front with his night vision binoculars. There he was heading towards him.

"Lamp-lighter, target in sight over and out."

A lone man walked along the road towards a blue Volvo. He crossed over and turned towards the entrance to James Fruit Farms. The man was the father of Richard James. He was now in full view of the driver of the Volvo.

"Shit," the driver muttered under his breath. "Lamp-lighter, Lamp-lighter, come in."

"Lamp-lighter, go ahead over."

"We have a possible problem. James senior on way over."

"Shit! Over."

"I'm going to intercept. Over."

"Be careful. Over and out."

The driver from the Volvo got out of the car and complete with map in hand walked towards the lone figure that was walking towards the farm. "Excuse me, I say, excuse me." He called after the man. The man stopped as the driver approached him. "Good evening, I wonder if you could help me." He said as he produced the map, "I seemed to have taken a wrong turn and have got myself lost."

"Where are you heading for?"

"A place called Chilham."

"Oh you're a long way from there. Here let me show you. Have you got a torch because the light out here is terrible?"

"Yes back in the car. Tell you what perhaps you could show me over there."

"Yes ok." They made their way back to the blue Volvo.

The driver opened the door in pretence to search for a torch. "Sorry about this, I thought I had one in here. Sorry, this is stupid. Look why don't you get in out of the cold and show me by the light in here."

Inside the house, the back door opened quietly and the first man manoeuvred his way into the kitchen blending in with the shadows. His feet travelled noiselessly across the floor as sure footed as a cat's as he made his way back into the front room.

"Ok, that's the car done. How are you getting on?"

"Just one more item to photograph then I'm done." There was a slight flash. "That's it. Lets go."

The two men checked that everything was as they had found it. All was correct. One last check as they silently pulled the door closed behind them.

As Mr James showed the driver the route on the map a white van with the name 'City Cleaners' on its side slowly pulled out from the entrance to James Fruit Farms and headed off passed a blue Volvo towards the main road.

"Thank you for your help. I can see where I went wrong now. Here let me let you out."

"Now don't forget up to the 'T' junction turn left and out onto the A2."

"Thank you Mr... sorry I didn't catch your name?"

"Mr James."

"Ah yes thank you Mr James. Good night now." With that the Volvo's engine roared into life and slowly moved off towards the 'T' junction.

"Lamp-lighter come in. Over."

"This is Lamp-lighter. Over."

"Target complete. Rendezvous at 'T' junction over and out."

"Roger. Well done out."

Just after eleven thirty Richard unlocked the front door to let Anne and Sean in.

"Sean that was a lovely meal and thank you very much."

"No problem, it's the least I can do. I hope you enjoyed it Anne and I'm sorry about the aggravation."

"It was lovely Sean and don't worry about the hassle. That's O'Flynn for you I've always said the man's a pain but Richard says that he's no trouble really, but there you are. I reserve my judgement. Does anybody want anything before we go to bed?"

"No thanks my love."

"Sean, what about you, tea or coffee?"

"No thanks Anne."

"Are you sure?"

"Honestly I'm fine."

"By the way Sean, you never did say what you did in the UDR, so what is it?"

"Didn't I Richard! Well I thought you had worked it out?"

"No."

"I can't say too much but let's say Military Intelligence and leave it at that."

Chapter 19

It was a little over a month since Sean had spent the weekend with us. The clocks had now gone back and winter fast approached. Normally this time of year we would be doing maintenance around the farm, but this year was different. The contracting business was taking off and unlike other farmers, who at this time of year would be cutting back on casual labour, we were in fact recruiting additional staff. We had become the victims of our own success. At long last I had managed, after a lot of juggling and a lot of interviewing, to put together two separate teams to take to Ireland. Paul would manage one team and head south of Dublin and the other team would accompany me up to the 'Holiday Camp'. The farm that was owned by the O'Connor brothers cousins of Breandán O'Shea, was situated just south of the border not that far from Louth.

"Can you think of anything I may have forgotten Paul?" "No I can't think of anything."

I went over everything one more time and ticked off each item as I did so.

"So when are we aiming to leave for Dublin?" Paul asked.

"I thought we ought to try to get on the afternoon ferry from Holyhead this Saturday. What do you reckon?"

"Well we certainly don't want to leave it much later than that do we? Have you spoken to O'Shea yet?"

"No not yet. I thought I'd get everything sorted out first before phoning him."

"Hmm. I suppose that's the best way."

"Well at least then we can give him an idea of when we expect to get to the Tara."

"Ok. Is there anything you want me to do?"

"Can't think of anything. We'll need to take your car as well as mine."

"That's fine. Right if there's nothing else then I'll get back to what I was doing."

"Ok Paul I'll catch up with you later." The door closed behind him.

I picked up the telephone and dialled the number of the travel agents, "Good afternoon, is that City Travel?"

Suddenly the tape recorder kicked into life and the man sitting there with headphones on stared impassively ahead as the metallic clicks of the relays in the exchange sounded through his headphones. He reached a hand up towards a small volume control on the loudspeaker above his head so his colleague could also hear what was going on. A thin blue line of smoke curled lazily upwards from the cigarette held between the nicotine stained fingers of the operator. The small cramped area in the back of the Transit van was crammed full of electronic wizardry. The clicks from the exchange stopped and on a digital counter a number displayed.

"Looks like a local number." The man wearing the cans said in a matter of fact way.

"Yeah." His colleague stated with total disinterest. "Can you run a check as to exactly where on this equipment?"

"Of course, but wait till they reply."

"Good afternoon Jane speaking at City Travel can I help you?" The disembodied female's voice sounded from the loudspeaker above their heads. There was a slight pause and the sound of someone breathing. Then a male voice crackled through the loudspeaker.

"Good afternoon is that City Travel?"

"Yes sir. What can I do for you?"

"I'd like to book two cars return passage on the Holyhead to Dublin ferry for Saturday afternoon if possible."

"Please hold a minute thank you." The line went dead as she put the call on hold.

The operator's colleague spoke for the first time. "So where is it?"

"There's no need to check it out," the operator replied. "I know exactly where City Travel is. It's near to the City centre down Sun Street. Do you know where I mean?"

"I think I do. Anyway you'd best advise control about this latest development."

"I'll wait a few minutes 'till we've something more definite to go on."

"Sure." He took a deep breath in exasperation and shook his head. "I didn't mean right at this moment, My God what do you think I am some sort of new boy?"

"No but you do rather..."

"Shh listen..."

The female's voice sounded through the loudspeaker.

"Sorry for keeping you sir. We only have places on the two fifteen sailing, would you like to take two on that?"

"Yes please."

"Thank you sir. How many people will be travelling apart from the drivers?"

"Two."

"Thank you sir, and in what name shall I book the passage?"

" Richard James and Mr Paul Jones."

"Thank you sir, and how do you wish to pay for the tickets?"

"Account."

"The name of the account please?"

"James Fruit Farms."

"Just a minute please." Once more there was silence as the girl put the call on hold. "Thank you sir, that's fine. Your booking is confirmed for two cars open return sailing on the 1415 Holyhead to Dublin Saturday afternoon. The return to be left open. The tickets are in the name of a Mr Paul Jones and Mr Richard James charged to James Fruit Farms. Now would you like me to post these off to you or do you wish to collect either from ourselves or the Port of departure?"

"I'll collect them from you. Can you confirm arrival time?"

"Certainly sir, one moment please." There was a short pause. "Yes sir the crossing time is about three and a half hours. Depart Holyhead 1415 and arrive Dublin Ferry Terminal at 1745."

"Thank you."

"Would that be all sir."

"Yes thank you."

"Thank you sir for booking with City Travel Goodbye."

"Goodbye." There was a metallic click as the receiver was replaced, followed by another click as the tape recorder switched automatically to standby. The man with the headphones pushed them from his ears so they hung loosely about his neck.

"Well there we are. I wonder where he is heading?" He pushed back his chair and took out another cigarette. His face was momentarily thrown into stark relief by the flare of the match as he lit it.

It was Friday night and a typical November night at that. Damp, foggy and cold. Because of the distance involved we had all ready loaded which meant we could get straight off at four in the morning without any hold ups.
"What time's the ferry?" asked Mike one of the guys travelling with Paul.
"Two fifteen, so that means we leave here at four in the morning!" I replied.
"You're joking. Aren't you?"
"No, I've never been more serious in my life."
"Holly shit. Is there such an unearthly hour?" He took a deep breath. "I best stay up in case I sleep in. It's not really worth going to bed is it?" He looked at me and grinned.
"It's all right for you Mike you're just a passenger and can sleep in the car. What about Paul and I. We've got to drive." He seemed to think about that.
Paul looked about him at the worsening weather. "I don't like the look of this fog. It seems to be getting thicker."
"I know. It's not very good at all."
"I hope it clears before we leave."
"So do I otherwise it'll be a long slow drive and we could even be struggling to catch the ferry." I grinned and winked at Paul. "What do you reckon then Paul, do you think we ought to leave at three?"
"Hmm. Maybe!"
"What! Three in the morning?" Mike exploded.
"Well if this gets much thicker we'll have major problems won't we Paul?"
"You bet."
"But, but..." Mike was lost for words. "Sod it, then I'm definitely not going to bed. Three o'clock in the morning, are you sure?"
"Sure."
"Shit man, that's bad news." Seeing Mike's face was a picture and I couldn't contain myself anymore. I exploded with laughter and so did Paul.
"You sods you really had me going there. I suppose it could be worse, it could be snowing."
"Many a true word Mike. Don't tempt providence. Anyway, thinking about it perhaps we ought to leave half an hour earlier than planned."
"Hang on I was only joking!"
"I know, I meant because of the fog not snow you prat."

It was only five thirty Saturday evening as the Holyhead to Dublin ferry tied up alongside the terminal in Dublin. We had arrived fifteen minutes early because of the strong tail winds we had encountered on the crossing. The ferry's very structure had shuddered from the shock of waves that crashed relentlessly against it as it ran ahead of the merciless sea. The bows would ride high on the crest of a wave, then in the next breath would rush headlong down into the greyish green depths of a massive trough, only to be spewed back up onto the crest of the next wave. In spite of all this we had arrived in one piece and ahead of schedule. There was a metallic clang that reverberated through the car deck as the ramp was lowered into place. Trucks and car engines roared into life ready for the off. Paul sat close on my tail as we broke out into the open. We now joined the steady stream of traffic away from the B & I terminal on to East Wall road, turning right towards Fairview Park and Tolka River to join the N1.

The passenger in the blue Volvo softly whistled 'Three Blind Mice' as he photographed the occupants of the two cars, with Maidstone registration plates, as they slowly drove passed where he was parked. The driver waited until some two or three other cars had passed before indicating to pull out and forced his way into the traffic. They followed the two cars at a discrete distance making their way towards Fairview Park and Tolka River.
"Control over." The transceiver crackled with white noise. The passenger, a man with a soft Irish accent, tried again. "Control over." This time he was successful.
"Control go ahead."
"This is Dublin. Targets moving along East Wall road. Now turning right northwards towards Fairview Park and Tolka River. Over."
"Roger Dublin."
The passenger resumed whistling 'Three Blind Mice'.

As we joined the N1 the traffic from the city ground to a halt. "I knew this would happen." I muttered to myself.
"Did you say something Richard?" One of the team in the back asked.
"No just muttering under my breath about this bloody traffic. I know it's not as bad as London is but nevertheless it's bad." Just then we started to move. Some forty-five minutes later we started to pick up speed, then at Santry the traffic disappeared and we had open road ahead of us for the first time since leaving the ferry terminal. I checked in my rear view mirror to make sure Paul was still with us and that I hadn't lost him on route. He was still there.
"Control. Over."
The disembodied voice of control sounded thin and tinny through his transceiver.
"Control. Go ahead. Over."
"Control this is Dublin. Targets not far from Santry heading towards border. Over."
"Roger Dublin. Standby for further instructions. Over."
"Roger Control standing by. Over" The transceiver went dead except for the 'whooshing' background sound of white noise.

It was not long before I was once more driving along the now familiar tree-lined lane towards the Tara Hotel's entrance. To both Paul and I it was home from home. Nothing much had changed since my last visit except that the trees, that had been full of foliage, now stood gaunt and bare. Their leaves dry and brown, lay like a carpet on the lane before me, were thrown up in the air by the turbulent slipstream of the car as we drove through them. I swung the car into the hotel car park with Paul not far behind.

"Dublin. Over." The small personal transceiver in the Volvo one again crackled into life.
"Dublin. Go ahead control. Over."

"Dublin this is Control, Area requests Sit. Rep. Over."

"Roger Control. Standby." There was a slight pause, "Control this is Dublin. Both cars still travelling towards border. Cancel, cancel. Both indicating to turn right into Tara Hotel. Repeat both cars right into Tara Hotel. Over."

"Roger Dublin. Did you say Tara? Over?"

"Roger Control. I repeat Tara Over."

"Roger Dublin. Area advised. Return base. Over."

"Roger Control. Confirm returning base? Over and Out." The driver of the blue Volvo accelerated passed the entrance to the Tara and continued heading northwards towards the border.

I got out of my car and stretched. "Well we're here at last."

A muted cheer went up. Having grabbed our bags and locked the car we all made our way to reception. I was shattered after our sixteen-hour journey but judging by the lack of conversation I was not the only one.

"See you all later," I half muttered to everyone and wearily trudged up the stairs to my room where I immediately slumped onto my welcoming bed.

"Well lads how do you feel now you've had a bite of something to eat and a bit of a rest after your long drive here?"

"Well I don't know about the rest but I'm certainly feeling lot better now thanks Mr O'Shea."

"Good. Now don't tell me you're Terry?"

"No I'm..."

"No of course not. Are you Mike?"

"Yeah, I'm Mike and he's Terry," Mike indicated the one sitting opposite.

"Yeah, I'm shorter than Mike, he's about six foot aren't you Mike?"

"Six two to be precise. Also I've got more hair than him!"

"Rubbish. It only looks that way because I've got a high forehead."

"Yeah so high it's nearly on top of your head."

"No it's not. Look!" Terry tipped his head down and tugged at his hair.

"Hey Terry you can't even see the join."

"Don't you start Barry I have enough with him." Terry pointed at Mike.

"Me? I don't know what you mean."

"Yes you. You long streak of..."

"Here you are lads." Paul interrupted their banter.

"What's yours Bas pint of Bitter?"

"No mild."

"I'll get it right one day. I don't know why I always mix yours and Terry's up. There you are Tes a pint of Smethwicks. Breandán there's yours and Barry you've got yours. Richard yours was a Smethwicks, Lager for you Mike, Smethwicks for you Frank and that must be my Lager. Everyone got a drink? Speak now or forever hold your peace!"

"Cheers lads may your stay here be a happy one. That brings me to a more serious note, work. Now who is working where Richard?"

"Paul's taking Frank and Barry with him down to the elderly guy's farm. Sorry his name escapes me for the moment."

"Don't worry I know who you mean. So does that mean you'll be going to the 'Holiday Camp' with Mike and Terry?"

"The Holiday Camp. Now Sounds good to me," said Mike.

"You've not seen it yet," Retorted Breandán, "You may not be smiling once you get there!" He winked at me. "As I was saying, I gather you'll be taking Mike and Terry with you then?"

"Yes. Then once we're finished up there I have to fit in the work at the college, but that won't be for some time yet."

"Right, then let me see." Breandán paused deep in thought.

"Is there a problem then?" I enquired.

"No. No not at all." He paused again. "Hmm. Tell you what." He looked over to Paul. "If you leave your car in the car park here I'll arrange to get you, Frank and Barry to old man Fitzpatricks place and Richard..." He paused again.

"What's wrong?" I asked.

"Nothing, it's just that they've only got an old van so you'll have to take your car."

"That's not a problem."

"Sure you don't mind? It's just that I can't see a way round it."

"No that's fine."

"Any questions Richard?"

"No I don't think so." I looked around the lads, "Anyone any questions?" They all shook their heads.

"Good. Oh there is one more thing. In the village there are two pubs. The one on the hill is strictly off limits to all of you."

"Why?" Asked Mike.

"Because there are certain people in my country who don't take too kindly to strangers, especially Englishmen."

"He means the IRA." Someone said. That caused a sobering thought among the newcomers.

"So just remember what I said, otherwise my two men," he pointed out two individuals sitting at a table a discreet distance from us, "Will be watching you!" I was determined not to let him get away with this. Sure the two guys he had pointed out to us I knew from my last visit were two top IRA men. In fact they were the two who, with him, had tried to recruit me into their service. I had to think of something to lighten the mood and to stop Breandán from getting away with this.

"Bah, watching us. They'd never be up early enough to keep an eye on us Englishmen, would they lads?" I looked around the table grinning.

"No chance!" They answered in unison.

"Touché Richard, touché. On that note I'll leave." With that he got up with a faint smile on his lips, raised his hand in acknowledgement and left.

Chapter 20

Suddenly I was wide-awake. My heart thumped deep inside my chest, something had disturbed what had been a really deep sleep. Every nerve in my body taut and stretched as I strained listening for the slightest sound. The room was still in darkness and I had no idea of what the time was as I scrabbled to switch on the bedside light. I screwed up my eyes up against the rude intrusion of the bright light and sat there listening. The phone rang again making me jump. So that was what had woken me, the bloody phone. I let out the breath that I had subconsciously being holding onto as I swung my legs out of the bed. My heart was still pounding as I picked up the phone.

"Yes, hello." I said into the mouthpiece testily, "Who?" I looked at my watch, "Noel, do you know what time it is. It's six o'clock in the morning and Sunday morning at that..."

"But he was very insistent Mr James."

"Don't call me Mr James," I said angrily, "I've told you before call me Richard understand. Richard." I took a deep breath, "Anyway who was very insistent Noel Mr O'Shea did you say?" My exasperation was showing. "What the hell does he want at this time in the morning?"

"I don't know sir, but shall I send him up or will you..."

"No you won't show him up here. Tell him to wait..." I paused.

"Will that be all sir?"

"No hang on Noel." I roughly pushed my fingers through my untidy hair before answering, "Please tell Mr O'Shea I'll be down just as soon as I've washed and dressed..." I had now calmed down, "Say about ten to fifteen minutes or so. Sorry about that."

"That's ok sir, sorry I had to wake you so early. There was a click as Noel cleared the line.

"Good morning Richard." Breandán greeted me full of the joys of spring, "Now I thought you said yesterday that you English would always be up before us Irish and my men would not be able to live with your hours! Hmm, well I think..."

"Breandán you're treading on very dangerous ground!" He caught my look and thought better of it, so he just smiled.

"I think perhaps we'll leave it then!" He said

"I think so don't you?"

"Coffee?" He asked indicating the empty cup before me.

"Yes please."

"One or two sugars?"

"This god forsaken hour on a Sunday morning I think I need two to sweeten me up." He put two spoonfuls of brown cane sugar into the steaming cup of fresh coffee.

"Sorry to call you at such an unearthly hour..."

"So what's the problem?"

"It's not so much of a problem, it's more of I needed to see you alone before you went off to Louth..."

"But Breandán, that's not for another couple of hours yet." I said in exasperation, "So

165

why couldn't it wait?"

"Sorry Richard, but please hear me out."

"Ok, so what's the urgency?"

"Well as I was saying, I needed to see you alone before my cousins arrived and as I've got to go out within the next half hour I was left with no alternative. Anyway when you get to the farm I'll need to pick you up so give Mike and Terry some excuse about having to go off with me about some other business all right?"

"What about my car? They'll think it strange that I don't take my car."

"Tell them it's easier to go in one car and you are going with me as I know the area."

"Why?"

"Richard, think of something."

"But why not my car?"

"Because you are in bandit country and have English number plates. Think Richard think."

"Ok. So I go with you to do what?"

"I'm going to take you to meet the local Area Commander."

"Why?"

"Because of protocol. If I don't introduce you then you are fair game for his soldiers."

"How do you mean, fair game for his soldiers?"

"Richard please trust me. Allow me to take you to meet him that way protocol is upheld and you and your men are left alone."

"Who is this man and what's his name?"

"I've already told you. He is the local Area Commander and in his own back yard he is in control. Believe me it's for the best." I thought about this whilst sipping my coffee, so this is why we're being paid so much.

"Ok, so what's this guys name?"

"His name doesn't matter."

"Maybe not to you, but to me it does."

"Why does it matter?"

"Because if I'm meeting this geezer then I need to know what to call him. Unless you expect me to stand to attention call him Sir and salute him. In which case you can piss off." Breandán sat in silence as I finished my coffee.

I poured myself another cup of coffee. "Anyway, what's the set up. If I don't meet this bloke what's the worst that happens? Or don't I ask?"

"Of course you can ask." He paused, "Well I suppose the worst is you could find yourself dragged off in the middle of the night and dealt with." He looked at me, "I don't really know as I said he is master in his own patch." He fell silent again.

"What's the least?" I asked.

"The very least is that you and your men would have to surrender a high percentage of your earnings as an insurance."

"Insurance against what?" I asked indignantly.

"Oh Richard, do yourself a favour and do as I request."

I ignored Breandán's comment and pressed my point. "Insurance against what?"

He gave an exasperated sigh. "Surely you know by now?"

"No Breandán, I want you to explain to me what will happen if I don't pay this, this umm insurance as you call it?"

"Well, oh this is stupid." He was getting impatient.

"No it's not. It's just that I need to know."

"Why, what difference will it make?"

"Because Mike and Terry may ask, so tell me."

"Ok. If you don't pay the insurance then things can happen."

"Like what for instance?"

"You could start having accidents at work. Damage to your stock so you'll need to replace it all these sort of things. Say you were a civil engineer building a road then you would require raw materials to be delivered on time. Machinery to be always in working order. Your gangs to have the necessary tools always available. No labour disputes or union troubles. Now any one of these things going wrong could cause major delays thus costing the main contractor tens of thousands of pounds in penalties. By paying the insurance dues you can avoid problems."

"A sort of protection racket then!"

"I prefer to call it an insurance policy myself."

"Who gets this money, or should I say where does this money go?"

"The local IRA funds." I looked at him in total disbelief. Oh sure, deep down I knew this but for him to be so blatant about it was something else. I just stared at him wondering to myself, what the hell was I doing here.

"Shit Breandán." I slammed my hand down on the table and started to shout, "You have the nerve to drag me out of bed at six in the morning, to calmly sit there and demand. Yes demand that I accompany you to see some fucking jumped up little bastard of a IRA commander, who you calmly announce unless I do he will drag me out in the middle of the night..."

"Slow down. I didn't say he would drag you out. You asked me the worst scenario and I was honest. That is the worst."

"Oh sure, that is the worst." I was on my feet now, "So you play that down and suggest the best is a protection racket..." He tried to interrupt me, "No, you listen to me Breandán, you called it insurance. It's a protection racket. Now we made a deal and that was I work for you. That's right you, no one else but you." I looked straight at him; it was too late to stop now. "Also as I pointed out to you last time I was over I am also in touch with some very senior people and should anything happen to me then you and your family have a major problem. Now do I make myself clear?" I had now run out of steam. I suddenly wondered had I overstepped the mark this time or would my previous hold over this man still be good? I don't mind saying I suddenly felt very scared. I sat back down and took a mouthful of coffee.

"Look Richard," his voice was soft, "All I want to do is take you to meet Eamonn the local IRA commander so as to avoid any misunderstandings and that way you won't have to pay anything."

"Are you saying we all won't pay anything?"

"Yes that's what I've been trying to tell you if you'd only listen." I took another mouthful of coffee as Breandán continued to talk. "All I was trying to do was to make it as easy as possible for you so as to avoid you having to tell Mike and Terry too much, that way everyone's happy. Anyway, I'll take you to meet the man then he'll know you're working for me and he will also advise you on where to go and not to go in his area. All right?"

"What about Terry and Mike will they have to go also?" I asked. "Because if they find out about this you'll not see them for dust."

Breandán thought about it for a few minutes.

"Hmm, could be a slight problem."

"Well, is it a problem or not?"

"Not one I can't get round."

"Ok, but they must never no about this conversation."

"I agree. Well that's settled then." He looked at his watch. "Jesus, it's time I wasn't here." He stood up to go "Don't forget we Irish can get up just as early as you English anytime," he chuckled, "See you later."

Paul and I had only just started breakfast with no sign of the others when the duty restaurant manageress approached our table.

"Mr James Reception have phoned through to advise me that there are two young men enquiring after you. Shall I arrange for them to be seated in the lounge or would you like them to join you in here?"

I looked at my watch; it was only nine fifteen. I looked at Paul. "It must be the cousins already." I addressed the young lady, "I think the lounge would be ideal."

"Thank you sir, I'll arrange for some coffee to be sent over to them. "

It had just turned nine forty-five when I tossed Mike the keys to my car.

"Here can you stick the gear in the boot whilst I go and find the cousins. "

I made my way to the lounge. Over in the corner I could see two young men drinking coffee and as they were the only ones in there I knew they were the O'Connor brothers.

"Hello I'm Richard James."

"Hi, I'm Patrick O'Connor and this is my younger brother Kelly."

"Pleased to meet you Pat and please call me Richard.

"Pleased to meet you Richard."

"Pleased to meet you, I'm Kelly."

"Oh yes, sorry Kelly. Pleased to meet you." I said as I took his outstretched hand.

"What time were you expecting us, I hope we're not too late?"

"No not at all Kelly. Breandán had said not before ten."

"There I told you Pat we were early. Sorry about that Richard."

"Yeah sorry Richard, I was sure Breandán had said we needed to be here before ten. Bloody hell Kelly that's a good start isn't it?"

"Don't blame me you were the one who kept on about getting here before ten."

"Right I'm ready when you are."

"Ok Richard, let's go. Come on Kelly leave that." He said to his younger brother indicating what remained of his coffee, and they followed me out to the car park.

The brother's set off up the lane towards the main road in an old red Post Office van. The faint outline of the Royal Mail logo was still visible through red paint somebody had crudely brushed on in a poor attempt to mask its áppearance. It even had an English registration so it would not look out of place in Belfast. Perhaps that was the idea! The little red van, once out on the open road, was not unlike Breandán's old Fiat.

One thing for sure it was no slouch! In no time at all we were travelling well in excess of eighty miles an hour.

"Bloody hell, what's he got in that van?" Mike asked.

"I think something a little more powerful than the norm!"

"You're not kidding Richard." He looked at my Speedo. "Eighty-five and they're pulling away from us, I don't believe it."

"It's true."

"That's got to have been breathed on, what do you reckon Terry?"

"Well let's say I've never known an old Postman's van capable of eighty. Seventy or seventy five, but eighty never."

"Wow, what are we doing now Richard?" I glanced at my Speedo.

"About ninety."

"So he must be doing ninety, a bloody old van at that and he's doing ninety. I'd love to know what's under that bonnet 'cause nobody can say that's your average van engine, can they? I'd love to have something like that." Mike said with a touch of reverence. "You know something that doesn't look what it was."

"You mean a wolf in sheep's clothing?"

"Yeah Richard. Yeah that sums it up just about right, a wolf in sheep's clothing."

"Yes he's not the only one Mike." I muttered to myself. "I can think of someone else who has a Fiat like that."

"Sorry what did you say Richard?"

"Oh, doesn't matter. It was nothing really I was just talking to myself."

"That's one of the first signs Richard, isn't it Mike?"

"Yeah I know."

"Yes but the second one is listening to yourself isn't Terry?"

"Ha-ha, very funny Mike."

We had now been following the two brothers for some distance and after that initial burst of speed we had settled down to a more leisurely pace. I glanced into my rear view mirror and noticed a blue Volvo not unlike Breandán's. Funny I thought he wasn't coming up this way until much later, on the other hand perhaps it wasn't him. I didn't think anymore of it until we reached Mullary and noticed that it was still there. It wasn't close enough to see the number, but close enough for me to be almost certain that we were being followed. I slowed down, dropping further and further back from the van and the blue Volvo did likewise. Always keeping just far enough away so as his number plate could not be seen.

"What's up Richard?"

"Nothing Mike."

"Then why are you slowing down?" He asked as the van drew away from us. "If you're not careful we'll lose sight of them.

"No we won't."

"Well I hope you know where we're going, because the van's disappeared."

"No it hasn't, they're not far away." I glanced in my mirror and floored the accelerator. The car leapt forward with a surge and for a moment the Volvo seemed not to respond. But I was wrong. I kept my foot hard down as the Speedo read sixty-five, seventy,

seventy-five, eighty, eighty-five then ninety. In the distance I could just make out the van. "There, I told you Mike. No problem." I glanced back in my mirror, "Shit."
"What's up Richard?"
"Oh nothing just that I thought I saw a patrol car," I lied, "Have a look Terry will you?"
"Ok." He turned round and looked out of the rear window. "No I can't see anything. Oh hang on, no it's ok, it's only a blue Volvo."
"Oh that's all right then. Phew, thank goodness for that." I said in mock relief.
"Well at least we're back in touch with the van again."
"Yeah." I replied, but I was preoccupied with the Volvo. I was now getting somewhat paranoid about it. I was certain he or she was tailing us, but why?

The Volvo had been tailing us for some miles now and despite whatever I did it stuck with us. As the miles rolled by I forgot about our tail and concentrated on keeping up with the brothers. There was no one more surprised than I when I saw it had gone. At first I couldn't believe it, but no matter how hard I looked it had gone, where I didn't know, but it was gone. Perhaps I had been wrong all the time and it had never been tailing us at all. Upon reaching Dunleer, we took a minor road to Ardee briefly joining the Dublin to Castleblayney road eventually to turn onto the N52 towards Dundalk. It was here that again I noticed a blue Volvo. I swear it was the very same one that had been following us for mile after mile.

About midway between Ardee and Dundalk we turned down a narrow winding road, no more than a farm track really, and headed for Tallanstown. Well that was what the signpost had said. As we entered Tallanstown we turned northwards, again, this time on a slightly wider road towards Louth. Suddenly out of the corner of my eye, there in my rear view mirror, I caught sight of the blue Volvo again.
"Shit, he's there again!"
"Who's there again?" Asked Mike.
"That bloody Volvo!" Terry turned in his seat to look out of the rear window to see who or what I was talking about. "I'm sure the bastard's following us."
"Do you know who it could be?" Asked Terry as he craned his neck round to look at the blue car following.
"I'm not sure but I think do!" I said glancing at the rear view mirror once again.
"Are you sure he's following us Richard?" Mike asked as he looked behind at the Volvo. "It could be just coincidence couldn't it?"
"Look Mike I think I can tell the difference between someone following us on purpose and someone who just happens to be following us, if you know what I mean."
"Yeah, but what makes you so certain that it's definitely following us? "
"Because since we left the hotel he's been there."
"Why didn't you say something before?" I didn't reply.
"Is that what all that slowing down and speeding up was all about back there?"
"Yes, so that's how I know we're being followed."
"He's been there all this time and you've kept it to yourself. Did you know Terry?"
Terry turned back to face the front. "No can't say I did. The only time I saw it was when Richard thought he saw a police car."

170

"So Richard?" Mike asked.

"So what?" I tried evading the issue, but Mike wasn't having any.

"So has he been there all the time?"

"No." I answered, "Just..."

"There you go then, if he hasn't been there all the time you can't be certain that it's even the same car. You're probably imagining it."

"Ah but he, she, it whatever was there most of the time except for..."

"For what?"

"Oh I don't know the last ten miles or so, I guess."

"Well there you go. As I said you're imagining things." Mike forced a laugh and fell silent.

Both my passengers now seemed a little on edge as knowing full well the implications that my discovery could mean.

Terry, in trying to reassure himself as well as Mike, was the first to speak. "It's probably nothing really, in fact it's more than likely two different Volvos painted the same colour." It was conceivable but I wasn't convinced. Eventually the van in front started to slow down as the road narrowed and the stone walls gave way to trees on either side of the road. Gradually the sprinkling of trees became much more prolific as we entered into a heavily wooded area with numerous little roads and byways branching off at different places. I glanced again in the mirror to check on our 'would be' tail.

"Well I'll be..." I left the rest unfinished.

"What?" Asked Mike.

"Our friend has disappeared again." Terry once again craned his neck round to look through the rear window and Mike did likewise this time.

"See anything?" I asked.

"Nope, not a thing. What about you Terry?" Asked Mike.

"No the road looks completely clear behind. He or she must have turned off down one of those side roads."

"Hmm they must have, but where. Or should I say, to where?"

"There I told you that you were imagining it, didn't I Terry?" Mike's nervousness had disappeared completely now as the thought of us being tailed had seemed to be a misconception.

"Yeah, see Richard we were right. It was a different Volvo. Mind you, the way you kept on about it I was beginning to believe that we were being tailed. Anyway, why would anyone be following us?"

I glanced in the mirror at Terry "Dunno really, but I was obviously wrong wasn't I?"

"Hang on Richard the van's he's turned off." Mike shouted. I slammed on the brakes and we slithered to a halt. With a crunch of the gearshift I selected reverse and accelerated back passed the narrow opening. With a quick check in my mirror I indicated and turned into the narrow lane. In those few seconds the van had disappeared from view. Suddenly the narrow track opened out into a clearing at the far end of which stood two solid wooden gates or doors, at least twenty feet high. The doors themselves were set into a solid granite archway within a wall of even greater dimension, and there immediately in front of the gates was the red post office van. As we entered the clearing a crudely painted sign nailed to one of the trees announced

'WELCOME TO THE HOLIDAY CAMP'. We had arrived.

Patrick gave three sharp blasts on the van's horn, which was instantly greeted by the two doors beginning to open. Very slowly at first but gradually they swung back to reveal a fully enclosed courtyard at the far end of which stood the house. As soon as the van and our car had passed through the portal and into the courtyard the doors swung shut. The house was sort of Gothic in appearance, with a flight of stone steps leading up to a large solid oak door with coach lights mounted at either side to afford illumination of both the steps and the entrance at night.

"Christ!" was all Mike could say. He sat there with his mouth open in disbelief.

Terry gave a low whistle. "What the hell. Some farmhouse."

Then something else caught my attention. There parked close to the steps was a blue Volvo.

As soon as I saw the Volvo I knew Breandán was there. Interesting I thought, I wonder how long he's been here. I slowly manoeuvred my car and parked alongside the Volvo.

"Well, well, well." I said out loud, "I wonder when Mr O'Shea arrived?"

"Sorry Richard, were you speaking to me?" Asked Mike.

"No not particularly, I was just saying I wondered how long it was since Mr O'Shea had arrived."

"Why, is he here then?"

"Oh yes he's here all right." I stated in a matter of fact way, "But how long that's the question?" I opened my door and got out of the car. As I walked passed the Volvo I casually brushed my hand across the bonnet, but to my surprise it was quite cool to the touch. At that precise moment Breandán appeared through the front door accompanied by a heavily pregnant young woman.

"Hello Richard, you made it then."

"Yeah, no problem."

He then saw Patrick and called across to him, "Hey Patrick, I've just been chatting to your lovely wife here. I gather it'll not be long before the great event."

"No Breandán just a little over six weeks, that's if the good doctor is right and of course if the little one's ready."

"Really?"

"Yeah all things being equal."

"That'll curtail your nights out a bit!"

"Like hell it will." Came his reply.

"Here Richard, let me introduce you. Richard this is Marie, Patrick's lovely wife and Marie this is Richard James my good friend from England."

"Pleased to meet you Richard."

"Likewise Marie."

"So you're going to be working here for a little while then."

"Yes." I leaned back against the Volvo placing my hands once more on its bonnet.

"Have you been here long Breandán?" I asked.

"What was that? Did you say how long since I arrived?"

"Yeah." I could now feel the heat beginning to percolate through the thick under-bonnet soundproofing to my hands.

"Oh, I guess about two hours or more. Why?"

"Just that I thought I saw you following us that's all."

"No, it wasn't me."

"Are you sure it wasn't?"

"Of course I'm sure. I'd tell you if it had been me. After all what reason would I have to lie?"

Exactly I thought, but the heat from your engine tells me you are lying about your arrival, so you could just as easily be lying about following us, but why? Had he been following us? I walked to the boot of my car and unlocked it as Breandán unlocked the Volvo.

"Would one of you two take my things inside when you go as I've now got to go off with Mr O'Shea."

" Sure Richard." Terry grabbed mine and his bag "So where you off then?"

"Oh it's just that I need to take Richard off to discuss some more business. We shouldn't be too long. If there's anything you need I'm sure Pat and Kelly will fix you up. Ok?"

"Ok lads?"

"All right Richard we'll see you later." Mike said as I got into the Volvo and Breandán started the engine.

"Why do you call it the 'Holiday Camp' Breandán?"

"It's just that it's always been known as that."

"Did it used to be a holiday camp then?" I asked.

"You're joking? No it's never been a holiday camp, we've had the occasional holiday for the IRA there but it's never been a holiday camp." I would or even could have believed him if I hadn't noticed that tell tale mischievous look about him and the faintest trace of a smile flicker across his lips.

"Ha, ha, ha tell me another one Breandán."

"What do you mean?" He asked with mock indignation, "Of course we have" but that was it he immediately spluttered with laughter.

"Ok, so why was it called the 'Holiday Camp' if it has never been such a thing?"

"Well the truth is those lads are so damned lazy and always have been when it comes down to hard work, that they've just let the place go, so I decided that as they treated life and the farm as one big holiday I would call it the 'Holiday Camp'. I'd hoped it would goad them into doing something with it, but no, they were so thick skinned that they didn't recognise that I was really taking the piss. Still that's life for you. They've had it handed on a plate to them so easy come easy go, one day they may wake up before it's too late."

Chapter 21

We entered the village and took the road towards Dundalk then after a couple of miles Breandán pulled up outside a small white bungalow with a meticulously maintained lawn and flowerbeds. The name of the bungalow 'An Ghaoth Aduaidh' (The North Wind) was created in a scrolled wrought iron plaque and mounted on the wall near to the front door. Breandán gave three sharp knocks with the heavy knocker and waited. A couple of minutes later the front door was opened by a bald headed man whose frame made even Breandán look small by comparison. The man greeted Breandán in Gaelic and after a very brief conversation we were ushered into the hallway and the front door closed behind us.

"Hello" I said. The bald headed 'goon' turned and looked me up and down with utter contempt then spat on the floor. I think I could safely say he didn't like me. In the meantime Breandán started talking to him in Gaelic, none of which conveyed any sense to me except for the name Eamonn, which cropped up on more than one occasion during the conversation. Then out of the blue the big 'goon' turned to me.

"I'm sorry for being so rude just now but I don't like your accent. However as you're with the man here I welcome you." His words were saying one thing, but the hatred in his eyes told the truth. Dismissing me with a look of complete disdain he once more turned his attention to Breandán. "Eamonn's expecting you both. Please follow me."

We were ushered into a room, where a slightly built man sat at a desk hunched over a map. His 'goon' coughed slightly and said, "Excuse me sir."

"Yes man what is it?" Eamonn asked without taking his eyes from the map.

"You have two visitors sir. Mr Breandán O'Shea and a Mr..."

"James, Richard James" Breandán interrupted. On hearing Breandán's voice Eamonn pushed the map to one side and got up from his desk.

"Why, what brings you here my friend." He then turned to his 'goon' "Thanks you can go," the tall bald headed one left the room closing the door behind him. "Now, I must say Breandán it's been a while now since you've graced me with your presence, how are you keeping?"

"Oh I'm fine, just fine. How's yourself Eamonn?"

"Not too bad. How are things in Dublin?"

"Much the same as they were when you were last down. I was down south talking to Paddy Macauley in Cork the other day; you know just going over one or two things with him. Working out a strategy on some fund raising. You know he's got a lot of relations out in New York and New Jersey, so he's been on to them to get something going among our American cousins. Still that's another story to be told another day."

"So why are you here, what brings the big man himself up here?"

"Oh I'm up here on a little business at my cousins place and I wanted to discuss it with you as the area commander."

"You're not meaning the 'Holiday Camp' are you?"

"The very same!"

"So how can I help?"

"Well Eamonn, it's more a case of helping Richard here. You see Richard is over here from England."

"England did you say?" Eamonn raised his eyebrows questioningly.

"Yes England. He's over here working for me at the 'Holiday Camp', in fact there's him and his two men, Mike and Terry. They're here to grub out and replant some orchards for me, so I want you to pay special attention to them and look after their welfare so to speak." Eamonn gave me a cursory once over.

"So you're from England. Hmm." He seemed deep in thought for a minute. He motioned us to sit down. "Well Richard, you and your men will see some things that are best ignored and there are certain places definitely to be avoided at all costs. Mind as you're at the 'Holiday Camp' a lot of the things won't affect you anyway which is quite useful really. But there is one thing to be remembered at all costs. In the village we have two public houses one is near the crossroads and the other is called O'Grady's which is passed the crossroads up the hill. Now if you or your lads wish to go for a drink always use the one at the crossroads, have you got that? I cannot stress this enough. Please remember it's very important; never ever go to O'Grady's. Which one is it you can use?"

"The one on the crossroads."

"Good, now don't forget because we live in uncertain times and the locals do not take kindly to strangers and that is very true of the pubs. Now as you're working for Breandán, the boss so to speak, I think it would be fair to say that you and your team can be regarded as fully paid up members of the club. So we will not be troubling you for additional dues. I'm sure my good friend Breandán has explained the system to you, haven't you Breandán?"

"To be sure I have Eamonn. As long as your men are aware then I think Richard will keep a wary eye out on his lads, won't you Richard?"

"You bet your life I will."

"Well Breandán, you can be rest assured we'll take very good care of Richard and his men in the usual Area Command way. I don't think there'll be any complaints, that is provided you stick to what I've said Richard. Do that and I don't think we'll have any problems, but if you or your men don't then I cannot guarantee your safety or well being. Ok?"

"Is there any questions Richard?" I looked at O'Shea then at Eamonn.

"No I don't think so."

"Good, then that's sorted that out. Anything else on your side Eamonn?"

"Only to say that I'll no doubt be seeing more of you in the not too distant future Richard. However, just in case you do have any problems, but I don't expect you will, then you had better take this." He pushed a small piece of paper into my hand on which he had neatly written a telephone number. "That's for your eyes only no-one else, understood?"

"Understood," I replied. "I assume this is for emergency use only?"

"Correct. Commit the number to memory then destroy the paper. Also remember that my name is Eamonn and I, just like a ferryman, am here to help carry you over the troubled water. To smooth your way so to speak, a bridge to enable traffic to pass. Mind you like all metaphors if people disobey the rules and 'the ferryman' doesn't get paid then he goes on strike and the ferry no longer runs. The bridge is closed to traffic and people will get hurt - so Richard, whatever you do, always remember the rules!" We all sat in silence for some moments. What the hell was he babbling on about I wondered. Then Breandán broke the spell.

"Well about time we made a move and thanks Eamonn I'm sure everything will be fine."

"Yes thanks Eamonn. I won't forget." Eamonn stood up proffering his hand as he did.

"Well Breandán it was nice to see you again. Don't leave it so long next time, ok?"

"Ok. Cheers Eamonn." He said as he shook his hand.

"Richard," Eamonn shook my hand and said, "Don't forget to memorise that number and remember the rules."

"What did he mean Breandán when he was on about ferrymen, bridges and the like?" I asked as we started to move off down the road.

"Oh that's Eamonn for you. He likes to wax lyrical from time to time. He just rambles on sometimes. What he was trying to say was that the IRA is a form of insurance and people around here buy that insurance to make sure the job gets completed. Like I said before, if as a businessman you didn't pay your subscription to the local area then things would accidentally happen to impose on your lifestyle. For example if you were in the haulage business and you refused to pay your prescribed amount then you'd quickly find lucrative contracts would start to dry up, then you may have union problems with your drivers. The Gardai could also start taking an unhealthy interest in your operations. All different things like this could and would happen."

"That's like the Mafia. It's extortion, protection money."

"No Richard it's insurance. If you pay your levy to the local area, the insurance company, then the local organisation is like the ferryman, once it is paid your goods get to the other side safely. So in that sense it's insurance."

"You call it insurance, I'll call it extortion."

"Well what are insurance companies but legalised extortionists?"

"Hmm, not quite the same thing."

"Isn't it?"

Chapter 22

Upon my return from Eamonn's bungalow, I was left with a bit of a quandary, how to explain to my two men about our situation and how we were working in IRA controlled countryside. Not the easiest of tasks but, as it happened, they took it better than I would ever have thought even in my wildest dreams.

"So you understand, if you do go into the village whatever you do steer clear of the pub called O'Grady's, That is a definite NO GO area. Ok?"

"Ok Richard."

"You ok with that Terry?"

"Yeah sure." He looked deep in thought.

"Problems Terry?" I asked.

"Hmm, I suppose not." I watched him closely he looked pensive.

"Come on Terry out with it. I know something's worrying you what is it?" I asked.

"Well it occurs to me that if we are sitting in the middle of bandit country as you put it how come we are being left alone, being English and all that?"

"That's a good point Richard, so why are they so keen to leave us alone?"

"I don't know." I said a little too hurriedly, but too late they sensed that I knew more than I was saying.

"I think you know more than you're letting on Richard. Would it be that the lads here, the brothers, are IRA themselves and so we are working for them indirectly?"

"That's..."

"Rubbish were you going to say?"

"No Mike, I was going to say that's not true." I lied

"Oh yeah." He said mockingly.

"Yes."

"So if that's not true how can you be so sure we are above being harmed?"

"Well, trust me I know these things."

"Come on Richard you've got to do better than that. You know something and you're not being totally honest with us. So out with it, what is it?" My mind raced, if I didn't tell them the truth they were bound to throw their hand in and if I did tell them they could still quite easily not want to know. I was in a dilemma.

"So what do you know?" Asked Terry. "If you don't tell us then you leave me no alternative, a thousand pounds or not, I'm out of here..."

"And if I do tell you what then, you'll still be out of here won't you?"

"Surely that's for us to decide isn't it, after all I have a wife and child to think of?" I knew deep down that Terry was right, but I foolishly had tried to conceal it from them and by doing that had made things worse. It was no good I had to take a gamble and tell them about O'Shea and how he fitted into this.

"I guess your right. You both deserve to know the facts." My mind went into overdrive damage limitation was desperately needed. "Like I said earlier we are in an area that is very much IRA territory, but I have the word of the local IRA commander that nothing will happen to us..."

"Who is this so called commander?"

"You don't need to know Mike. So like I was saying..."

177

"Why don't I need to know?" I gave him a withering look.

"Shh Mike, stop interrupting, you don't need to know the guy's name do you now?"

"Well it might be useful Terry, you never know do you?"

"When will you need it?

"Listen both of you. You wanted me to tell you what was going on, I'm trying but all you do is interrupt me."

"Sorry Richard carry on."

"As I was saying. I went to see the local IRA commander, and before you say anything Mike you don't need to know who it is. He has given his word to leave us alone all the time we are working here. But one thing we must do and that is obey his wishes..."

"But how do we know we can trust him?"

"Ok." I thought about this for a minute, "because I have paid out protection money for all of us..."

"But..."

"No buts ok. That's the deal."

"What stops them still taking us anyway?"

"Good question Mike. The answer is Breandán O'Shea." The room fell silent whilst they took what I had said on board. Mike was the first to speak.

"What's O'Shea got to do with all this?"

"O'Shea is probably the most powerful man in Eire, not only is he one of the wealthiest men in Eire he also has friends in high places. It's surprising who he knows."

"Is he IRA then?"

"I didn't say that Terry. What I said was he knows a number of people in high places. The last trip over he introduced me to the Taoiseach himself."

"Who's the Tao hmm whatever it was called?" asked Mike. I laughed at his pronunciation. "So what did you call it?"

"Taoiseach." I said again. "The Taoiseach is the Prime Minister of Eire."

"So he knows the Tao whatever, the Prime Minister then?"

"And the Minister for Agriculture and many others. How else do you think I got all the contracts."

"So he is a very powerful man then."

"Oh yes indeed. So you see with Breandán O'Shea on our side we have effectively got the best protection we could have. Don't forget that whilst we are here the brothers are his cousins so it is still his family." I could see the worry starting to evaporate. I continued, eager to push home my advantage. "Still I think we should get the contract done as quickly as possible, we really don't want to outstay our welcome do we? So how do you feel about staying" I asked.

"Now I know the full facts; no problem. In fact there never really was a problem."

"What: you're telling me that there never really was a problem. I don't believe you."

"Well I may have had slight doubts, but you know me, I always trust your judgement anyway."

"Bullshit! Absolute rubbish." Terry winked and smiled.

"It's true." He said, "Honestly I never doubted you one little bit!"

"What about you Mike?" I asked.

"No problems, I stay. Like Terry I never doubted a thing!"

"You pair of lying, conniving old toe rags. Get out of it." I smiled to myself and thought, 'Yes!' well done Richard. Give yourself a pat on the back.

Monday saw the three of us eager to start work at first light. I poked my head around the kitchen door in a forlorn hope that the O'Connor brothers would turn up but deep down I knew that would be unlikely. In any event all three of us grabbed our warm coats and left for the orchards. It was whilst walking towards the small door in the perimeter wall that I noticed what looked like a brand new dog compound. This was partially hidden by bushes and tucked away at the rear corner of the house. Strange, I thought, especially as the brothers didn't have any dogs. Then as I got closer to it I noticed a tractor and trailer had been carefully parked close to the open gate of the compound and to some extent hidden from view of the casual observer. As we approached the door, the trailer and its load were clearly visible to us, as was the man whom I assumed to be the driver. The load was a mixture of stacked nitrogen top dressing fertiliser, forty-gallon drums of oil and a number of milk churns. At that time in the morning the question of why the milk churns never occurred to me. Mind you, the driver was a strange one, he looked out of place on a farm. There he was, a tall slim bloke, reasonably dressed, not jeans or the like, leaning against the perimeter wall having a smoke. The lads nodded to him in acknowledgement as they passed by.

"Morning. Nice morning. Bit cool mind but nice." I said to him as I approached the door. He didn't even acknowledge the greeting. Surly sod I thought. He just stared at me, his eyes full of hatred. Then he spat at my feet as he pushed himself away from the wall and walked off towards the dog compound. Well 'stuff you then' I thought, 'you ignorant sod' and left it at that.

As I walked up the field I felt something was not right. I couldn't put my finger on it, but I knew something was wrong. Try as I might, I just couldn't push the scene from my mind. The lads were chatting on about something and nothing, but I wasn't really listening.

"Hey Richard, you're very quiet, what's up?"

"Huh, what did you say Mike?" I tried to concentrate on the conversation and to push the guy and what I had seen to the back of my mind, but the scene still kept coming back into focus. "Sorry Mike, I was miles away. What did you say?"

"It must be good, wherever you are, because twice I've asked you where you want us to start. Say what's bugging you?" Then it hit me like a brick.

"That's it; the milk churns!"

"What? Milk churns, what are you on about Richard?"

"Sorry. Yes where to start. Err, why don't you both start in the far orchard. Damn, you two carry on; I need to go back. I've just remembered something." I hurriedly set off back towards the house.

"What?" Mike called after me.

"Oh nothing much, just something I should have done before we left."

"Where did you say, was it the far orchard?" Terry shouted after me.

I stopped and shouted back to him. "Yes that's right, the far orchard."

I carefully and slowly opened the door in the wall inch by inch until I had a good view of the compound and the trailer. There were two men plus the surly one manhandling the last of the forty-gallon oil drums off the side. I pulled the door closed and waited. "Jesus and mother of god they were bloody heavy to say the least." I heard one of them say.

"To be sure they were. They were bloody full, so what d'you expect you daft bugger."

"Well you know what I mean, what with the bags of fertiliser and the milk churns as well it was a helluva lot to shift all in one go."

"Are, you be getting old Seamus that's a fact."

"Oh, and I suppose you're not then Joseph O'Flaherty?"

"When you two have finished discussing your age will you be telling the brothers we'll be needing a load of finished mix soon plus detonators." I assume the voice belonged to the 'happy' looking slim bloke.

"Ok we'll tell them." That must be Joseph I thought. Suddenly the tractor started and all other conversation was drowned out.

The sound of the tractor gradually melted away to become a slight drone in the distance. I gave it a couple more minutes then slowly and carefully edged the door open. I listened intently for the slightest sound but there was nothing save for the sound of crows over head. With the door opened fully I could see the house, the compound and part of the yard. There was nobody around everywhere was deserted. I darted through the door. I ran towards the bush. I paused here for a moment. I listened carefully. I checked to see the coast was clear. Nothing stirred. Now for the compound. The gate was unlocked. I was in. I pulled the gate closed and headed for the door. The door yielded and I slipped quietly inside pulling it closed behind me. I could feel my heart pounding, was it a dog run? Would some large snarling dog suddenly confront me? I paused, and listened. Nothing. I moved forward in the pitch black. There was a loud crash as I banged into something. I froze expecting the door to be opened at any minute. Nothing, only the noise of my breathing. "There must be a light here somewhere?" I muttered to myself as I felt around. I slid my hand along the rough texture of the granite, stretching my fingertips up and along in all directions, first to my right then to my left. "Ah, what's this?" I could feel the outline of a rectangular metal box. "Yes there it is. Let there be light." I said to myself as my fingers flicked the small switch down. A low wattage bulb started to glow giving off just enough light for me to see that I was in some sort of storeroom. On both sides of the room stacked three deep and two high were milk churns, about sixty in all. I kicked one and judging by the ring they were empty. I moved along the centre aisle and it wasn't long before the milk churns gave way to the large oil drums. I tried to move one but it was no good they were definitely full of something, the label on the side showed it to be diesel not oil as I had originally assumed. "Bloody hell," I said to myself, "There's got to be well over a thousand or more gallons here." I made my way towards the end wall, the oil drums gave way to plastic sacks of nitrogen fertiliser stacked one on top of the other from floor to ceiling. "Phew. God knows how much top dressing they've got here." I muttered to myself, "Must be tons of the stuff." This begged a question. With all this fertiliser then why are the trees looking short of nitrogen? Now that is interesting I thought. I was now at the end of the kennel block and in the dim light could see the outline of yet another door. This door like the entrance was unlocked and opened easily. There was just sufficient light that spilled through the open doorway for me to make out that it led into some form of cellar. It was make your mind up time. Had I seen enough or do I risk the possibility of getting caught in here and venture through? A good question. I nervously looked back along the aisle to the far end and wondered how long it would be before someone came in. I looked at my watch it was still relatively early. I once again looked towards the outer door. Should I go on or should I leave? "Oh sod it." I said out aloud, "Go for it." With my mind made up I passed through into the other area, there's no going back now I thought. Although the light that spilled through was very dim, it was still bright enough for me to see another light switch. Suddenly everywhere was bathed in brilliant light and after the dim light in the storeroom, my eyes took a little while to adjust.

I could now see that the area I was standing in was under the main body of the house. There were a number of granite columns stretching up to support a vaulted roof. There were some stairs carved out of stone leading nowhere. In fact upon closer examination I could see that at one time they must have served as a means of entry from the main body of the house, but were now redundant and ended up against a blank stone wall. The wall must have been erected in recent times, as it looked a lot newer than the surrounding stonework. I took some time to look around at this vaulted cellar and bearing in mind the design of the house and its age I assumed this at one time would have been the wine cellar. Suddenly I thought I heard a movement. I held my breath straining my ears to listen. My heart thumped deep inside my chest. I slowly reached my hand back through the door into the storeroom feeling around for another light switch. I dare not move too much just in case. My fingers closed over the switch and plunged the storeroom into darkness and I withdrew my arm hurriedly back to my side of the door. I closed the entry door to the cellar, flicked off the light where I was and waited. Just in time. I could now here muffled voices as they approached the door. My nerves were stretched to breaking. I expected the cellar door to open at any minute. There was a thud from the other side. More talking. Another thud. Beads of sweat on my brow. A scraping sound near the door. Voices clear now. Another thud. Then quiet. I waited for what seemed an eternity before I risked opening the adjoining door to listen. The storeroom was again in total darkness. I closed the door again and switched on the light. Once more the cellar was filled by a blaze of light.

Under one of the archways I discovered a workbench with several reels of different coloured instrument wire stacked at one end. An old AVO 8 was stood on the bench along with a number of different tools, from screwdrivers, pliers to wire strippers. At the back of the bench were a number of plastic storage boxes. Each one contained different electronic components. For example there were batteries in one, small digital clocks in another and Printed Circuit Boards (PCB) complete with battery holder and flying leads in a third. Then placed in the centre of the bench, was an illuminated magnifying lens beneath which was an upturned milk churn lid. Already mounted on a purpose made bracket and nestling in the upturned lid was one of the digital clocks and the small PCB with its flying leads soldered to a small transformer. Also on the bench was a small pile of different coloured lead lengths with ends tinned and stripped ready for soldering. Some leads had already been soldered in place on the circuit board. On a rack adjacent to the workbench were a number of upturned lids, which looked as if all the necessary wiring had been finished. Adjacent to the rack were a number of milk churns all packed solid with a pinkish powder. Further into the cellar under another Arch I discovered another bench. This one had a good electronic balance set up on the top. A measuring jug and a large container full of the Pink powder. The measuring jug had traces of pinkish liquid clinging to its base, which upon further examination appeared to be oily. A sniff confirmed what I had thought it was agricultural diesel. I began to wonder what all this meant. The bench was flanked on either side by milk churns, some were empty but others already were partially filled with the powder. Not too far from this bench I could see a number of forty-gallon oil drums one of which had a hand pump fitted to enable the diesel to be drawn off. In a corner, convenient to the oil drums, a number of full fertiliser sacks had been stacked. On the floor in front of the pile stood a bag that had been opened and some of the contents had already been removed. To my horror I suddenly realised that I was standing in the middle of a manufacturing plant for the crude yet very efficient milk churn bombs and the pink powder was in fact 'Northern Ireland Mix' or 'HME'. My mind started to work overtime. What was I to do? Who was I to tell? Where was I to go? All these things rushed into my head. The very thought of all this below where I was staying made me come out into a cold sweat. I really didn't know what I was going to do, but what I did know was that I needed to get out of here. Out of this IRA factory of death. The very thought of the death and destruction that surrounded me in this cellar nauseated me. Christ I needed some air. Suddenly the cellar had become very claustrophobic and I needed to get out. I hurriedly walked to the door that would lead to the storeroom I had seen enough. Now I could see why the O'Connor brothers had bought an old Post Office van and left the English registration plates on. What better vehicle to drive through Ulster with and above suspicion. You bastards I thought, you low down bastards. I was through into the storeroom, pulled the door closed behind me and running along the aisle between the churns. Suddenly I stopped. Shit, had I switched off the light? Sweating now I ran back along the aisle clattering against the odd churn as I did but I couldn't care less. All I wanted to do was to get out as soon as I could. I threw open the door to be greeted by pitch black. I had switched off the light automatically without realising. I pulled the door closed again, must get out, must tell someone was all I could think about. I reached the outer door that led to the compound. I remember switching the light off, but the next thing I recollect was half walking half running across the field towards the orchard. The time from leaving the storeroom to getting to the field was a blur. I looked at my watch I had been much longer than I had anticipated, and I began to wonder what the lads would be thinking. Would they be wondering what had happened to me? I slowed down to regain my composure. So who could I tell about my find? My first reaction was the Gardai but then I remembered O'Shea's connection with them. Perhaps that was not such a good idea. I wondered if I could get a message to Paul, possible I thought, then what could he do? Go to the British Consul in Dublin I suppose? Then what would they do more to the point what could they do? In the end I had to discount that idea. The more I thought about it the more of a problem I seemed to have. It had to be of interest to our security forces. Then it came to me. Sean, yes that's it I thought, Sean's the man. Somehow I would have to get a message to him.

As I reached the second orchard I could see Mike and Terry had already made considerable in roads on the re-planting.

"Sorry I've been so long lads. Still you seem be doing well enough without me. I reckon if the weather holds up then at this rate we could have this area all wrapped up with straw on by the middle of next week, what d'you think?"

"Possibly if the weather holds."

"It'll hold Mike. Have faith."

"Yeah, yeah, yeah. I've heard it all before Terry!"

"Come on lads take five, you've earned it." Terry took out a pack of cigarettes and lit one as he walked towards the edge of the field.

"Hey guys," he called back to us. "Come over here."

"What for Terry?" I called across to him.

"I thought you said we were still in the Republic Richard?" He shouted back.

"We are why?"

"Well if you come here I'll show you." At this Mike got up and walked over to join Terry.

"What is it Mike?" I called.

"Look over there Mike. See them?" said Terry.

"Yeah, I can see."

"See what?" I called to them.

"Well it looks like a squad of our lads out on patrol and heading this way." Hearing this I quickly got to my feet, the pictures of the wine cellar came rushing back to me. Perhaps this was my chance. I got to where they were standing.

"Where you looking lads?" I asked.

"Over there." I followed the direction of Terry's outstretched arm pointing towards the far side of the adjoining field. I could now just make out a squad of men dressed in black berets and camouflage gear heading across the field towards the dividing hedgerow. As they got closer we could see that each man was fully kitted out with standard army issue weapons and kit. Suddenly the dulcet tones of 'Squad, squad left wheel' could be heard. The squad turned to their left and marched along the side of the hedge towards us. As they drew level with where we were stood the voice was more boomed out.

"Squad, squad halt." Their timing was impeccable.

"Squad, squad left turn." In unison they turned with their backs to us. A little guy marched round to face the squad; he was obviously the owner of the big voice.

"Squad, squad dismiss." The guys were slick as they broke rank. Laying their weapons on the ground, some sat down, some stood around in small groups talking among themselves, whilst others lit up cigarettes and just stood there having a welcome smoke. The idea that these may have been our lads soon faded. Any idea that I may have had in telling them about what I had seen were soon dispelled when the guy with the 'big' voice came over to the hedge and started talking to us in a broad Irish accent.

"Hello there, so you're the Englishmen working at the 'Holiday Camp' then."

"Yes, I'm Richard and this is Terry," Terry reached over the hedge.

"Hi." He said shaking the Irishman's hand.

"This is Mike." I indicated Michael standing nearby. He nodded in acknowledgement. There was a pregnant pause. "To what do we owe this pleasure?" I enquired politely.

"What pleasure?" He asked.

"Well you," I answered. "You and your squad of men."

"Oh, sorry I see what you mean." He answered smiling at me "It's orders from area command. We've been asked to just keep an eye on you."

"How do you mean, an eye on us?"

"Why, what have we done wrong?" Asked Mike.

"Oh nothing, nothing at all. Sorry I didn't mean to offend. What I meant was that we have been ordered just to make sure there's no problems; you don't get into difficulties. Don't get lost around here. You know the sort of thing." Yes I'm sure you have I thought to myself. What you really mean is you've been told to make sure we don't go anywhere we shouldn't.

"Oh that's very thoughtful of your commander." I said, "Please convey our thanks to him for being so helpful and of course our thanks to you." I can play this game as well I thought.

"How long are you here for?" Innocent enough question I thought.

"Hmm, depends on the weather really. We've got two orchards to replant and some winter pruning to do so could be some time."

"We should see a fair bit of each other then. Oh sorry my name's Ciaran. Did you say your name's Richard?" He asked stretching across the hedge to shake my hand.

"Yes that's right. Pleased to meet you Ciaran." I said shaking the proffered hand. "Well Ciaran we've still got a lot to do so we must get on, so if you'll excuse us?"

"To be sure I will. Probably see you again." He called after me as I signalled to Mike and Terry to follow me back to where we'd left off.

"I expect so." I called back to him.

"Squad, squad fall in. Squad, squad 'shun. By the left, quick march. Left, left, left right left." I heard his voice keeping time as he marched his patrol away.

As we closed the small door in the perimeter wall we were greeted by one of the casual workers employed by the O'Connor brothers.

"Hello there," he called across the yard to us. "I don't expect you'll find anyone in."

"Where've they gone?" I called back to him.

"Sorry hang on a minute, I'll come over as I didn't quite catch what you said." He briskly walked in our direction. "Now what was it you said?"

"I asked you where had they gone?"

"I'm not too sure, but I think they went up north to visit the boys' parents."

"All three?"

"No. Marie hasn't gone with them. I think Patrick took her to her mums for a couple of days."

"Where does her mum live in the village?"

184

"No, she lives out at Swords I think."

"So when will the lads be back?" I asked.

"Oh be Jesus, there be no telling with those two when they get up into the north. It's like asking how long is a piece of string."

"Hmm, that's handy." I said to myself as much as anything.

"Why, was there anything in particular?"

"Sorry, what did you say?" I asked.

"I just wondered if there was anything in particular or was it something I could help with?"

"Oh I see. No, not really. I was just thinking out aloud," realising what I had said about it being handy them not being there, I hurried on. "About whether Marie had left us out anything to eat or not. That was all."

"Couldn't tell you, but I'd have thought so. Still if not there's always the village shop, they sell most things." He hovered for a minute or two waiting for me to say something, then shrugged his shoulders as he said, "Well if there's nothing I can help you with I'll be away home then my wife will wonder what's happened to me.'" He grinned and nodded to the lads, "So I'll see you lads later." He turned and walked off in the direction of the small door.

"Oh, excuse me?" I called after him.

"Was there something after all?"

"Yes, can you tell me how far is it to the border from here?" He frowned as he looked as if he was trying to calculate the distance.

"Hmm, I don't rightly know, but I would say if you went by the main roads it would take about twenty minutes or so."

"Not that long then?"

"Oh no and if you were to know the lanes you could be over the border in no time at all."

"What would you call no time at all?" I asked.

"Ten minutes at the most."

"Ten minutes?" I asked incredulously.

"To be sure, unless you were the Kelly driving then it would be less. Jesus he drives around these lanes as if he was the only one in the world. One of these days that lad will come a cropper, he's mad. Mad I tell you absolutely mad. Do you know only the other day he took me down to the village..." At this point I was no longer listening to his story, I knew with those sort of times there was only one thing for it, I had to contact Sean and arrange a meeting, but how? That was the question. "...So you see I won't go with him now. To be sure he's as mad as a hatter that one."

"I'm sorry, what was it you were saying. I was thinking about what still needs doing tomorrow."

"Oh nothing really, I was just saying how mad the Kelly was when he drove me into the village the other day, so if he was driving rather than Patrick then it would probably take less than ten minutes to get over the border. Anyway I'll be off now. Goodnight to you all now."

"Goodnight and thanks."

"He was a nice old boy wasn't he?" Terry said addressing no one in particular as we made our way towards the steps.

"Well he was certainly better than that bloke this morning." I said.

"Which bloke?" asked Mike.

"That slim bloke who was over near the tractor and trailer."

"Oh him. Yeah I should say so. A right miserable bastard he was wasn't he?"

"Yeah a real bundle of laughs. Here Mike," I tossed him the keys to the car, "You and Terry go down to the shop and get some stores whilst I go in and get the kettle on. It shouldn't take you that long and I'll have a nice brew made by the time you get back."

"What do you want us to get."

"Better get some bacon and eggs for breakfast and whatever for tonight. Sausages, peas and some potatoes, you know the sort of thing. Oh and best get some bread and a few cans of beer"

"Ok."

"Mike," I shouted after them, "Stay out of the pub called O'Grady's."

"What did you say?" He called back as he wound down the driver's window.

"Stay out of the pub..."

"Ok got it." He shouted as the engine kicked into life, "See you later." With a blip on the accelerator and a blast on the horn he was out through the gate and down the lane.

Chapter 23

By the light of my torch I checked my watch one more time. I had already checked it several times even in the last ten minutes and been down to the gate on numerous occasions. Once again I set off to go through the same routine as before. At the gate I stopped and listened for any sounds then by torchlight I carefully made my way along the lane for a short distance where once again the whole charade was repeated. It was now well over two hours since Mike and Terry had taken the car and gone off into the village. I was worried.

"Where the hell are you?" I shouted into the blackness at the top of my voice. It didn't achieve a lot except to give vent to my feelings and disturb some small woodland creature, which scrabbled off through the undergrowth. Once again I headed back towards the gate, then froze certain that I had heard the sound of an approaching vehicle. Holding my breath and listening for the slightest noise I peered down the lane beyond where the beam from my torch petered out trying, even willing, to catch a glimpse of headlights through the trees, but nothing. Obviously I was mistaken because all I could hear was the plaintive screech of an owl somewhere deep inside the woods. I turned and had started to retrace my footsteps when there was the definite sound of an approaching car. Once more I searched the darkness of the lane for the tell tale glimpse of light, this time it was there, I could see it, the faint flash of the headlights bouncing around through the trees. At last they're back, I thought, and not before time. As I reached the gateway the headlights came into full view as the van emerged from the trees. Damn, I thought, why you? I had been banking on it being the lads. I turned as the old post office van pulled up alongside me.

"Hello Richard what are you doing out here?" Patrick's voice called to me from the confines of the van. "Is everything all right?" He enquired.

"No it isn't all right," I replied my anger spilling over.

"What's up?" He asked hearing the anger in my voice. I must have sounded really off but didn't care. Even though it wasn't his fault I didn't reply.

"Hey come on Richard, it's obvious something's upset you what is it?"

"Oh it's nothing really, it's my problem."

"Well maybe we can help?" I thought about that for a minute then started to tell him. "It's the lads..."

"What about them?"

"I sent them off over a good couple of hours ago in my car to get some food and they've not returned. It's probably nothing really but just that without any transport I can't go and look for them if they are lost." Then an idea occurred to me, "I don't suppose you'd lend me the van would you?"

"Of course, here take it." Patrick got out and held the door open for me to get in.

"Wait a minute Richard," I paused before getting in. "How about if I drive you?" Asked Kelly, "At least that way I know all the different routes and some short cuts." That made sense to me. "Ok Kelly sounds good to me." With that he settled himself in the driving seat and I went to the passenger's side. The engine gave a throaty roar.

"Right where to first?"

"Well I sent them to the village shop so perhaps we had better start there."

"Ok let's go." With a blast on the horn, wheels spinning wildly to get a grip we roared off into the night.

The van squealed to a halt and even before I got out I could see that the shop was closed so it was really a bit of a lost cause, but nonetheless I still tried the door on the off chance.

"Any luck?" Kelly shouted to me from the van.

"No," I called back as I rattled on the handle. Just then someone moved the blind on the door aside and a face appeared.

"What do you want? I'm closed for the night."

"Excuse me can you tell..." but the blind slammed back in place. Kelly heard me shout through the window to the face.

"Any luck Richard?"

"There's someone in there but he just shouted that they were closed and that was it." I rattled the door handle and banged on the window all to no avail. I gave one last rattle to the door then thumped on the glass for a last time before calling it a day. I ran back to the van and jumped in. With a squeal from the spinning wheels we were already accelerating away as I grabbed the door handle to slam it shut.

"Shit Kelly, hold on! Give me chance to get in."

"Ah to be sure Richard, when I'm driving there's no hanging about!" I could see that, and I appreciated now what their worker had meant when he'd said, 'Unless Kelly is driving then it would be less than ten minutes to the border!'

"Where to now Richard?" He asked as he completed a racing change down and slung the van into a tight bend. A controlled four-wheel drift and slight correction on the wheel completed the manoeuvre as he powered out of the bend. I grabbed the dashboard to stop me being thrown into him by the sudden change of direction.

"Well I suppose we could try the pub."

"Which one?" He asked.

"The one at the crossroads."

"Ok hold tight." He slammed on the brakes. Quick look in the mirror indicated and spun the wheel. There was a squeal of protest from the tyres as we veered off the road down a cobblestone ally, which ran behind the old terrace houses. Suddenly we bounced over the kerb at the end and in the next minute were bouncing across open land. We hurtled headlong down a rough cart track bounced across potholes, bumped up another kerb and we were now on a small housing estate. I hadn't a clue where we were. Suddenly Kelly braked and we slithered to a halt. Now I recognised the crossroads but from a different approach. The pub was just around the corner.

"I'll wait for you here while you go and check it out."

"All right, I won't be long." I said as I opened the passenger door. It only took me a minute to the car park and a cursory look around confirmed that the car was not there, but just to make certain I went in.

"Good evening to you and what could I be getting for you?"

"Good evening, I wonder if you could help me?"

"I'll try my best sir?"

"Well I'm looking for two friends of mine. Two Englishmen one about twenty the other mid twenties."

"Englishmen you say sir?"

"Yeah, English have they been in?"

"No I'm sorry sir. Have you tried O'Grady's up the hill, not that they'd be made very welcome there though?"

"No I can't say that I have."

"Well if you're going there just a word of warning to you, they don't take kindly to strangers especially Englishmen. So be careful or you could find yourself in trouble now."

"Well thanks anyway."

"You're welcome. I hope they haven't gone in there for their sakes as much as anything. Goodnight to you now." I headed back to the van. So where now I asked myself.

"They weren't there then?" Kelly asked.

"No, and according to the barman they hadn't been in there at all."

"Where to now?"

"Well there's only one other place to try." I said looking at Kelly and he knew as well as I did where I meant. This time we drove at a reasonable pace up the hill to O'Grady's, the pub that was 'off limits'. We cruised passed very slowly as I checked to see if the car was anywhere to be seen.

"Anything?"

"No."

"Any sign of your car in the car park?"

"No." I heaved a sigh. "Any suggestions Kelly?" I asked grabbing at straws.

"We could check down the side roads to see if they parked there if you like?"

"I suppose so." I fell silent. They can't have gone in there I thought to myself, surely not after what I'd told them. Kelly took the road off to the right. We drove slowly along this road into another small housing estate. He checked his side as I checked mine.

"Anything Kelly?"

"No, what about you?"

"Me neither." We drove on a little further and still nothing.

"Well Kelly I can't see them parking all this way away from the pub, if in fact they've gone in there."

"Ok. I'll just go up a little further and I'll turn round. There's one more road further up the hill which we could check in if you like."

"All right lets do that then." I answered but I wasn't convinced that we would find them there. Kelly swung into a little side road where there was a parade of shops to turn round, when I caught sight of a telephone box. That gave me an idea.

"Tell you what Kelly, if we draw a blank in the next road come back here and I'll give Eamonn a ring."

"Have you got his phone number then?"

"Yeah, he gave it me in case I needed to contact him in an emergency." We turned into the other road and slowly cruised along it for a short distance following the same procedure as before. Nothing, as before we drew a blank.

"Well back to the telephone Kelly. That's got to be our only chance."

I tried the number three times each time I got through but as soon as I spoke I was cut off. This left me with only one option and that was to persuade Kelly to take me to Eamonn's place. I got back into the van.

"Well any luck Richard?" He asked as he started the engine.

"Can you take me up to Eamonn's place?" I asked.

"I can but why, couldn't you get through?"

"Oh I got through all right. In fact I got through three times, but every time I spoke they put the phone down on me."

"Ok so it's Eamonn's then."

"Yeah if you don't mind." He checked the main road for traffic before pulling out.

"I don't mind at all. Do you know the name of his bungalow?"

"Yeah, it's An..."

"An Ghaoth Aduaidh is the name. In other words 'The North Wind'."

"You know where he lives then." I said, then realised how stupid I was.

"Of course I know where he lives." Kelly retorted with disdain, "It's out on the Chanonrock to Dundalk road."

Within minutes we were slithering to a halt outside Eamonn's bungalow. Before the van was at a standstill I had the door open and was running up the path. Hammering on the front door I then waited for what seemed like an eternity. Just as I was about to knock again the door opened.

"Richard, what are you doing here?"

"I'm sorry Eamonn. I don't really know how to put this but..." I paused to get my breath, "But I need your help."

"Whatever is the problem? Here you had better come in and tell me what's going on." With that he stood to one side closing the door after me. "Go through, go through." He said to me cheerily. I entered the room that I had left less than twenty-four hours previously.

"Now make yourself comfortable and tell me what on earth has happened." I sat down on the settee and he sat facing me in one of the armchairs. "I must admit I hadn't expected to see you so soon after our last meeting. Now what's the problem?"

"Well about two and a half hours ago Mike and Terry, you know the two lads I brought with me, went off to the shop to get some bits and pieces and have not returned. Well they hadn't by the time we left."

"Why have you left it so long?"

"Because I had no means of getting into the village before Patrick came back."

"What about your car?"

"They have my car."

"Ah I see. So you were without transport until the brothers got back?"

"Yes that's right" He thought about it for a minute then asked, "I'm sorry if this sounds obvious but have you checked the shop?"

"Yes but it was closed and no amount of rattling on the handle got me anywhere."

"Hmm." He paused as if deep in thought then went on, "So where else have you tried?"

"Well Kelly has very kindly run me around all over the place. We tried the pub, in fact both pubs..."

"And?"

"Nothing."

"Did you go in the pub?"

"Yeah, well should I say only the one."

"Which one?"

"Not the one on the hill called O'Grady's."

"Fair enough. Hmm." Eamonn was silent.

"So what are you thinking?" I asked.

"Did you tell Mike and Terry to stay away from the pub called O'Grady's?"

"Sure I did, why?"

"You're certain that you told them to stay away?"

"Of course I did." He looked at me intently.

"Hey Eamonn hang on. I definitely told them to stay away. So what do you think?"

"Me, I don't think anything. Just making sure of all the facts first. Now, how do you know they haven't gone to the pub called O'Grady's, did you check the car park?"

"Of course I did." I was beginning to get annoyed at the inference that I had not checked thoroughly.

"Look don't you think I would have seen the car there had it been, or is that you don't think I would recognise it. Christ Eamonn it was my car." He gave me a stony stare, but that didn't worry me. "Yes that's right, my car so I'm damned sure I would know it if I had seen it." He looked totally unmoved by my outburst.

"Ok, so you've checked the shop, been in the pub at the crossroads and checked the car park at O'Grady's."

"Plus the streets nearby."

"Streets nearby you say, what for?"

"Well just in case they had parked there instead of in O'Grady's car park."

"My you have been thorough." Once more he was silent, then he suddenly got up out of his chair. "All right," he said, "I'll make a few phone calls." He opened the door that was my signal to leave. "Now in the meantime I suggest you wait out in the van until I have some news." He opened the front door and ushered me out into the cold night air. "Now you're sure you've told me everything?" He asked.

"Yes, there's nothing else to tell."

"Ok I'll be as quick as I can." With that he shut the door. I slowly walked back to the van and got in.

"Well, what did he say?"

"Nothing much, he asked if I'd checked the pub and the shop. Where we had looked and so on and so forth."

"Did you tell him we'd checked the nearby streets?"

"Yeah."

"So what are we to do now go back or what?"

"He just said wait here in the van whilst he made some phone calls."

In the control centre the outside line rang. The duty controller answered.

"TCG Duty Operations."

"Could I speak to mother please?" A voice with an Irish accent said.

"Who's calling?"

"This is the Ferry Pilot."

"Just a minute whilst I try to connect you." The telephonist passed it through to the controller.

"Ferry Pilot on line three."

"Hello Foxtrot Papa this is control, problems?"

"Nothing major. Just to let you know target has been in contact with me."

"So soon?"

"Yeah, he has a slight problem. The other two with him have gone missing with target's car. Can you check, trace and advise?"

"Hold a second." The controller put the line on hold whilst he dialled another extension. "Hello, this is extension 110 Foxtrot Papa's controller can you advise me on whereabouts Operation Ferryman's car?" He waited only a few seconds before the voice on the other line came back. "Thanks." He switched back to Ferry Pilot.

"Fox trot Papa are you there?"

"Yes I'm here."

"Target's car is in Louth area, just checked the grid reference which indicates it is to the rear of a public house north of the crossroads."

"Thank you control."

"Anything else?"

"No that's all I'll handle my end." The line clicked as the phone was put down.

It wasn't that long before the front door opened and Eamonn re-emerged and beckoned to me. I looked at Kelly.

"Well maybe it's good news." Then made my way up the path. "After what you had told me I tried around my contacts but drew a blank. Zilch, nothing, in fact nobody had seen them anywhere nor the car."

"So what's happened to them?" I asked, "They can't have just vanished into thin air complete with car and all. They've got to be around here somewhere." I protested.

"Your absolutely right. In fact I've now located them they're..." I cut him short.

"Whereabouts?"

"Where they should never have been. In the pub."

"But I checked in there."

"Not that one, but the one on the hill called O'Grady's. The one I stressed that under no circumstances must any of you go in. I thought you said you had told them to stay away from there?"

"I did."

"Well they are exceedingly lucky, that's all I can say. Fortunately for them the only lads in there were the ones who you saw earlier today. It could just as easily have been an IRA patrol that were far less tolerant then who knows what could have happened!"

"How come I didn't see the car?" Eamonn shrugged his shoulders.

"I don't know. I suppose I should have phoned there straightaway but when you said the car wasn't there and you were so adamant that they couldn't be there I assumed they would not be there. Still all's well that ends well!"

"Thanks again Eamonn."

"Glad to be of service. This time they were lucky, next time..." He just looked at me, I knew what he meant when he said, "Well let's just say there will not be a next time ok Richard?" I nodded in agreement. "Right, that's that then. By the way I've told the lads to escort them back to the 'Holiday Camp' so they should get back fairly soon and they won't get lost on the way this time." He smiled and gave a wink. I thanked him once again and turned to go. "Richard," he called after me, "Don't forget now. Stress to them that whatever has happened tonight, that pub is off limits. The next time they may not be so lucky."

"Yeah I sure will and Eamonn," I paused.

"Yes Richard?" he looked at me quizzically, "Is there something else you wanted?"

"No, not really just thanks."

The engine sprung into life as I closed the passenger door and with a quick glance in the rear view mirror to ascertain all was clear Kelly spun the wheel on full lock. With a squeal of protest from the front tyres scrubbing across the surface of the road Kelly swung the van in an arc and once again we were racing off into the night.

"How did you get on?" He asked, but I wasn't listening, I was too busy wondering how we had missed them.

"Sorry Kelly, I was miles away how did I get on did you ask?"

"Yes, with Eamonn, any news?"

"Oh yes. Yes of course Eamonn." I repeated still only half concentrating on the conversation. I was still wondering how we had missed the car. I was certain it wasn't there.

"Well how did you get on?" He asked again.

"Sorry Kelly." I pushed any further thoughts about the car to the back of my mind. "Yes Eamonn came up trumps. He tracked them down to the pub."

"Which pub, I thought you said that they hadn't been there?"

"The one called O'Grady's, not the one I went in."

"Oh I see." He fell silent for a moment before going on, "You checked there anyway." He stated in a matter of fact way, then added, "Well I mean, we looked for the car there."

"I know and I swear it wasn't there."

"So where was it?"

"I don't know and it's been niggling me. Don't get me wrong, I am pleased and relieved to know the lads are safe, but where was the car?" I like Kelly had not seen it anywhere. "Kelly, I'm not convinced. They won't have left yet can we have another look around near the pub. We must have missed it, I know it wasn't there so it must be parked on one of the side roads somewhere."

"Ok, but I don't know where unless it was further down on the housing estate." We continued the journey in silence.

"Can we check down there again?" So Kelly once again swung into the road leading to the housing estate. We drew a blank.

"Where else?"

"Well it only leaves the second housing estate and we'll have been everywhere within reason." With that he swung the van into the road where the houses were and slowed down so we could check both sides. We had driven down a fair length of the road but still nothing. "What do you reckon Richard?"

"Drive down to the shops and if it's not there well then I just don't know." We crawled our way to the shops passing by the telephone box where I had stopped earlier to phone Eamonn, but still nothing.

As we turned into the small parade of shops the silhouette of an old milk churn, casually tossed onto a rough piece of ground and thrown into relief by the lights of the van, suddenly reminded me of the cellar back at the 'Holiday Camp'. The memories of all those milk churns, detonators and explosive mix came flooding back. With the lads disappearance and the ensuing chasing around looking for them everything else had been temporarily forgotten. My God, I thought to myself. Then I remembered the phone box. I promptly forgot all about looking for my car, as this was more important now. I needed to think of some excuse to use the telephone and phone Sean. Something that sounds convincing, something that sounds plausible. I thought about it for a moment or two and came up with an idea.

"Well it doesn't seem to be anywhere around here, so what now Richard?"

"Let's call it a night. At least we know they're safe. I'll have to ask them where they hid it when they get back." Just then we passed by the telephone box. "Hang on Kelly." He slammed on the brakes.

"Have you seen it?"

"No sorry. It's just that I saw the phone box and I ought to give Anne a ring."

"No problem." With that he slammed the van into reverse and with a high pitched whine from the gearbox Kelly accelerated backwards to where the telephone box was. "Shouldn't be too long." I said as I got out and slammed the door shut behind me. Once inside the phone box I put in a quick call home to get hold of Sean's number. Then hoping that Kelly had not noticed I quickly dialled Sean's number.

"Hello." It was a soft female voice that answered. "Is Sean there please?"

"Who is it?"

"Tell him that it's Richard."

"Hang on a minute then." There was a clattering noise as she put the receiver down then I heard her calling his name.

"Sean it's for you. Someone called Richard." I heard a muffled voice in the background then Sean was on the line.

"Hello there Richard, how are you keeping?"

"I'm fine, now listen carefully Sean as I've not much money and I'm calling from a call box in the Republic. I need your help."

"What's the problem?"

"I'm working down near Louth and Chanonrock at a place they call the 'Holiday Camp', I'm here with two of my lads on a contract. The place is something to do with O'Shea but I don't know whether he owns it or not but his two cousins live here..." Sean cut across my conversation.

"What's their name?"

"O'Connor, but that's not important..." He interrupted me again.

"Don't know them, sorry Richard go on."

"Like I said their name isn't important for now, but what is, is that I've discovered that where we are working is just a front for a big IRA bomb production area. They're packing milk churns with explosive and so on. Sean we need to talk officially..." The pips started to go. I pushed in some more money. "Sean, hello. Sean are you still there?"

"Yes I'm still here. Go on Richard." I took a quick look over towards the van to see what Kelly was doing. He was oblivious as two young girls were chatting to him. "Richard go on."

"Sorry Sean. I was just making certain I was not outstaying my welcome."

"Are you with someone then?"

"Yeah, one of the O'Connor brothers."

"Shit man, why didn't you say?"

"Don't worry some of the local talent is keeping him amused."

"Ok, so what are you saying Richard. Is it that you want me to act as a go between or something?"

"No it has got to be more than that. That's why I say we need to talk officially. I am in the ideal situation. Here I am, in the south, working in close proximity with the IRA. I am trusted, I see things and I overhear things and now this bomb factory. All this information must be useful to somebody up there."

"Sure it is so you could pass it to me?"

"Now come on Sean you know better than that. If I get caught passing information then I am spying and it is good night nurse. Then what's going to happen to Anne? No Sean I need some form of insurance not only for me, but also for Anne and the future. I need to be on the payroll. I need to become a soldier again. Remember when you were over in Kent you tried to persuade me to join the TA. Well is that still an option?"

"It's a possibility, but I can only get you into the UDR, which is a long way from your home."

"Well can you look at the options for me because if I'm to become the whistle blower on the IRA I need some firm reassurances. Sean I'm not prepared to take the risks with out any commitment from the British Government, ok?"

"Ok. I understand. Leave it with me Richard. Perhaps if I spoke with my senior officer he could suggest something."

"Then what?" I asked.

"Then I'll get back to you."

"How?"

"Somehow, somebody will get a message to you. Don't worry Richard. I'll get back to you." With that the rapid pips cut across the conversation. "Sean, I must go. Hear from you soon."

"Yeah cheers Richard we'll be..." The phone went dead. All I could do now was to sit tight and wait for either him or someone else to contact me.

Chapter 24

Inside the barracks, a Sergeant kept a wary eye on the weather as he briskly made his way across the camp. In his hand, he clasped a buff envelope file as he walked through the outer door of the nondescript two-story building identified as A3. A3 was the nerve centre for field operations and inside was a hive of activity. It was here that all information gathered by the intelligence service was collated and sifted through. Photographs studied in minute detail. Where taped conversations obtained through covert surveillance and secure signals were all analysed. This was all very necessary to keep Her Majesty's Government informed of an ever-changing military world.

The Sergeant made his way through the door marked Sector 2 F/Ops & Planning. Walking along the short corridor with doors either side he eventually came to a door marked 'Colonel D. Ash (Field Ops)'. He tapped on the open door and a booming voice summoned.
"Enter."
Behind the desk sat a man in his mid forties with slightly greying hair thinning on top. He had a round face of ruddy complexion and sported a moustache. He was of average build and known to his friends as Dash.
"Good morning Sergeant, is that the file on Operation Ferryman?" he asked.
"Yes sir. I was told it was required urgently so I brought it over straight away." He placed the envelope file marked 'Classified Operation Ferryman' on the desk.
"Thank you sergeant." Just then the secure telephone on his desk rang. He picked up the phone.
"Hello, Ash speaking, just hold for one." He looked up at the Sergeant. "Thank you Sergeant that'll be all for now. He saluted the Colonel and left. "Sorry about that. Yes any news about our target Ferryman?"
"A contact was made with his home this morning." A voice at the end of the phone said.
"And?"
"Nothing much, only to ask his wife for our players phone number."
"Nothing more than that?"
"No Sir."
"What about from the other side, anything?"
"Not as yet. We definitely know he entered via Dublin. We know there are two additions. We also know target has moved from last known base to Louth area. Close surveillance reveals he has reached destination known locally as the 'Holiday Camp'. Whilst we talk we are receiving a report from sector would you like me to call back?"
"Please, how long?"
"Oh a couple of minutes."
"Fine." He replaced the phone and opened the file and studied its contents.

Down in the control centre another outside line rang.
"TCG Duty Operations."
"Mother please?" A voice with an Irish accent said.

"Who's calling?"

"Ferry Captain."

"Just a minute whilst I try to connect you." The telephonist passed it through to the controller.

"Ferry Captain on line one."

"Hello Foxtrot Charlie control speaking"

"Had a phone call from target requesting to join the circus. He's uncovered vital information."

"What sort of info?"

"Implications are that it's of major importance. Possible Northern Ireland Mix."

"Whereabouts are you Foxtrot Charlie as I need to discuss further and come back to you?"

"I'm at home base, but can come in out of the cold if you want?"

"We'll let you know. By the way we've had report from Pilot. Target had problems, did you know?"

"Yeah he mentioned briefly but I believe cleared up. He couldn't say too much as he was with opposing player and phoning from call box."

"Ok understood. How serious is he about joining?"

"Very. You know I've been cultivating him for some time don't you?"

"Yeah. I believe you've been to his house as well haven't you?"

"Yes I was over there a little while back. Had the place cleaned whilst there and I understood that he was to be P-V checked, or am I wrong?"

"No you're right. HQ handled. Anyway I'll come back to you soon. We'll call you on the net if we want you. Ok?"

"Sure. Cheers." The phone clicked as the receiver was replaced.

The secure phone on the desk rang and Dick Ash instinctively reached out and picked it up as he continued to read the manila file in front of him.

"Ash. Who?" He quickly put down the file. Now he was interested. "Right, so you say we've had a positive response according to our man." He paused to listen to what the other person was telling him. "Good, hmm how about setting up a meeting with our key players after all we definitely need someone. Can I leave you to organise something? Oh I guess the sooner the better. Ok a week then, yes let Sheila know the actual date and time and I'll be there. Thanks speak with you soon." He put down the phone, looked down at the file and idly tapped on the desk deep in thought.

The blue Volvo with a Dublin registration was indicating to turn right. It moved to the centre of the road slowed then stopped. The driver, a slightly built man, sat waiting patiently for a break in the oncoming traffic as the radio softly played background music. It was precisely a week since the field operatives had been in contact with their control, and here he was waiting to attend a meeting with other senior people at the circus to discus Operation Ferryman. An oncoming driver slowed and flashed his headlights and the Volvo driver raised his hand in acknowledgement as he turned across in front of him. He stopped just inside the entrance to Gough Barracks. An armed soldier approached the driver's window.

197

"Good morning sir." The soldier looked at the identity card that the man proffered whilst a sergeant checked the registration against his list then gave a slight nod of his head to the soldier and raised the barrier. He parked the blue Volvo in the visitors car park alongside another a vehicle with a Belfast registration, then walked towards an unmarked door some fifty yards or so away.

Colonel Dick Ash was preparing himself for the meeting with the main players from sector. The meeting was to take place later that day and it was very necessary he was fully informed on the latest developments within the circus and 'Operation Ferryman'.
"Well Frank, what's your feeling about our target?"
"In what way Sir?"
"Well you're in charge of Sector, it's your M R F (Military Reaction Force) that's been looking after this one. So what's your feel? What's the input from Gough on this?"
"Well 14 Int. and SB haven't had a lot to go on. We know the target was in the Para's..."
"Served in Ulster?"
"Yes sir but came out prior to Jan '72."
"What else about his military background, anything there?"
"His record is good."
"Any weakness, any blemish?"
"Not particularly."
"From RUC, anything?"
"Nothing specific."
"What about links with known targets, anything there?"
"No, unless we consider Leonard?" Dick's brow furrowed in a frown.
"Leonard?" He shot up one eyebrow questioningly.
"Yes Sir, a Major Paul Leonard at Dorking."
"Oh yes, wasn't he some sort mercenary?"
"Yes that's right. He was recruiting a mercenary force for Angola before the PM got wind of it and had it squashed. Could have had certain repercussions you know the sort of thing."
"Have you spoken with our counterparts in other agencies?"
"Yes Sir."
"And?"
"Nothing, he's clean.
"What about family?"
"As per the file, parents still alive, a brother and his wife Anne. No children."
"Friends and people he knows?"
"Main one is Paul Jones his partner. Went to school with him, joined the army together, served together in the Para's and nothing really known except military record."
"Overall how do you view him as a candidate?"
"Well I feel he has a lot to offer. He is in the area we want operatives. He has offered his services with provisos."
"Would that be a problem?"
"No I don't think so Sir. I'm sure we could re-enlist him, fix him up with papers and

a rank. No problem."

"How would we operate with him, would it be via our own circus or would it be via RUC SB; MRF or Stormont and one of their TCG's?"

"I would expect it to be through MI6 control either via 14.Int or MRF. I would not want him controlled through another agency." The Colonel considered this for a minute or two. "Hmm. Yes I think your right. I agree, we don't want him working outside our control, otherwise we won't get first hand information." He thought some more about what Frank had told him about the target before he made up his mind. "Ok Frank. I've heard what you've said and I agree. We go with him. We present the facts to the meeting and my recommendation is that 'Operation Ferryman' goes ahead. We need to arrange a meeting at the safe house. Thank you Frank and well done."

"Will that be all Sir."

"Yes thank you Frank, it's been most enlightening and very useful. Yes very useful indeed."

The noise of the helicopter's approach grew to crescendo. It circled the square once then came in to land. No sooner had it touched down and the pilot killed the engine. The door opened and a slightly built man wearing sunglasses and civilian clothes stepped down onto the square followed by a Major from the UDR. They were both met by a Sergeant who escorted them to the building marked A3 and into the briefing room for the forthcoming briefing. Operation Ferryman was about to begin.

Colonel Ash greeted the two newcomers and welcomed them to the meeting. "Gentlemen, I'd like to introduce you to our visitors, Major O'Rourke, otherwise known as 'J' from Military Intelligence 'Special Operations and MRF' and on my left I'll refer to this gentlemen as agent 'X'. 'X' does have some bearing on the subject of today's briefing and as part of the RUC SB network, operating undercover for them within Eire, his input is valuable." At this last comment a murmur of dissent went around the room as the agent looked on impassively. "Gentlemen if you would allow me to finish." Gradually the murmuring subsided and order returned to the meeting. "As I was about to say, I know the RUC Special Branch and ourselves do not always see eye to eye, but in this instance 'X' is our man within the RUC SB."

"A question Colonel."

"Yes Belchar."

"Are you saying he is a liaison operative within SB?"

"Yes and no. The facts are that X is our operative, a member of our group albeit the RUC think that they are his taskmasters we are privy to all information and we filter off what we require and they get the info after us."

"In other words Colonel are you suggesting he is Military Intelligence?"

"That's exactly what I'm suggesting, but it goes even further than that, X is also a highly respected IRA operative. A double agent!" This disclosure immediately caused an excited buzz around the briefing. "Gentleman, gentleman if you would allow me to continue." Ash waited patiently for the meeting to come to order before continuing. "As I was saying, X, whom some will also know as Foxtrot Papa or Ferry Pilot, has a crucial role to play in our circus and has for many months, no years passed us a lot of useful intelligence from the Republic about the senior members of the IRA. However we could always do with more intelligence about our enemies, especially the top persons within their operation and ideally get to know more about their plans, their targets etc. Unfortunately it is not always possible to obtain sufficient data because of logistical problems and as you know we do suffer to a certain extent because of this. Anyway I think that this situation could well be changed in the not too distant future and with the help of Ferry Pilot and others we can go a long way to resolving the problems we have been encountering in the past. I will now like to hand you over to Frank to bring you up to date on some very important developments over in Eire. So Frank would you please continue."

"Thank you Sir. As you know we have for a long time now had our ideas about the target known as O'Shea." Frank pressed the button on the projector and an enlarged picture of O'Shea was projected on the screen for all to see. "As far as we can ascertain, and that is with help from our contacts within the Republic, O'Shea is a key person, if not the key person within the IRA. This has been recognised over a period of time and has since been confirmed by various reports received back from the field. In fact even Ferry Pilot has a fair in depth knowledge of O'Shea. Am I correct?" Frank looked at the civilian. He gave a slight inclination of his head as confirmation. "So we have for quite some time had the target under surveillance. Then earlier this year a second target came into the frame. Our man in Dublin alerted us that a car bearing a Maidstone registration had been seen in the vicinity of the Tara Hotel, a hotel believed to be owned by O'Shea. We arranged for an operative to stay at the Tara and carry out a covert surveillance of target number two, who can be seen in this picture." Frank depressed the button on the remote control and a picture of Richard James was thrown up on the screen. "The question is how does he fit in with O'Shea? We thought we could tie him in with O'Shea as a possible link, but an added complication came into the frame in the shape of a third target as seen here." A picture of Paul Jones was thrown up on the screen. "This person we now know is definitely connected with target two and both parties are newcomers to this circus. We needed to know their involvement if any with our known target. We do know that soon after arrival they were implicated in some sort of trouble at the Tara nightclub, but having checked that further we can be certain that they were caught up in something as innocent bystanders. What our man did manage to ascertain was that targets two and three were both over in Eire working for O'Shea on his farm and that was all. Our man has checked as much as he possibly can but has not any conclusive proof that they are involved with the IRA, here or over there. We have of course checked with five on this as well as CRO but there is nothing to link either to any known activist, sleeping cell or IRA sympathiser. However, we did get a lucky break, just as we thought we were going nowhere on this one. O'Shea - target one - decided to take target two to his farm in Ulster. We do now know that target two is one Richard James. We also know he is married, with one brother but no children. Both parents are still living and he works with his father in the family business known as James Fruit Farms here in Kent. Whilst in Ulster O'Shea introduced target two to the neighbouring farmers." Frank picked the file off the desk in front of him and quickly flicked over some pages. "Ah got it. He was introduced to the Devlin boys, Ross O'Toole and Mike McCluskey. The latter two being ex B Specials."

"How was that a lucky break Frank?"

"Through meeting target two O'Toole and McCluskey came over here to England with a third party - a very good friend of theirs - who by coincidence was non other than our man code name Ferry Captain. Through the chance meeting in Ulster and their subsequent trip over here Ferry Captain was introduced to target two. Another lucky break was that both targets are both ex-Para's and this gave our man something in common - a talking point. Then when our man came over on manoeuvres he had an excuse to invite himself to target two's home for the weekend and this gave us the opportunity we had been waiting for. Our man managed to get us a small window where he, target two and his wife were away from the farm. This window was sufficiently large enough to allow us enough time to call in our cleansing department. We had also sufficient warning to enable us to carry out thorough surveillance op, and the rest is history. There was only one fly in the ointment and that was for some reason RUC SB took more than just a passing interest in our operation. In fact the cleansing department reported two Irishmen appearing on the scene in a blue Volvo. These two as yet are unconfirmed operators from another circus but whose we are not totally sure as yet."

"Perhaps I could help." Ferry Pilot' spoke with a soft Irish accent. Frank looked at the visitor, then back to Ash. Colonel Ash nodded his approval.

"Ok fire away."

"The two men in question were from Sector and under direct command of Mother. In other words they were friendly but part of Six operating out of Gough Barracks."

"What the hell were they doing there? Didn't they think for a moment that they could have jeopardised the whole Operation?"

"Steady Frank. Before everyone gets too excited on this score. They were there at our request. They had been pulled in with my authorisation and were briefed to operate as independents as a back up to our resources. They are in fact part of 14 Int. Company operating under extreme circumstances. After all we were looking at a possible candidate for recruitment at that time. We had, through our man, fostered a possible working relationship but needed all the data we could lay our hands on I hope that dispels some of the misgivings. I accept that we do not like using other agencies but in this case I felt it would be useful. Ok?"

"Sorry Sir, I did not realise."

"That's fine Frank you were not to know, anyway please continue."

"So in light of what we've just heard we can now say that the Volvo was friendly. By the way Sir, have you had any feedback from them?"

"Yes Frank and I'll cover that in a minute."

"So, the cleaners had chance to sweep the property and to install an eavesdropping system plus we've managed to attach a tracking device to the target's car. Once his job had been done our man returned to his unit. Colonel Ash will bring you up to date on the latest."

"Thank you Frank. Right gentlemen, on the table in front of you, you will find a resume of target two's life. You will note that he returned to the Republic on his own earlier this year, in fact our people at Heathrow advised us he took a flight to Dublin where he was met by O'Shea. Our man kept them under surveillance and we know he returned to the Tara Hotel. Later a high powered delegation held a meeting at the Tara, the meeting included the Taoiseach and a number of other Ministers. It was because of this meeting we managed to obtain further details about our possible, with the help of the Special Branch and our man in Dublin. Our man managed a clean sweep of his bedroom at the Hotel and obtained some items, which are copied, into his file. The present situation is that target two returned to the Republic with his partner and four additional men. Both vehicles were checked through the Ferry terminal at Dublin and tailed to the Tara. Since then we now know that target two has moved into the Louth region whilst target three is south of Dublin. Any questions so far?" Dick paused and looked around the briefing room. "No questions?" He waited a couple of seconds before proceeding. "So we now know he has moved to another of O'Shea's family farms. This is known as the 'Holiday Camp' and the O'Connor brothers live there." A picture showing Patrick and Kelly O'Connor with Marie in the centre flashed onto the screen. "The female pictured in the centre is Marie O'Connor, the wife of Patrick the eldest of the two brothers. The younger one is Kelly O'Connor. We know both these men as IRA. What we did not know until seven days ago was they're position within the organisation. Any questions so far?"

"Yes Sir, are you at liberty to say what they're role is within the IRA?"

"Well first of all we ought to be aware that the O'Connor's drive an old Royal Mail van complete with English registration. The importance of this is that it does not look out of place in Ulster. Also I am told that provided one knows the area there are so many byways and tracks around that part of the country that anyone could be over the border in under ten minutes. Imagine the advantage of that?" He paused to let his point sink in. "Add to that the fact that target two made contact with Ferry Captain seven days ago advising him that the 'Holiday Camp' was a front for the mass production of milk churn bombs. These bombs we know all about in Ulster. This I feel is extremely valuable information and something we did not know previously." He looked about the room to see that the seriousness of this discovery was not lost on anyone. "I think that it is fair to say and that everyone here would agree that for some time now we have wanted someone in the Republic who was close to O'Shea. Unfortunately this would mean either turning someone within his organisation, which because of his position and those around him would be extremely unlikely, or recruiting someone whom we could perhaps install at the Tara. Neither of these options would really fit the bill. Well that was until we had this break with target two. The latest situation is that target two has not only provided us with good information, but he is liked and trusted by O'Shea. Add to this that he has offered his services to Her Majesty's Government, provided we enlist him back into the military." A definite murmur of approval went around the room. "Also, I would add, he has already had a military background within the Para's so he is used to discipline. On top of this he joined the Angola lot as a mercenary so obviously he is happy to go back to a military type background. It is with these things in mind that I propose to enlist this individual as part of our team subject to my meeting with him at our safe house over there. The operation is for your eyes and ears only and gentlemen, I should not have to remind you that it is classified information. From now on target two will be known as code name Ferryman. This whole operation is to be known as Operation Ferryman. Gentlemen that concludes the briefing and thank you."

A hum of conversation developed as people chatted about what they had heard.

"Frank, I need to speak with both you and Ferry Pilot to discus the arrangements for over the other side. Shall we say ten minutes in my office?"

"Yes Sir."

Chapter 25

In the control centre at Gough Barracks the TCG Duty Officer for Sector and MRF had just been passed a message addressed to 'Mother' code Red.

'Mother, we're coming over on flying visit. Could you please put us up at you're house overnight. Also thought we could go to the Captain's table for dinner and don't forget to bring my cousin the Pilot and his friend, can't think of his name but you know whom I mean, the Ferryman. Expect to see you in forty-eight hours.'

He read the message carefully before picking up the telephone.
"Comms Duty Officer please." He waited to be put through.
"Sector Duty Officer, 'Operation Ferryman' is at level Red so need to send following message addressed to Fox trot Charlie and Foxtrot Papa. Ok I'll hold." He waited a few minutes whilst he was transferred through to a Communications Clerk who would take the details.
"Message coded level Red." He paused, "Addressed to Foxtrot Charlie and Fox trot Papa." He paused again. "Message reads, we have 'Go' on Ferryman. Confirm Ferryman is 'Go'. Friends arrive in forty-eight hours and will meet at home. Foxtrot Charlie to make arrangements for collection. Mother. Message ends. Please read it back." He listened patiently as the message was read back to him. "Right thank you that's all." He replaced the handset. He had one further call to make before leaving for the night.
"Sorry to trouble you at home Sir, it's the TCG Sector and MRF Duty Officer, just to let you know we've been advised by HQ that 'Operation Ferryman' has moved to a positive." He paused whilst his superior Officer spoke. "Yes Sir, I have followed Standing Orders, everything will be in place tomorrow. Sorry Sir what was that?" He paused again, "Yes that's right Sir, by special delivery tomorrow. Thank you Sir, goodnight." He replaced the secure phone. The TCG Duty Office door opened and his relief came in.
"Hi Steve not too much to hand over. Ten minutes ago had a positive on 'Operation Ferryman' from HQ. I've advised the old man and communications. Logistics are being handled by Sector, Safe house already on standby. We will need to confirm once we know we have our target en route. Both Captain and Pilot have been advised that it's a go for Ferryman. So all info has been circulated to those who need to know. Oh ETA from HQ is day after tomorrow, which gives a realistic time for delivery to target. And that's it. I'm out of here. Good night Steve."
"Goodnight Ray." The TCG Duty Officer settled down to what he hoped would be a quiet night.

It had been nine days since my call to Sean and I still hadn't heard a word and now it was the start of the weekend. I took a look at my watch it was already getting on for three-thirty and we had just finished off the first orchard. The sky looked grey and overcast so I thought, there's no point in making a start on the second orchard today, we'll leave it for now and make a fresh start in the morning.

"Right lads, we'll call it a day then. Come on Terry you and I on the trailer Mike you're driving."

There was a puff of black smoke from the tractor's exhaust as Mike started the engine and we were off bumping our way towards the house. As we entered the courtyard Patrick was stood there looking somewhat preoccupied with whatever he was holding in his hand. Hearing our approach whatever had preoccupied his thoughts was lost as he looked up and with a grin called across to us.

"Richard this is for you." He waved a brown flimsy object in the air. "It's a letter Special Delivery." I got off the trailer and walked over wondering what that could be about.

"Thanks Patrick." I reached out to take the letter from him, but he snatched it away.

"Nothing wrong is there Richard?" For a minute there I could have sworn there was a cold murderous look in those eyes then it was gone. He was grinning at me as he passed the letter to me. "Sorry Richard, only joking!" I took the letter and slowly turned it over in my hands looking for some sort of clue.

"I wonder what this is all about?" I said more to myself than anyone else. "Came special delivery you say?"

"Yes arrived just before you got here. Brought out by a young lad from Dundalk. I hope everything's all right at home."

"Hmm, so do I." I muttered as I pushed the letter in my pocket and started to walk towards the front door.

"Aren't you going to open it then?" I stopped and said quite sarcastically.

"Yes, later if that's all right with you."

"Oh I'm sorry," he said smiling. "How rude of me. It's just that not having a phone here I was a little concerned in case it was from your home. I wondered if something had happened that was all." I shot him a sideways glance. "Well, it's very unusual for us to get special deliveries out here and I just thought that if something was wrong and you needed to phone home then maybe Kelly or I..." I cut him short.

"Could get me there quicker. Is that what you were going to say?"

"Yes that's right," he said quite lamely. Yeah I bet, I thought to myself, more like you wanted to know what's going on sunshine.

"No it's all right thanks Pat." My voice was tinged with sarcasm "It'll keep until I've got tidied up." With that I turned and disappeared inside. I went straight to my room and closed the door behind me, taking the letter from my pocket I, once more, looked at the envelope. It had an Eire stamp on it and a sticker, which read Speisialta Seachaid (Special Delivery). Now who in the Republic would be sending me something Special Delivery? I turned the letter over but there were no clues as to where it was from or the sender's name, therefore the only way I was going to find out was to open it. I paused only for a moment then tore the envelope open. Inside was a neatly folded single sheet of white notepaper upon which the following short note was written.

URGENT need to meet tonight to discuss business details. I have arranged car to pick you up at 7.30 p.m. outside O'Grady's, the pub on the hill. Imperative you are there on time, as car will not wait. Cater for at least one possible night away.

'S'

I assumed that the S stood for Sean, but there was no address or anything else to confirm its origin, therefore it could well have come from anyone. It could in fact be an IRA trap, although I had to admit the handwriting looked like Sean's but I couldn't be certain. I read and re-read the note over and over again. I was still not totally convinced that it was all it purported to be. Perhaps someone had seen me go into the cellars and told the brothers who then set me up. But if so who? Was it the one who was a bundle of laughs, spat on the ground, and gave me that murderous stare? Or maybe I had been careless and left the storeroom light on when whoever it was had entered whilst I was in the cellar. All these thoughts and a hundred and one others came to mind. What should I do? The more I dwelt on the question, the more confused I became. If I decided the note was aboveboard then I would have to involve the lads, either way a decision was needed. Suddenly I knew what was expected of me. I decided to go, which would mean taking either Terry or Mike into my confidence. Just then I heard voices approaching, so stuffing the envelope and the note back into my pocket I opened my door feigning surprise at seeing the lads.

"Hello, I was just about to come down and find you two. Mike, have you a minute?" My mind was made up; it was now or never.

"Yeah sure."

"See you in a minute Terry."

"Ok."

"What's up Richard?"

"Here." I beckoned to him to follow me into my room.

"Problems?" He asked. I put my finger to my lips. Once inside the room I closed the door.

"Shh, listen carefully to what I say and no questions, ok?"

"Depends on what you say!"

"Can I trust you?" I asked.

He looked at me with indignation. "Of course you can." He sounded annoyed at first then when he saw my look he relented.

"Why? Is there something wrong? I know you said we were in bandit country and I know both Terry and I caused a problem the other night by going into O'Grady's pub but I thought that was all sorted?"

"It is."

"So what's happened?"

"Nothing." I paused I didn't really know what to say without implicating Mike. "Look Mike, I need to get out this weekend I have a very important meeting with some Protestant farmers but because we are here and you both were seen in O'Grady's it makes life a little difficult..."

He interrupted me. "How does it?"

"Well the local IRA know my car now so I can't drive out to meet these people otherwise the local IRA will know where I've been." I said bending the truth.

"How will that matter?"

"I don't know, but I think it would be better if they didn't. Had they not seen my car then I think I could have gone without any repercussions but I just don't want to risk it and rock the boat. After all we have a lot of contracts over here and a lot of money riding on this work. So I need your help." He thought for a moment or two before answering.

"Hmm." He didn't sound that confident. "Go on, how can I help?"

"Well first of all you must not breathe a word to a soul and that includes Terry."

"Why, Terry's with us isn't he?"

He seemed to smell a rat. "I know. But all the more reason why he should not know, just trust me on this."

Once again he fell silent and I was beginning to think he wasn't going to play, then suddenly he nodded. "All right. So what do you want me to do?"

"So you promise not to say a word?"

"Yes you have my word on it."

"Shh. Hang on a minute." I got up from my bed and moved to do door. I opened the door as quietly as possible and checked the corridor in both directions; nobody. I listened for the slightest sound; nothing. I carefully closed the door again and quietly crossed back to my bed. Then in a subdued voice continued. "Tonight, I have to go to the O'Grady's pub where I am being met by a business acquaintance. They will pick me up from there..." He again interrupted me. "I thought you said an acquaintance?"

"I did why?" I couldn't see what his point was.

"It's just that you said they'll pick you up so there's more than one then?"

So that was where he was coming from, although I couldn't see what difference it would make. "There could be for all I know." I said, "Does it really matter, he, they, what's the difference?"

He thought for a moment before answering, looked at his fingernails then looked back at me. "None really I guess, just that it sounds a bit suspicious to me. Firstly outside O'Grady's an IRA pub, then being picked up. Who is this mystery person or persons then?"

I didn't want to tell him too much. "Mike they are important people, lets leave it like that." We sat there in silence whilst Mike considered this last statement, then he must have decided not to press the point.

"Ok."

I felt a weight lift and heaved an inward sigh of relief. That's the first hurdle over with I thought to my self as I continued with my slight fabrication. "Right, as I was saying, I don't want you to say a word to anyone and that includes Terry. Now as they are picking me up and I'm not too sure when I'll be back I'm going to ask you to cover for me whilst I'm away. If I'm not back by Sunday night get one of the brothers to run you into Louth and phone this number." I wrote down the number that Eamonn had given me for emergency use. "But remember the number I've given to you must not under any circumstances be communicated or shown to anybody else, do you understand, nobody and that includes Terry?" I passed him the piece of paper. Mike looked at the number, nodded and then folded it up placing it carefully inside his wallet.

"One thing Richard."

"What's that?" Now comes the crunch.

"What, if anything, has this to do with that Special Delivery letter you received today?" I shook my head and was, shall I say, economical with the truth.

"Nothing at all, why do you ask?"

He gave me a knowing look and a half smile. "Ok Richard if you say so. Have it your own way then." He got up from the single chair in my room and walked towards the door. "My lips are sealed then until Sunday." He opened the bedroom door and checked the corridor in both directions and said in a low voice that was almost a whisper, "Good luck and don't worry I'll cover for you." Then he was gone closing the door behind.

"Well that was a great meal, thanks for that. Now if you'll all excuse me I have some business I need to attend to." I pushed my chair back and looked over to Patrick and said mainly for his benefit. "I've got to meet another bloke this weekend about some more work." I smiled as I said, "That's what we get for being so good. Obviously our reputation has spread." Then I added as an after thought, "By the way Pat, that was what the Special Delivery was. So you see, it's not all bad news after all." I got up and made my way to the door, "Oh by the way Mike just in case I do get held up with this bloke you know what to do, as I said earlier, start in the lower orchard tomorrow if I'm not back. If I should be longer and you need anything I'm sure Patrick or Kelly will give you a lift to the phone box." I winked at Mike then looked across to Patrick.
"Won't you Pat."
"Oh yes, sure." He answered taken off his guard, "No problem. Are you anticipating being away then?"
"Well you never know do you." I smiled and left it at that. "Now if you'll excuse me I must get on. Mike can I have a quick word?"
"Sure, excuse me all." With that Mike followed me out of the room as I headed towards the stairs.
"Nothing's changed has it?" He spoke in a low whisper.
I shook my head and pointed upwards to signal my room and put my finger to my lips. Once inside my bedroom I spoke. "No it's still on for tonight, in fact I'll have to leave soon if I'm to be there in time. Now you're happy with everything?"
"Yes."
"No problems? You know what to do if I'm not back?"
"Yes, phone the number which I've got here." He said patting the back pocket in his jeans, which held his wallet. "What about Terry, what do I tell him?"
"About what?"
"Work wise?"
"Jesus, Mike use you imagination. Just tell him... tell him what I said downstairs that we are starting on the lower orchard. Something along those lines, it doesn't really matter. In fact yes that's a good idea." I said thinking out loud, "Why don't you literally make a start on the lower orchard because it needs pruning anyway."
"What about the replanting though?"
"We can do that afterwards, besides the lower orchard is only about an acre so with both of you on it, it should take you nicely through to Sunday. Then on Monday morning we'll start on the replanting again. Now if Terry should query it, and I doubt he will, just say that I felt it best we left the replanting until Monday just in case we needed anything from the local agricultural suppliers at short notice. Ok?"
"All right. So, if you're not back by Sunday I'll phone this number?"
I nodded. "That's right."
"I assume somebody will be there?"

208

"Should be."

"What do I do if there isn't anyone there?" I fished in my pocket and found a scrappy piece of paper.

"If not then..." I hastily scribbled down Eamonn's address plus the telephone number again. "Then get Kelly to run you to this address and ask for Eamonn. Now remember his name and tell whoever you see that you're working at the 'Holiday Camp'. So don't forget." I repeated his name again to emphasise my point. "Eamonn ok got that?"

"Eamonn." He said as he checked what I had written on the paper.

"Yes that's right."

He took out his wallet and the other piece of paper I had given him earlier to make sure he kept them together when he noticed the telephone number. "These telephone numbers are the same." He said looking at the both pieces of paper.

"Yes I know, so set fire to that one," I said indicating the piece I had written the phone number on earlier. "Here drop it in this before you burn your bloody fingers" I held out a bent and battered old metal waste bin for him. Mike dropped the flaming paper just before the last remnant went up in flames. "Good, that takes care of that." I looked at my watch; "Right it's time for me to go. See you Mike and with a bit of luck I should be back later and if not, well, definitely before Sunday."

"Yeah, ok cheers mate and good luck."

"Thanks. See you." I left him framed in the doorway to my room as I made my way towards the stairs.

209

Chapter 26

As I stood outside O'Grady's I nervously checked my watch again. It was seven twenty-eight and I was feeling more than just a little vulnerable standing outside this IRA pub. The road in both directions remained deserted.

"Come on, where are you?" I muttered under my breath nervously. "Let's get on with it." My mind was beginning to work overtime. What if this was some sort of trap? What if it wasn't Sean who had sent the note? "Come on pull yourself together man." I said to myself. Of course it was Sean, who else could it have been? I looked at my watch again. It was now seven thirty. I was really getting paranoid about my situation. Once more I looked up the hill in desperation just as the headlights of a car came into view. I held my breath as it started its descent. Was this it I wondered as the car slowed right down until it almost stopped opposite where I stood? I was just about to cross the road when it suddenly accelerated off at high speed. "What the...?" That spooked me even more and it was now seven thirty-one. "Well Richard," I said to myself, "Sod this ...get the hell..." I didn't even have time to think as suddenly out of the blue there was the roar of an engine, the screech of tyres braking, and a thud as car doors were thrown open. The next thing I knew was some guy wearing a black ski mask over his face who jammed the barrel of a small automatic in my ribs. He thumped me in the middle of my shoulder blades and sent me spinning towards the open rear door of the car. "Fucking move. Get in the back before I blow your lights out." As I stumbled towards the rear door he brought the butt of the gun down across my shoulders. The next thing I was aware of was a hood of some description being roughly pulled down over my head. Car doors being slammed as the engine screamed and the smell of burning rubber as the tyres squealed from wheels spinning and we accelerated away up the hill. It had all happened so quickly that I didn't even have a chance to catch my breath, never mind be afraid. I vaguely remember the car was a blue Volvo. Slowly realisation dawned on me, Breandán O'Shea had a blue Volvo and he was IRA, and what's more I had been lifted from outside an IRA pub. So was this O'Shea's doing? If it was then I was well and truly in the shit. As the fuzziness started to clear my thoughts became more lucid. Two things were apparent: one my hands were securely tied so I must have blacked out and two; how stupid of me to be so easily fooled by that 'special delivery' letter. It could only mean one thing, O'Shea had found out that I knew what the 'Holiday Camp' really was. Just how, I wasn't sure unless I had I been careless and left the light on in the storeroom by mistake when I heard the voices there. Or had the thin bloke seen me go to the compound? Did the O'Connor brothers know all along about my discovering their bomb making in the cellar and tell O'Shea? All these thoughts tumbled through my mind. Obviously something had gone dramatically wrong and alerted O'Shea now this was the result. Shit was the only word that readily came to mind.

I was not sure, but it seemed as if the car was now travelling at a more leisurely pace and the tension that I had sensed earlier in the car was starting to slowly ebb away. The guy in the front seat seemed to be in charge of the operation as it was a voice from that direction that said.

"Ok we're clear. Well done everybody." Then the guy sitting next to me spoke for the very first time.

"What about his hands Rick?"

"How do you mean?"

"Well, shall I untie them now?"

"Yeah I don't see why not."

"Richard, it is Richard isn't it?" He asked.

"Yes." The hood muffling my reply.

"Right, I want you to turn slightly to your left so I can untie your hands. Good that's fine. There you are mate I expect that's better for you?"

I rubbed my wrists to encourage the circulation. "Yeah thanks." I grunted to him through a mouthful of material. "Now what about the hood?" I asked.

"What do you reckon Rick?"

"No that has to remain in place."

"But why?" I asked.

"Because those, my friend, are the orders."

In the Sector office briefing room at Gough Barracks Major O'Rourke was playing his part in briefing the Duty Officer, Ferry Pilot and Ferry Captain. He spoke with a slight Irish accent as he outlined the final details of 'Operation Ferryman' that was zero plus thirty minutes away.

"The car should be arriving about now at O'Grady's where the subject is waiting. The idea is that the team will pick up our man from under the noses of the local IRA and bring him over the border to the house, where both you Ferry Captain and you Ferry Pilot will meet with him. The ETA of the car carrying the subject is when Mike?" He raised a questioning eyebrow at the duty officer.

"The journey should take approximately thirty to forty minutes Sir."

"Fine, so ETA should be twenty hundred hours. In which case we need to be in the house by nineteen fifty hours at the latest. Colonel Ash from HQ will join us. Has anyone any questions so far?" He looked to each person in turn. "No one? Good. Well gentlemen it will take us fifteen minutes to reach our destination in which case we have five minutes before we leave. Please make sure you have everything you require and don't forget the duty officer co-ordinates the whole operation from Sector office. So Mike are you clear on your details as Duty?"

"Yes Sir."

"What about you two gentlemen, are you both clear on what is expected?"

"Yes Sir."

"Good, then we go. Mike 'Operation Ferryman' takes priority over anything else as far as you are concerned so please advise your number two. Also advise the team and the backup that 'Operation Ferryman' is now under way."

"Yes Sir, anything else Sir?"

"No that'll be all."

"Very good Sir."

"Gentlemen, the time is now nineteen thirty-five and 'Operation Ferryman' has now started, so let's go." Major O'Rourke led the way from the briefing room.

We started to slow down after what I estimated had been about twenty minutes. Eventually we came to a halt and I heard what I assumed was the driver's window being lowered. I could here someone talking in a low voice but because of the thick hood over my head I couldn't quite make out what was being said. We were only stopped for what seemed like seconds whilst whoever it was spoke to the driver, then we were on the move again. I assume that we had just crossed over the border and we were now in Ulster and still travelling northwards.

"Ok Barry, in a couple of hundred yards you need to take a right, do you see where I mean?" Asked the one in front whom I assumed was called Rick.

"Where?" I assumed that was Barry replying.

"There, near to that tree coming up on the right?"

"Got it."

"I should slow right down now otherwise you may overshoot it as it's only a narrow track?" I felt the car turn to the right, as it did so we slowed to a walking pace. The surface was far from smooth as we bounced from one pothole to the next. Then I felt the car swing round in an arc and heard the crunch of gravel under the tyres as we come to rest. I heard the door alongside me open and felt someone assist me to get out then guide me up some steps into a building.

"Good evening Mr James." A well-spoken voice with the trace of an Irish accent greeted me. "I'm sorry to have to bring you here like this, but for security purposes it had to be. I trust you will forgive us our little stage managed operation and I sincerely hope we have not inconvenienced you too much?" He then addressed someone else in the room. "Please, remove the blindfold from Mr James. I'm sorry Mr James, a slight oversight on my behalf." As they quickly removed the hood, the brightness of my surroundings caused me to blink against the light. I did not say anything immediately but took careful stock of my surroundings. I found myself in a moderate sized room, with fitted carpet and heavy drawn velvet curtains. The furniture consisted of one long wall unit, two easy chairs, a settee, and a small occasional table. Opposite me sat who I assumed was the owner of the voice, that had been addressing me. Although the furnishings were sparse, it had the appearance of being of good quality. On the small table in front of me a freshly poured cup of steaming black coffee; a tray containing a pot of freshly made coffee; a small jug of cream and a bowl of brown sugar. To my left was the long sideboard or unit on top of which stood a tray of drinks. The decor was plain and simple. One thing I did notice was a small camera discretely placed in the far corner of the room just below the ceiling and angled to take in the scenario before it. Sitting in the chair opposite me was a smartly dressed youngish looking man, with fair hair and a freshly scrubbed look about him. At the side of his chair stood a tired looking worn leather brief case.

"Coffee Mr James," he enquired, or would you prefer something a little stronger?" his voice was one that exuded confidence. He had an aura of quiet authority about him.

"Thank you," I answered, "I'll stick with coffee."

"Help yourself to cream and sugar. Oh, would you like some biscuits? Fetch some biscuits would you." He addressed someone standing behind me; I turned in my chair just in time to catch the glimpse of a body as it disappeared through the door. I turned back to face the young man opposite me.

"Where am I?" I asked.

"I'm sorry Mr James that's not for me to say, well not at present any way. I am sure you will forgive me for not telling you, but what I can say is that you are here more as a friend than as an enemy. All I ask of you is to give us a fair hearing and then, if having heard us out you feel that what we are proposing is not for you, you are free to go. Unfortunately you will, of course, have to be blindfolded once again."

The door opened and another man who sat down on the settee joined us. He placed a plate of biscuits on the table in front of me.

"Please help yourself to a biscuit Richard." The man who had just joined us said.

"I'm sorry, should I know you?" I enquired.

"I don't think so Richard," was his reply, "But I know a lot about you," he paused and studied my face, before continuing. "I trust that your journey was not too tedious and like my colleague I must apologise for the method by which you were picked up." I didn't answer; I just sat there quietly studying the man. He had a round face with rosy cheeks, which gave the impression of youth. However, closer examination revealed crows feet at the corner of his eyes and the thinning hair tinged with grey at the temples indicated that he was perhaps older than first appearance. I, upon reflection, put him at mid to late forties. He spoke with a quiet authority; a man who was used to dealing with others; a man who was used to giving orders. Even from what little he had said it was easy to discern he was a man from a public school background. Well educated and judging by the accent probably graduated from Cambridge.

"More coffee Richard?" He asked as he proffered the coffeepot.

"No thank you."

"Perhaps a large Bushmill whisky would be more acceptable?" Without waiting for my reply he got up and made his way over to the drinks tray and poured two large drinks.

"Now Richard, let me continue." He made his way back to the settee placing the tumblers on the table in front of us. "I believe you know a Sean O'Donald?" I tried to ask him a question, but he held up his hand and hurried on. "Please Richard let me finish, I know there must be a lot of question marks in your mind, but I think everything will become clear as we go on. As I was saying I believe you know Sean O'Donald," he paused as if waiting for an answer. "Well do you know O'Donald?"

"Yes," I said hesitantly, "yes I know Sean, why?"

"Good, now, as I said Richard things will become more apparent as we progress," he then addressed his colleague. "Have you got the 'Ferryman' file?" His colleague reached down to pick up the well worn leather brief case situated on the floor beside his chair and very quickly he produced a buff coloured envelope file and passed it over to him. "Thank you." He opened the file and for a moment he paused as if to read its contents.

"What is going on?" I asked.

"Patience Richard. You know Sean O'Donald and you have recently contacted him. You were a member of the Parachute Regiment I do believe before joining a Major Paul Leonard and his Angola boys, it says here that you got disenchanted with that. Why was that Richard?"

213

"I don't see what any of this has got to do with you and unless you tell me why I'm here or who you are then..." But he cut me short.

"Then what Richard? I would be very interested to know what you will do?" He looked at me his eyes seemed to pierce my very soul. "Yes I would be very interested to know what you would do and where you would go without transport? What's more, you do not even know where you are." His voice contained a slight note of resigned irritation as if he had heard this so many times before. "Now having got that out of the way shall we continue?" He asked.

"Just a minute. Your friend over there," I said indicating his colleague, "told me if I wished I could call a halt to the proceedings and leave at any time."

He sighed. "Quite true Richard so you can, after all you are not a prisoner. But a word of caution before you make what could be a catastrophic error of judgement, let me just point out a few things to you. First of all you are not at home in your little secure world, you are over here working in the Republic of Ireland, an Englishman..." I latched onto the bit about the Republic and cut him short.

"Ah, so I am still in the south then?" I was eager to get some idea of my whereabouts.

"I didn't say that, what I did say..."

I interrupted him again, "So are you telling me I'm not in the south and that I'm in the north?"

He sighed again. "Richard," he said patiently. "If you will let me continue your questions will be answered in due course." He looked at me.

"All right then, I'm listening," I said rather petulantly.

"As I was saying, you are free to go at any time, but perhaps you ought to hear me out then consider your options. Now where was I? Ah yes, you were a member of the Parachute Regiment then having served your time you then joined the Angola lot. You also have knowledge of bomb disposal and explosives. Since leaving the military and your abortive time as a mercenary, you have rejoined your father in Kent working as a fruit farmer. Currently you are over here, on your second tour, working for one Breandán O'Shea, correct so far?"

I nodded.

"Good, now I believe on Monday you made a telephone call to Sean O'Donald purporting to have discovered a bomb making factory at your present place of work; is this correct? Your wife's name is Anne and you live at James Fruit Farms in Kent"

"Yes," I said quietly. "How do you know all this?"

"Never mind how we know; suffice it to say we do know. Now Mr James, is this your wife?" With that he showed me the picture of Anne that had disappeared from my room in the Tara.

"Yes, how the hell..."

He held up his hand. "Mr James please just answer the questions, and this letter, is it from your wife?"

He passed me a copy of the letter that had also disappeared from my room at the same time. "Yes it is, but I demand to know how you came by those. Those were in my drawer at the Tara Hotel so how come you've got them?" I was indignant, no, more than that I was fuming at the thought of them having my personal items and it showed.

"Mr James, as I said we have our methods and let's leave it at that otherwise we are not going to get anywhere. Now as I was saying before you interrupted me, did you ask or propose to Mr O'Donald that you should become part of the security force over here?" He looked at me and raised an eyebrow which served to underline his question. "Yes I did."

"Good, I'm pleased that we agree on that. Now Mr James, I have a proposition to make to you. However, before I do I think you ought to meet two people. All I now say to you is, trust me." He beckoned to someone behind me.

"Hello Richard," a softly spoken Irish voice came from behind me. I swung round to look in the direction of the voice and to my horror, standing just inside the door was the slight build of the local IRA commander Eamonn. My mind went into overdrive; so I was right it was Breandán O'Shea's Volvo. Eamonn crossed the room and sat on the settee. I turned to face the three men. I felt numb, what was I to do? Somewhere through the numbness, as if in the distance I heard another voice, one that certainly sounded familiar.

"Hello Richard." I froze; I didn't dare to look round. Who was it? Was it going to be Breandán? It didn't sound like his voice. The spell was broken when a strong hand squeezed my shoulder. The voice continued "How you doing my friend, glad you could come. I did say I would speak to my boss," Sean made his way over to the settee and joined the others. Boy was I relieved to see the big man.

"Hey Sean, am I glad to see you; I was beginning to think that I had been lifted by the IRA." Suddenly I panicked. In my moment of elation, I had forgotten Eamonn. "Sean," I started uncertainly. "If I'm among friends then what's he doing here?" I pointed at Eamonn. "Or are you..." the words would not come.

"No Mr James, we are not the IRA, we are the British Army, allow me to introduce myself and my colleagues," with that the young man in the chair stood up.

"I'm Major Liam O'Rourke of Military Intelligence otherwise known as 'J' and this gentleman is my boss, Colonel Richard Ash from Military Intelligence HQ and the other two gentlemen you know."

"Now Richard, first of all another drink, Liam would you see to it? Thank you." Colonel Ash paused, "As I was saying, you spoke to O'Donald on Monday indicating that you wish to become part of the circus. I'm sorry, I mean our operation out here, but only if you were on the pay-roll of the security forces?" I nodded in agreement. Ash looked at me studying my face in detail. "Hmm." He flicked through the file again. "Well," he paused and looked round the room at the others as if gauging their feelings. I followed his stare looking from one face to the next, but their faces were impassive. Ash continued. "What I've in mind is to enlist you initially into the UDR as a territorial but seconded to Military Intelligence HQ." He looked towards Liam, "Would that create any problems?"

"No sir, I do not foresee any problems."

"Good that's settled then. This will mean that whilst in Ireland you will be regarded as part of the UDR. However, you will be operating under cover for us at HQ. You will automatically hold the rank of Captain in the UDR. The code name for this covert operation is 'Ferryman' and your local controller whilst you are working at the 'Holiday Camp' is to be Sean, code name Ferry Captain but your overall operational control is through Sector. Ferry Captain will be your field link with Sector at all times.

Eamonn, code name Ferry Pilot, will be there as back up in emergency. It is Ferry Captain's job and responsibility for co-ordinating the information both received from you at local level and passed back to you from Sector. The information you communicate to Ferry Captain will then be passed up the line to Sector Duty Office where it will be analysed and decimated through the circus accordingly. Major Liam O'Rourke, otherwise known as 'J' heads up Sector. The Duty Officer is known as Mother and it is he that will always be responsible for your safe operation, his orders of course come from 'J'. It will be Sector, in conjunction with Mother and Ferry Captain who will decide if and when to pull you out. Do you understand?" I nodded. "At all times you must keep in touch at least once a week with Ferry Captain on a pre-arranged schedule. Should you not be able to keep to the schedule then all telephone numbers you have will instantaneously be killed and you will need to get a message back via the emergency route, we will of course brief you on that drill. Ok?" I once again acknowledged my understanding. "Have you any questions?" I thought about what he had said and felt that I had a good grasp of it.

"No I don't think so." I replied.

"Good, because it's very important that you understand how the circus operates. Sean will brief you along with 'J' and make sure you have all the necessary contact numbers once he has sorted out your papers. Sean I trust you have the UDR papers with you?"

"Yes sir."

"Good. Oh, there is one other thing."

"What's that?" I asked.

"You will of course have to go through the swearing of your allegiance, signing the 'Official Secret Act' and so on, but I am sure you understand the procedure Richard"

"Yes sure I do."

"Good. Once we have you up and running we will of course send you on a specialised training course when you get back home."

"What does that entail?"

"You will spend some time at our training establishment where you will be instructed in various techniques of covert surveillance, methodology in obtaining good information and a number of other interesting things. Once you have gone through the schooling you will become a valued member of a specialist group known as 14th Int., but that's for the future. First of all, welcome to the circus Ferryman and good luck."

Sean went over the necessary documents with me and I swore my allegiance to Queen and country signed the set of papers for my enlistment into the UDR. I was then taken into another room where a photographer took my photograph and my new forces ID card showing name, rank and number.

"Ok Richard, this is what is now required from you whilst over here. First of all we need full information on Breandán O'Shea. As much as possible: names; contacts and people he deals with, his business and how it is set-up; the relationship he has with the IRA and if possible its organisation at the top. Once again names contacts and so on. What other business interests does he have, all these sorts of things are of interest to us."

"But how do I know what's useful and what's not?"

"Don't concern yourself about that, let us worry about that score ok?"

"All right."

"Cultivate him. From what you say he already trusts you and by all accounts this is born out by what was said to Ferry Pilot when he took you to meet him. That's correct isn't it?" He turned to Eamonn who nodded giving his reassurance. "Also we need detailed information about the O'Connor brothers and the 'Holiday Camp'. Obviously we know some of what goes on but the details are a little sketchy. Also how does the Tara Hotel and night-club figure in the overall picture? For instance, is it a front for other operations or is it a legitimate business."

"How would I know that?"

"You wouldn't, but what I'm trying to impress on you is any little detail could be important no matter how insignificant it seems."

"Ok. Well there is one thing..." But I thought better of it, I was going to tell them about the fruit being loaded, but I still was not too sure about Eamonn.

"Well Richard, you were going to say?"

"Oh, it's nothing."

"Now I said even what seems insignificant, so what was it?"

"Honestly it was nothing." Ash just fixed me with a stare.

"Well if you're sure then we'll leave it at that. Now for the future, if we want to get hold of you we'll use the trade magazine, what's it called Liam?"

" 'The Grower' Sir."

"Ah yes 'The Grower' that's the one. Well as I was saying if we want to get hold of you we'll put an advertisement in 'The Grower', have you got a copy of what we'll use?"

"It's in the file Sir."

"Is it?" He said thumbing quickly through the pages. "Got it. Here Richard this is what it will look like." He passed me a sheet of paper on which appeared the following advertisement.

'Regular Journeys Abroad will Make Earnings Stretch.'

"Now that will appear in the classified section, I believe I'm right aren't I Liam?" He looked to 'J' for confirmation.

"Yes that's correct Sir, it will appear in the classified section under the heading 'Work overseas'. As you can see each capital letter when put together spells R James. Now if you see that appear then you will need to contact Mother with all haste as we have something urgent for you. All right?"

"I understand."

"Any further questions Richard?" asked the Colonel.

"Yes, who does the blue Volvo belong to?"

"Ah, that's my car," answered Eamonn. "Why?"

"Two things then. First of all was it you or Breandán who followed me on my trip to the Holiday Camp?"

"It was me, now what's your second question?"

"Ok Eamonn, I was introduced to you by Breandán as the local IRA commander," I

217

paused and looked straight into those piercing blue eyes of his, "So what's your game?" He didn't reply. He just sat there and stared back at me. I repeated the question again. "So what is your game?" Still he did not reply. The silence was unbearable. I didn't know what to think, or do. I blinked and looked away. I could feel the frustration building up inside and being unable to contain myself, I exploded with anger, "Come on Eamonn. Tell me. Who do you really work for?" I once again found myself staring deep into those piercing blue eyes of his. I held my breath. Then the silence was broken.

"It is really quite simple Richard, remember the rules."

"Damn the rules Eamonn, who are you and who is your task master?" I asked him vehemently.

"Like I said before all the time the Ferryman is paid the ferry runs. If the Ferryman does not get paid then the ferry ceases to run."

"So who pays the Ferryman is it Breandán O'Shea or England?"

"That's a very good question in these uncertain times, but let me put your mind at rest. In my book it's the UDR, what does it say in yours. Who is going to pay you?" The Colonel intervened. "Gentlemen, gentlemen let me put everyone at ease. Eamonn, trained by British Intelligence, has a foot in both camps so to speak. He is one of our top operators over here. In order for him to stay effective, he needs to remain in the trust of the IRA, just as you Richard have to cultivate the trust of Breandán O'Shea and his contacts. Therefore it's fair to say Operation Ferryman needs us all."